DemonPride

Prideland Series: Book 1

Theo Mann

Invisible Publishing Company

Prideland Series

Contents

Chapter 1

Captain Doyle laid a star chart on the briefing table and pointed to the small red dot in the upper corner. "What do you know about that planet, Lieutenant?"

Every face at the table turned to stare at Dina Dyer. She knew and trusted everyone present and her long-time sweetheart Tom stood straight across from her.

His eyes encouraged her. Everyone's eyes encouraged her, even the captain's

"It's never been incorporated on the Coalition roll," she began, "so no one's conducted a full survey. Passing ships take regular scans of the surface, but I can only tell you what's in the official record."

"Tell me everything there is to know about it."

Dina's fingers flew over her handpad. She pulled up the official record on the planet. "The scanning crews named the planet Daustina. It has an oxygen atmosphere and most of the surface is either jungle or rainforest. It supports several large mammalian species and it has a sizable human population. So why hasn't the Coalition incorporated them before?"

"Anything else, Lieutenant?"

Dina held up the image on her handpad screen for everyone to see. "This scan here shows a major architectural development. Either the human population constructed it themselves or they're occupying some older settlement."

"How recent is this scan?"

"It's three years old. The record lists the human population as three hundred thousand people, so they must have a stable social structure. This planet is close enough to the Inner Corridor. You wouldn't expect the Coalition to pass up a population that big without making at least an initial reconnaissance foray."

"They're making it now," the captain replied. "You and the rest of the landing team will prepare the population for incorporation into the Coalition. You've worked together so many times, this mission should be a snap. First Officer Tom Sharples will carry out all the political negotiations on behalf of the Coalition. Commander Matthew Geromi will do a full psychological profile of the population. Commander Tania Barnes will act as linguist. Lieutenant Commander Marcus Harte will make the anthropological report and you'll conduct a complete biological survey. You'll report to the Coalition on the human population's condition. Are they incredibly inbred from living so long in isolation? How good is their nutrition? The Coalition will want to know as much about these people and their lifestyle as possible."

"They've got large game species available so their health should be pretty good. Then again, depending on what weapons they use, they may not be making very good use of available resources."

"There's one more crucial task you'll need to accomplish," the captain added. "Six months ago, a shuttle crashed on this planet. The distress signal from the wreckage indicates the entire passenger and crew complement survived the crash. Your objective will be to find the survivors and bring them back."

"The record shows other ships crashing on the planet before this," Tom pointed out. "The Coalition never launched any rescue mission for them."

"Alexander Mathus was on this shuttle along with his wife and children. His father, Coalition Chancellor Peter Mathus, gave direct orders to mount this mission to bring his son back. Rescuing Alexander Mathus and his family takes priority over incorporating the rest of the population. Incorporation is just a pretext for getting our people down onto the surface to look for the Chancellor's son."

"Yes, Sir."

"You'll have three weeks before the podcraft's power packs run down. I'll keep the *Savannah* in orbit around the planet and you'll contact me to arrange the next stage of your operation. We'll have one more briefing and you'll leave by morning watch tomorrow."

Dina's head shot up. "So soon?"

Captain Doyle fixed her with his bushy-browed glare. He could make anybody pull their head in with one glance. "Is there a problem, Lieutenant? I just said this is a rescue operation."

"You said this was an incorporation. The Mathus family has been on the surface for six months. If we want to incorporate this planet, we should conduct more detailed scans to get an accurate picture of what's going on down there. Morning watch tomorrow is too soon. We should be having daily briefings for weeks, not just two."

The captain surveyed the circle of faces. "Does anyone else have any objections to raise?"

Of course no one said anything and Dina squirmed. No one else expressed the slightest concern about this mission.

Tom broke the long silence. "This team has faced dangerous missions before. We can handle whatever we find down there."

"No two planets are alike. We've incorporated enough of them to know that." Dina held up her handpad showing the most recent scan. "This scan shows a high concentration of large carnivores living in the middle of the cities. They must be living side by side with human beings. We have no idea what's going on down there. We could be walking into a trap."

"It couldn't be a trap," Tom countered. "The population has no idea we're coming."

Dina held up both hands. "The time frame is too short. That's all I'm saying. We should take extra precautions with this planet."

"The time frame came directly from Chancellor Mathus," the captain replied.

Dina lowered her eyes. "Yes, Sir."

The door opened and an elderly lady entered the room. Her white hair touched her shoulders in a perfect bob.

"Dr. Joyce Galvin will conduct your psych evaluations and clear you for active duty," the captain went on.

Dr. Galvin smiled at everyone, but her presence sent a chill through the landing team. Dina stepped away to make room for Dr. Galvin at the briefing table.

"Report back here at eight bells for your final briefing," the captain ordered. "By then, I'll have Dr. Galvin's report that you're all clear for duty."

Every eye gravitated to Dr. Galvin. She never stopped smiling. "Who would like to go first?"

No one answered. No one moved.

"Very well, then, let's start with you, Tom. I'll call each of you up in descending rank order. That means you're next, Matthew, so don't go too far away." Dr. Galvin waved her hand. "The rest of you are dismissed."

The other officers headed for the door. Dina paused on the threshold and looked back at Tom. She would have liked to exchange a smile or a nod with him before his evaluation, but he didn't notice her watching him. He remained rooted to the spot, his hazel eyes fixed on Dr. Galvin. The lights over the table shone on his dark curls. His muscular shoulders made him look powerful compared to tiny Dr. Galvin.

The door closed and cut off Dina's view. She turned away with a sigh and found Tania Barnes waiting for her on the landing. Tall and blonde, always beautiful, always graceful, Tania was an excellent linguist and remained undefeated in the *Savannah's* combat training arena.

Tania fell in next to Dina on the way down the corridor. They couldn't be more different even though they were the same height.

Tania's blonde hair touched her shoulders with her bangs cut straight across her forehead. Dina's dark brown hair hung down her back with layers framing her face. Tania's crisp blue eyes measured every detail of the corridor.

Dina faced front while her mind wandered back to the briefing. A thousand questions nagged her, but she would probably never get them answered. She would have to go down to the planet's surface for that. She sure wouldn't get them answered here.

Tania's voice broke in on her thoughts. "How about a match in the training studio while we wait for our turns?"

Dina looked back toward the briefing room. "Now? You heard Dr. Galvin. We have to be ready when she calls us up. We've only got until eight bells to complete our evaluations."

"She said she'll evaluate us in descending rank order so she'll evaluate you and me last. We've got time. Come on. Forget the evaluation for a little while. Nothing calms my nerves like a good workout."

Dina had to grin at her friend. "All right, but don't blame me if Dr. Galvin strikes you from the landing party for showing up for your evaluation with a black eye."

"A black eye—me? Not likely. If someone shows up for their evaluation with a black eye, it will be you."

Dina snorted. "I would love to see you try to get close enough to give me a black eye. You're dreaming, as usual."

They turned the corner on their way down the corridor. Dina spotted Matthew waiting by the lift. He kept his back to the two women so she couldn't see his face.

Dina started forward to join him, but Tania grabbed her arm to hold her back. Tania pressed a finger to her lips and drew Dina back to the corner where Matthew couldn't see them.

Dina stared at her in surprise, but she didn't dare break the silence. What did this cloak-and-dagger stuff mean? Why was Tania hiding from her own husband?

Dina peeked out to steal a glance at Matthew. He stood with his legs planted wide and his hands clasped behind his back. An eerie stillness surrounded him. He didn't look right or left. What was he doing?

The lift door slid open. Matthew stepped into the car and disappeared. Tania let go of Dina's arm and both women stepped into the open to approach the lift. "What's wrong?" Dina asked. "Why did you hide from him like that?"

Tania pressed the button to call the lift back. "When he stands like that, he's focusing his concentration. It's his way of dealing with stressful situations. "

"He didn't look stressed to me. I wish I was that calm heading into my evaluation. These things wrack my nerves. I wish Matthew was evaluating us instead of the Ice Queen."

"You don't understand. Matthew would never admit it, but Dr. Galvin's probably the one person on board—maybe even in the whole Armada—that he's really afraid of. She's the only other psychologist on board, so she's the only person qualified to evaluate Matthew. He can't stand psych evaluations."

"He's evaluated dozens of people himself. He should know what to expect."

"He can't stand facing Dr. Galvin as a subject being questioned and analyzed the way he analyzes others.

"I don't like Dr. Galvin, either," Dina remarked. "She makes my skin crawl."

"What are you talking about? Dr. Galvin loves you. She always makes evaluations easy for you."

Dina made a face. "She's always trying to be my friend. The harder she tries, the more she makes me want to scream and run the other way."

Tania gave Dina's shoulder a playful shove. "I think she wants to be your mother."

"So why is Matthew afraid of her? With his combat skill, he could break her in half."

"His mother's parents were traditional Japanese. His mother became a psychologist and married a psychoanalytic researcher. Matthew barely knew his father, even though they lived in the same house. His grandfather taught him everything, including the martial arts. He taught Matthew to control his thoughts and emotions and Matthew takes that very seriously. He has to keep every piece of his life under control at all times. He keeps a rigid schedule with separate time slots for recreation, combat training practice—even relationship time. He can't stand anything unknown and being evaluated is the ultimate unknown."

"What's he doing on the landing team, then? He gets into all kinds of unknown situations on incorporation missions and he's never lost his head in combat."

"He sees life and death situations as the best possible combat training where he has to keep his mind calm and rational under extreme conditions. He won't allow fear to defeat him."

"What about you?" Dina asked. "I wish I had a collection of trophies like yours. You must have started competing when you were young."

"I got into martial arts in high school. I was always good at sports, and the next thing I knew, I was competing in the international championship. I met Matthew at the All-Armada Combat Championship."

"What did your parents think about you going into the military?"

"They loved it. Both my parents worked on military bases in San Antonio. My father made a joke about me joining the family business. Somehow, my whole life revolved around combat. It's in my blood."

"How did you become a linguist?"

"In high school, I discovered I had a natural ability with languages. I used to practice them during training breaks. The Armada brass decided my ability with languages plus my combat training made me a good choice for the incorporation team."

"They were right. We never could have survived the last incorporation without you. You covered all of us long enough to escape."

Tania turned aside. "Here's the training studio. I'll impress you some more by giving you that black eye."

Chapter 2

Tania and Dina stepped out of the training studio with their cheeks flushed, their hair in disarray, and sweat beaded on their foreheads. Tania clapped Dina on the shoulder on their way down the corridor. "You're getting better. You came close to giving me a black eye that time."

"I'll never be a martial arts champion like you."

"Maybe not, but you're good enough to hold your own against me. That's saying a lot."

"You still beat me every time," Dina returned. "Maybe you could give me some hints to help me beat you."

"You're just overcautious. You need to take more risks. You can't land blows if you don't try them."

They took the lift back to the crew quarters. When the doors opened, they spotted Marcus Harte coming their way. "I wonder how *he* deals with evaluations," Dina murmured. "He doesn't look too worried."

Tania turned away. "You find out and tell me later."

Dina grabbed her arm. "Don't run off. He's all right once you get to know him."

"You must like him flirting with you. He never stops talking. I think he suffers from Short Man Syndrome."

"You can't blame him for trying to talk to us. We're his closest colleagues on board. Who's he supposed to talk to if not to us?"

"There are lots of other women on board."

"None of them are near him in rank or they're already taken—like us. He just had the bad luck to get assigned to a team with two established couples."

"Then you can stand here and listen to him talk. I'm going home. I'll see you later." Tania walked away.

Marcus stopped in front of the lift just as Tania turned into her quarters. He smiled at Dina. "Another disappearing colleague."

Dina changed the subject. He couldn't help but notice his teammates avoiding him. "Are you ready for your evaluation, Marcus?"

"I have nothing to hide. These psychologists can search for psychosis until doomsday. They'll never find anything on me."

"It must be nice not to have anything to worry about."

"You don't have anything to worry about, either, Dina. You know you'll pass. Dr. Galvin wouldn't exclude you. The team needs a biologist. It doesn't need an anthropologist."

Dina had to look down to make eye contact with him. "We need an anthropologist, too. The team wouldn't include one if we didn't. You have no reason to doubt your place on the team."

He faced the lift, but he didn't push the button. He ran his fingertips distractedly over the console. "I joined the Armada to get assigned to the incorporation team. I always wanted to study other cultures and species."

"How did you get into anthropology?"

"I had a charmed childhood. I spent summers exploring the Vermont woods around my house. I always liked science and digging old things up out of the ground."

"How are you enjoying the *Savannah* since you came on board?"

"It's like other Armada ships, I guess. I didn't grow up military like some of these people. We need some leadership, but I'm not cut out for this rigid command structure. I don't mind telling you this, Dina, even though you're dating the First Officer. Tom's a natural leader. I can see why you're attracted to him instead of someone like me."

Dina blushed. "You're very attractive, Marcus. You're going to make someone very happy one of these days."

"That's nice of you to say, but it won't happen on this team."

"The team respects you. You kept your head under fire on our last few missions. That's the most important quality on any incorporation team."

"They might respect me, but I won't make anyone happy on this team. You and Tania are already in long-term relationships and I don't enjoy combat the way the others do. It's a necessary evil. The fighting we did only made me want to get closer to my teammates and that's a dead end."

"What about your family back on Earth? Do they support your work?"

"They want me to get married. I want to start a family, but I'm not ready to give up exploring the galaxy yet. When I finish my commission with the Armada, I'd like to enter politics."

Dina's mouth fell open. "You would?"

"I know what you're thinking. You think I'm not political material. I'm not cut out for cutthroat power struggles and intrigue the way Tom is."

"I never said that."

He tried to bite back a smile and failed. "I'm too much of a homebody. I like the simple pleasures and little joys of ordinary relationships. I'm happy reading and writing with a round of golf thrown in and maybe a game of chess. I only want to be comfortable, not rule the world."

"That's not what I heard," Dina countered. "You might think combat is a necessary evil, but when the time comes to write your anthropological surveys, that's when you really shine. Captain Doyle says Coalition brass are impressed with your ideas and recommendations. They recognize a political mind at work. They're only waiting for you to establish yourself on the *Savannah* before they move you up."

He cocked his head. "Did he really say that?"

Dina nodded.

Marcus burst into a huge smile. "Thanks, Dina. I appreciate you telling me. I really needed to hear that right now."

Chapter 3

Marcus punched the button to call the lift. A different crew compartment opened while they waited and two men stepped into the corridor. Both men dwarfed Dina and Marcus, but one stood a head taller than the other. Tom Sharples smiled at Dina, but she and Marcus stiffened to attention when they saw the other man.

Tom nodded to Dina and Marcus. "At ease. Dina, this is my father, General Maurice Sharples. This is Lieutenant Dina Dyer, the biologist I told you about."

Dina's heart pounded in her chest. Tom's father—a general! Cold sweat broke out on the back of her neck when she held out her hand. "It's a pleasure to meet you, General."

He returned her handshake with warm muscular fingers. His black eyes sparkled and he surveyed her up and down with one glance. "Likewise, Lieutenant."

"I was just showing Dad around the ship," Tom added. "He's never visited the *Savannah* before."

"How are you finding it so far, Sir?" Dina asked.

"Satisfactory so far. I'm a little concerned about my son's career, though."

Dina froze. "You are? What concerns you, Sir?" She already knew what he was talking about.

"My son has big ambitions." The general's eyes blazed and he skewered her with a glance. "I would hate to see anything jeopardize that."

She shot a glance at Tom. "I don't think anything *could* jeopardize it now, Sir."

"There's only one thing I can think of. Scandal could cost him everything."

Dina gulped. Why did this conversation sound so familiar? "By scandal, do you mean...?"

"I mean," the general interrupted, "the wrong relationship with the wrong woman could destroy everything he's worked so hard to achieve. I would hate to see him throw his future away on a passing flirt, especially if that flirt will end with the changing seasons, just like Judith McCurdy did."

"Who's Judith McCurdy?"

The lift bell dinged and the doors slid open. The general nodded to her without answering. "As you were, Lieutenant." He stepped into the lift.

Tom followed him and Dina caught his eye. "Who's Judith McCurdy?"

He didn't answer. He ducked into the lift and the doors closed. Dina found herself staring at the plain grey metal doors.

She turned to Marcus. She had to swallow the lump in her throat to get her throat working. "Who's Judith McCurdy?"

He turned away to take the stairs. "I honestly don't know."

Dina watched the number change on the lift control panel, but she hardly noticed them. Her head spun through a thousand possibilities. Judith McCurdy? A passing flirt who jeopardized Tom's political ambitions? What did the general mean by that?

She shrugged off her confusion and stepped forward to touch the computer console on the wall. She keyed in her search code: *Judith McCurdy.*

Bright characters streamed across the screen:

Judith McCurdy Commander

Staff Anthropologist

Assigned Destroyer Savannah 53872-53875

Resigned Commission 53875

Replaced by Marcus Harte Lieutenant 53875

Dina frowned at the readouts. So Judith McCurdy served as staff anthropologist on the *Savannah* before Marcus came on board. Tom must have gotten involved with her and that involvement threatened his ambitions—at least, his father thought so.

The writing on the screen vanished and a loud chime startled Dina back to reality. Another stream of characters crossed the screen.

Lieutenant Dina Dyer report to Briefing Room immediately by order of Staff Psychologist Doctor Joyce Galvin Commander.

Dina jumped. Her evaluation callup! That was fast. The lift opened and she stepped inside. She knitted her fingers behind her back trying to steady her nerves. Workouts in the training studio might relax Tania, but they did nothing for Dina.

She rode the lift back upstairs to the briefing room and found Dr. Galvin waiting for her outside the room. When Dina tried to go inside, Dr. Galvin stopped her. "Let's take a walk instead."

"Aren't you going to evaluate me?"

"I don't really need to evaluate you. I know you're fit for duty. I thought we'd just have a little talk about how things are going for you since the last mission."

Dina eased a few extra inches farther away from the woman. "Things are going fine for me. I don't want any special treatment. If you evaluated the others, you should do the same to me."

"I didn't do anything to the others I won't do to you. This is just a formality to get you down onto the planet as soon as possible."

"So what do you want to talk about?"

Dr. Galvin started down the corridor and gestured for Dina to join her. "How is everything going between you and Tom?"

Dina refused to look at her. "Everything's fine between me and Tom."

"I hear his father is on board."

"Yes, he is."

"You haven't met General Sharples before, have you?"

"I haven't met any of Tom's family before. I told you that."

"Have you met the general yet?"

The blood rushed to Dina's cheeks. "I just met him outside the lift."

"How did that go?"

Dina thought fast. These psychologists never asked a question they didn't already know the answer to. "It went fine. He said he was very pleased to meet me."

"Did you know he was coming on board?"

Dina stole a sidelong glance at Dr. Galvin and threw caution to the wind. What the heck? Why not go for broke? "Did you know Judith McCurdy?"

Dr. Galvin stopped dead in her tracks. The self-satisfied smile evaporated off her face. "How did you find out about Judith?"

"General Sharples mentioned her. He called her a passing flirt. He said the wrong relationship with the wrong woman could ruin Tom's chance for advancement. Tom was involved with Judith, wasn't he? She threatened his prospects, didn't she?"

Dr. Galvin shook her hair out of her eyes and started walking again, but she didn't regain her cheery demeanor. "I think you better ask Tom about Judith."

Dina grabbed Dr. Galvin's arm and pulled her back so hard she nearly jerked the old lady off her feet. "I'm not asking Tom. I'm asking you. Who was she and what happened between her and Tom?"

"I've always liked you, Dina, even when everyone said you shouldn't get involved with your superior officer."

"What's that got to do with this?"

"I always thought of you like my own daughter even though I don't have one. I want to protect you, but I can't do that very well in this job. Your being on the landing team is dangerous enough without you searching for threats on board this ship."

"I'm not searching for threats. I only want someone to tell me the truth. You asked how things are going between me and Tom. They would be going fine if I only knew what connection he had to Judith."

"You don't have to worry about Judith. I would be stepping out of line if I told you something you should hear from Tom. I can promise you that his connection with Judith has nothing to do with his relationship with you. You have no reason to suspect him."

Dina smacked her lips in annoyance. "I guess you're not going to tell me anything more than that."

Dr. Galvin started walking again. "Tom's a sore subject for you just now, so let's talk about something else. Have you heard from any of your family back on Earth since you came back from the last mission?"

Dina's shoulders slumped in defeat. She had no choice but to fall in at Dr. Galvin's side and answer these questions. Dr. Galvin could pull Dina from the landing team otherwise. "I heard from my brother. He's still managing that foundry on Lake Baikal."

"You must be proud of him."

"He's done well for himself."

"So have you, Dina. You've exceeded all your goals of joining the Armada and traveling through the stars."

"The Armada let me get away from home. I can study alien biology in interesting places. My brother and I always loved plants and animals. Tom reminds me of him sometimes."

"Tom's a nice man," Dr. Galvin breezed. "I can see why you love him so much."

"I would be friends with Tom even if we weren't dating. I know a good man when I see one."

"You make friends more easily with men than women."

Dina's head shot up. "What makes you say that?"

"You told me that yourself once. You have more male friends on board than female ones."

"I'm friends with Tania."

"You train with Tania. There's a difference. You're starting to make friends with her, but you can't deny you trust men more than women. You don't love or trust Tania and you don't trust me."

"I never trusted you," Dina growled. "I told you that many times, but that's not because you're a woman."

"Why is it, then?"

"You're the psychologist here. Why don't you tell me?"

"You trust male authority figures like Tom, Matthew, and Captain Doyle. Women don't have the authority to command your respect."

Dina focused her gaze on a spot down the corridor. How did this conversation turn against her so fast? For someone who just wanted to talk, Dr. Galvin seemed to be doing plenty of psychological evaluation. "I don't like men analyzing me any better than I like you doing it."

"Are you sure about that?"

"Maybe that's why I love Tom. He never analyzes me, and even if he did, he always approves of me."

Dr. Galvin hooked her arm through Dina's elbow. Dina fought the urge to pull away. "How about I put you at ease by talking about myself? You don't want anyone analyzing you. I can understand that, so we'll analyze me instead."

Dina whipped around. "What?"

Dr. Galvin laughed. "I can be just as ruthless with myself as I am with my other subjects. Listen and I'll tell you everything you need to know to analyze me yourself. I'll give you enough dirt on me so you never have to dread another psych evaluation again."

Dina stared at her. "You can do that?"

"You know I like you, Dina. You're like a younger version of myself. I grew up in the Southern US, too, and I escaped to college to get away from my drunken father."

Dina held her breath waiting for the doctor's next words. Where was this going?

"I got interested in human relations watching my mother navigate a marriage to an alcoholic. That's why I studied psychology—to find out what made people act the way they did. I married another psychology student in college, but after graduation, he turned cold and analytical. He wouldn't stop analyzing me, so I left him. A few years later, I married a gruff grandfather type, a military man like Captain Doyle."

"Did you have any children?"

"Sadly, no."

"So how did you wind up in the Armada?"

"After graduation, I spent a few years in private practice. Then I met one of my college professors at a conference. He invited me to work with him on a research project interviewing returned prisoners from the Anrove Nebula War. I spent two years talking to them and learning about their experiences. After the project ended, the Armada funded two years of intensive rehabilitation for the prisoners. I already knew them and their stories and the issues they faced, so the Armada hired me. After two more years, they renewed the funding to give the prisoners follow-up support. That's when I saw an opportunity to help the Armada staff by working as a frontline psychologist. I wanted to share their experiences and understand them better."

"That's a long way from helping returned prisoners," Dina remarked. "I guess your experience with them doesn't help you much here."

"You'd be surprised. The military causes psychological trauma in ways you can't imagine."

"Trauma? It's not that dangerous. Our landing team has faced more danger in the past year than the rest of the *Savannah* crew combined, but none of us have suffered any trauma."

"The military doesn't cause trauma by being dangerous. It quashes the free thinking that would make people truly resilient. That makes ordinary, safe situations psychologically traumatic when they don't need to be."

Chapter 4

Dina left Dr. Galvin at the briefing room where she would meet and evaluate Tania. Dina waited until the lift door closed before she let herself relax.

Her evaluation was over. She could go home and relax until eight bells. Then Captain Doyle would brief the team one more time before they left for the planet.

Dina started to enter her destination on the lift's control console, but she changed her mind and exited instead on the upper Engineering concourse. Engineering staff clustered below her on the main floor. They crowded around a tall man with a thick topknot of black curls. He towered over the others. He had to stoop to hear each person over the engine noise.

He spotted her on the upper concourse and his head shot up. Even after five years together, his sharp eyes sent a shiver through her. He signaled to her in the engine room sign language. *Wait for me. I'm almost finished here.*

Tom Sharples wasn't as husky as Captain Doyle, but his height gave him a commanding air over everyone, even those of higher rank. He sized up people and situations with lightning speed and unerring accuracy.

A few more years as Captain Doyle's First Officer would earn him command of his own ship and Dina would join him. Someday, he might get to be an admiral or even a congressman. Everyone admired Tom Sharples and even Captain Doyle delegated important decisions to him.

Tom gave orders to each member of the engineering team. One by one, they left to carry on their work. Tom tucked his handpad under his arm, stepped into the lift, and joined Dina on the upper concourse.

He didn't try to speak to her over the noise. He escorted her out of Engineering and into the corridor. Quiet enfolded them and they walked in silence to the crew quarters. He slid aside a compartment door between the medical ward and the starboard access shaft and Dina entered her own quarters.

As soon as the door closed, Tom wrapped his arms around her from behind and crushed her against his body. He nuzzled his face into her neck. "You don't usually come down to Engineering in the middle of a shift. What's on your mind?"

Dina breathed a heavy sigh and sheltered in his embrace. "This could be our last chance to be alone like this."

He raised his head. "What do you mean?"

"We're leaving tomorrow and we'll be down on that planet for at least three weeks. We won't get much chance to be alone down there."

He closed his arms around her again. "Then we should take advantage of it."

His mouth covered hers. They breathed in unison and Dina pressed her body against his. The nectar of his kiss flooded her mind until she pulled away. "We both have to get back on shift in a minute."

"We still have tonight together."

Her heart wrenched when she pulled away from him. "Something about this mission doesn't sit right with me."

"You mentioned that at the briefing."

"We ought to study the planet before we launch a landing mission. We should take weeks to prepare for a landing like this."

"The word came down from the Coalition Chancellor to get a team down there right away," he pointed out. "We're rushing to rescue the Chancellor's son. That's the real reason behind this mission. The Coalition doesn't really care about this planet."

"Are you telling me you don't have any misgivings about this mission at all?" she asked.

He shrugged and straightened his jacket. "Landing missions are always uncertain. It's not ideal, but we can handle it. We'll be armed and we have our contingency plans. We've done it dozens of times before. If anything goes wrong, we'll fall back to the *Savannah*. That's the way we always work it."

Dina turned away to straighten her hair in front of the mirror on the opposite wall. At twenty-five years of age, she stood almost two meters tall, not much shorter than Tom. A scar traced the corner of her upper lip.

She finished her hair and fiddled with the knick-knacks on the shelf below the mirror. She didn't want to turn around to continue her conversation with Tom.

A ragdoll of a little girl in a dress occupied the central position on the shelf. The doll's unblinking button eyes stared straight out into the room. Dina smoothed down her gingham skirt and arranged her yarn hair.

"I'll be spearheading the negotiations with their political leadership," Tom told her. "The records show these people living in cities, so they must have an advanced civilization."

Dina still didn't turn around. "That's what I thought."

"We don't know what we'll find until we get down there. Incorporations completely reorganize the population's culture, but I don't let it worry me. We've been on enough of these runs to know we can handle anything."

"I'm not worried about that."

"What are you worried about, then?"

"Nothing. Forget I mentioned it. We'll be busy between now and tomorrow with your briefing and fitting out the pod for launch. I just wanted a minute alone with you before we go."

He didn't come back to her the way she hoped. He watched her from across the room. "Don't discount your instincts. If something doesn't sit right, you should tell Doyle."

"I already did that. He would take me off the mission if I brought it up again. That would mean staying behind while you go down to the planet. I don't want to back out. Besides, I'm the ranking biologist on board. No one else can report to the Coalition."

"True. If you don't go, the whole mission would probably be scrapped."

"There you go."

"I still think you should listen to your instincts. If something doesn't sit right with you, you should act on it."

"We shouldn't have to run Chancellor Mathus's errands for him."

Tom chuckled. "That's life in uniform. I don't like it, either. I'm supposed to be in command of this mission, but I'm really just a grunt for someone farther up the food chain. We all are. Being in command isn't all it's cracked up to be, you know."

"That's easy for you to say. You went straight from Cadet Camp to being First Officer of the *Savannah*. You've been in command all your life."

Tom ran his fingers through his hair and straightened his jacket again. "You should try it sometime."

"No, thanks. I'll be your grunt instead."

He finally came up to her and wrapped her in his arms. "Good."

"Who's Judith McCurdy?"

His head shot up and he dropped his arms instantly. "It seems like you already know who she is."

"Why didn't you tell me about her before?"

"There was nothing to tell."

"Tell me now."

He puffed out his cheeks and sighed. "She worked on the team for three years. She was our anthropologist before Marcus came on board."

"She was more to you than an anthropologist. Your father called her a passing flirt."

"She was a lot more than a passing flirt, but he never knew that," Tom snarled. "He never visited me once in all that time. None of my family visited me. They were all too busy with their own careers or they would have known I was as serious about Judith as I am about you."

"So what happened? Why did she leave the *Savannah*?"

He looked her straight in the eye. "She wanted to settle on Earth to raise children, so it didn't work out between us."

"I see. So settling on Earth didn't fit with your political ambitions. Now I know what your father meant about me jeopardizing your future."

He softened and put his arms around her again. "My relationship with Judith ended long before you came on board the *Savannah*. You've been the only woman in my heart since the day I met you. You have my word of honor on that."

He pulled her close, and this time, she let it happen. She relaxed into him and her fears started to fade. "Your father didn't seem to think much of me."

"I don't care what he thinks. I don't care what anybody thinks."

"You have to care if you want to rise in the political world. What will you do if they don't accept me?"

"Do you mean my family or the political world?"

"Either one."

"They'll accept you as soon as they get to know you. They'll love you as much as I do."

Dina rested her head on his chest. "I hope you're right."

"I am right. Trust me. You can adapt to any situation and I won't do this without you." He kissed her hair. "I'll make them love you."

She leaned back to study him. "Do you have history with any other women on board I should know about?"

"Of course not! I would tell you if I did. You know that."

She shook her doubts out of her head. "Maybe my evaluation with Dr. Galvin got to me more than I realized."

"Don't give it another thought. Psychology is for screwed up people. It has nothing to do with us."

"Except when we have to get evaluated, you mean."

"I don't pay them the slightest attention. No psychologist will ever turn up anything screwed up about me."

"Some of us have to pay attention to them."

Tom kissed her on the forehead and took a step toward the door. "I'll tell you what. When we get back from this mission, let's get married."

Dina spun around and gasped. "What?"

"We've been together for five years and we both want to stay together. When we get back from this mission, we'll both be in line for promotion, which means I'll have my own command. If we're married, the Armada will make sure we stay together. Come on, Dina. Marry me. You know you want to."

"Of course, I want to. You just never mentioned it before. I didn't know *you* wanted to."

"I didn't mention it, but I thought about it. I thought about it a lot and I want us to stick together no matter what. I'll get my own command soon no matter what happens with this mission and I want you to come with me. Come on. Tell me you'll marry me."

She beamed at him. "Okay. I'll marry you when we get back from this mission."

He laughed out loud and swept her off her feet. He spun her around before putting her back down. "Let's celebrate! Let's have a special dinner, just you and me, here in your quarters tonight, to celebrate our engagement."

"Okay, but let's keep the engagement quiet for now. We can tell everyone when we get back from the planet."

Tom bit back a grin. "Of course, Lieutenant. I'll be the picture of professionalism."

Chapter 5

The podcraft skimmed the treetops. Dina studied the jungle through her porthole, but it concealed the planet's secrets under a carpet of foliage. Tom leaned over her shoulder to check the display console. His smell wafted into Dina's nostrils. Memories of last night calmed her nerves.

He pointed to a clear patch on the screen. "That's our spot. It's big enough to land the pod safely and the jungle will hide it from prying eyes. Set us down, Lieutenant."

Dina touched the controls to stabilize the rudders and keyed in the landing sequence. The pod banked, leveled out, and dropped through the canopy. The engine wash tore at the branches.

She cut the engines and peace returned to the jungle. Tom raised his eyes to the ceiling and listened. "Scan the area. Make sure there's no one nearby."

Dina pressed a button and scanned a one-kilometer radius around the pod. "There are some large carnivores nearby, but no sign of humans. We're a dozen kilometers from any human habitation."

Tom waved to the rest of the team. "Stand by to defend the door."

Tania, Matthew, and Marcus unbuckled their restraint harnesses and climbed out of their seats. Dina charged her weapon and the electric vibration buzzed up her arm.

She dropped to one knee and trained her weapon at the door. Tania took the position next to her. Tania, Dina, and Marcus formed a defensive arch around the door while Tom and Matthew flattened themselves to the walls on either side of the doorway. Every nerve tensed in anticipation of what they would find on the other side of that door.

Tom's hand hovered over the door release. His shoulders tightened and his voice split the silence with a sharp edge of command. "Stand by."

He shot the lever to break the hatch seal and the door swung open. Compressed air hissed out and warm jungle humidity flooded the pod. The pungent aroma of wet vegetation stung Dina's nostrils.

Tom took a deep breath and strode out first. He sealed his back to the pod's hull and slid down it to the far end. He trained his weapon out at the jungle searching on all sides. The others followed until all five stood with their backs against the pod.

Then Tania inched forward and the others moved out one at a time to form a semi-circle. Tania strode straight out into the jungle with Marcus on one side and Dina on the other. Tom and Matthew kept their backs against the Pod to cover the sides.

Animal voices rang through the dripping canopy. Tree lizards flitted through the branches and chirped to each other. Iridescent moths opened and closed their wings in silent rhythm.

The arch widened and pushed forward until Tom and Matthew turned their weapons backward to close the arch into a circle behind Tania. The circle widened to ring the pod, but there was nothing here. Nothing threatened the team or the pod. Nothing but tree lizards surrounded the pod in every direction.

Tom straightened up. His shoulders relaxed and he lowered his weapon. "Stand down."

The landing party softened their stance and started to look around. Dina scanned the area with her handpad. "It's almost exactly like some parts of Earth. The human population must have brought plants with them when they landed. They may have brought animals, too."

Tom cast a hard glance over the undergrowth. "Which way is it to the human settlement?"

"The nearest village is twelve kilometers that way. I'll get a reckoning from the pod's computer to find the road leading to the village."

"Let's get moving. We're attracting too much attention to the pod." He signaled to Tania and Matthew. "Landing protocols! Put your handpads away. Conceal your weapons and move out. We don't know how the population will react to our arrival, so be ready for anything."

He watched them hide their weapons under their clothes and set off through the trees. They followed the contours of the land until they found a trickle of water, which led them to a footpath. Tom kept the lead position and Dina brought up the rear with Tania, Matthew, and Marcus between them.

They walked for two hours climbing hills and crossing ravines. They pushed through solid walls of vegetation and forded streams.

The jungle hypnotized Dina into a steady, marching rhythm. It erased all memory of the *Savannah* with its sanitized air. The *Savannah* and its biology lab ceased to exist. She might have lived on this planet her whole life.

The trees thinned out and the streams widened into irrigation ditches. More signs of human life appeared on both sides. Foliage no longer blocked their path and human footprints marked the soil.

They found the road after another hour. Fell deer and water oxen dotted cultivated fields on both sides. A river flowed next to the road, but Dina didn't see any boats.

The first sod house popped out of the middle of a field. From a distance, she mistook it for a mound of dirt sprouting grass and bushes. Smoke rising out of the roof gave it away.

Something caught Dina's attention from behind, but when she looked back, she didn't see anything except the empty road stretching behind her.

Late afternoon progressed toward evening, but the team still didn't see any people. Another hint of movement made Dina glance back over her shoulder again.

This time, she couldn't mistake a shape moving in the undergrowth between the river and the road. The branches parted and two giant male jaguars padded out of the undergrowth on broad, soft paws. Their spotted coats rippled with muscle and their eyes didn't miss a single detail of the surroundings.

Dina snapped out of her reverie and her hand shifted instinctively to her weapon. The cats stalked into the road with their heads lowered and nostrils flaring.

They didn't even try to hide their presence. Dina's mind went into a tailspin. These couldn't be jaguars from Earth. Jaguars didn't hunt in pairs. They didn't hunt during the day and they didn't walk right out into the open like that. They crept on their bellies and then pounced. These cats didn't care who saw them.

The cats fixed their eyes on her. Her hand closed on her weapon and the cats broke into a sprint heading straight for her.

Dina shouted to her teammates, "Look out!" but the cats were already halfway across the road. She brought up her weapon and leveled it at them, but they were too fast. One of them launched into the air coming straight for her. She fired and the blast hit him in the shoulder.

The cat bellowed in pain and surprise. Dina didn't have time to fire again before his wide-open mouth blocked out her whole field of view. His weight flattened her and her weapon sailed out of her hand.

The other cat sprang at Marcus and hit him with his hand still gripping the weapon concealed under his shirt. He didn't have time to draw it before the cat knocked him over.

Weapon blasts rent the air on every side, but Dina couldn't see anything beyond the big head and dripping jaws looming in her face. She managed to throw her arms up between her face and the cat's fangs. He drove for her neck, but she fought him away and curled under his chest for protection.

The cat bounded back to catch her again, but she rolled to one side and jumped to her feet. The cat batted his paw at her. His claws flashed in the sun and she didn't hesitate. She set off running down the road as fast as she could go. Where were her friends? They would drive this cat off with their weapons if only she could find them.

She got one glimpse of the other cat dragging Marcus toward the bushes. Blood speckled the cat's jaws and chest. Marcus's head lolled sideways at a sickening angle and a gaping red hole opened in his neck.

The cat dragged him several yards before Tom fired at the creature. The shot clipped the cat's ear and the animal let go of Marcus with a growl. The next moment, the cat sprang at Tom with teeth bared.

Dina couldn't help Tom and she didn't have time to look around for Matthew or Tania. The first cat recovered from his surprise and chased her down the road. That cat could easily run down any human. He didn't even have to run at full speed to overtake her.

She had to run until her lungs exploded to get away from him. If only closing her eyes could block out the sight of Marcus's broken neck. She charged down the road toward where she hoped she would find the village. The people on this planet must have some way to combat these animals.

She glanced over her shoulder and immediately wished she hadn't. The second cat leapt and landed on Tom's shoulders. It knocked Tom face down in the road. The cat's blood-splattered jaws closed on her fiancé's neck. She couldn't watch anymore and she ran on in blind panic.

Houses and fences flanked the road. Pastures and gardens lay closer together everywhere. One by one, people appeared in their doors to stare at her. Children ran through the yards and gardens. They pointed at the cat chasing her, but not a single person stepped out to help her.

She tripped on a pebble and staggered off her feet. There was nowhere left to run but farther down the road. Her stumble encouraged the cat. He put on a burst of speed and sprang. This was the end of her life. She was a meal for a cat. Would her family back home ever find out how she died?

She felt herself flying through the air. An almighty thud thumped through her body and she inspected tiny pebbles on the road at close range. She lay on her stomach with blood seeping out of a gash in her chin. The cat's jaws close on her neck and she went limp waiting for the end.

Chapter 6

To Dina's surprise, the cat didn't bite her. His teeth pressed into her skin, but instead of breaking her neck, he just held her still. Two human feet stepped in front of her eyes. She examined the microscopic detail of the grain in the leather boots. "Are these the slags Hector told us about?"

She couldn't see anyone else, but another voice answered the first. "Pack them up and send them to the market. I'll find places for them."

"Consider it done," the first voice replied.

She couldn't figure it out, but she could have cried in relief when the cat let go of her neck and his weight lifted off her back. Her ribs expanded and her lungs filled with air. She looked around and gulped when she saw one of the jaguars dragging Marcus's body into the bushes and out of sight.

"You can stand up now."

The person standing in front of her must be talking to her. Dina got to her feet and discovered a sandy-haired man regarding her with a blank stare.

A ring of faces surrounded her. They all eyed her with the same empty expression. The men wore their hair short and their faces clean-shaven. The women kept their hair tied back in long twisted braids down their backs. Everyone wore heavy leather boots with laces crisscrossing up to their knees.

"Thank you," she told the man.

"What for?"

"For whatever you did to scare that cat off me."

The man frowned. "I didn't do anything."

"You must have done something. He wouldn't just run off like that if you didn't do something to scare him."

She bent down to pick up her weapon, but he picked it up first. He could move with surprising speed when he wanted to. "You won't need this."

Dina stiffened. "I might not need it, but it's mine. Can I have it back?"

The man squinched up his wrinkled face, but he didn't give it back. "I think you better come to the village."

"Isn't this the village?"

"No, this isn't it, but we aren't far away. Come to my house. We have a lot to do."

She looked around for the rest of the team. That's when she spotted Tom lying face down in the middle of the road.

Her heart skipped a beat. She hated to see him mauled and destroyed, but she had to face the hard truth. She couldn't leave him lying here on a strange planet. She had to figure out what to do with him. She had to get him back to the *Savannah*. The medical staff would take care of his body until the ship returned to Earth. They would deliver him to his family.

She dragged her feet back to the spot where he lay, but she couldn't look. She turned away with a lump in her throat. Her Tom, her love—he was gone. She would never marry him now. She made up her mind to call off the mission. Her instincts were right. This planet was too dangerous.

Then she noticed the small hairs curled against his skin on the back of his neck. They were still wet from the cat's jaws, but they weren't wet with blood. In fact, there was no blood on him at all.

She touched his neck to find the bite marks. He startled her out of her skin by stirring and rolling over. "Dina, you're all right!"

She gasped out loud. "You're all right! You aren't dead!"

"I'm okay. I guess that cat just wanted something to chase. I saw him bite you and I thought you were gone."

Dina helped him up and threw her arms around him. She would never let him go again. "This man wants to take us back to the village. He scared that cat off me."

"I told you I didn't," the man broke in.

Tania and Matthew appeared at the roadside surrounded by village people. "What happened to you guys?" Dina asked Tania. "Why didn't you fire on those cats when they attacked us?"

Tania glanced at the villagers. "We never had a chance. These people...." She broke off.

"We never got a clear shot," Matthew added. "These people surrounded us and blocked our fire It makes no sense. When the cats saw the people surrounding us, the cats ignored us."

"I raised my weapon to fire," Tania told her, "but one of the men stopped me. He stood in front of me so I couldn't shoot."

Dina studied the villagers more closely. They stared back at the landing team without offering a word of explanation. Even the children kept their distance. They stared at everything with the same wary reserve. They never smiled at the strangers or talked to each other.

Tom glanced toward the bushes where the jaguars disappeared. "We can't go after them. We'll have to wait for another chance to get Marcus's body back." He headed down the road toward the village.

Dina put out her hand, but she stopped herself from touching him here. "Wait a minute, Tom. We have to fall back to the *Savannah*. We've lost one of our team. We have to switch to our contingency plan."

Tom shook his head. His voice told her not to argue. "We've made contact with the human population. We lost Marcus, but we can still accomplish our mission." He followed the man who invited them to his house.

Dina hesitated, but when Tania and Matthew fell in line behind Tom, she had no choice but to go along. What else could she do? She couldn't fall back to the *Savannah* alone and Tom was the ranking officer on this mission.

The man led them to another conical dirt house. More people crowded around the strangers until the who crowd stopped at a garden bed in the middle of the road.

Cheerless faces stared out from every doorway and from every fence and gate. The villagers discussed the strangers in whispers, but no one made any move to interact with them.

No one offered hospitality. The houses didn't have a single identifying mark or artistic decoration to distinguish one from the next. Only farm implements and hand tools hung from the walls and leaned in corners.

"This must be the village," Tom remarked

"Where's the man who scared the cat away?" Dina looked around, but the man had disappeared into the crowd. "He must their leader. We can negotiate with him."

Tom lowered his voice and grimaced at the lackluster crowd. "They don't look all that interested in talking to us. Someone should have at least asked who we are and what we want. I'd rather deal with outright hostility than this."

"Maybe they're waiting for us to go away," Matthew suggested. "Maybe this is their way of expressing hostility."

"We aren't going away. We have a mission to complete here. We have to find Alexander Mathus."

"Let's ask the children where to find their leaders. They'll tell us." Tania waved and smiled at a gang of children behind the nearest fence. The children scowled back at her and muttered to each other.

"Come on, Tania," Dina exclaimed. "They might not find two women together so threatening."

Tania and Dina walked over to the fence under the children's watchful eyes. They stood in a stiff, straight line. Not a sparkle enlivened their eyes.

Dina did her best to smile at them. "Hi there. Who's in charge here?"

Something stirred in their expressions, but no one answered. The younger ones exchanged glances, but they didn't reply.

She tried again. "You must have some leaders in this village. Just tell me who they are. I just want to talk to them."

Whispered conversation passed through the adult onlookers. Dina waved to them, too, but they didn't return the simplest greeting. She pursed her lips. "I know you can understand our language. Just tell me who's in charge here and I'll leave you alone."

Tania nudged Dina and nodded behind her. The man who scared the cat away was elbowing his way through the crowd toward them.

Dina smiled at him. "Are you the leader of this village? We have a proposal to make to you on behalf of your people."

"You're making people uncomfortable talking to these children. You should leave them alone."

"We aren't doing them any harm by talking to them. We just want to find out who's in charge here. Maybe you can tell us."

"If you have to talk to someone, you can talk to me, but leave the children alone. They could get visited for this."

"What do you mean by 'visited'? Visited by whom?"

"They could get in trouble."

"How could they get in trouble? We aren't doing anything. We just walked into this village."

"They won't talk to you," he told her. "They won't talk to anyone. They aren't even supposed to talk to each other, but I guess there's no way to stop children from doing that."

His words made no sense to her. "Why aren't they supposed to talk to people?"

"That's the understanding we have," he replied. "The less they talk to people, the better."

Dina blinked at him. "I don't understand you. Everybody has to talk to everybody else. It's the human way."

"Not here. It's safer if they keep to themselves."

She couldn't stop her voice from rising. "But you live in a village. Why do you live in such a close-knit community if you want to keep to yourselves?"

"We live in a village because we have to. We have business to transact as a group, but we try to keep to ourselves. The children don't understand it, either. They come to an understanding as they grow up why it has to be this way, but they learn not to talk to people they don't know. They learn that from a very early age."

"Then who should we talk to? Who speaks on behalf of the group?"

"No one. You shouldn't even talk to me, but you can't stay here. You can't stand here talking to the children like this. They'll get visited and so will you. If you can't stop talking, come with me. You might as well come to my house. At least you'll be out of the street."

He shuffled away. He walked hunched over. His strange gait made him look older than his years. Dina glanced back at Tom, but he only shrugged. She followed the man and Tom joined her. Tania and Matthew came last.

The crowd parted to let them pass back up the road to a house on the main street. The man opened the door, crossed the threshold, and let the door bang closed behind him without inviting the team inside.

They waited, but the man didn't come back out. This must be the house where he wanted to take them, but he didn't return to invite them in. Dina exchanged glances with her comrades, but after a long wait, she plucked up her courage. She pulled the door open and stepped into the house.

Chapter 7

L ight slanted into the house through the hole in the conical roof. A fire smoldered in the middle of one big room and smoke billowed up into the beams.

A platform attached to one wall served as a bed. Low wooden chests lined the walls. A few pots and pans hung from the rafters along with bundles of plants and joints of meat. Hand tools hung from pegs on the walls.

The man sat on the ground next to his fire, but he still offered no word of greeting when the landing team entered.

They copied him and crossed their legs to sit on the floor. Dina sat on one side of him and Tom took the other. More people snuck into the room to listen to their conversation and to glare at the strangers, but they kept to the room's outer walls and didn't come near the visitors.

Tom cleared his throat and broke the silence. "My name is Tom Sharples. I'm Second in Command of a starship. It's called the *Savannah* and it's in orbit around this planet. This is Dina Dyer, our biologist. Our people want to form diplomatic relations with you and we're here to make peaceful first contact with you."

"I don't have the authority to talk to you about any of that," the man countered. "I told you I could get visited for talking to you."

"Who would visit you?" Dina asked.

The man shook his head. "You don't understand. It's best if we don't talk about it."

"You're right. We don't understand," Tom told him. "Why don't you explain it to us? If we shouldn't be talking to you or to the children, who should we be talking to?"

"No one."

"Don't you have leaders?" Dina asked. "Don't you have some representatives of some kind?"

"No, we don't."

"You must have some social structure," she argued. "How do you make decisions if there's no one in charge?"

"We don't make decisions—not that way, anyway. No one sticks his neck out like that if he knows what's good for him."

"We have to talk to someone," Tom insisted. "How else can we communicate our intentions?"

"We don't want to hear your intentions. It doesn't matter what your intentions are or who you are or where you came from. Just keep all that to yourself. It can't do anybody any good here."

"But we came here to talk to you—to all of you." Tom waved his hand at the people sitting around the room. "It would be easier if we spoke to your representatives to negotiate our offer, but we could talk to each of you individually if that would work better for you. It would certainly take a lot longer, though."

"We don't want to talk to you. None of us wants to talk to you—about anything. It doesn't matter what you came here for or what it is you want to negotiate. We aren't interested. It would be better if you went back where you came from, but now that you're here, we can't let you go."

Dina froze. "We'll leave if you want us to, but we'd prefer to complete our mission first. We have an attractive offer to make to you and your people."

"You keep your offers to yourselves. We can't let you go. You'll have to stay here until we turn you over to the Pride."

A siren went off in Dina's head. "What's the Pride?"

"The cats."

"What?!" The nightmare of the two jaguars flooded back.

"We have an understanding with the cats. Any stranger coming here has to be turned over to the Pride. We'd get visited if we didn't."

Dina couldn't think. His words made no sense, but in another way, they made too much sense—in the worst possible way. "What is the Pride?"

The man turned on her. "You're a biologist. You should know what that word means. It's a group of cats living together. They live and hunt together. They're a pride of cats and this is Prideland."

Dina stared at him hardly daring to believe the words coming out of his mouth. "Do you mean to tell me those cats have some kind of influence here?"

"You've seen them. You saw them on the road."

"Those two jaguars tried to kill us."

"They didn't try to kill you. If they wanted to kill you, they could have done it with just a little more pressure from their jaws. They were just playing around. They were probably just saying hello."

"Maybe they didn't kill us, but they certainly weren't saying hello. One of them tore our friend's throat out."

"Your friend tried to fire on them. What do you expect?"

"I fired on them, too. I even hit one of them in the shoulder, but they didn't kill me."

"You got away from him. By the time he caught you, he must have recovered from the surprise. He didn't want to kill you. He wanted you turned over to the Pride."

"How do you know that?"

"He told me, of course. You heard him."

"Who told you?"

"Hector. Who else?"

"Who is Hector?" She dreaded hearing the answer.

"I already told you. For a trained biologist on a starship, you aren't very bright, are you? Hector is the jaguar who reduced your friend."

Dina frowned. "What do you mean by 'reduced?"

"What I just said! Your friend was going to fire his weapon and Hector reduced him. Then he told me to send you to the Pride."

Tom and Matthew stared at the man from his other side. They listened in stunned horror to his conversation with Dina. Neither of the two officers interrupted. Dina half-hoped they would because she felt herself sinking deeper and deeper into some black pit she couldn't get out of. "But how could he tell you?"

The man glared at her. "What is wrong with you? How do you think he told me? He told me with his voice. How else? You were right there. You heard him as well as I did."

She gasped out loud. "Do you mean he can talk?"

"Of course, he can talk! All the cats of the Pride can talk and they can think better than you and I can."

"I never heard of cats who can talk and think."

"We would still have to turn you over even if Hector and his brother hadn't caught you on the road and reduced your friend. They found your landing craft and sniffed all around it. They got the scent of all five of you and tracked you to this village. We would still have to turn you over even if they hadn't done all that. We have an understanding with them. If they found out we kept you hidden or let you go, we'd all get visited or worse."

"His brother?"

"Oh, you didn't know, did you?" He laughed in her face. "They're twins, those two. They always travel and hunt together. They live together in the city with their mates and their young. Hector and Victor. You don't see one without the other."

Dina shot a look at Tom for help, but he just kept listening with his mouth open. This conversation had the same effect on him as it did on her.

"They know the whole story," the man went on. "They told us a craft landed in the jungle. They told us the exact location, even, and they told us five people were traveling this way. Then they spotted you on the road. They didn't have time to deal with you on their own. That's our job. They were heading back to the city."

"Why didn't they just wait for us to come into the village?" she asked.

The man shrugged. "They must have come upon you on their way out of the village and decided to catch you themselves. Maybe they did it for the fun."

Her eyes widened. "Fun!?"

He turned away and gazed into the smoldering embers before him. "You heard Hector tell me to send you to the Pride."

Dina shook her head in confusion, but she couldn't clear her thoughts. "I thought it was a person. I didn't know he could talk."

"So we'll turn you over. It's the only thing we can do."

A general scuffle interrupted the exchange. People jumped to their feet and flooded outside. Dina and her teammates went along with the crowd to find the villagers lined along the fences. They gazed up the road toward the jungle.

The same two jaguars stalked up the road. They strode through the middle of the street without taking any notice of anyone. They showed not the slightest hesitation at entering a human habitation.

They paid the landing party no more attention than the villagers even though the visitors stood at the fence in plain view. The cats walked through the village with their big heads lowered and their broad paws stirring up dust. They went around the flower bed and onward out of sight.

"You see?" their host went on when they returned to his house. "They haven't left after all. They want to see if we followed their orders."

"If they wanted us," Dina asked, "why didn't they take us themselves?"

"How could they take you? They are two and you are four. No, they couldn't take you and they have to see if we do our duty. Someone else will take custody of you."

"Who?"

The man shrugged. "Who knows? Whoever has the time and inclination to take you."

He pulled a rope down from the rafter and hung a pot of water over his fire pit. He poked up the coals to make a blaze under the pot. He tossed a handful of dried plant material into the steaming water and set out a row of cups.

The ritual of preparing the drink softened him. "We have an understanding with the cats. We live according to that understanding. You'll come to your own understanding with the Pride in time."

His words piqued Dina's curiosity. If she had her handpad, she would have recorded this. "Tell us about your understanding with them."

"The cats are superior to us in every way. They're stronger, faster, and smarter. We've learned over the years to acknowledge their superiority. We're lucky to have such a close relationship with them."

"What happens if you break the agreement?"

"We never break the agreement. Only people with an understanding enjoy the benefits of living with the cats and following the laws of the Pride."

The man lifted his pot off the fire and poured steaming tea into the cups. He passed them to the four teammates before taking the last one for himself. Dina touched the fragrant liquid to her lips. "Isn't there anything you can do to help us?"

"I'm sorry."

Tom spoke up from the other side of the fire. "What's to stop us from going back to our pod, getting into it, and flying away? We could even pretend to beat you up to make it look like you didn't help us."

Their host stared into his teacup and shrugged. "We can't let that happen. We could get visited if we did and no one wants to risk that."

"What happens if you got visited?" Dina asked.

"You'll be much better off with them, anyway. The Pride can give you everything you need and they can handle any business with your people. The Pride can handle any situation like this."

Dina tried one last time. "There's someone here who knows about our people. If we find him, maybe he can explain things better than we can."

"Who is he?"

"His name is Alexander Mathus. Do you know who he is?"

The man stood up. He towered over her. "I am Alexander Mathus."

Chapter 8

Dina's jaw dropped. "You're Alexander Mathus? Then you know all about the Coalition."

He nodded. "I know all about it."

"Then you can't turn us over to these cats. We're on a diplomatic mission. You can help us negotiate with these people. Your father sent us here to find you. We're here to take you home."

He shook his head. "It doesn't matter who you are or what you're doing here. We'll turn you over. If you have anything to say about what goes on here, you can say it to the Pride." He walked away and left them alone with the villagers lining the walls.

Dina waited until the door banged shut. Then she whispered to Tom, "Let's get out of here."

Tom shook his head. "We're not leaving until we fulfill our mission. Even if we can't incorporate them, we have to take Mathus back. We can't go back without him."

"You heard what he said. They're going to turn us over to those cats. We can't let that happen. We have to leave now."

Matthew spoke up. "We wouldn't get away. There are hundreds of villagers here. They would overpower us and stop us from leaving."

"We have our weapons," Dina whispered. "These people don't have anything but knives and clubs. We could fight our way out."

"I'm with Dina," Tania added. "We already lost Marcus and these people refuse to negotiate with us. Even Mathus is against us. We should fall back while we have a chance."

"I'll make that decision," Tom countered, "and we're not leaving. They're taking us to this Pride, so we'll find someone we can negotiate with. They know we're diplomatic representatives. They wouldn't dare hurt us."

"They already hurt Marcus," Dina pointed out. "We could be next."

Tom didn't budge. Dina recognized the expression on his face. There was no point arguing. Mathus took her weapon away. It left a hollow place inside her jacket, but Tom still had his. Maybe he was right and they should stick out the mission a little longer.

Mathus came back, but he didn't sit down again. Five other men entered behind him and they formed a line. They scowled down at the strangers. Tom met their eyes with his own direct gaze. "If we're going to the Pride, we better go now. We have important work to do."

Mathus shook his head. "We have procedures to follow. We have to have a class."

"What kind of class?"

"To teach you about the Pride. You don't have any understanding with the Pride, so we have to teach you."

"I don't like the sound of that," Tom murmured.

"You will like it," Mathus replied. "The class will help you come to your own understanding with the Pride. Whenever something like this happens, we have a class. It strengthens our understanding of our place in the Pride. You'll see."

Tom shrugged. "I won't argue against it if you think it will help us communicate with the Pride. We need to learn about it."

At a nod from Mathus, the other men stepped forward. At some unseen signal, they swooped down as one and stuck their hands inside the team's shirts. They pulled out the three remaining weapons so fast no one could react fast enough to stop them.

Tom reared back. "Hey!" His hand shot out for his weapon, but the man over him yanked the gun out of reach. No one could do anything. The landing team was totally defenseless.

Tom looked over at Dina with a very different expression on his face. He glanced at Matthew and Tania, too, but it was too late. They'd missed the only chance they would ever have to fight their way out.

The men gave the visitors no time to change their minds. They laid hold of the strangers and dragged Dina, Tania, and Matthew toward the door. Dina struggled in vain to fight her way back to Tom. "Tom, hold onto me!"

Tom went wild. He tore at the hands holding him and yelled at the top of his lungs, "You can't do this! Dina, give me your hand. Hold onto me! You can't do this! We're diplomatic representatives! You can't do this!"

Two men held him down and eventually punched him into submission while the others dragged Dina and her comrades kicking and screaming from the house. Dina scratched and fought, but the men overpowered her by main force. The door slammed shut and she gave vent to wordless howls.

They dragged her through the dust by her arms. She bit and flailed, but she couldn't get her feet on the ground to put up a decent struggle. They hauled her to a neighboring house and tossed her through the door where they locked her in and left her there.

She crashed to the floor screaming toothless threats about diplomatic protocol. She called for Tom. She threatened these people with everything she could think of, but every word fell on deaf ears.

Hours passed and night blotted out any light coming through the roof hole. No fire burned in that room. No one came to see her or talk to her.

After hours of sitting alone on the cold hard ground, she started to wish someone would come. Even someone threatening and dangerous would be better than no one. She couldn't see or hear anything, so after a while, she curled up on the floor and nursed her bruises.

She must have lain there in the dark for half the night. A thousand doubts and nightmares played through her mind. What did they plan to do to her? Would she ever see any of her teammates alive again?

Maybe they would never get off this planet. Maybe she would never get a chance to marry Tom. They were so happy together just a few hours ago, so secure in their plans for their future.

Hunger gnawed at her insides and thirst tore at her throat. She closed her eyes to go to sleep when a rustling sound outside startled her awake. She sat bolt upright and stared into the darkness.

The door opened and Alexander Mathus came in carrying a lighted lantern. He held the lantern over his head and peered down at her.

Without a word to her, walked back to the door and barred it behind him to lock himself in with her. Then he hung the lantern from a post and sat down in front of her. "You aren't hurt, are you?"

She looked away. "A lot you care."

His voice softened. "I do care. How could I not care? You're from the Coalition, so you're my own people."

"How could you do this to us? You should be helping us, not holding us prisoners like this."

His voice caressed her shattered nerves. "It's because I care about you as my own people that I'm here now. I'm here to help you. I'm here to make sure you get the best treatment possible."

She shook her head. "I wish I could believe you. I wish none of this was happening."

"None of this would be happening if you and your friends hadn't come into Prideland with hostile intentions. You invaded the Pride's territory armed with weapons and intent on subverting the Pride's sovereignty. Then you fired your weapons at those cats and tried to kill them."

"How could we not fire on them? They attacked us on the open road and they killed our friend. We fired on them to defend ourselves."

"They didn't attack you. Hector and Victor went into the jungle to investigate a spacecraft landing. They didn't plan to kill anyone. When they saw you on the road, they had to investigate you, too. You drew your weapons and you fired on them. You hit Hector in the shoulder and your friend Marcus could have killed Victor. It's the cats who had to defend themselves. You must understand that."

"They didn't have to kill him." The memory of Marcus on the *Savannah* hovered before her eyes. He was so vital and optimistic just a few hours ago. Now he was gone.

"They didn't have to, but they did. We can't change that now. You can't blame them for doing it. They're cats. They fight and they kill. Anyway, they didn't kill you or your friend, Tom. That should prove to you that they don't just go around killing everything in sight."

She stared down at her hands. "I guess not."

"These are intelligent creatures. They know what they're doing. When you have your own understanding with them, you'll see I'm right. The best thing you can do is to entrust yourself to them entirely. They're so superior to us in every way that you'll never regret it."

"I can't do that," she murmured, "not yet."

Alexander smiled. "I know how it is. Believe me. I was like you when I first came here. I couldn't get it into my head that humans were inferior to some animals. To me, human beings were the crown of biological evolution. After a while, though, I realized these cats were better than us in every way. Once I realized that, I turned my life over to them and I've never looked back."

"I'm not turning my life over to anyone," Dina snapped, "especially not to a bunch of cats."

"That's all right. No one's asking you to do anything you don't want to do, but pretty soon, you'll do it of your own free will. You're a biologist. You of the whole group can understand these cats the best."

"What do you mean?" she asked.

"You know people aren't the greatest thing in the universe as far as biological fitness goes. We're actually quite inferior in the overall scheme of things. We might have big brains and a sophisticated social system, but physically, we're weak and vulnerable."

"That doesn't make us inferior."

"It would make us inferior if another species had all our strengths and none of our weaknesses," he pointed out. "Imagine an entire race as intelligent as we are, with all our social structure, all our sophisticated language, and at the same time, the physical power, speed, and agility of a full-grown tiger. Human beings wouldn't stand a chance against such an animal."

"We might not stand a chance in a physical confrontation. That still doesn't make us inferior."

"Now you're just being stubborn," he countered. "The cats' superiority goes way beyond physical prowess and you know it. You can do better than this. Stop throwing obstacles in your own way. The sooner you realize you don't have to fight the Pride, the happier you'll be. You're a reasonable person. That's why I'm here talking to you."

Dina squirmed. "You should be talking to Tom, not me. He's my superior officer and he's the Coalition representative on this mission. Whatever you have to say, you should say to him."

"Your friends are all in different houses now. Different people are talking to each of them the way I'm talking to you. I chose to come here to talk to you. You're a biologist. You must realize how remarkable and majestic these cats are. You'll make a valuable asset to the Pride and I want to help you come to an understanding with them. As soon as you do that, you'll be on your way to a more meaningful and fulfilling life."

"I don't want a more meaningful and fulfilling life. I'm perfectly happy with my life the way it is. I'm happy being an officer on a starship. I'm happy with my relationships with my friends and coworkers and my sweetheart and I don't want to change any of that. I don't care how superior these cats are."

"Dina," Alexander murmured. "Do you mind if I call you Dina? You introduced yourself to me a little while ago and I think we can talk on a first-name basis. Dina, try just for a little while to step out of your little world and see something greater. You could be a part of a revolutionary advancement in the evolution of the human race."

"How?"

"These cats are superior to us. You just said so yourself. They give us a completely different way to live our lives that gives new meaning to being human. Living with an understanding with the Pride gives us the kind of purpose and belonging humans throughout history have only been able to dream about. The religions of Earth promised this kind of fulfillment, but they only ever held out a dim hope for it. Now we have it. We can take our places in the Pride and fulfill our destiny as human beings."

Dina snorted. "You must be joking. How can a race of cats, however intelligent and advanced, hold the fulfillment of human destiny? How can they take the place of religion? They aren't even in the same category of experience."

"We live our best, most complete lives in harmony with the Pride. You'll see. Nothing in human existence compares with it. I've found this fulfillment for myself. I speak from personal experience."

"What have you experienced? Tell me."

"I understand so much more now than I did before I came here. I understand where I belong and what I'm supposed to do with my life. I don't doubt anymore about who I'm supposed to be and what I'm supposed to believe. That's all gone. I don't have to worry anymore about living my best life. As long as I'm a part of the Pride, I'm doing what I'm supposed to do. My life is dedicated to helping other people achieve the same sense of belonging and purpose. You will, too, as soon as you come to an understanding with the Pride."

"I'm not so sure," she muttered.

"I am. As soon as I met you, I knew you were the kind of person who would see the value and potential of the Pride. I knew you would realize your full potential by embracing the Pride and finding your place in it." He held out his hand to her. "Come on. I'm taking you back to my house. Your friends are waiting for you there."

"You said they were all in different houses."

"They were, but they'll be back now. They've been talking to the other factors."

"Factors? What's that?"

"I'm a factor of this village. It means I'm responsible for people who need help coming to an understanding with the Pride. That's my job."

"You said you don't have any leaders or any influence over these people. Now you're telling me the opposite."

"I don't have any power to negotiate between the Pride and the Coalition. None of us does. You have to take that up with the Pride."

"How will we do that?"

"When you get to the city, you'll learn how things work, but leave that until later. Come back to my house for now. We have more to discuss there."

He took her hand and smiled. That smile eased her fears. He was finally talking to her and opening up about his life here. She was making some progress toward fulfilling their mission.

He led her out into the street. A sea of stars floated overhead and Dina paused on the doorstep to breathe in the night air. She couldn't see anyone else nearby.

Alexander paused to let her look up at the sky. "You see? Prideland isn't all bad. We have a lot of love and beauty and goodness here."

"I hope you're right."

"Of course I'm right. I've been here long enough to know. You can take my word for it."

He led her across the street to his house. They crossed the threshold holding hands as though they'd known each other all their lives. Tom saw her holding hands with Alexander and his eyes popped. She dropped Alexander's hand in an instant, but it was too late.

Chapter 9

Dina sat down in her old place by the fire with Tom and Matthew and Tania. Exhaustion weighed her down to the floor. She needed sleep. Hopefully, this negotiation would end soon and then she could get something to eat and go to sleep. It must be after midnight. Her friends gazed back at her with hollow eyes and pinched faces. Did she look as worn out as they did?

The same five village men stood against the opposite wall with their arms folded. They must be the other factors.

The instant Alexander Mathus joined them, his demeanor changed. "Stand up!" he ordered.

The landing team jumped to their feet, even Tom.

"Form a line!" Alexander snapped. "Right here! Face front!"

They formed a line and faced front pressing their arms to their sides. They held their breath and waited. The factors came forward and lined up opposite them with their brows knit and their eyes flashing.

"You landed on this planet illegally," Alexander barked. "You invaded the sovereign territory of Prideland for the express purpose of overthrowing the native government. Admit it!"

Tom opened his mouth to explain, but Mathus cut him off. "No one told you to speak. You'll be silent until you're told to answer. You're a prisoner here and you'll keep your place. You have no right to respond. You'll answer when you're invited to, not before."

Tom tried to say something else, but Mathus shouted over him. "Keep quiet! You're international terrorists planning to overthrow the sovereign government of Prideland. You've admitted your guilt more than once, so don't waste time denying it. Stand up straight! You're on trial here!"

The rapid-fire orders worked magic on the team. They snapped to attention every time Alexander ordered them to and they held their tongues. Only Tom rallied to defend them.

"This is no trial. A trial involves defense counsel and an independent judge. I don't see any of that here."

"You better control your mouth if you know what's good for you!" Alexander snarled. "You landed in the jungle to conceal your arrival. You wanted to subvert our society by inciting domestic unrest. Don't deny it."

A second man stepped forward and opened up in an even more cutting tone. "You're slags. You aren't fit to enter decent people's houses until you come to an understanding with the Pride. No one will have anything to do with you until you do."

"You'd be better off dead than to live without an understanding with the Pride," a third man added. "Do you want to be slags for the rest of your lives? Do you want to eat mud and slugs and snails off the jungle floor with the rest of the slags? I wouldn't let my children come within a hundred miles of any slag."

On and on it went through the small hours until Dina couldn't tell one man from the next. She actually tricked herself into thinking Alexander might be a friend. Now she couldn't tell when he or some other man shouted abuse and insults at her.

The night blurred into a haze of hunger, exhaustion, and despair. Dina stopped trying to understand what the men said. She couldn't make head or tail of their arguments, much less think clearly enough to counter them. Were they making any sense at all or was her brain just addled from lack of sleep.

All at once, the shouting stopped. Dina floundered out of her daze just in time. Before she knew what was happening, the men jumped on the landing party and beat them all senseless.

Two big men attacked her and Tania. The others doubled up on Tom and Matthew in pairs. Blows struck Dina's body all over. Even then, she couldn't understand what was happening or why the factors were doing this. Maybe she was just hallucinating.

The men dumped the landing team back in their places. Then the factors worked over each prisoner individually, starting with Tom. He was the biggest and strongest and the leader of the party. The factors had to make an example of him.

They dragged him into the middle of the room, kicked him and thumped him with sticks, and lashed him with leather straps. Between blows, they shouted, "You're a slag! Say you're a slag! You're here to overthrow the Pride. Admit it!"

Blood ran from his nose and ears. His face became one solid mass of pulpy purple flesh. He tried to curl up to protect his head and body under his arms, but they held him down and stomped on his face with their boot heels.

Tom held up under the torment as long as he could, but in the end, he said what they wanted him to say. He had to say it to get them to stop before they beat him to death.

He admitted he was a worthless slag who wanted to overthrow the Pride. He acknowledged the cats were superior to humans. He said he wanted nothing more in the world than to come to an understanding with the Pride. Once he said it, they threw him back into his place on the floor. Then they started on Tania.

No training could protect the team from fractured ribs and bruised kidneys and broken noses. Tania kept quiet as long as she could, but after an hour or more of continuous attack, she broke down and admitted everything they wanted her to admit. She said she would come to any understanding with the Pride that they wanted her to come to, but they beat her just as much, if not more.

The men surrounded Dina next. It was her turn. At least she didn't have to watch Matthew going through the same ordeal. The waiting was worse than the actual beating. By the time her turn came, she was almost glad to get hit just so she wouldn't have to wait anymore.

Alexander Mathus's face stood out from the others. She saw him coming nearer out of the surreal haze. He couldn't hit her, not after everything he said about helping her.

He met her eyes and read her thoughts. He smiled at her the same way he smiled when they sat alone and he held her hand. Then, slowly and deliberately so she could see the movement of his arm, he raised his fist and smashed her in the face.

She saw it all happen to Tom and Tania, but she still couldn't comprehend it. What did they expect from her? How could Alexander win her trust and then deliberately violate it this way? How could he deceive her like this?

Did they want her to embrace the Pride or reject it? Did they want her to worship it or fear it? She couldn't do both. Beating the team like this contradicted everything they said before about coming to an understanding with the Pride. How could anyone come to an understanding with a system that brutalized people this way?

Dina tried to be strong and defiant, but in the end, she caved. She said she was a slag and not worth the flesh on her bones. She said they landed in the remote jungle to conceal their arrival, which was true. She said they planned to overthrow the sovereign authority of the Pride in favor of a foreign government, which was also true.

What else could incorporating this planet into the Coalition mean but overthrowing the native government? The people would have to give up their autonomy and accept the Coalition's governance, wouldn't they?

She said she wanted to come to an understanding with the Pride and serve the cats for the rest of her life. By the time the factors got through with her, she meant every word. She wanted nothing more than to come to an understanding with the Pride so she could get out of this house.

They beat her until she couldn't really open her eyes, so she didn't see what they did to Matthew. It must have been the same. After they finished with him, they beat all four again just to wrap up the lesson, but Dina didn't remember that. She only remembered the early morning light coming through the door when the men left the house.

The factors left different men to guard the four teammates. Dina and her friends lay in silence on the cold floor for several more hours. Every time any of them groaned or turned over, the sentries kicked them until they lay still.

Dina swung between devastating pain and a blissful cocktail of sleep and unconsciousness. When she revived enough to wake up, she could only pray to pass out again to get away from the pain in her head and body.

Thus she spent her first night on the planet.

Chapter 10

Daylight shone through the hole in the roof and Dina saw her teammates for the first time. The others looked a lot worse than Dina felt, but she must have looked just as bad.

Matthew wheezed every time he exhaled. Tania kept licking a cut on her lower lip. Tom's eyes darted around the room, over his teammates, the sentries, the door, and up to the roof. Dried blood clumped his ears and nostrils. His lips pouted in swollen, battered balloons.

Dina let her eye slip around the room, too. How could a simple landing mission go so wrong so fast? She'd been on enough of these incorporation runs to expect the worst, but this one took the cake. In all her years on the team, she never met anyone so hostile from the very first contact.

These people's hostility started even before the team landed. They hated any and all outsiders. Alexander Mathus might have taught them to feel this way, but Dina didn't think so. These people had a policy of turning over all outsiders to the Pride. No one wanted to see, hear, or have anything to do with anyone outside their world. They wanted to know nothing about them.

She couldn't understand them. It flew in the face of everything she knew and believed. Her team met plenty of people who decided not to join the Coalition. Some even drove the team out at gunpoint, but at least they listened to the team's proposal first. These people wouldn't even talk about it.

The sentries stood impassive through the night. They glared down at the strangers and kicked and beat anyone who talked or stirred in their sleep.

The guard changed twice to keep the men fresh and alert. Their vigilance never once slipped. The landing party never got another chance to escape. No one bothered to feed the prisoners or offer them water and no one tended the fire to keep them warm.

Alexander Mathus came back late in the morning and this time he left the door propped open. Dina's spirits soared at the sight of daylight streaming in from outside. At last she would be able to stretch her legs and get something to eat, but several more hours passed with no change. The team stayed inside the house long into the afternoon.

Dina resigned herself to spending another night on the floor when a different man came in with an armload of rope. The sentries brightened up and went to work.

They tied up the prisoners from head to foot so Dina and her friends couldn't move a muscle. The sentries paid no attention to the prisoners' injuries.

The men checked and double-checked the knots again and again. Then the guards turned away and left the team on the floor for more endless waiting. The sentries never slackened their watch for an instant. Most of the day passed with no food, no water, and no rest.

Alexander came back a third time, and at a nod from him, the sentries advanced on the prisoners. Dina cringed in anticipation of another beating, but instead, the men laid hold of the team and hauled them outside into the clear day.

The ropes held the prisoners so immobile that the men had to carry each person out one at a time. Four men carried Tom and two carried Dina outside where a wagon yoked with two water oxen waited at the gate.

The sentries dumped the prisoners into it and then climbed on board themselves. Alexander Mathus mounted to the driver's seat. He picked up the reins and urged the oxen into a slow, steady plod out of the village.

Dina couldn't find a comfortable position on the hard wooden boards. She rolled from one side to another and got another kick for her trouble. She yelped in pain.

She couldn't see anything outside the wagon, but the sentries sure could. They smiled and shouted at unseen people. Tom took the risk of sitting up, but the guards paid no attention. After a long, tense wait, Dina copied him and the sentries ignored her, too.

Alexander drove down the long dirt road until it changed to a busy city street. The city walls, windows, doorways, and arches of chiseled beige stone all followed the same distinctive architectural design.

Men, women, and children of all ages crowded the streets. Their colorful clothes looked so different from the village men in their drab leather clothes.

The sun inched across the sky and the wagon wheels bumped through cobblestone streets. People carried out their daily business in the streets. They went in and out of houses and called to each other across the squares. Every sound rang off the stone walls and played the music of a thriving and prosperous human population.

Dina saw cats everywhere she looked. She never saw so many cats in one place in her life. Cats occupied every surface, every wall and windowsill, and every street corner. They crowded in doorways, lounged under trees in the parks, and stalked up the middle of the street.

Thousands of cats of every species, size, and color lived in that city. Fully grown lions with bushy manes watched the wagon pass. Cougars strutted down the sidewalk. Tabby house cats washed their paws in the sunshine. A tiny Mexican Hairless perched in a window overlooking the main square.

At first Dina thought the people mostly ignored the cats. The cats' presence was no more remarkable to them than the tree lizards chirping overhead. These people didn't stare like Dina and her teammates did and no one even tried to communicate with the cats. The two groups kept apart, at least in public.

After a while, Dina noticed people giving way to the cats on the streets and sidewalks. The cats might disregard people and vehicles blocking their path, but the people took pains to yield to the cats whenever possible.

The scene presented a fascinating study for Dina's biologist brain. A group of children ran down the sidewalk. Their voices and footfalls rang off the walls, but they flattened themselves against the wall to give a bunch of house cats room to pass. Those cats stood no taller than the children's knees. The children resumed their play only after the cats passed out of sight around the next corner.

Alexander Mathus drove to the city's main square. One of the sentries hopped out of the wagon and disappeared into the crowd. Mathus parked his wagon and reclined in his seat to wait. The other guards relaxed, too, so Dina and her friends could look around as much as they liked.

Wagons loaded with food and livestock packed the square. Cats and people strolled through the jumbled collection of goods. Animals and bags changed hands in no predictable order and the cats took their pick of the merchandise on sale.

A little cheetah cub with a ridge of grey fur down his neck pounced on a tree lizard tethered to a vendor's stall. The cub crushed the lizard in his jaws. The lizard squawked out loud before the cub crushed its rib cage with his teeth.

Then the little cat sat down on the cobbles and devoured the lizard in full view of the lizard's late owner. The man didn't bat an eye. He just went on talking to another customer.

Three lionesses strolled through the market. They examined all the livestock before deciding on a cow tied to a wagon.

They surrounded the cow and jumped on her as one coordinated killing machine. One lioness grabbed the cow by the snout while a second snapped the cow's foreleg in her jaws to cripple it.

The third lioness leapt onto the cow's neck. In a few minutes, they pulled the helpless animal to the ground and one lioness crushed the cow's throat in her jaws. The other two lionesses tore into the cow's flesh even before it stopped thrashing.

By the time the cow lay completely dead, dozens of cats of every size gathered around to share the feast. They formed a ring around the lionesses and watched them gorge on the carcass. When the lionesses walked away with their bellies sagging, more cats moved in and demolished what was left.

Several fights broke out over the scraps and bones. Cats ran from the scene with tufts of fur missing and bloody ears and faces.

The people in the market paid no attention to this incident and many others just like it. The cats ate what they wanted with no interference from anyone. A few vendors left the market empty-handed after cats devoured their goods or killed their stock and no one offered a word of complaint.

Chapter 11

The sun slanted low between the buildings and the market dwindled to a close. A young woman with a country girl's sturdy frame approached Alexander's wagon. She shook back her golden hair and smiled up at him. "Good evening, Factor Mathus."

The guards flew into action. They cut Tania's ropes and set her on her feet next to the wagon. The girl scrutinized her. "Is this her?"

"That's the one, Maddy," Alexander replied. "She doesn't look like much, but she might be good for something."

"Why do we have to take her, anyway?" Maddy complained.

Mathus held out both hands. "Hector ordered us to split them up. They already tried to kill him and his brother. We can't keep them in the village."

"They should have been reduced as soon as they were caught," Maddy returned. "They'll only make trouble."

"I'm just glad to get them off my hands. I have work to do back home, and the sooner the others come to collect these three, the sooner I can get on down the road."

Maddy sighed. "I guess I have to take her. Khalid can figure out what to do with her." She cocked her head at Tania. "Can you understand our language?"

"Yes, I understand you," Tania's replied.

"Then come with me. I don't know what we'll do with you, but I guess I have no choice but to take you."

Maddy walked away leaving Tania to hurry after her. Just before Tania turned the corner and disappeared, she looked back over her shoulder toward the wagon. Matthew stared straight ahead and didn't look at her. Then Tania turned away and her teammates lost sight of her.

Dina glanced at Tom and found him gazing back at her. Would they be separated, too? How long would it be before they saw each other again?

Tom pursed his lips and glared at their sentries. "What are you going to do with us?"

Alexander didn't take his eyes off the market. "You'll be divided up until you come to an understanding with the Pride. That's all you need to know."

"It sounds to me like coming to an understanding with the Pride means more than you think it does."

"You should be grateful the Pride is giving you a chance to come to an understanding," Alexander replied. "You should be grateful they didn't reduce you the minute you landed. They've done it before. I'm surprised the Pride gave you a second chance. If I was you, I'd make an effort to come to an understanding with them as soon as possible. They might not be so generous in the future."

"Which houses are we going to?" Tom asked.

"I don't know. Hector arranged it all. Each house will send someone to get you. That's all I know."

A young man approached the wagon and greeted Mathus. The sentries slashed the rope binding Matthew's feet, but he left his wrists and arms tied.

The village men dragged Matthew out of the wagon box and stood him in front of the young man. Mathus looped the rope through Matthew's wrist bonds to make a leash and placed it in the young man's hands. The young man yanked the leash and hauled Matthew out of the square.

Dina's mind went into overdrive. If only she could get Alexander to open up to her the way he did last night, he might help her. "How did you come to an understanding with the Pride?"

"I suppose I did it the same way you'll do it. After we crashed here, we found our way to the village. It took us a while to understand how the Pride works. Some tried to leave and we had classes just like you."

"Are the other shuttle passengers in the village with you?"

"Most are. Some are in the city. I don't know where some of them are. Different people handle the process differently. Almost all these people were born here, of course. They've seen classes all their lives, so they grow up with an understanding of the Pride. They get it from their parents. My children will have a much easier time than I had."

Dina gasped. "Your children!"

"Of course." Alexander twisted around in the wagon seat to study her. "You said my father sent you here to get me. He must have told you my wife and children were with me on the shuttle."

"He did. I just never thought about a child going through a class. It must be awful for them."

"It's not so bad. When they're little, they watch other people having classes, so they get the idea without going through it themselves. It's only when they get older that they run the risk of saying the wrong thing or making a mistake."

"How could you stand by and watch your children being beaten?" Dina exclaimed. "I couldn't stand a child going through what we went through last night."

"I admit it's not the most pleasant experience. I went through the same thing when we first came. It's no more pleasant for me to have to do it to you, but I got through it. Just about everyone in Prideland has gone through it at some point in their lives. If my children go through it, they'll survive and it will help them come to a better understanding with the Pride."

"I wouldn't let my children go through that," Dina muttered more to herself than to him.

"I thought the same thing when we first came here. That's why I became a factor. I thought I could protect them better if I took a position of responsibility in the village."

"Do you still feel that way?"

"Now I know that going to a class or anything else that might happen isn't the worst thing that could happen to my children. It's better for them to come to an understanding with the Pride and take their place in this society than anything else that could happen to them. It's better for them to go through all of that than to be a slag in the jungle. I'd do anything to prevent that."

"What's so bad about being a slag in the jungle?"

"They don't have an understanding with the Pride. I can't think of anything worse than that. When you find out how the slags live, you realize why living without an understanding with the Pride is so bad."

"How do the slags live?"

Alexander growled low under his breath. "They're worse than the lowest animal. They're walking corpses. They don't take any care of themselves or their children. They breed like rabbits, but they don't bother to feed their children. They let their children starve to death when the cold weather comes. The children run around with their teeth rotting in their heads and weeping sores all over their bodies. The slags don't even teach their children to speak properly. They communicate with grunts and snorts. That's what we hear, anyway."

"And you believe that?" Dina asked. "No human being would live like that."

"That's what living without an understanding with the Pride will do to you. That's what it means to be a slag."

This conversation was going nowhere so Dina decided to change the subject. "Do you know how humans came to live with these cats? Have you learned anything about their history?"

"All I know is that the people came to an understanding with the cats. That's all we ever hear about how it happened—that people came to an understanding with the cats. That says it all, doesn't it? The cats are so superior to us in every way, it only makes sense that people would come to live with them. We're lucky to have an understanding with them."

"You said that already," she murmured, but he didn't hear her or pretended not to.

"That's the way everybody tells the story. As far back in history as anyone can remember, everybody says the people came to an understanding with the cats and that's how we live today."

Tom broke in on their discussion. "Where was Matthew taken? You knew the man who took him, didn't you?"

Mathus nodded. "He helps a cat called Fallon. He lives near here."

Dina brightened up. "Then we might see him sometime."

Alexander shrugged. "That depends if your benefactor lets you go, but they probably won't."

"Why wouldn't they let us see our friends?"

"I only meant the decision rests with your benefactor."

Tom frowned. "What do you mean by 'benefactor'?"

"The cat who takes custody of you. Your benefactor will decide whether you can go see your friends, but I'm sure Hector told them all about you and how you tried to kill him and his brother. They won't give you a chance to do it again. They'll keep a close eye on you until you come to an understanding with the Pride."

"We didn't try to kill him or his brother," Tom countered. "We only tried to defend ourselves."

Alexander turned away. "It doesn't matter. The Pride can't risk you causing any more trouble, so you'll be separated. Hector arranged for you to go to the houses of influential cats. They'll make sure you come to an understanding with the Pride before you go running around on your own. I would tread lightly these next few weeks if I was you."

Chapter 12

A girl barely taller than the wagon wheel skipped through the crowd. "Where's the slag for Elyse's house?"

Mathus pointed to Tom. "Right here! Wait a minute while I cut him free. Can you handle him or should I keep his hands tied for you?"

She laughed and tossed her head. "I can handle anything! Just cut him loose so I don't have to carry him. Elyse can't wait to see him and find out all about where he comes from and who he is. It will be so exciting having a new face in the house! We get so bored with the same old helpers all the time."

Mathus freed Tom.

"Come with me, slag!" the girl sang out. "You're going home!"

Before Tom and Dina could say goodbye, a stout, sweaty woman shouldered her way through the market and distracted Alexander. "What have you got for Renfroe's house?"

Alexander pointed at Dina. "The last one. I'll cut her loose for you."

"Not so fast," the woman snapped. "Cut her legs free, but leave her hands tied. I don't want to take any chances."

Alexander held up a scrap of rope. "I can tie this to her wrists to give you something to hold onto."

"Do it." The woman swung a net bag in her hands and her knot of grey hair wobbled on top of her head. "I have all this to carry and I don't have more than one hand free to control her. I hear she tried to escape yesterday. Well, she won't get away from me. Renfroe can do what he wants with her, but I'll do my duty."

Alexander tied the rope to Dina's wrists and handed the leash to the woman. She tugged on the rope to drag Dina out of the wagon "Come on. We don't have all night."

"I'm coming," Dina replied.

"No backtalk!" The woman gave the rope a vicious jerk. "I won't put up with any nonsense from a slag like you. If you know what's good for you, you'll keep your mouth shut and do what you're told or I'll make sure you get visited."

She yanked the rope so hard that she almost knocked Dina off her feet. She stomped away with Dina stumbling after her. By the time Dina remembered to look back to see what happened to Tom, she and her guide had already turned the corner. The wagon, Alexander, Tom, and the market slipped away into the past. She might never see any of them again.

Every time she paused to look around, the woman jerked the rope so Dina almost fell on top of her. If Dina bumped into her, the woman shoved her back with all her strength. "Get off me, slag!"

Dina fell back to the end of the leash. She did her best to keep up without bumping into the woman or falling behind. The rope cut into her wrists, but the woman took no notice. She wrenched the rope again with another brutal, "Come on!"

Dina got so absorbed in obeying the woman that she didn't pay any attention to where she was going. The woman turned into the courtyard of a grand house in a quiet neighborhood. By then, Dina didn't know where she was.

She couldn't retrace her steps to the market or to the road leading back to the village even if she found a way to escape. She couldn't run away without her teammates anyway. She would have to wait until they escaped together as a group.

It was really more of a mansion than a house. Ornamented cornices surrounded every doorway and windowpane. A fountain tinkled in the courtyard.

A brick walkway led to a carved wooden door set in a stone archway, but the woman didn't enter through that door. She towed Dina from the courtyard around to a different door on the side of the house.

This door swung open on cracked leather hinges and led into a low, dim passage. The woman hooked her meaty paw around the back of Dina's neck and shoved her in. The woman let go of the leash and shot a wooden bolt to lock the door from the inside.

Dina sprawled hard across the stone floor and instantly broke out in a sweat from the stifling heat. A roaring fire blazed in the enormous fireplace and heated the room to an oppressive temperature.

Haunches of meat, bundles of herbs, bunches of vegetables, and every kind of cooking utensil hung from the rafters. A massive hewn wooden table occupied the center of the room with giant cleavers and pointed knives embedded in the table's surface.

The woman set her bag on the table, picked up a knife, and with one swift stroke, slashed the ropes binding Dina's hands. Then the woman stabbed the knife back into the table, took a fistful of Dina's shirt, and pushed her onto a wooden stool by the fire. "Sit there and don't move."

The woman took down vegetables, cheeses, and herbs from the rafters and went to work chopping, mixing, and rolling. She wasn't preparing anything for a cat.

After a while, the fire started to die down. Without thinking, Dina picked up a stray log lying at her feet and pitched it into the coals.

She turned around to find the woman staring at her. Instead of scolding her for daring to move without permission, the woman pursed her lips and snapped, "Thanks." Dina smiled back, but the woman only turned away and went back to work.

She ladled the food into a dozen wooden plates. A cauldron on the fire started to boil and Dina put out her hand to take it off the hook. "Stop!" the woman yelled. She hurried over and took the handle out of Dina's hand. The woman puffed and panted and lifted the pot onto the brick hearth.

"Let me help you," Dina urged.

The woman stabbed the air with her finger. "You stay where you are! I have enough to do without babysitting you!"

"I won't try to escape Let me do something besides sit here. If you have so much to do. At least let me help you. I give you my word of honor I won't do anything other than help you."

The cook scowled. "No, I can't. If I got caught, I could get visited. You stay where you are. Renfroe will decide what to do with you."

"Who's Renfroe?"

"Our benefactor. This is his house."

"Who is he?"

The cook puffed herself up. "He's only the most important cat in the whole Pride. He's Chairman of the Senate, you know."

"I didn't know."

"You'll meet him soon. He'll talk to you himself as soon as he can. He's very busy, what with Senate business and everything else. He's involved in just about everything that happens in all of Prideland."

"He sounds like the closest thing to a leader I've found since we landed."

"No, he's not a leader. The Pride doesn't have leaders."

"Somebody has to be the leader," Dina argued. "Every society has to have somebody in charge."

"Not the Pride. They work together as a group. No cat has any more authority than any other. Renfroe isn't a leader, even if he is Chairman of the Senate. He's just very highly thought of. The other cats respect him and they trust his judgment. That's how he came to be Chairman, but he doesn't exercise any authority over them. Each cat follows his own whims. You'll see. You'll come to an understanding with the Pride and then you'll fit right in."

"Are there many other human beings living here?" Dina glanced at the plates of food on the table. "In this house, I mean?"

"No, just you and me."

"Then who's the food for?"

"Oh, that!" The cook laughed. Her laughter sounded strange after the way she'd been acting just a few minutes ago. "The subsidiaries can't always spare adults to bring their subscription to the market, so they send their children. The children spend all day at the market with their subscription and they have nothing to eat, so they leave for home very hungry. Then they walk for hours before they get to their villages. So Renfroe lets them stop by here and have something to eat before they leave for home. Isn't that kind of him?"

"I don't understand much of what you just said, but, yes, it is very generous of him."

"Renfroe's the kindest, most caring benefactor any helper could ask for. You're very lucky to be sent to him."

"I hope you're right," Dina murmured.

"Here." The woman set a plate in Dina's hands. "You better eat some. You may not get another chance and I understand you had a pretty long day."

"Yes, I did."

The woman stuck a spoon into the food. "You'll need this."

"Thank you."

Dina spooned the hot mixture of vegetables and cheese into her mouth. After more than thirty-six hours without food or sleep, the concoction intoxicated her exhausted brain with visions of home and comfortable beds. "Does Renfroe normally give out charity like this to people?"

"This particular group of subsidiary children comes every evening. They eat as fast as they can before they start for home. Other than that, I can't recall Renfroe taking much notice of the subsidiaries, except when he goes to the market to get their subscription."

"What's the subscription....and what are subsidiaries?"

Before the woman could answer, a clang sounded somewhere in the depths of the house. Dina barely heard it, but the woman instantly dropped her knife and trained her ear toward the sound. "That's him! He's calling for you!"

"Who?"

"Renfroe! Who else? Go!"

Dina jumped off her stool. "Go where?"

"There!" The woman shoved her across the kitchen to a corner behind some shelves. Another door opened there and led into the house itself. The woman pushed Dina through it and slammed the door behind her.

Dina could never imagine a scene as different from the kitchen as the room on the other side of that door. Potted trees and statuary decorated a large hall made of beige stone. The marble floor rang underfoot. Wide, decorated, porticoes opened on both sides into gardens lined with stone benches and flagstone walkways.

Dina wandered down the hall gazing through each portico at the elegance all around her. She came to the end of the hall. Where should she go now? What would Renfroe do when she didn't answer his call?

She looked through the last archway and froze in her tracks. In another manicured garden beyond the arch sat an enormous tiger.

Chapter 13

The tiger swiveled his ears toward Dina and flared his nostrils to catch her scent. His yellow eyes scanned her from head to foot. He must have outweighed her by hundreds of pounds. He could crush her with one swipe of his paw.

He spoke in a purr with a raspy undertone. "There you are. I'm told you've been tied up in the back of a wagon all day. Did Belinda give you something to eat?"

Dina shuffled her feet fighting to keep herself calm. Now she knew what a mouse felt like when facing a cat. This must be Renfroe, the cat who owned this house.

She couldn't lurk in the shadows all night, so she dared to advance into the garden. "If you mean the cook, then yes, she did. Thank you very much for asking."

He inclined his head to one side and examined her more closely. "Think nothing of it."

At that moment, a church bell tolled in the distance and Dina cocked her ear to listen. The sound died over the treetops and drifted away. "What's that?"

"That's just the curfew bell."

Dina started in surprise. "Curfew?"

"Is there a problem?"

Renfroe let out a puff of air from his nostrils. "I'm told you come from a starship. Is that true?"

"Yes. Our landing party came to this planet to invite the human population to join our Coalition of Inhabited Planets. We didn't know they lived with cats."

"Of course you didn't. How could you know?"

"We knew large carnivore species lived on this planet. Our scans showed what types of animals live here, but we couldn't tell from the scans that you were sentient cats. We also couldn't tell that you lived with people. If we had known, we would have re-evaluated our strategy."

A deep chuckle rumbled out of his broad chest. "I'm sure you would have. As it is, now that you know, you are stuck here. The Pride won't let you go."

"Why won't they let us go? We don't belong here."

"We just don't do it. Anyone who lands here stays here. That's the understanding we have with the humans on this planet."

His manners gave her courage and she started talking faster. "I keep hearing about this understanding between the people and the cats, but no one ever explains it. It seems like a way of saying something without saying it."

"You're right. It is a way of saying something without saying it."

"So what is it that you aren't saying?"

"You'll come to an understanding with the Pride and then it will be clear to you. Until then, you'll stay here with me. I need someone like you to talk to."

Dina stiffened. "What do you mean—someone like me?"

"I mean someone intelligent who thinks for herself. That is a quality in painfully short supply around here. No one can think clearly about anything or speak clearly about what they do think about."

"Do you mean the people," Dina asked, "or the cats?"

Renfroe flicked his tail through the air. "All of them. Even some of the more advanced Senators can't formulate their thoughts coherently. Talking to them is like talking to a hollow shaft in the ground. You call down it and only an echo of what you just said comes back up to you."

Dina grinned in spite of herself. At least one person in this crazy place understood.

Renfroe blinked his big eyes at her. "You think it's funny, but you'll see I'm right. You come from outside Prideland. You come from a starship, so you must know about things no one else here knows about."

"What about Alexander Mathus? He comes from outside Prideland, too. He knows as much about the Coalition as I do and he's been here six months. You could ask him anything you wanted to know."

Renfroe half-closed his eyes and scanned the garden. "I don't know that person. Who is Alexander Mathus?"

"He lives in the village. He called himself a factor, whatever that means."

"I don't have much to do with the subsidiaries. They keep to the village. Anyway, you're here now, so I'll talk to you instead. You're a trained scientist—a biologist, I'm told. You must have studied a wide range of subjects and learned how to think critically about them. I look for these things in a helper. None of the other helpers get any education at all. It makes them very dull indeed."

"Who are the helpers?"

"The human people who live with the cats in the city. They perform essential functions of city life, so they are called helpers."

"What functions do they perform?"

He flared his nostrils in her direction for the second time. "Just what you'd imagine. If you spend any time at all in this city, you'll soon see for yourself and then you'll understand."

"Don't the cats of the Pride get any education?"

"Not as much as they ought to. I would like our Pride to interact with other sentient races, but the others don't agree with me. The education our young receive focuses more on the realities of this planet. It doesn't cover all the information they need to look beyond it. Perhaps your coming here will change that."

"Do you really think so?" Dina asked.

Renfroe sighed heavily. "No, I don't. I don't think anything will change it, but I can still enjoy the company of someone from outside Prideland who thinks about something other than our narrow little world."

"I'd be glad to talk to you about anything you want to talk about. I don't often meet someone who hasn't been off their home world. Almost everyone in the Coalition has traveled to at least one other planet. The Armada crews have all traveled to dozens of worlds. I'm not even a senior officer and I've been to over fifty. Tom Sharples—he's our First Officer—he's been to thousands and he's interacted with hundreds of different races. He's the one you should talk to about life outside your world."

"Hmm. He's the one who went to Elyse. I will inquire about him later."

"And there's Tania, our linguist," Dina went on. "She speaks about eighty different languages. I'm sure she would teach you or anyone else who cared to learn. She could teach you to communicate with other sentient races."

"Hmm," he purred. "She went to Khalid. I won't find him so agreeable to interaction with his new helper. He'll want to keep her away from you and the rest of her slag friends."

Dina bristled at that word. "What's that supposed to mean?"

"I mean he won't want me or anyone else talking to her about her life outside of Prideland. He'll want her to come to a firm understanding with the Pride and he'll want to keep her as far away from counterproductive influences as possible. Then again, we all want the same thing for the rest of you. We all want what's best for you."

"Shouldn't I be the one to decide what's best for me?" she asked.

"What's best for you is what's best for Prideland. Look around you at the helpers in the city and the subsidiaries in the villages. Do you really think they would choose a way of life destructive to themselves? Of course not. They come to an understanding with the Pride. What they most need and want are the same things the Pride most needs and wants. We understand each other and we live together in harmony."

"But they're afraid," she argued. "They're all afraid to get visited, whatever that means. It must be some kind of punishment."

"I don't know what being visited means, but whatever it is, it's something the humans do among themselves. It has nothing to do with the Pride."

Dina shifted her feet again. He hadn't told her to sit down. "Belinda said you're Chairman of the Senate."

"That is correct."

"Tell me more about your society. You must be the only sentient cats in the galaxy. How did you come to evolve such complex intelligence?"

"I couldn't tell you that. As far as I know, we've always been this way."

"I find that hard to believe. You're too similar to the cats we have on Earth. You're even the same species and subspecies and individual breeds. You must have been transported here and then developed your intelligence after that. Maybe some sort of mutation changed the way your brains work."

He shrugged. "I can't think of any cat knowing anything about it or I would have heard. I've been around the Senate long enough."

"Have you? You don't look that old to me."

"I'm flattered you think so. I'm fifty years old."

Dina's eyes widened. "Do all the cats of the Pride live that long? The cats on Earth don't live so long."

"We live just as long as humans. Some cats live much longer, what with the wear and tear some people take around here. I'm sure you could make a more careful study of our lifespans if you looked into the public records."

"Tell me about your social structure. I'm supposed to make a report for my captain about everything on the planet's surface."

"There isn't much to tell. The Senate is really nothing more than a venue for the Pride to meet and discuss issues we face by living together. Lions are the only cat species that naturally live together as a group. Tigers like me live alone except when mothers rear their young. We don't even live with our mates, although here in the city it's much more common than among wild cats living in the jungle."

"A large number of small cats living in one place will form a social group."

"That is true, but this conglomeration of large cats in such close proximity to each other creates an artificial structure of its own. We call it a Pride for lack of a better word. We created the Senate to meet and air our differences and hopefully come to some agreement about how to handle them. That's all the Senate is. As Chairman, I'm little more than a referee. I'm not even that since I have no power to arbitrate disputes."

"It sounds a little less than ideal," she remarked.

"That's putting it mildly. Fights often break out on the Senate floor and cats have ripped each other to shreds just as if they were brawling in the street."

"What happens when the humans bring their issues to the Senate?"

"Humans never address the Senate. Sometimes a cat brings his helper along, but never to participate in Senate business. That would be most inappropriate."

"Then what social structure do the humans have? They must have some leadership of their own or at least a set of rules they follow. They couldn't live together if they didn't."

"I'm sure they do, but I don't concern myself with human affairs. I don't know how they order their lives among themselves. It doesn't concern me."

"What about your helpers? Don't they concern you?"

"Only insofar as their lives intersect with mine. When they do, I communicate my wishes to them and that's the last I hear of it. How they deal with other helpers or with subsidiaries—I don't consider that at all."

"I thought you took more interest in the lives of your associates," Dina countered.

"Associates? My helpers aren't associates. The cats of the Pride—yes. Helpers—no."

"But isn't that what the term 'helpers' means?"

"No, it doesn't. I don't associate with helpers."

"But that's what you're suggesting you and I do. When we talk about the Coalition and life off this planet, isn't that associating? Aren't I a helper?"

"You may be a helper and we may be talking about your Coalition, but I don't associate with helpers. I'm making use of a resource that has fallen into my lap through fortunate circumstances. You represent a treasure trove of information that happens to interest me. I will investigate it by talking to you, but I wouldn't go so far as to call that associating with a helper."

Dina pulled her head down between her shoulders. "You don't make the situation sound very advantageous to me."

"It's very advantageous to you. No other cat in the whole Pride would allow you to discuss these things with another human being, let alone a cat. You're very lucky to have me for a benefactor."

Dina turned away. "That's what everybody keeps telling me."

"Take Khalid, for instance," he went on. "He took your friend Tania as a helper, but you can be certain he won't take the slightest interest in her expertise in languages or her experience off this planet. He'll put her to work along with his other domestic helpers. In all likelihood, he won't exchange a single word with her in the time she spends in his house. He'll make use of those things that do interest him, which is entirely up to him."

"That's a bit mercenary, don't you think?"

Renfroe shrugged. "That is the nature of our Pride. Each cat follows his or her own course without interference from anyone else. None of us holds any power over any other, not even the power to suggest someone behave differently."

"If that's true, then you don't have any social structure at all."

"We are not human beings with a complex set of social rules. We are cats. Our connection through our Pride is a loose one. We only have a Pride at all because we live in such close proximity to each other. Beyond that, we barely speak to one another. We share space with each other, but we don't impinge upon one another the way human beings do. If you think about it, the helpers are the ones who make this a city—a city infested with cats."

"It's like no other city I've ever seen," Dina remarked. "Even the humans are like no other people I've met. They behave very strangely."

Chapter 14

Renfroe got up and stretched. "That's enough talk about this planet. We have all the time in the world to talk about this planet and its populations. Tell me about your own people and your life. Start by telling me your name because I do not know it."

"I'm Lieutenant Dina Dyer of the Coalition Armada Vessel *Savannah*." Those words meant exactly nothing in this enchanted garden. They fell into a vast pit of silent meaningless nothing. They became nothing, which is exactly what they were worth. "I'm the staff exo-biologist on board."

"And I am Renfroe." He bowed his head to her. "I am pleased to make your acquaintance."

Dina bowed in return. "The pleasure is all mine."

"Of course it is," he rumbled. "Now tell me exactly how you managed to come here."

Dina skimmed over the events of their landing and their encounter with the village people.

Renfroe nodded. "I heard from Hector that he and Victor found a craft in the jungle. He said he caught four slags and wanted them divided up between houses in the city where they could be kept more safely than in the village."

"What are 'slags'?"

"People who haven't come to an understanding with the Pride, or else they've come to an understanding and then broken it. It can mean either one."

Dina's eyes widened. "Are there people who don't have an understanding with the Pride? Are there others like us who don't understand?"

"Something like that."

Dina looked around the garden. "Where are they?"

"The slags skulk around in the jungle. Neither the subsidiaries nor the helpers will have anything to do with them since the slags don't have an understanding with the Pride. People who have an understanding with the Pride guard their positions very carefully. They keep away from harmful influences. If the slags want to turn their backs on everything the Pride has to offer, that's their loss."

"The village people don't have anything nice to say about them."

"There isn't anything nice to say about them. They live in the most wretched conditions. Their cantons are little more than mud wallows and I understand they can barely speak anymore, they've fallen so far from being human. They eat worms and insects and they sleep out in the rain on the bare wet ground. They're completely insensible to the hardships of their condition and their young starve to death every winter when the food runs low. You wouldn't want to be a slag."

"But you just called me one!"

"That's because you haven't come to an understanding with the Pride, but you'll come to an understanding very quickly. Then you won't be in any danger of becoming a slag. Slags are dangerous. I've even heard of them eating their own kind when they can't find any other food. They're worse than the lowest worms in the mud. You'd be better off dead than to be a slag."

"I didn't realize some people lived away from the cats. I'll have to find out more about them for my report. If they really are living in such terrible conditions, the Coalition will want to do something about that."

"You would be better off having nothing to do with them and you don't have to compile a report for your Coalition. You'll be staying here indefinitely."

Dina bristled again. "I won't stay here. I have to get back to my ship. You can't hold us here against our will."

"I don't intend to hold you here against your will. You'll come to an understanding with the Pride and then you'll realize that staying here is the best possible choice you can make."

"I will not!" she shot back.

Renfroe half-closed his eyes. "Let's not argue about it right now. I see we've strayed back into talking about this planet. Come with me, Dina dear. We'll take a walk through the other garden and talk about your world."

Renfroe padded over to the fountain and lapped up the cool water rippling into its pool. Then he sauntered across the lawn to an opening in the wall. He slipped through it and Dina followed him.

They strolled along the flagstone walk into a much larger garden lined with flowering shrubs and weeping trees. In the fading evening light, Dina told Renfroe all about the

Coalition's laws and customs. She told him how it formed from a few closely related humanoid species on planets in the same star system. Then she told him how it grew to encompass hundreds of inhabited planets with dozens of species and hundreds of languages.

She lost herself in the memory of her home culture. Another life waited for her once she got back to the *Savannah*. The memory erased her anxiety. Her ordeal on this planet faded into a bad dream.

She warmed to her subject. Before she knew it, she found herself gushing. She bragged about the Coalition's accomplishments as if they were her own. Renfroe hung on her every word. He asked questions and made insightful observations at appropriate places.

If other cats of the Pride wanted their people to interact with sentient populations the way Renfroe did, this mission stood a good chance of success. Dina turned the problem over in her mind in search of a way to bring it about. The close relationship between humans and cats presented a curious puzzle for the team to solve.

Twilight enveloped the garden and stars came out to dot the sky. The garden softened her toward him and she put her reservations aside. He posed no danger to her. She thought at first that this society had no concept of hospitality, yet here was Renfroe offering it to her.

Lights flickered on in the windows and Dina looked in on the house from outside. A sharp breeze rustled the trees and she rubbed her arms to keep warm. Overpowering exhaustion caught up with her and her strength started to ebb.

"You're cold," Renfroe observed. "Let's go inside. You can sit down and relax somewhere more comfortable."

"Thank you," she croaked. "I don't think I can stand up any longer."

Renfroe retraced his steps through the gap in the wall and into the house. He entered a carpeted parlor furnished with cushions and drapery, but not a single chair. A fire crackled in the fireplace.

Renfroe stretched out on the floor in front of the flames. He extended his limbs across the carpet and gave a loud yawn. His whole face stretched to show his teeth.

He blinked once and nodded toward some cushions on the floor next to him. "Have a seat." Dina took a step into the room and stopped. A fly would have been as safe in a spider's web. He was a tiger, a predator, and she was some defenseless prey he could kill with one bat of his claws. "Don't worry. You're perfectly safe here."

He examined her with hypnotic eyes and twitched his nose. No amount of reassurance from him could convince her to move closer to him. Her muscles refused to relax. She kept a safe distance from him in constant readiness to run or defend herself. She kept one eye on the door, but overwhelming fatigue broke her resolve. She inched forward and sat down across the room.

Renfroe laid his head on his paws with another long sigh. "You'll get used to me in time. All the helpers go through an adjustment period when they come to the city for the first time. I understand your alarm at being so near a predator. It takes time to overcome it."

How could she sit with him and talk to him, all while holding herself ready to run from him at any moment? "I'm sorry."

"Don't apologize. Let's return to a lighter topic. I appreciate your insights on your home world and its history. I hope we can close the gap between us through a mutual exchange of ideas."

"I hope so, too. I'm glad to find someone who wants to hear about it. I gave up our mission for lost before I met you."

"I'm only one individual. Don't give yourself false hope. Everyone on this planet—cats as well as humans—are happy to keep things the way they are. I've introduced the idea of contacting other populations before on the Senate floor."

"They didn't like that suggestion?"

"Your plan to incorporate us essentially requires us to give up our autonomy to a foreign government. That plan will not meet with support here. I can assure you of that."

"We can try. At least we can present our proposal."

"I hesitate to dash your hopes by telling you it's impossible. Anything is possible. We'll leave it at that."

Dina hugged her shoulders. She shuddered from a different kind of cold, a cold that came from inside herself. "Okay. We'll leave it at that. I don't think I can talk anymore, anyway."

Renfroe cocked his head. "Why don't you lie down for a while? You've had a long day."

Even with the blazing fire warming her face, Dina couldn't stop her teeth from chattering. Renfroe blinked at her. His eyelids seemed to take forever to dip and his nose and whiskers twitched.

Dina's eyelids weighed a ton, but she didn't trust him or herself to close them. She tugged her lip.

Renfroe watched her with his piercing eyes, which made her more nervous. "Where did you get that scar on your lip?"

She yanked her hand away from her mouth and turned her head away from him.

He studied all her movements. "I hear you had a class in the village."

"It wasn't like any class I ever went to before," she mumbled.

"The subsidiaries call them that."

"And you wonder why no one on this planet has any education. If that's a class, then no one is going to learn anything."

"Tell me what happened."

"You know exactly what happened. We didn't sit around reciting our multiplication tables. They berated us all night long about how worthless and disgusting and degenerate we are and how fortunate we are to finally find ourselves in a civilized society where we can learn the error of our ways. They yammered on at great length about the superiority of the cats and how blessed everyone is to be associated with them."

"That sounds like a typical class."

"They told us the understanding between people and the Pride was the greatest development in the history of human evolution."

Renfroe chuckled. "Indeed."

"And then they topped the whole thing off with repeated beatings."

"Mm-hmm." She wasn't telling him anything he didn't already know.

Dina clenched her jaw to stop the shudders racking her body. She couldn't keep up her defenses much longer. Renfroe could see her in the darkness much better than she could see him. Her vision swam. She couldn't keep her eyes open.

"Lie down, Dina." His voice rattled her bones. The mixture of command and benign suggestion shot to the center of her brain. She tried to resist, but she had to obey him. "You're tired and sore. You need sleep. You'll feel better in the morning. Lie down here and get warm. You're safe here."

She could barely distinguish one word from the next. The low rumble hummed in her ears and her last crumb of strength trickled away. She stretched out on her side on the carpet. She would fall asleep here. No feline presence could keep her awake, no matter how dangerous.

Renfroe sighed on her behalf. "There. That's better."

The last thing Dina saw before her eyes closed was Renfroe blinking at her in the firelight. He would have her by the throat in a second. She would die before she woke up in the morning.

Chapter 15

D ina didn't die before morning.

She woke up to daylight streaming through the parlor window. She sat up to find a light blanket draped over her. The fire had burned down to charcoal. She crept through the house's corridors and chambers and admired the furnishings in the light of day. The sunshine blurred her memory of last night.

How could the brutality of the village exist side by side, on the same planet, with this luxurious and charming house? Cats and people couldn't live side by side together. Matter and anti-matter canceled each other out. Didn't they?

Dina paused in the portico. She was gazing out into the garden when Belinda bustled up in her usual sweat. "Ah, you're awake. Renfroe told me to show you a room where you can stay. Follow me."

Belinda strode away and Dina hurried to keep up. Belinda led her down the hall and through a doorway into another carpeted room. A single divan sat under a window overlooking the garden.

"This is the only room with anything that could serve as a bed for you," Belinda told her. "Renfroe wants you to be comfortable here and you wouldn't be comfortable in the servant's quarters where Buck and I sleep."

"Who's Buck?"

"He's the gardener."

"You said you and I were the only people living here."

"Did I?" Belinda rubbed her chin. "Well, Buck lives here, too. Maybe when you meet him you'll understand why I forgot all about him. He moves around like a shadow. You won't even notice him. No one does."

"It's a very nice room. Thank you."

Belinda moved toward the door. "You stay here. Renfroe wants you to. You let me know if you need anything else. That blanket you used last night will serve until we can find you some more suitable bedding."

"Thank you."

"Renfroe never entertains human guests, so the house isn't set up for it. You understand! It's unusual for a helper to stay in a room like this, but that's the way Renfroe wants it, so that's the way it is."

"Where is Renfroe?"

"He's down at the Senate."

Belinda started again to leave, but Dina held her back. "When will he be back?"

"He won't be back until this evening. Now I have to leave you here. I have to fly back to the kitchen. You come there, too, just as soon as you can, because Buck and I will be having breakfast in a few minutes. You can join us."

Belinda sailed out of the room leaving Dina to ponder. Belinda represented the paradox of Prideland better than anything else.

When she brought Dina from the market, she wouldn't even let Dina help with the kitchen chores. Now she attended her like a guest of honor. The two Belindas could hardly be the same person. Dina would have avoided the kitchen without Belinda's invitation to join her for breakfast.

Belinda didn't offer the invitation only on Renfroe's orders, either. Something changed her opinion. Yesterday Dina was a slag. Today she was a helper. Dina began to understand the difference. One had an understanding with the Pride. The other did not. Could she live up to the new title, at least until she fully understood?

The cats of the Pride must be superior to human beings. Dina couldn't argue with that. They were just as intelligent and they possessed strength and power that humans could only dream of. She had only to look at Renfroe to see proof of that.

How did these cats develop sentient intelligence? How did they develop the capacity for speech? Such a miracle and the miracle of the Pride's relationship with people—these miracles existed nowhere else in the galaxy, possibly even the universe.

The villagers were right. They were lucky to live in such close communion with these cats. Dina would come to an understanding with the Pride as quickly as possible. She would get as much information as she could about Prideland from the nearest available source: Belinda.

Dina returned to the stifling hot kitchen, where she found Belinda setting breakfast plates in front of three chairs. She served into each plate a steaming brew curiously similar to last night's dinner. "That's yours." She pointed to the chair nearest the fireplace.

Dina sat down and waited for Belinda to finish before she started eating. Belinda hustled around the kitchen putting utensils away and attending to last-minute business.

She was just wiping her hands on her apron when a grizzled old man shuffled through the side door and slumped into the chair nearest the exit. He offered no greeting and he kept his eyes down. He didn't eat until Belinda took her seat. At some invisible signal, all three helpers started eating at the same time.

Dina watched for a chance to talk to them. After a few minutes of silent eating, she turned to Belinda. "Does Renfroe has any special task he wants me to do today?"

Belinda gasped at the sound of Dina's voice. "Oh! I really don't know. Renfroe didn't mention anything this morning before he left. I really don't know."

"Then maybe I could help you in here. I'd like to make myself useful—that is, if it's all right with you."

"It doesn't matter whether it's all right with me. I don't know if Renfroe wants you working in here."

"He probably wouldn't mind if I did."

"Oh, I don't know!" Belinda threw back her shoulders. "But you shouldn't do it without his permission."

"But he hasn't given any indication that he wants me to do anything. I might as well do this."

"Maybe he wants you to do nothing," Belinda countered. "We don't know and we shouldn't second-guess him."

"I can make my own decision about what I'm going to do."

Belinda pursed her lips. "I don't think so."

"You don't think I can make up my own mind about what I'm going to do? Why not?"

"You're Renfroe's helper. Make sure you know what he wants before you do anything. You could get visited if you don't."

Dina seized her chance to finally get her questions answered. "Who would visit me?"

"I'm just saying you could get visited if you did something Renfroe didn't want you to do."

"It doesn't make sense for me to sit around and do nothing all day. You said yourself that he won't be back until evening. He would never find out."

"*I* could get visited if I tried to pull something like that. If he found out I went behind his back, I could lose my position here. Renfroe's too good a benefactor to risk that and that's not saying anything about the chance of getting visited if word got out."

"Who would visit you? Not Renfroe."

"It doesn't matter who. Getting visited is bad enough without worrying about who does the visiting. I'm not going to do anything that could get me visited and that's all there is to it. You should be more careful yourself, young lady!"

"But I don't even know what I did that's so wrong. All I asked was if there was anything I could do today until Renfroe comes back and tells me what to do. I don't see what's so wrong about helping you in the kitchen."

"What's wrong with it is that you don't know for certain that Renfroe wants you working in the kitchen. You could get visited for doing what he doesn't want you to do."

Dina heard her voice rising and fought to control it. "But I don't know what he wants me to do!"

"Since you don't know what he wants, you shouldn't do anything."

"But that makes no sense at all!"

"It makes perfect sense. I've been helping Renfroe for almost ten years, and in all that time, no one—I mean *no one*—has ever slept here overnight. Do you hear me? No other helper, either Renfroe's or any other cat's, has slept here."

Dina couldn't stop her hands from shaking. "I hear you."

"I saw you walking through the house just now. Did you notice that none of the rooms have any chairs in them? That's because human beings don't come here and sit down. Buck and I are Renfroe's only helpers—until you came along, that is—and we certainly never sit down. We work all day and then we go to our quarters and sleep. Human beings don't sit down here and they don't sleep here, either."

Dina gulped. "What are you saying?"

"I'm saying that in the last ten years—since I've been here, anyways—Buck and I have been Renfroe's only helpers. Then along comes you, and before we know what happened, you're sleeping in the only room in the house with somewhere to sit and somewhere to sleep. Don't you see? You're special—or at least Renfroe thinks so."

"I never asked him to give me special treatment."

"I didn't say you did, but if I had to guess, I'd say he probably doesn't want you working up a sweat in the kitchen. That's what I'm here for. To tell you the truth, I really don't know what he wants. He didn't tell me and I didn't ask, so if I was you, I would just sit tight until you know what he wants. That way, you'll be sure to do exactly what he wants you to do."

Dina let out a sigh. "Okay. You've been here ten years. Renfroe must value you if he's kept you on so long."

"Value? I don't think Renfroe values any helper. I'm the one who values him. He's the best benefactor a helper could ask for."

Dina put a spoonful of food into her mouth. "You said that yesterday."

"It's true. I wouldn't do anything to jeopardize my position here, even apart from the risk of getting visited."

"The pay must be pretty good. Renfroe must be wealthy if he keeps a house like this."

"There is no pay."

Dina's jaw dropped "What do you mean there's no pay? You must get something. You work all day, so you must get paid."

"None of the helpers get paid. We're lucky to give our lives to the Pride. That's compensation enough."

"That's not right."

"Of course it's right. That's the way Prideland works."

Dina clenched her teeth fighting down the urge to lose her composure. "Where I come from, we have a word for working without pay. It's called slavery."

"There is no slavery in Prideland. We serve the Pride and we're honored to do it. Ask any helper. They'll tell you the same thing. Helpers have the most privileged position in all of Prideland. We live in such close contact with the cats that everyone envies us. Only those people with the best understanding with the Pride get to work as helpers."

Dina sighed again and shook her head. "I don't understand. None of this makes any sense to me."

Belinda patted her hand. "Don't worry. You don't understand now, but you will in time. Once you come to an understanding with the Pride, everything will become clear to you."

"I certainly hope so. If it makes life here any easier, I'll do everything I can to come to an understanding with the Pride as quickly as I can."

"That's the way!" Belinda clapped her hands and went back to eating. "The cats of the Pride are so superior to us humans in every way."

"That's what they told us in the village."

"They're the most remarkable creatures anywhere. They can outwit any human and no one stands a chance against them physically. They're the pinnacle of evolution."

"I don't know about that," Dina mumbled.

Belinda's face flushed and the words tripped and fell over each other in their haste to get out of her mouth. "We should all be very grateful to be helpers. The subsidiaries in the villages have their assigned places. Even the slags have a role to play in the Pride."

"What role do the slags play?"

"If you just watch the cats for a little while, you realize how magical and captivating they really are." Belinda flapped her hands in excitement. "The Pride can teach us all the right way to live. The Pride can elevate us as a species. If human beings established contact with the Pride earlier in our evolution, we could have avoided all the misery of war and starvation and conflict long ago."

Dina chose her next words very carefully. "Is that what they tell you? What else do they tell you about the history of humanity?"

Belinda wagged her finger in Dina's face. "So you remember that and make sure you don't do anything to anger Renfroe."

"I'm sure he won't be angry. He seems reasonable enough to me."

"Well, don't say I didn't warn you." Belinda compressed her lips and scowled. "You don't want to get visited, do you?"

"I don't know what you mean when you use that word."

Belinda glanced across the table at Buck. "I don't know what it means, either, and I don't want to know."

Dina blinked at her in stupid shock. "What do you mean, you don't know? Haven't you ever been visited?"

"Of course, I've never been visited! I make sure I never do anything that could get me visited. If you're smart, you'll do the same."

"All right. If it makes you uncomfortable, I won't do it."

Belinda relaxed and smiled again. "That's a girl!"

Dina tried a different approach. "I won't help you in the kitchen, but at least let me keep you company while you work in the rest of the house. I'm sure Renfroe doesn't want me to spend the whole day without human contact."

Belinda studied her and took another bite of her food. "No, I guess he doesn't. I guess that would be okay. You can keep me company while I work as long as you stay in the house."

Dina burst into a radiant smile. "Thank you so much! I'll do exactly what you tell me to do."

"You'd better! Now finish your breakfast and go back out to your room. I'll come and get you when I finish in here."

Chapter 16

D ina went back to her new bedroom, but she didn't stay there. Insatiable curiosity drove her to inspect every detail of the room. Afterward, she ventured into the hall. That led her back to the main corridor.

Belinda was right. The house contained no chairs, no sofas, no seating of any kind. No pictures hung on the walls. No curtains covered the windows.

Besides every surface and every windowpane being perfectly clean, the house could have been utterly empty. Not one cat hair soiled the carpet anywhere. How could anyone, especially a single housekeeper like Belinda, keep a house occupied by a cat so clean?

Dina wandered the halls for hours. Only the tree lizards' chirps broke the silence.

The quiet rang in her ears. She hadn't been alone like this since leaving the *Savannah*. She couldn't even remember being alone like this *on* the *Savannah*. Someone was always hanging around and there was always someone to talk to there.

She paused under the arched portico and gazed out at the garden. The sunshine soothed her eyes and the soreness in her face. The luxury of the house and Renfroe's kindness pushed the previous days' nightmare farther out of her mind.

If the other cats of the Pride were as sensible and insightful as Renfroe, this mission would certainly succeed. He would overcome any backward tendencies. Once the cats realized the mission's galactic implications, they would jump at the chance to incorporate. Then the Coalition would rein in those half-witted villagers.

A side gate opened in the garden wall to one side and four scruffy men pushed a crude wooden wheelbarrow into the garden. Large wooden barrels rested in the wheelbarrow and the men strained at their work.

Hand-stitched patches covered the knees and elbows of their shabby clothes. These men upended everything Dina thought she knew about this planet. Even the village children kept their hair trimmed and combed and their clothing in good repair.

The men pushed their cart to the garden's very back corner where they disappeared among the trees. Dina stepped onto the grass to follow them when Buck appeared at the same gate and shuffled to a nearby flowerbed. Dina changed course and strode over to him. "Good morning, Buck. Isn't it a beautiful day?"

He pruned the bush in front of him without looking up.

"Who were those men who just went by? I haven't seen anyone like them before."

He didn't see where she was pointing, but he knew exactly who she meant. "The Elite Battalion." His voice cracked when he spoke.

"Who are they?"

He didn't answer. Dina began to see a pattern between questions that brought no answer or an indirect non-answer. She made up her mind to find those answers, but she wouldn't get any answers from Buck.

She fell back on simple questions she knew he would answer. "Belinda says you've been helping Renfroe for a long time. You must be very happy here."

He cleared his throat. When in the last ten or twenty years had he spoken to anyone? "I have an understanding with the Pride."

Dina closed her eyes and raised her face into the sunshine. "I could be happy for the rest of my life, working as the gardener in this garden. It's so beautiful and you make it beautiful every time you work in it. It must be heavenly."

Buck grunted. "I'm lucky to be Renfroe's helper. The closer a person lives to the cats, the more he benefits from an understanding with the Pride."

"Do you come from this city? Were you born here?"

"My parents were subsidiaries. They had their own understanding with the Pride."

"So how did you become Renfroe's helper?"

As soon as the question came out of her mouth, she read in his face she'd made a mistake. He closed up in front of her eyes. "I have an understanding with the Pride. I wouldn't be a slag for the world."

"Who said anything about you being a slag?"

The damage was done. He wouldn't talk again no matter what she said. In the end, she walked away.

She followed the flagstone path through the trees to find out where the scruffy men went with their wheelbarrow. If Buck wouldn't answer her questions, she would have to find out for herself. She found the barrow tracks in the sod and followed them.

She found them at work in the farthest back corner of the garden. The four men bent over shovels and rakes in a wide square of grey sand that had been constructed into an angle of the wall. She couldn't think of one good explanation for what they were doing.

She approached them. "Excuse me?"

All four immediately stopped what they were doing and glared at her. Dina drew back in horror at the pure hatred in their faces. Their wild hair and wretched clothes made them look even more ferocious.

At that moment, Belinda called her from the house. Dina spun on her heel and raced back the way she came. Belinda barely glanced up when Dina burst into the corridor. Belinda fluttered down the corridor dusting every corner with a cloth attached to a stick.

Dina pulled up short to catch her breath. "Who is the Elite Battalion?"

Belinda stopped dead in her tracks and her mouth dropped open. The duster fell out of her hand and clattered to the floor. "What?"

Dina pointed over her shoulder. "I saw them in the garden. They came in through that gate over there. I followed them to try to find out what they were doing."

Belinda narrowed her eyes at Dina. "And what did you see?"

"They were digging up a pit of sand in the back corner of the garden. It sounds crazy, but they looked like they were digging for buried treasure or something. I asked Buck who they were. He told me they were the Elite Battalion, but he wouldn't say anything more."

Belinda gasped in horror. "You.... you talked to Buck?"

"He came into the garden right after the Elite Battalion. I just wanted to talk to him, to get to know him better, you know. It's the natural thing to do when you live with another person. You must know that."

Belinda shook her head and went back to her dusting. "You shouldn't talk to Buck."

"Why not? He's a human being. I'm not going to pretend he doesn't exist. That wouldn't be right."

Belinda compressed her lips and shook her head. "You don't understand. You *will* understand someday, but until then, you better stay away from Buck."

"Why? No one will tell me anything."

"It's better that way. Just stay away from him."

Dina exploded. "What is wrong with you people? Why won't you answer any of my questions? You keep saying over and over that I'll understand everything someday. Well, how am I supposed to understand if you won't explain anything to me?"

Belinda stopped her work and regarded her. "All right. I'll answer your questions. What do you want to know? You want to know about the Elite Battalion and what they're doing in Renfroe's garden."

"Yes," Dina croaked. "Is that too much to ask?"

"Okay. I'll tell you who they are." Belinda squared her shoulders. "They go around cleaning up the city."

Dina waited for more, but no more came. "What do you mean? Do you mean like clearing leaves out of gutters and drains....or do you mean mowing lawns and trimming the bushes?"

Belinda blushed. "You still don't understand. The cats...they...relieve themselves."

Dina stared at her. "What are you talking about?"

"You know!" Belinda flapped her hands. "They...empty themselves. I don't know what words you use in your language, but we don't have any other words to describe it. They have to answer the call of nature."

Dina burst out laughing. "You mean when they have to urinate and empty their bowels? Why didn't you just say so in the first place?"

"Yes! That's it!" Belinda laughed, too. "That's what I'm trying to tell you. The Elite Battalion goes around cleaning up the city. The nicer cats—the more sophisticated ones like Renfroe—they have certain places where they go. They dig a hole and bury it...when they finish."

A light bulb came on in Dina's head. "Is that what the sand pit is for? I saw the...Elite Battalion digging in a sand pit in the back corner of the garden."

"Yes!" Belinda clapped her hands. "Yes! You've got it now. Anyway, the other cats—they just go anywhere they please. They don't care about covering it up or keeping the city clean. They don't have to care. The Elite Battalion cleans up after them."

"Is that what the barrels are for—the barrels on their wheelbarrow?"

"That's right." Belinda went to her dusting.

Dina couldn't resist poking fun at Belinda. "They look like treasure hunters. They dig up their treasure and take it away with them. Where do they take it—the Museum of Antiquities?" She burst out laughing again.

Belinda stared at her and a kaleidoscope of emotions crossed Belinda's face. Then she pursed her lips again. "You shouldn't make fun of the Elite Battalion. They perform a very important function in this city."

"They certainly do!" Dina couldn't stop laughing. "Elite Battalion? I'll bet it's elite! No one wants to join that crew."

Belinda scowled even more furiously. "I hope you didn't act like this in front of Buck. He wouldn't appreciate that nonsense at all."

Dina sobered up real quick. "I wouldn't play around like this in front of Buck. Actually, he wouldn't even answer my questions. What's wrong with him, anyway? Why won't he talk?"

"He got into some trouble when he was young. His father was a village factor, and when Buck grew up, he rebelled and went a little wild. You know how it is."

"I know how it is. Everyone goes through that. It's normal."

"Not in Prideland, they don't. No one can stand against the factors. They make sure everyone keeps the understanding with the Pride. They have to be especially tough on their own children. They wouldn't let them break the understanding for anything!"

"No parent wants their child to rebel, but what can they do about it? My father tried to crack down on me and my brother when we got to our teenage years, but it didn't work. The harder he tried, the more wild and unruly we got. Eventually, we both left home and there was nothing he could do. He had to admit defeat."

"Not in Prideland. The factors would never admit defeat and there's nowhere to run, either."

"But what can they do about it? In the end, what can they really do?"

"They can visit you. That's what I'm telling you. That's what happened to Buck."

"So that's what 'visiting' means? They punish you for stepping out of line?"

"Yes." Belinda dusted off her hands, satisfied at last.

"I understand that perfectly well. You should have told me in the first place."

"Buck tried to break away from his father, even though he knew it was useless. He ran off to the jungle to live with the slags."

Dina frowned. "The slags?"

"Of course his father wasn't having any of that. He and some other factors went out to the canton. They brought Buck back to the village and he got visited. He hasn't been the same since. He doesn't speak unless he's spoken to. When he does speak, he just repeats that he has an understanding with the Pride. That's the understanding he has."

Chapter 17

D ina sat in the little courtyard where she first met Renfroe. The fountain water falling through the late afternoon sun brought back so many images and impressions from her time on the planet.

She couldn't reconcile the fountains and glittering tree lizards with the horror of Marcus's death. She had to think and decide what to do. Should she accept Renfroe's hospitality or work out a way to escape.... or both?

She closed her eyes, but a low rumble made her snap them open again. That sound struck deep into her soul. She didn't need to look up to know that Renfroe was back.

He padded into the courtyard and sat down next to her knee. "There you are. I trust you had a nice day."

"It was a lot better than yesterday."

"I'm glad to hear it."

"What about you?" she asked. "Belinda said you went to the Senate, but you've been gone all day."

Renfroe started licking his paw. "I had to go see about some of the younger males. They're causing trouble in the city and other cats have complained about them. I had to go have a word with them."

"Have a word with them? That doesn't sound good."

He put his foot down. "Young male cats only understand one thing and that is the dominance of bigger, older males. You're a biologist so you know all about that. When they step out of line, the older males show them their place in the Pride. It's the natural order of things."

Dina went back to gazing into the fountain pool. "I guess so."

"Is something bothering you?"

"I don't know. A lot happened before I came to live with you. Maybe it's all catching up with me."

Renfroe stared at her until she squirmed in her seat. She still couldn't relax around him. "I understand. You need time, but that's not a problem. You can take as much time as you need to settle in here. That's what you're here for. That's why I wanted you to come and stay here. I wanted you to feel at home here and to settle into your new life."

"I don't want a new life here," Dina murmured. "That's what I'm saying."

Renfroe paused. He wouldn't stop staring at her. "I want you to feel at home here, so I want you to do something for me." Dina's head shot up. "Don't worry. It's nothing that will compromise your integrity at all. I know better than to ask you to do that."

"You don't have to make my integrity sound like a joke."

"I don't think your integrity is a joke—quite the opposite. That's why I wouldn't ask you to do anything to compromise it. Your integrity is very important to me. At least hear what I have to say before you make up your mind."

"Okay. Go ahead and tell me what you want me to do."

"I want you to have dinner with me."

Her eyes popped. "What? You mean—associate with a helper?"

A speck of dust landed on his ear and he flicked it. "Call it what you like. I want us to sit down together, just you and me, and share a meal. We can talk some more about your home world if you like or we can talk about Prideland—whichever you prefer. How would you like that?" Dina stared at him. He turned his head and blinked at her. "Is there a problem? I asked you to eat dinner with me."

Dina turned back to the fountain. "I heard you."

"And then I asked you how you would like that? Did you hear that, too?"

Dina nodded. "I heard it."

"So what do you say? Will you have dinner with me?"

"Do I really have a choice?"

"You always have a choice. If you really want to sit alone in your room tonight and stare at the wall, I won't force you to do anything else."

Dina blushed. "I would love to have dinner with you. I don't know what I was thinking."

Renfroe let out a puff of air through his nostrils. "Very well. That's settled, then. I'll give Belinda instructions."

Dina looked around. "Where will we eat? You don't have a table and chairs. There's one in the kitchen, but I guess you don't go in there."

"I hadn't thought about where we would sit. The fact is you will probably be the one who eats while I just keep you company."

"Then we aren't really sharing a meal, are we? I thought that was the whole point."

"You don't want to eat while I'm crunching up a nice tasty fell deer fawn and swallowing it whole, do you? I thought you'd be more comfortable eating your meal while we talk."

"Oh. Okay."

"I have only your comfort and well-being in mind. I thought you would be more at ease if we do it this way."

Dina took a deep breath. "What exactly do you want me to do here?"

Renfroe tilted his head to one side. "What do you mean?"

"I mean do you want me to just sit around the house all day or is there something specific I'm supposed to do?"

"I still don't understand what you mean. You can do whatever you want."

"If that was the case, I wouldn't be here at all. I would be free to walk around the city and so would my friends. We wouldn't be split up and we would be free to address the Senate about our mission. We wouldn't be expected to come to an understanding with the Pride before everyone told us what is happening on this planet. So don't tell me I can do whatever I want."

Renfroe sighed. "What is it you want to do that you can't do?"

"I just told you, but since you don't really mean that I can do whatever I want, how about me helping Belinda in the kitchen?"

He narrowed his eyes. "Why would you want to do that?"

"I can't sit here doing nothing all day. I have to do something. If you won't let me go out and explore on my own, then you have to let me do something here in the house. I've never had people waiting on me before in my life and Belinda has a lot of work to do. I could help her and we could keep each other company."

"I don't know why you would want to keep company with Belinda. She isn't exactly the kind of person a trained scientist would find any commonality with."

"I want to keep company with her because there's no one else to keep company with. I've never spent this much time alone and you can't keep me locked up in this house all the time without someone to talk to."

"You have me to talk to. You have a lot more in common with me than with Belinda."

"You're a cat. She's human."

"What difference does that make? You would have a lot more to talk about with me than with just about any other helper in Prideland."

"Maybe so, but you're still not human. Nothing can take the place of your own kind."

Renfroe paced around the courtyard. "That's true, but you don't need to work in the kitchen. That's not what I brought you here for."

"What did you bring me here for?"

"I told you last night. I brought you here so I could talk to an intelligent person about subjects larger than Prideland. Life can get so dull talking about all the same old things with all the same old people. I hoped you might be a delightful companion for me."

"So does that mean I can't work in the kitchen?"

"I'm not going to tell you that you can't. I'm not going to tell you to do anything, but you would be making a big mistake working in the kitchen with Belinda. You could be doing so much more. You *are* so much more. If I wanted another helper to work in the kitchen, I could get one anywhere. I didn't have to get a starship biologist for that."

"Don't you see? I may be a starship biologist, but I'm no better than Belinda. She's a woman and I'm a woman. She has a lot of work to do and I would rather work in the kitchen than do nothing. I'm not working as a biologist here, am I?"

Renfroe stopped in front of the portico. "If you really want to waste your life working in the kitchen, I won't stop you, but I'd be very disappointed if you did. I would wonder why I brought you here in the first place. You think you're not working as a biologist, but you are. That's exactly why I'm feeding and housing you and asking you to have dinner with me."

Dina wilted. "All right. I won't do it. If you feel that strongly about it, I better not."

"Good. Now, if you'll excuse me, I'll go discuss the situation with Belinda. It's nearly dinnertime."

He disappeared into the house and Dina went back to staring at the fountain, but she didn't think about her experiences of the past few days. She replayed the conversation she just had over and over in her mind.

What was it that made Renfroe impossible to resist? Why did she care so much about disappointing him?

His glowing yellow eyes hung before her, even when she shut her eyes to block out the sight of them. She saw those eyes whether she kept her own eyes open or closed. She saw them in her sleep. His low, grumbling voice mesmerized her with even hours after they parted company.

What would happen when she went back to the *Savannah*? Would she dream about Renfroe when she curled up in Tom's arms? Would she see and hear and feel Renfroe when Tom bit her neck?

Did she hate Renfroe or fear him? How could a human be drawn to a cat? How could a human woman think of her sweetheart in the same thought as a cat?

She couldn't get Renfroe out of her mind no matter how hard she tried. He couldn't be any substitute for Tom. He was a cat. He mesmerized her as a tiger staring down his helpless prey before he broke her neck. If she let that fact slip out of her mind for an instant, she was utterly lost.

Chapter 18

Renfroe flared his nostrils and sniffed. Dina put a bite of food into her mouth, but she couldn't taste it. "Maybe this wasn't such a good idea."

"Why not?"

"I can't eat with you watching me."

"What's wrong? You're eating just fine."

She stuck her spoon into the bowl. "It's no good."

"What do you want me to do? Do you want me to move so I'm not looking at you?"

He stretched out in front of the fire. She sat on a cushion opposite him. "Don't bother. It wouldn't do any good."

"There must be something we can do. I only want to set your mind at ease." He stood up and paced back toward the door. "Does this help?"

"It would help if you were eating, too, but even then, it's not the same as eating with another person."

"I am a person, Dina."

"You know what I mean. It's not the same as eating with another human being."

"You said that before. I don't see the difference. You want company. Here I am. You want to talk to someone. That's what I want, too. So let's talk."

"You don't understand. I didn't ask to come here. I'm a prisoner here."

"You didn't ask to come here. You came here on a starship, didn't you? You came to this planet of your own free will. No one forced you."

"But someone forced me to come to your house and I can't leave. I'm stuck here. That makes it hard to enjoy your company." She passed her hand across her eyes. "Would you please sit down? You're giving me a headache with all that pacing."

He sat down by the door, but he still towered over her. "I'm sorry. I thought you wanted me to stop looking at you."

"You're looking at me now." She set her bowl down. "Anyway, I'm not eating anymore. I guess I'm not going to be comfortable around you no matter what you do."

Renfroe let out his breath. "I've been thinking about what you said before."

"Which part?"

"The part about what you would do if you were free to do whatever you wanted. I said you could do anything you wanted, and you said, if that was true, you would be exploring Prideland with your friends and working toward accomplishing your mission."

"Yeah? What about it?"

"I've been thinking about that and I've decided to take you into the city tomorrow. I'm going to take you to visit your friends."

She stared at him. "Do you really mean it?"

"I wouldn't say it if I didn't mean it. We'll go around to all the houses where your friends are staying. You'll be able to see them and talk to them just the way you want to."

"How much time will I have to spend with them?"

"That depends on their benefactors. Their benefactors have very different personalities and attitudes toward their helpers."

"These aren't helpers. These are starship officers. They deserve more consideration than your average helpers."

"I might agree with you on that, but others don't. Fallon, for example, believes exactly the opposite."

"Doesn't he realize all your future dealings with the Coalition depend on you treating us according to interplanetary diplomatic standards?"

Renfroe shook his head and turned away. "Dina, Dina, Dina. How can I ever explain?"

"Explain what? Surely you must understand that. All of you must."

"Dina," he murmured, "there will be no future dealings between your Coalition and Prideland. I hesitated to put the matter in those blunt terms, but the sooner you realize that, the better off you'll be. The Pride won't have anything to do with the Coalition. Cats like Fallon will treat you and your friends as cruelly as they can just to get those ideas of interplanetary diplomatic standards out of your heads."

Dina started to her feet. "But they can't! *You* can't! We have a mission to accomplish here. We're offering you membership in the most cohesive, most productive political and economic bloc in the galaxy. The Coalition has a laundry list as long as my arm of planets waiting to join. You're lucky the Chancellor intervened to incorporate you."

"I've been trying to tell you ever since you got here, Dina. The Pride doesn't want to incorporate with your Coalition. Get that fact into your head now or the other cats will make life very unpleasant for you until you do. Why do you think I'm making your stay here so pleasant and easy? The other cats won't give you the same consideration. You'll see that when you visit your friends tomorrow."

Dina shook her head. Now she started pacing while he sat still. "This is impossible! Our mission can't be a total failure. We can't go back to the ship with nothing to show for it."

"Dina," he breathed, "you won't be going back to the ship. You're here and you're staying here. There's nothing I can do about that."

She heard the words, but they didn't penetrate her mind. The terrible truth was just too horrific to comprehend. Her chin fell onto her chest "I said it this morning. When Belinda told me that she and Buck never got paid for the work they did, I said they were slaves. We're all slaves."

"There are no slaves in Prideland—only helpers."

"That's what Belinda said."

Renfroe studied her with his head on one side. Then he got to his feet and padded across the carpet to where she sat. "Dina."

She didn't move.

"Dina." The air rushed in and out of his nose. His warm fur radiated heat toward her. "Dina, I care for you or I wouldn't have brought you into my house. Even in the short time you've been here, I've come to value you for the strong, intelligent woman you are. That's why I've made every effort to see that you're treated well and your unique gifts cherished. I would do anything to help you, but there's only so much a single individual can do. Don't you understand that?"

Dina shook off her stupor. "I understand."

"You want to see your friends, so I'm taking you there. I don't want to see you unhappy, but seeing your friends won't bring you any closer to coming to an understanding with the Pride."

"What if I don't want to come to an understanding with the Pride? What then?"

"Then you'll be out with the slags. Is that what you want?"

She didn't answer. He started to move away, but Dina's head shot up. "Wait! Don't go!"

He glanced backward at her over his shoulder. "If you don't want to come to an understanding with the Pride, then there's nothing I can do to help you. I *am* the Pride,

Dina. Not only am I a cat, but I'm Chairman of the Senate. If you don't come to an understanding with the Pride, then there's nothing for you and me to say to each other. I might as well walk out of here right now and forget all about you."

"Don't leave!" she whispered. "If you leave, I'll be completely alone."

"Then, please, for both our sakes, at least try to come to an understanding with the Pride. I only want to help you. I'm taking you out into the city. I'll show you everything you want to see and I'll take you to see your friends, but you have to help me, too. You have to help me help you."

Dina's lips trembled while she floundered to hold it all together. It couldn't be as hopeless as he made it out to be. "I'm trying! I just can't handle people living in slavery and beating everyone who happens to drop in and worshiping animals like gods. It's insanity!"

"Whatever the subsidiaries did to you before you came to the city doesn't have anything to do with the Pride. If you don't like what the subsidiaries do, you take it up with them."

"How can I take it up with them? I'm here and they're in the village. Who knows if I'll ever get back there—not that I really want to—except that negotiating with them is part of our mission. How am I ever going to accomplish that?"

"Let's not talk about that anymore. You're still fresh off your ship. I won't tell you any more about Prideland and I won't tell you any more about your mission."

"But I want to know about Prideland! That's exactly what I want."

"That's why I'm taking you out tomorrow," he replied. "You'll understand much better if you see it for yourself."

"Is that what you mean by coming to an understanding with the Pride?"

"Yes. That's what I mean."

Dina brightened up. "If that's what you mean, then I'm happy to go. I'll be happy to come to an understanding with the Pride."

Renfroe sighed. "Good. I'm glad we got that cleared up."

She rubbed her eyes. "I think I'll go to my room. I'm tired. Thank you for setting aside that room for me. I know it's out of the ordinary for a helper to have a room to herself and it's a very nice room. I appreciate you thinking of me."

Renfroe sat down at her side. Cat smell pricked her nose. "Think nothing of it. It's the least I could do for you. You deserve much better."

"Belinda says you think I'm special. That's why she thinks you're going to so much trouble."

"You are special. Don't you know that?"

Dina stared down at the carpet. She couldn't look at him. "I'm nothing special. I'm just a country girl from Tennessee."

"I don't know where that is, but you're definitely special. You're the most special woman I've ever met."

She closed her eyes and turned away. "Stop it."

"It's true. There are no other human women like you here. Of that I am quite certain."

"I'm sure there are lots of women just like me."

Renfroe shook his head. "No, you're the only one. I'm sure you have all the men on your starship chasing after you."

"No, I don't. I have a fiancé."

He inclined his head to one side. "What's that?"

She thought of a comparable word that he would understand. "I have a mate, a permanent mate. He's my superior officer. None of the other men would dare to go after me with him around."

"Oh, I see. Your mate is the alpha male. That explains everything."

Dina blushed in spite of herself. "That's one way of putting it."

"But he isn't here," Renfroe pointed out. "I am. That makes you mine."

She froze at those words. Where was this going? "I'm here now, but I'm still his."

Renfroe didn't answer. He stood up and walked around her. She sat on the floor, so she couldn't exactly jump up and run away.

He paced around her with slow, deliberate strides. He was marking her off, laying claim to her as his own possession. She fought the urge to run. He would be on top of her before she got to her feet.

He stalked in a complete circle around her. Then he cut in closer to her shoulder and slid his whole body along her back. He leaned against her so hard she tipped over at the waist.

He passed his full length across her back and his tail flicked around to tap her chin. A charge of electric tension passed from his sleek coat through her spine and into her.

She sprang to her feet and rocketed across the room in a flash. Renfroe's eyes glittered in the firelight. "What's the matter, Dina?"

Her breath grated through her clenched teeth. "Don't do that."

"Don't do what?"

"What you just did," she snarled. "You know what you did. Don't do it again."

"All I did was rub against you. I didn't hurt you."

Her voice cracked. "But you could have."

"I could have killed you the very first night you came here, but I didn't. Doesn't that prove to you that I have no plans to hurt you?"

Dina shook her head, but she couldn't clear her mind. She couldn't let her guard down around him for an instant. "You could be toying with me. You could be waiting until I trust you enough to relax. Then you'll attack and kill me."

"I wouldn't do that. I value you too much."

"You're a cat," she spat out. "Cats play with their prey before they kill it."

He sat back on his haunches and blinked. "I didn't bring you here to kill you, Dina. You're much too valuable for that. I simply want to be close to you. I didn't mean to frighten you. If it bothers you so much, I won't do it again."

"Good," she snapped. "Don't do it again."

"I thought you might want physical affection. I thought, after your experience in the village and being separated from your friends, that you might be lonely. I thought I might offer you some contact. I thought I could comfort you somehow, but I can see you don't want that."

"I don't want it from you!" she shot back. "I'm human and you're a cat. We're completely different species. We can never be together like that and you can never take the place of a human companion."

He studied her out of the corner of his eye. "Why not? Why shouldn't we comfort each other just because you are human and I am a cat? There is no law against it."

A shudder ran down her spine. "It's against nature. Each individual should mate with a member of its own species. They shouldn't cross the natural boundary between species. It's not natural. It's abomination."

"Abomination?" he repeated. "That's not a very scientific word."

"It is so scientific!" she shrieked. "You can't seriously expect me to mate with you. We're completely different."

"I never said anything about mating with me. All I said was that we could give each other some physical comfort. What's wrong with that? Don't tell me your people don't have companion animals. I know it's true because I've seen the subsidiaries do it. Some of the children walk around with tree lizards on their shoulders and some of the adults show affection for their milk cows and cart oxen. I've seen it many times."

Dina closed her eyes to clear her head. Which confused her more—his arguments or the fixed stare of his yellow eyes?

She couldn't think when she talked to him. His voice vibrated to the bottom of her soul and took root there until her own thoughts rang through her head with his low rumbling voice. "It's true that we have companion animals, but we don't get intimate with them. It isn't normal. It's pathological. It's sick."

He turned away. He must know the effect his gaze had on her. His presence held her captive even when he wasn't looking at her. "I was walking once through one of the villages—I can't remember which one. I was walking down the road on my way somewhere else, so the surroundings didn't interest me much. I saw a young man resting in the shade under a tree. A shaggy old ox lay on its stomach with its legs folded under it and the man sat with his back leaning against the animal's side. They both had their eyes closed. I understood then that humans have a natural affinity for animals. Do you understand?"

Dina nodded. He had a point, but she still couldn't stop shaking. "I know what you mean. It seems like people can't live with animals without bonding with them. I understand what you mean now about it being natural."

"That's how cats and humans live on this planet. We live together in harmony. The cats benefit from the humans and the humans benefit from the cats. It's a mutually advantageous relationship."

"I see."

"That's all I'm suggesting we do. Lean against me the way that man leaned against his ox. We're tied together by circumstance and common interest. Why shouldn't we offer each other comfort? It can't do us any harm and it can only benefit us both."

"I understand."

"Such an arrangement would give us the comfort and companionship we both desire. Wouldn't you like some physical comfort since your mate isn't here?"

Dina snapped out of her trance. "Don't talk about him. He's none of your business."

Renfroe let out a long breath. "Dina dear, you really are going to have to calm down. I won't stop talking about your mate. I'm not threatening him. He's nowhere near here. I'm talking about you. I have no intention of coming between you and him, but he isn't here right now. I am. I'm offering you the comfort of physical contact. You're alone here, you're separated from your mate, and I'm here offering it to you in his place. What is so threatening about that?"

Her teeth chattered and tension racked her body. "I can't. I might want physical contact. I might want to rest in the shade and lean against your side, but I can't. I can't rest."

He lowered his eyelids. "I understand. Believe me, I understand. You just got here. You'll get used to me, and in time, you may grow comfortable enough to lean on me. I'll be waiting, and when that time comes, I will welcome you."

Chapter 19

D ina stopped in the doorway of her room and stared down at Renfroe. He was waiting for her. "Good morning, Dina dear."

"Good morning. What are you doing here?"

"I'm taking you into the city today to visit your friends. Don't you remember?"

She stopped herself from throwing her arms around his neck. "Thank you. You don't know what this means to me."

He bobbed his head and she walked at his side. "That's why I'm doing it. It will give you a chance to get out of the house, anyway." They passed down the corridor to the portico into his favorite garden. Dina stopped in front of a table set up by the stone bench. "Is anything the matter?"

"I'm supposed to eat in the kitchen with Buck and Belinda."

He sat down next to the fountain and peered around him. "Not anymore. We'll eat here together."

Dina glanced toward the kitchen. "They won't like this."

"Who?"

"Buck and Belinda. They already think you're giving me special treatment."

Renfroe's eyes went hard and cold. "Is that what they told you?"

"They didn't say it. Buck never says anything. Belinda only said she thought I must be special to you or you wouldn't have given me a room with a bed in it."

"That is true."

"She said no one ever sat down in this house before I came. Now I'm eating with you here instead of in the kitchen with them. They can only come to one conclusion from that."

Renfroe sniffed. "If Buck or Belinda or any other helper says anything to you about my treatment of you, you must tell me. I'll be the one to decide what happens in this house. No helper has a right to object to it."

"I wouldn't want to get anyone in trouble."

"They would get themselves in trouble talking like that," he growled.

"You said you weren't involved in visiting people."

"I'm not talking about visiting anyone. I don't visit. No cat visits. The subsidiaries and helpers do that between themselves, but if any helper steps out of line, the Pride has its own ways of dealing with them. We demand a high standard of behavior from our helpers. We couldn't live with them if we didn't."

"I wouldn't feel right telling on someone. I wouldn't want to be responsible for anything bad happening to someone else."

"If you didn't tell me and I found out later that you kept it to yourself, you would wind up in a much worse situation. Don't ever think about protecting someone by keeping it to yourself. That's the most important rule you can learn about Prideland."

"You make it sound like everyone is spying on everyone else," she pointed out.

"It isn't spying. Everyone is responsible for everyone else. Everyone is responsible for making sure nothing threatens our understanding."

Dina looked away. Just then, Belinda came out with a tray balanced on one hand. She set it down on the table. She turned to leave without a word or even a glance at Dina.

"Excuse me, Belinda," Renfroe called. "If you'll wait a moment, I'd like a word with you."

Belinda stopped dead and looked around with wild eyes.

"I'm taking Dina out to see her friends later this afternoon," Renfroe told her, "but before that happens, I want you to take her with you to the festival."

"What festival?" Dina asked.

"There's a festival for the helpers in the city this morning. You'll go to that first and Belinda will show you the way."

Dina brightened up. "A festival for the helpers?"

"Yes. We have them on a regular basis. You'll see for yourself."

"It sounds great," she exclaimed. "Will the others be there?"

"What others?"

"My teammates—Tom and Matthew and Tania."

"I don't see why they wouldn't be. The festival is not optional. All the helpers attend the festivals. Belinda will show you where to go. When you get back, we'll go see your friends at their benefactors' homes." He turned back to Belinda. "You may go. Make sure you take Dina with you when you go."

Dina watched Belinda out of sight. "She's afraid of you."

Renfroe shrugged. "That's her business."

"Why have you taken such pains to make me comfortable here when you haven't done the same for her? Don't you care to make her comfortable in your own house?"

"She isn't here to be comfortable. I don't care if she's comfortable and I don't care if she's afraid of me. She's here to cook and clean—nothing more. Those words I just had with her about taking you with her to the festival are probably the longest conversation I've ever had with her. I told you I don't associate with helpers."

"You could be a little kinder to her. She is human, after all. You didn't have to stare at her like that."

"Like what?"

"You know very well like what!" she shot back. "You deliberately stared at her in the eyes so she would be afraid. I saw you as plain as I'm standing here."

"I don't have to deliberately stare at her to scare her. If she's scared of me, she has no one to blame but herself."

"How can she be anything but scared of you? She's a human woman and you're a tiger twice her size—maybe bigger. She couldn't help but be scared."

"*You* aren't scared of me and we've spent quite a bit of time together over the last couple of days. If I'm so frightening, you should be scared, too."

"I *am* scared. I'm scared out of my wits and that's even with you turning your head away so you don't stare at me so much. I've seen you doing it, so don't deny it."

He snorted through his nose. "Listen, Dina. It's precisely because she is human that I treat Belinda the way I do. She has her own understanding with the Pride. That means I and every other cat on this planet treats her a certain way so she knows her place and her duty to the Pride. These relationships have been established for eons and they work perfectly well. I wouldn't be doing Belinda or any other helper any favors by treating them differently. You ask any one of them and they'll tell you the same thing. They don't want anything different. They're happy with the arrangement the way it is."

"That's easy for you to say. You're the one with all the power."

He twitched his whiskers. "All of that is by the by. I've told you what's going to happen today, so now you know."

Dina turned away. "Now I know."

The fountain trickled and the tree lizards chirped in the branches. They sounded so loud in the silence that followed.

How did Renfroe make himself so infuriating? Why couldn't Dina resist his effect on her? She couldn't hate him in spite of all the evidence that Prideland wasn't as he made it out. She gravitated to him in spite of herself, maybe out of sheer loneliness.

She raised her face to the sunshine and closed her eyes. Blue sky and green leaves glanced across her eyelids and soothed her exhausted brain. If only she could see those colors and not the rest of Prideland.

Renfroe's deep purr brought her back to the present just in time to see him moving toward her, but she already knew what was coming.

He padded over to her and ran his side across the backs of her legs. Each rib knocked against muscle followed by his soft flank all the way to his hip bones. He curled his tail around her thigh so it whipped against her hip.

She didn't jump away this time. She wasn't afraid of him anymore. How could she fall into slavery at the first kind touch he gave her? She wasn't any better than anyone else on this planet.

Renfroe must have known she wasn't afraid anymore. What would replace that fear? What would she feel the next time he touched her like that? She didn't have to ask. She already knew.

He walked a short distance away and sat down. He extended his head toward Belinda's tray and sniffed. "You haven't touched your breakfast."

Dina couldn't move. Renfroe stared at her with his glittering golden eyes. How pathetically weak human beings were compared to him!

"Eat your breakfast, Dina," he told her. "You can't go to the festival without eating something."

After five years in the Armada, she knew a direct order when she heard one. She strode over to the bench and sat down without looking at him. She didn't have to look at the food, either. She just had to eat it.

She shoved the bread and meat into her mouth. She stared at the glories of the garden while she chewed. Renfroe observed her without interrupting her meal. Then he came toward her. She didn't pay any attention. He could do what he liked with her. Thinking about it made no difference.

He stretched out on the ground on top of her feet with his spine against her shins. He didn't try to talk to her anymore. He was just there, near her, touching her, sharing the same space with her.

That was all it took. They might be different species, but they could still sit together. What did it matter what everyone else was doing outside these walls? Dina and Renfroe could still find some peace and friendship together. Couldn't they? Why couldn't they?

Dina relaxed into his presence and she started to taste the food she was putting into her mouth. It really was delicious.

Everything about Renfroe's house was excellent. The village wasn't very charming, but a society couldn't function if everyone in Prideland was living a nightmare. She and Renfroe couldn't be the only ones on the whole planet enjoying a life of pleasure and ease.

Chapter 20

Dina studied the city while Belinda led her through leafy neighborhoods lined with towering mansions and high garden walls. Wrought-iron gates separated the street from beautiful gardens surrounding almost every house. Someone spent a lot of time and effort maintaining these gardens and all these magnificent houses were home to cats.

"This is a fine neighborhood," she remarked. "Do you know everyone who lives here?"

"Most everyone," Belinda replied.

"Do all the cats have human helpers living with them the way Renfroe does?"

Belinda didn't look up. She kept her face turned far enough away to stop Dina from making eye contact. "Uh-huh."

"The helpers in these houses must live pretty well. They live a lot better than the people in the villages."

Belinda didn't say anything.

"Don't you think the helpers in the city are doing better than the people in the villages?"

"I don't know anything about the subsidiaries," Belinda muttered.

"Didn't you say all those village children come to your kitchen for food after they come to the market? You must have talked to some of them about their lives."

"No, I haven't. Helpers keep away from the subsidiaries. The less they say to each other, the better."

Dina gasped. "Don't tell me you don't even talk to them! You must know *something* about them."

Belinda quickened her pace. "If the subsidiaries have such hard lives and the helpers are living so well, that explains why they all want to become helpers. The closer a person lives to the Pride, the better off they are. That's the understanding we have with the cats."

"Then why do they live in villages? Why don't they all pack up and move to the city if it's so great?"

Belinda smacked her lips and stopped in the middle of the street. She rounded on Dina with her hands on her hips. "Don't talk to me anymore, okay? I don't want to talk to you. Renfroe told me to bring you to the festival and that's what I'm doing. He didn't tell me to discuss my life with you or to explain every detail of Prideland to you. Just be quiet. I don't want to talk to you anymore."

Dina's jaw dropped. "Why not? How am I supposed to understand what's going on here if I don't talk to people about it?"

"You talk to anyone you like so long as you don't talk to me," Belinda snapped. "I don't want to talk to you about anything ever again. Just keep your mouth shut around me."

Dina couldn't speak above a whisper. "But why?"

Belinda whirled away and started walking again. Dina had to jog to keep up with her. "You're trouble," Belinda spat out of the side of her mouth. "The more you talk, the more trouble you are. Don't talk to me anymore. Just shut your mouth."

Dina was too stunned to argue. She tried to keep abreast of Belinda, but after a while, Dina dropped back and followed a pace or two behind. She definitely didn't try to talk to Belinda anymore.

At least Dina would see her teammates at this festival. She would draw them off by themselves and talk strategy. Tom especially must be thinking of ways to break loose. His head stuck up well above any crowd. He'd be impossible to miss, and wherever Tania and Matthew were, they would most likely be together.

Belinda led her out of the neighborhood into the city center. Mansions and villas gave way to stately buildings. Their sweeping steps led up to towering entrances.

Dina studied every detail of the city. She hadn't seen it since she entered the city in Alexander Mathus's wagon. The place looked different now. The buildings showed off their grand nobility despite their age, but this time, not a living soul, neither human nor cat, occupied the streets. "Where is everyone?"

"They're at the festival," Belinda replied.

Dina's head shot up. "All of them?"

Belinda nodded. "They wouldn't miss it."

Dina looked around again. "I thought some of them would be on the street. What if somebody comes late?"

Belinda shook her head. "They wouldn't be caught dead coming late to a festival—never in a million years."

Belinda turned off the main street to an old building. Eons of weather had stained its stone exterior and the decorative parapet crumbled at the corners.

"What is this place?" Dina whispered.

Belinda whispered back, "Helion House."

The building was nothing but a disused gymnasium with parquet wooden floors and vaulted ceilings. Wooden bleachers lined the four walls and ancient exercise equipment still rusted in the corners. No festive banners or balloons decorated the place. No gaiety or happy music livened the atmosphere.

Dina didn't see any signs of festivity at all except for hundreds, probably thousands, of people packed into the main room. Every man, woman, and child in the city crowded into the gymnasium until the bleachers overflowed.

Latecomers stood body to body around the floor and overflowed into the hallway. Not a single face glimmered with cheer or merriment. The people all craned their necks toward the platform against one wall.

Belinda grabbed Dina's arm and yanked her toward the bleachers. "Come on. We have to find a place to sit."

The room was full to the ceiling. "Where?"

"It doesn't matter. We have to find a place to sit down."

Dina hesitated. "We might as well stand."

"We can't," Belinda insisted. "We have to sit."

Dina didn't understand why sitting down was so important and she didn't ask. Somehow, she and Belinda jammed their hips into a tiny space and turned their faces toward the platform.

Dina tried to look for her friends, but she couldn't see beyond the few faces on either side. Belinda elbowed her in the ribs. "Pay attention!"

A group of men gathered on the platform and Dina gasped. "Look! There's Buck. What's he doing up there?"

Belinda elbowed her again. "Shh!"

A man moved to the edge of the platform and the whole gymnasium fell silent.

"Welcome, all of you," he began, "to this festive occasion where we celebrate our good fortune at sharing the destiny of this Pride. Those of us who've come to an understanding with the Pride enjoy a special quality of life no one else in the known universe can share."

No one made a sound, but he held up both hands as if he needed to quiet the audience. "I know some of you don't feel as strongly about this as I do, but no one is as lucky as we are. We have the most blessed position in the world. I'm here to call on each of you to embrace this destiny along with me. No one else has a chance to live this life. We can even shape the future of humankind."

Dina glanced right and left, but she couldn't tell whether people agreed or disagreed with him.

The man gritted his teeth. "Some people call the cats all kinds of terrible names. They call the cats cruel and capricious and uncaring. It's up to us to change that. If you know anyone who says those things or even thinks them—maybe someone sitting right next to you right now—I'm begging you to help them. Show them how wrong they are. Do your part to convince them how superior the cats are and how much the Pride does to make our lives better."

A murmur ran through the crowd. The man nodded in answer.

"I know, I know," he continued. "It's terrible, isn't it? It's hard to believe a person could be so ungrateful. I find it hard to believe a person could be completely insensitive to the beauty and glory of the Pride—and do you know the most amazing part? The most amazing part is that these people have grown up in Prideland just like us. They've been to the same classes and festivals. Their poor parents have given everything to educate them in a proper understanding with the Pride and this is how they act. I can't believe it!"

The crowd heaved in wordless agreement.

"You might wonder how I know these people do and say and think these things. You might wonder how anyone could be so rude as to say these things out loud. You would think everyone in Prideland would know how to mind their manners. You would think, after everything they've learned, if they really think those things, at least to keep their mouths shut."

Dina's ears burned. Who could he be talking about but her?

"But no! These people actually have the nerve to say these things out loud. They actually say these things to other people and try to spread their lies among those of us who love the Pride with all our hearts. They try to turn us against the Pride and rob us of our understanding with the cats. Can you believe anyone would be so despicable? I don't know how anyone could stoop so low."

Half the audience nodded back at him. The other half listened in silence. Was Dina the only person in the auditorium who got the sense that he was talking directly to them?

"Well, I won't put up with it a moment longer!" he thundered. "I won't rest until I deal with these people! If I hear them spreading their lies, I'll tell them to their faces that I won't stand for it! I won't allow them to degrade Prideland and destroy the understanding we have with these cats. This understanding is the best thing to happen to human beings in the whole course of our evolution. We should stand up and say so to anyone who says otherwise!"

A few people shouted their agreement from the stands and the man shouted back over their voices. "We should defend the Pride with our lives! We should attack these slags in the streets and drive them out of our cities and villages! We should tell the world who these people are and who their families and friends are! We should burn their houses and kill their children and their livestock! We should cleanse Prideland of the filth of their existence so the rest of us can live in peace!"

The responding murmur rose to a fevered pitch. More people called in answer to every statement he made until the whole assembly exploded into an uproar. People surged to their feet on all sides. The man shouted over the noise to kill the slags and wipe every trace of them out of existence.

Somewhere, someone got to his feet. In an instant, everyone else in the crowd jumped up. Dina sat transfixed until Belinda grabbed her arm and forced her to stand up, too.

The shouts and screams rose to a deafening roar. Waves of energy washed through the crowd. People waved their hands in a frenzy at the man on the platform until no one could hear a word from any direction.

A woman on Dina's left wiped tears off her cheeks. A smile of wild ecstasy lit up another face. The man on the platform surveyed his audience, smiled, nodded, and called out to them, but the noise swallowed whatever he was saying. At last, he raised his hand for quiet. The crowd fell back into their seats and every other sound died.

He heaved a heavy sigh. "I can see some of you still aren't convinced. I can see some of you still won't take my word for it, so we're going to hear from someone who's been there and experienced the slags' nastiness for himself. I won't keep you waiting by telling you his story. I'll step aside and let him tell you himself."

No one breathed. No one fidgeted. No one coughed or sneezed or even scratched their faces. Everyone sat perfectly still waiting for whatever came next.

The next speaker wasn't young. He glanced at the other men flanking him on both sides. They gave him no space to move except forward to the edge of the platform. He sighed and came forward while his listeners perched on the edges of their seats.

"Well, here I am." He glanced over his shoulder at the men behind him. One of them nodded. He surveyed the crowd and then dropped his eyes to the floor. "I never thought I'd be standing here, talking to you all like this. I thought I was safe, but I was wrong."

He stared down at his shoes. No one helped him. He looked behind him again, and this time, the man who nodded frowned at him and pointed toward the crowd.

The speaker sighed again and his shoulders sagged. "I guess this is it. This is where it all ends. I had such hopes, but this is what became of them all."

He sighed one more time. Then he raised his eyes to the crowd and they flashed in defiance. "All you people, look at me. This is what happens to anyone who speaks against the Pride. This is what happens to anyone who tries to leave. This is where you end up."

Dina held her breath hanging on his every word. Was it possible that someone had the courage to speak up against this insanity?

The man crushed her hopes with his next words. "Everything they tell you is true. No one can escape Prideland. I thought I could run away and live with the slags in the cantons. I thought I could be free. I thought I didn't have to bring in my subscription. I thought I didn't have to send my children to the city to be helpers. I thought I didn't have to go to classes or help the factors with their village visits. I thought I could get away from all of that."

A murmur rippled through the crowd.

"I was wrong. You can't run away. I came up with a great plan—at least, I thought it was a great plan. I found a way to leave my village without letting anyone know. I found a way to leave so my wife and children would be taken care of. No one knew I left and I never told anyone why."

A few voices answered and encouraged him. He talked louder and faster and stronger. "But it was no use. I found out the truth about the cantons. Once I got there, I couldn't believe what I saw. I couldn't believe any human could live like that. I wanted to get there and then bring my wife and children out after me, but once I saw what it was really like, I made up my mind."

The crowd surged forward as one body. The noise crashed back and forth between the bleachers and the platform, calling and answering.

"I made up my mind never to let my children see the cantons, not even to reduce them. I made up my mind to come back and give everything I had to the Pride. It's the best thing I could do. My children and my wife would never get any better life than the one we have in Prideland. The only hope they have of anything better is to come to the city and work as helpers."

Heads nodded, arms stretched out to embrace him, and voices cheered him.

"You people," he called even louder, "you listen to these men here. They're your fathers. They know what's best for you. You don't have to run away to the cantons to find out how bad it is. I already did that for you. I'm telling you from my own experience that everything they say is true."

The men standing behind him smiled and nodded some more.

"This Pride," the speaker boomed, "this is the best any human being can hope for. These cats give us the best life any human being could want. What are you going to do? Are you going to run off to the canton, just so you can find that out for yourself? Are you so stubborn that you won't listen when someone tells you what it's like out there? Are you going to fly away to another planet, away from your families and your friends? Are you going to live like a rat in a hole among strangers, just so you can save yourself the price of a cow for your subscription?"

People leapt to their feet again, calling out and weeping and answering him with prayers and entreaties.

"I'll do everything in my power, even at the cost of my own life, to protect this Pride. I'll make sure the understanding between us and the cats stays strong and nothing threatens it. I'll do it for my children, if for nothing else. I'll make certain they're part of the Pride as long as they live and I'll kill anyone who stands in their way!"

The crowd broke into cheers at his last words. The speaker walked back to the men. They patted him on the back, but he didn't smile. He shuffled off the platform and disappeared somewhere.

The cheering lasted longer than the first eruption. Dina started to wonder if it was going on longer than it should. Finally, the first speaker waved his hand for silence and got it. "Most of you know our next speaker. Harmon Farley travels around to all the cities and makes sure we all understand our place in the Pride. Every one of us owes him a debt of gratitude for his tireless efforts to improve our lives. Please give him your undivided attention."

He stepped aside and an aging, heavy-set man took his place. The audience didn't applaud him. He approached the edge of the stage in rapt silence.

"You all know me," he began. "I've told my story so many times I can't even remember where and when I've told it, so I guess I have to start from the beginning. I was born in this city. I was born the son of two helpers to a pair of cats down along the river. My parents helped those cats all their lives and no one could ask for better benefactors."

The crowd nodded in answer and he warmed to his topic. "I went through my boyhood without much trouble. I would have to be pretty worthless if I got into trouble with an upbringing like that. My parents and my benefactors gave me everything a boy could wish for. When I got old enough, my benefactors took me on as a helper along with my parents. That tells you what caring and generous benefactors they were. They took me on out of generosity to my parents."

The crowd murmured and nodded in agreement.

"But do you think I would appreciate that sort of thing? Not me. That was the greatest gift a young man could ask for in life and I had to throw it back in their faces. Just a few days after I started helping those cats, I met a man down by the river. I never met that man before and I never saw his face again after that. I can't even remember his name, but I remember what he looked like. I'll remember him 'til the day I die, and if I ever lay eyes on that man again, I'll know what to do with him. I learned my lesson. You can count on that, but I was young and stupid then. He could see that just from looking at me. He had my number from his very first glance. He smiled and spun my head full of all kinds of wild stories."

Exclamations of shock and horror broke out from the assembly, even though everyone must have heard the story thousands of times. Maybe the story wasn't even true.

"He told me what a pack of demons the Pride was. He told me how wonderful life was in the cantons with the slags. Can you believe that? That's how confused and foolish I was then. I actually believed him. I believed a slag's life was good and a helper's life was bad." He shook his head and lowered his eyes. He sniffed and wiped away a tear on his sleeve.

"I only talked to that man...." He raised his finger. "I call him a man in the loosest sense, you understand. I only talked to him for about an hour at the most, but that was all it took. I went home to my beautiful house with my loving parents and my generous benefactors, but I couldn't see what was right in front of my eyes. I couldn't love it or admire it anymore. Every time my benefactors asked me to do something, I burned in my heart to get away from them. I had to find a way to get out to the jungle with the slags.

"No matter what I did or where I went, I had to find out about them. I searched the city from one corner to the other for anyone who could tell me something about them. I tried talking to everyone I ever heard about who went out to the cantons and came back. Of course there were always a few around who had done it. They all told me the same thing. They all said to stay where I was and be grateful for what I had. They all told me I could get visited just for asking."

The audience growled in hatred for the jungle people who had no understanding with the Pride and Dina's mind churned. What were they really like? They couldn't be as bad as everyone made out. Either way, the landing team would have to contact the jungle people before the *Savannah* team could complete its mission.

"After about six months, I couldn't stand it anymore. I had to find a way to get away from Prideland. Beautiful, harmonious, peaceful Prideland—I had to leave it. I was so confused I couldn't understand what was good for me. I might as well have drunk poison. I had to throw away what was good for me and drink what was bad. I had to stab my poor parents in the heart and leave the best benefactors in all of Prideland. I had to go out to the jungle to sleep on the cold ground and eat lizard droppings and wood grubs—and that's what I did."

A woman's cry broke the silence. The whole crowd looked toward the sound. A white-haired old lady rose from her seat, pressed the back of her hand to her forehead, and collapsed into her neighbors' arms.

Farley saw her and a flush spread over his cheeks. "Well, I guess the rest isn't so different from my friend's story." He waved behind him. "I won't bore you with the same story all over again, but I didn't come back right away the way he did. I had to torture myself for six whole months before I saw the light."

The audience couldn't sit still much longer. People started to yell back at him and the noise grew louder.

"I'll admit to you I slept on the cold, wet ground. I ate grubs and lizard droppings. I even helped them get rid of their dead babies. I saw all the same things everyone else saw. We all know what sort of life the slags live. Enough people come back from there. We don't have to doubt them. I'm just one of dozens who tells the same story, but I came back. What choice did I have? What kind of life is that compared to the life of a helper? How could you stand a slag's life when you know what the Pride has to offer?"

The crowd started to rise.

"We can't stand the life of a slag and we don't have to! We're helpers. We have our place in the Pride and none of us has to give that up. We can all do our part to make the Pride great. We can keep our understanding with the Pride and we can make sure those around us do the same thing. I'll leave you with that and I hope you have a pleasant day."

It wasn't exactly the invitation they were hoping for and the crowd stood there waiting for some big finish. Only when Farley walked away did they realize they were free to react. A soft murmur surged into an almighty crash of shouting, singing, weeping, and arm-waving.

Belinda pulled Dina to her feet again. Dina didn't have to ask why she had to stand up every time. One glance at Belinda's face told Dina all she needed to know.

Belinda shouted and waved and raised her eyes to the ceiling along with everyone else, but something in her gaze told Dina that Belinda didn't quite share the rapture. She caught Dina's eye and jerked her head toward the platform. Dina got the message, raised her arms over her head, and shouted to the rafters, too.

She didn't know what to say, so she didn't say anything. She just shouted and waved. She had to do something and she did. She didn't stop until the first speaker lifted his hands and the audience sat down again.

"You all go back to your homes now. Go back to your work helping the cats. That's the best thing you can do with your lives. There is no life for human beings on this planet outside of Prideland. Life outside of Prideland is a living death. It's not fit for humans to live. Let's all agree right here and now that no more people will ever leave Prideland. The slags out in the jungle will die and the only people left on this planet will be those with an understanding with the Pride. That's the way it should be."

The crowd burst into wild cheering and the festival broke up. Dina did her part and shouted herself hoarse until Belinda dragged her out of the building.

Throngs of people glutted the streets. Dina looked around for Tom, but Belinda wouldn't let her hang around long enough to find him. She took Dina back through the tree-lined neighborhoods to Renfroe's house.

Chapter 21

Dina and Belinda found Renfroe waiting for them in the main corridor of his house. Belinda fled to the kitchen.

Renfroe greeted Dina. "So that's out of the way."

Dina stopped in front of him, but she didn't say anything.

"How did you find it?" he asked. "Was it what you expected?"

"Of course not!" Dina snapped. "How can you even ask me that?"

"What's the matter now? It's not my fault you have to go to the festivals. If you didn't care for it, you don't have to take it out on me."

"You didn't have to lie to me about it. If you had told me the truth, at least I would have known what to expect."

"How could I know what you would expect? How could I know you wouldn't like it?"

"How could I like it? You called it a festival. It was just about the farthest thing in the world from a festival. It was a mass brow-beating session." Renfroe chuckled, but his response only made her angrier. "Why can't you just call it what it is? Why do you have to use some ridiculous word like 'festival', which means nothing and actually means exactly the opposite of what it really is?"

He turned away. "It's not up to me what to call it. If you don't like it, I can't help that."

"Using these words is the same as lying. It's the same as calling a late-night beating a 'class', or a slave a 'helper', or a tribute a 'subscription', or...."

Renfroe took two paces towards her. He didn't threaten her, but his movements made her close her mouth with a snap.

"It's up to you to take exception to those words, Dina," he growled. "I didn't make them up and I can't change them to suit you. If you want to get mad about them, you're going to have a hard time coming to an understanding with the Pride. If that happens, you might have to leave here and I wouldn't like that."

She stared at him, right in his gleaming yellow eyes. She would have preferred to look down at the floor, but his eyes wouldn't let her look anywhere but into his face. Then he broke his gaze and released her. "I'm sorry to hear you didn't enjoy the festival."

"I didn't enjoy it," she muttered. "I don't ever want to go to another one."

"There's nothing either one of us can do about that. You have to go to the festivals whether you like it or not. All the helpers have to go, but at least now you know what to expect. I would hate to lose you over a misunderstanding about the words we use. Besides, you wanted to know how people come to their understanding with the Pride. A festival is the perfect place to find out."

She nodded. "I think I know now what you mean when you talk about the understanding."

"You do?" Renfroe perked up. "I'm glad to hear that."

"Just don't ask me to explain it. I don't think I could put it into words if I tried, but it's clearer to me, now that I've been to the festival. What I saw and heard there made it clear—at least, more clear than it was."

"And do you think you can come to an understanding of your own now?"

She nodded. "I can't explain that, either, but I think I know now what I have to do to come to an understanding with it."

He leaned his warm weight against her legs, rested his shoulder against one thigh, and rubbed his head against the other. "You don't know how pleased I am to hear that. I worried you might never come to an understanding with the Pride."

She couldn't move with him leaning against her like this. She stared down at the top of his head. "Would they take me away from you if I didn't?"

"It isn't like that. No one would take you away, but you couldn't stay here. If you didn't come to an understanding with the Pride, you wouldn't stay. You would leave of your own accord."

"I would never do that." The words came from somewhere deep inside her. "No one could make me leave."

"We couldn't stay together without the understanding."

Dina raised her hand, but she hesitated to let it fall. How did she develop feelings for this creature in such a short time?

He was just an animal. How could she give him the slightest consideration?

She had to admit the truth, though. She cared for him more than she ever intended. He wasn't just an animal. Whatever else happened, she never wanted to be separated from him. He was her only lifeline to sanity—if she could call it that.

Her hand hung suspended in the air. In the end, she surrendered to the inevitable. She couldn't stay on this planet without him. She couldn't do anything, not even live her own life, without him. He had won her.

She let her hand fall and it came to rest on his head. A deep purr vibrated out of his chest and he pushed his head into her hand. She ran her fingers through his thick fur and her fingertips nestled around his ears. "I won't leave you. I'll come to an understanding with the Pride. If only to stay with you, I'll do it."

"Do it for me, Dina," he rumbled. "You don't know how much you mean to me. I couldn't live here without you. You're like no other woman on this planet. I never thought I'd find someone like you or feel this way about anyone. I couldn't stand to lose you now, especially over some stupid misunderstanding."

Dina closed her eyes, but something besides his words took hold of her heart. It was the touch—the simple touch. She never knew until that moment how much it meant. He was right. In all the world, the two of them had only each other. Their companionship was the only thing she could rely on.

Chapter 22

Renfroe escorted Dina to the city, but he took a different route than Belinda took.

Market stalls offered their wares for sale in the central square. People bought and traded while the cats took what they wanted. When they found something they liked, they killed it and ate it on the spot. Splattered blood flowed in the gutters. Cats chased lizards, oxen, and fell deer through the streets. The bellows of dying animals rang off the city walls.

Dina and Renfroe watched from a safe distance. Renfroe chuckled at the squawking of dying animals and the flying blood and fur when the cats caught them.

"Where do these animals come from?" Dina asked.

"What? Oh, that. The subsidiaries bring their subscriptions into the city. That's how they contribute to the Pride—by bringing subscriptions."

Dina's shook her head and snorted. "You really are a consummate politician, aren't you? You're a master of saying something while saying nothing."

"You asked, so I told you."

He started walking and Dina followed him. "Why don't you just say exactly what you mean? Why do you have to use these meaningless slogans for everything?"

"I *did* say what I mean. You asked where the animals came from. I told you the subsidiaries bring their subscriptions to the city as contributions to the Pride. Where's the meaningless slogan in that?"

"That's what you said, but what you really mean is the villagers bring these animals as tribute to the Pride. They have to pay to pacify the Pride. The animals the cats eat keep the Pride from taking out their aggressions on the people. That's what you really mean."

"Why do you have to make everything so ugly? You put the worst possible construction on everything. Why can't you see the situation for what it is?"

"I *am* seeing it. *You're* the ones who paint it as something different. I'm just telling the truth."

Renfroe sighed. "I can see you haven't come to an understanding with the Pride yet, Dina."

Beyond the square, he climbed into the hills where the houses overlooked the river. Men tended the gardens and repaired the houses. Women hung laundry out to dry and walked back and forth from the market. They carried bags and baskets on their hips and slung over their shoulders.

Dina and Renfroe hiked up the highest hill to where an enormous white villa dominated the pinnacle overlooking the city. Dozens of cats and people of all ages clambered in and out of the doors.

Dina and Renfroe passed through a gate into a well-tended garden and Dina cried out in surprise "Tania! How are you?"

Tania didn't move to meet Dina or even smile. Her eyes shifted back and forth between Dina and a young woman standing near her. It was Maddy, the same girl who took Tania from the market.

Tania cast quick glances all around at the bushes and chewed her lower lip. Her hands trembled when she took a freshly laundered sheet out of Maddy's hands. Tania turned away to hide her face and hung the sheet on the clothesline.

"Khalid isn't at home," Maddy told Renfroe. "I don't know where he is or when he'll be back, but I'll tell him you came to see him."

Renfroe scanned the garden, flared his nostrils, and twitched his whiskers. "Very well. I'll speak to him another time."

Dina tried again. "Tania, how are you? Tell me everything you've been doing since I last saw you."

Tania glanced at Maddy. Her voice trembled when she finally summoned the will to speak. "It's good to see you again, Dina. You look like you're doing well."

"I am. Renfroe's been very kind to me. He was especially kind to bring me around to check on you. I couldn't think about anything but seeing you again."

Tania scanned the garden one more time. "That was nice of him."

Dina waited, but Tania didn't say anything else and Renfroe turned away. "Come along, Dina. We'll go now. Maybe we can catch up with Khalid another time."

He strolled out of the garden without looking back. Dina paused at the gate to glance back at Tania. Tania bit her lip again and her hands shook so badly she couldn't hold the laundry.

Dina hesitated. She would have run back to comfort Tania, but Maddy picked up the laundry basket and said something to Tania. Both women strode up the sloping lawn toward the house before Dina got a chance to move.

Tania stole one last look toward Dina and walked away. Dina watched her out of sight before she caught up with Renfroe on the street. "I wonder what's wrong with her."

"I didn't notice anything wrong with her."

"What are you talking about? I've never seen Tania so frightened before. You must have noticed it. I've known Tania long enough to know when something's bothering her. She's as tough as they come. Nothing rattles her. Now she can't stop her hands from shaking and she's chewing her lip to shreds. She's scared of something."

Renfroe sniffed. "That's natural."

"Natural? That kind of fear isn't natural. She's scared out of her mind. Something must be wrong with her. We have to find out what it is."

"Dina," Renfroe murmured, "when are you going to understand? Your friend is afraid of Khalid, and to be perfectly honest with you, I don't blame her. I've known him for decades and even I'm afraid of him."

"You! You're a Bengal tiger. What do you have to be afraid of? You don't have anything to fear from any creature in the world, not even another cat. Why would you be afraid of him?"

"Khalid is a fearsome and dangerous cat. He could easily kill me in a fight. I would never cross him under any circumstances. He might very well be the deadliest cat in the whole Pride and I'll tell you something else. He hates human beings. He can barely stand his own helpers."

"How could he hate them? He lives with them in his house."

Renfroe nodded. "All the helpers in his house are afraid of him, even after helping him for years. They live in constant fear of him. He could turn against any of them at any time. I'm sure your friend has found that out in the few days she's been in his house."

"If you know that, how can you let her live with him? Tania's not another village maid. She's a highly trained linguist and a starship officer. She's a diplomat of the highest order. How could you turn her over to a cat like him?"

"I had no choice in the matter. Hector arranged all the benefactors for you and your friends. I only found out about it after the fact."

"We have to get her out of there. We have to find another place for her to stay."

"None of you is going anywhere." He set off down the hill. "Too bad Khalid wasn't there. I wanted to talk to him about her."

"Why didn't you talk to her yourself? She was standing right there."

"No," he replied. "That is protected."

"Protected? What do you mean, protected?"

"It means it isn't allowed. It's...how do you say it? It's frowned-upon. She is Khalid's helper. I couldn't question her without his permission."

"That's not what the word 'protected' means. It doesn't mean 'frowned-upon' at all. That's another one of your meaningless formulas for saying something without saying anything at all."

"The factors come up with all the rules related to the helpers. They came up with the word 'protected'. They made the rule that no one should speak to a helper without their benefactor's permission. Some cats want to hear what their helpers talk about. That's the reason for the rule."

"Are you sure the rules come from the factors and not from the Pride?"

"The Pride had nothing to do with it. As a matter of fact, the factors make the rules for the subsidiaries and the slags as well."

"I find that difficult to believe. Why would they restrict people for no reason? It makes more sense that the cats don't want people speaking without permission from their...what's the word you use? 'Owners'?"

"We prefer 'benefactors'. These people aren't doing anything they don't want to do."

Dina laughed out loud. "You really are something else, you know that?"

Renfroe eyed her. "Is there a problem?"

"You cats really are some piece of work. I couldn't make this nonsense up if I wanted to. I say 'villager'. You say 'subsidiary'. I say 'tribute'. You say 'subscription'. I say 'owner'. You say 'benefactor'. Do you see a pattern here?"

"The only pattern I see is that you use the ugliest, most offensive word you can think of to describe these people whereas I use the words our society finds most acceptable and appropriate. You make the situation out to be negative when it isn't."

"Of course, *you're* going to say that. You're one of the benefactors."

"These people have an understanding with the cats of the Pride. That understanding dictates what they do and don't do. These are simple social conventions. All societies have them." He turned away with another shake of his head and started down the hill. "Come along, Dina. We have a couple more stops to make and the next one is to visit your friend, Tom. I think when you see how he is living with Elyse, you'll agree the humans on this planet have a very satisfactory arrangement with their cat benefactors."

Her heart skipped a beat. She could talk to Tom. He would understand. He would have some idea about how to get off this planet.

She started after Renfroe, but as she turned into the street, a shape caught her eye and she sucked in her breath.

"What is it?" Renfroe asked.

"Something's up in that tree over there," she whispered. "I think we're being watched."

At the top of the hill, a formless shape darkened the fork between two tree branches. Dina couldn't stop staring at it. Some magnetic force held her hypnotized.

Renfroe followed her line of sight up the hill. "It's Khalid."

Two yellow eyes blinked out of the shapeless mass of black. "What is he?"

"He's a black panther. That's his favorite tree. He probably heard our entire conversation."

"Aren't you going to go talk to him? You came all this way to see him. Now's your chance."

Renfroe turned away. "No. He told his helpers he wasn't at home. He doesn't want company. He's seen me. He'll come and find me when he's ready to talk. Come on. We'll make our next call."

Chapter 23

Dina caught up with Renfroe on their way down the hill. "Who were all those other cats at Khalid's house?"

"Just cats."

"Are they his relatives?"

"No, they just live there."

"Cats don't normally live together like that."

"Some do. Some don't. After we visit your friends, we'll stop into Helion House."

"Helion House," she repeated. "That's where Belinda took me for the festival."

"That's right."

"There weren't any cats there. It was just a big gymnasium."

"It's the biggest building in the city. That's why the helpers hold their festivals there. It's actually home to a family of lions—the Helion family. They are the original Pride and they're the most powerful cats in the Pride. Lord Helion, the old patriarch, is the most powerful cat in all of Prideland. He virtually controls the Senate."

"Belinda said *you* were the most influential cat in the Senate. You're the Chairman, aren't you?"

"I'm the Chairman, but I'm not the most powerful Senator—not by a long shot. No cat can twitch a whisker in Prideland without Lord Helion's approval."

"So the Helion family lives together at the gymnasium. How many of them are there?"

Renfroe thought it over. "I would estimate about three hundred."

Dina gasped. "Three hundred!"

He nodded. "They're a big family and they enjoy each other's company. I don't understand it myself. I prefer to live alone."

"Khalid must enjoy the company of all those other cats, too."

"No. He prefers to be alone as well. He simply allows other cats to use his house. He keeps to himself in the trees and on the rooftops."

"And you have your helpers," she pointed out.

"That is true, but I keep only a bare minimum of helpers. I wouldn't keep any if I had my way. Belinda keeps the house and Buck keeps the grounds. That's the only reason I keep them and I don't associate with them at all."

"Why do you keep me, then?"

"Originally, Hector decided to separate you and your friends in the city and he asked me to take you. That's how you wound up at my house. I thought the arrangement would be temporary, at least until the Pride decided what to do with you, but it didn't work out that way."

"Does that mean the Pride *has* decided what to do with us?"

"We haven't decided what to do with you, but we know we can't let you leave. That's all we know, so there's nothing else to do except to keep you here."

"Why can't you let us leave? We haven't done anything wrong."

"You landed here. That's what you did. Anyone who lands here stays here. That's the understanding we have with the humans on this planet, but I would keep you anyway. I've become attached to you."

"I'm attached to you, too, but I would be a lot more attached to you if I had the freedom to come and go as I please. You can't expect someone to care for you if you hold power over them."

"It isn't up to me. I don't make the rules."

They walked on in silence until they came to a house overlooking the river. Rambling gardens surrounded it on all sides, all of them meticulously tended by human gardeners. The gardeners watched Dina and Renfroe approach, but they didn't stop weeding the flower beds and trimming the shrubs.

"This is Elyse's house. Knock on the door, will you please, Dina?"

A pretty blonde girl ushered them into a parlor. To Dina's surprise, the room contained several wing-backed chairs, upholstered couches, and other seats for human beings. Tom lounged in the most luxurious chair of all.

A white Persian cat perched on a leather couch opposite him while she groomed her downy fur. Tom and the cat broke off their conversation when Renfroe and Dina entered.

"Oh, it's Dina!" Tom jumped out of his chair and swept Dina up in a bear hug. "I've been wondering how you were getting along. This is Elyse." He waved his hand toward the Persian.

"And this," the white cat crooned back, "is Renfroe, Dina's benefactor. How are you, old man?"

Renfroe growled in his usual way. "I'm fine, Elyse. I'm glad to see you and Tom getting along so well."

Elyse narrowed her eyes at Tom. "Who could fail to get along with such a handsome specimen as this? I really must thank Dina for delivering him to me. I didn't realize what I was missing until he came along."

Tom grinned at the white cat. "I was just telling Elyse all about you, Dina."

Dina's every nerve stiffened. "What were you telling her?"

"I was telling her about our mission and how you and I have worked together on landing parties before. I was telling her that you're really the most vital member of our team. I might be the Coalition negotiator, but you'll be making the biological survey."

"It really is fascinating," Elyse purred. "I'm amazed such a complex society as this Coalition can exist outside our planet and we know nothing about it."

"That's why I came to see you," Renfroe replied. "Dina wanted to see Tom, but I also wanted to discuss with you the possibility of accepting this embassy and incorporating Prideland into their Coalition."

Dina couldn't help but interrupt. "When did you decide to do that? Just this morning, you told me it would never happen."

"I changed my mind." He turned back to Elyse. "This proposed incorporation could be a golden opportunity for our people to move beyond this planet into the wider galactic community."

Elyse sniffed. "That will be a matter for the Senate."

"You and I sit in the Senate. I plan to speak to Lord Helion after we leave here. Between the three of us, we hold enough influence to sway the Senate in favor of incorporation."

"We'll see about that. I won't commit myself to anything at the moment. I'm enjoying myself too much with my new helper." Elyse twitched her whiskers at Tom.

"I agree," Tom told her. "Let's keep business and pleasure separate. There will be plenty of time to negotiate later."

"And our time together has been so pleasant," Elyse added.

She strutted along the couch seat and sprang onto Tom's chair. She trod on his lap and sat down between his legs. Tom ran his fingers through her silky white fur. He rubbed around her ears and under her chin. Elyse purred and kneaded her paws into his lap.

Dina stared at them. Was she really seeing what she thought she was seeing? She'd seen people petting cats thousands of times, but never like this.

Elyse prodded her paws into Tom's genitals and his penis started to swell inside his pants. Elyse pushed her hips into his hand and flicked her pelvis back and forth.

Dina gulped down a lump in her throat. "I'm glad to see you're doing well."

"How could I not be doing well?" Tom replied. "I've never been treated so well in all my life."

Dina struggled to clear her thoughts. "I just came from visiting Tania at Khalid's house. I didn't get a chance to talk to her, but she looked frightened. It made me worry about the rest of the team—especially you."

"There's nothing to worry about. I'm doing just fine."

"Yes," Elyse agreed. "We have a very clear understanding between us—Tom and me. Don't we, my dear?"

"We sure do," he exclaimed. "We understand each other perfectly."

Dina could see what kind of understanding they had. "Would you mind if I had a few words with Tom in private?"

Elyse glared at her. Then she glanced at Renfroe. She sniffed again and jumped down. "Go ahead. I won't stop you."

Tom got to his feet and crossed to an open double door leading into a different garden behind the house. "Come out into the garden, Dina. We can talk there."

He led her down a path toward a pond in the distance, but she couldn't help glancing back toward the house. Did she just imagine the sexual tension between Tom and Elyse? "What do you want to talk to me about?" he asked.

"We're on a mission here. We're here to negotiate incorporating with these people and to bring back Alexander Mathus."

"I know," Tom replied. "What makes you think I forgot it?"

"Are you sure you're not enjoying yourself a little too much?"

He cocked his head to one side. "What makes you think that?"

"The way you were acting with Elyse in there. I didn't like it at all."

"That doesn't mean I've forgotten about our mission. You heard her. They'll discuss our proposal in the Senate. What more can we ask for?"

"Have you made any effort to talk to any other people about it?"

"No," he replied. "You know we aren't allowed to talk to other people without our benefactor's permission and I haven't had any opportunity to talk to anyone other than Elyse and her helpers. To be honest, I don't see the point."

"We have to get back to the village. We have to talk to a large number of people without the cats present."

"That would be unwise. We could get visited for that."

"Do you know what that word means?" she asked.

"No, I don't and I'm not about to find out."

"Could you get permission from Elyse to talk to the villagers about incorporating?" she asked. "She might help us if you ask her."

"I'm not going to do anything to cross Elyse. She's been too good to me since I got here. Things could be a lot worse."

"She seems favorable to our mission and she likes you. We could use that to our advantage."

"I'm not going to use Elyse to our advantage," Tom countered. "You should be ashamed of yourself for even suggesting it."

"All right," Dina conceded. "I won't suggest it again, but this is the first chance I've seen to accomplish our mission."

Tom curled his arm around her shoulders and pulled her against him. "Can't we talk about something other than the mission? I haven't seen you for days."

She melted into his embrace and his lips covered her mouth. His breath warmed her face and she let his tongue glide into her mouth. She leaned her body against him. His breath quickened in her nostrils and he ran his hands up and down her body.

"You don't know how much I've wanted you!" he murmured. "I've been going crazy without you." His hand cupped her breast and she pushed her chest up into his grasp.

At that moment, a bell rang in the house and Tom caught his breath. "Elyse is calling me." He tore himself turned away and raced back to the house.

Dina stared after him. Her body ached for him. Aching need for him burned her skin and face where he kissed and touched her.

In answer to her body's silent call, Renfroe strolled through the trees to fill that gaping hole. "Let's go, Dina. We can't accomplish anything more here today. You can come back another time to see Tom."

Dina stood rooted to the spot and stared toward the open door where Tom disappeared. What was he doing in there? Was he comforting himself with Elyse?

At least Elyse had other helpers that Tom could talk to. He wasn't locked in a room all day, but he needed companionship and bodily contact, too. He would get it from Elyse if he couldn't get it from her.

She felt Renfroe studying her and she tore herself away. She followed him out of the garden in numb silence.

He led her through a gap in the hedge onto the street overlooking the river. Her mind still revolved around Tom when the Elite Battalion passed on the opposite side of the street. They pushed their wheelbarrow up the hill going the other way. They were heading toward the river.

The sight snapped Dina out of her trance. "It's the treasure hunters."

"Who?"

"The Elite Battalion. They're taking their treasure to the safety deposit vault at the bank." She chuckled to herself.

Renfroe frowned at her and then at the Elite Battalion. "No, they're cleaning up the city. That's their job."

The Elite Battalion pushed their cart up the hill to a square, windowless building on the riverbank. "What is that place?"

"It's an old power mill. That's their headquarters."

"Headquarters? What do they do there? Do they practice their digging and scooping techniques? Do they review the latest industry developments? Maybe they give each other pep talks to improve morale."

She burst out in hysterical laughter. The whole thing seemed too ridiculous to take seriously, and on top of all the horror she encountered recently, she couldn't hold back her mirth.

"No, they live there. They sleep there at night and they leave from there every morning."

"They must hide their treasure there," she remarked.

"I don't know what they do with their...findings." Renfroe turned away. "I don't want to know."

Dina chuckled to herself again. "It's the Museum of Antiquities."

Chapter 24

H elion House was jammed from wall to wall with hundreds of lions. They lounged on the floor in piles, strutted around and stepped on one another, and groomed themselves on the bleachers. Litters of cubs tumbled around the adults. The cubs gnawed their elders' faces and pounced on any twitching ear or tail.

Dozens of men, women, and children carried trays of food through the vast building. The helpers carried basins of water and blankets to the lions.

Some of these people brushed the lions and combed their manes. One big male held his mouth open while an elderly man cleaned between his teeth with a pointed stick.

A large cub almost collided with Dina when she walked through the door. He ran around and tussled with his playmates. He bounded from mauling his fellow cubs and pounced on one of the attendants as the man passed with a bucket of hot soapy water.

The man sprawled across several lions covering the floor beneath him. The bucket sailed out of his hands and soapy water splashed across the room. The water drenched another group of lions and saturated their blankets. The cub rode his prey to the ground and gnawed the man's leg.

Dina moved into the room watching the whole scene. "Look, Renfroe. That man's in trouble." She would have dragged the cub off, but the mass of bodies covering the floor stopped her from going anywhere.

"Leave them alone, Dina. Don't interfere."

"But he could get hurt. We have to do something." She couldn't do anything without stepping on lions.

"The young of every species are all the same. They have to learn by testing themselves. Look, there's Lord Helion. I'll go talk to him. You wait here."

Renfroe waded into the sea of cats until he sat down at the foot of the bleachers next to a grizzled old male with a huge mane. The two cats surveyed the Pride and fell into conversation.

The man with the bucket cowered under his attacker and didn't move. The cub came to his senses and let go of the man's leg, wrinkled his nose, and went back to playing with his friends.

The man waited until the cubs moved away before he stirred and got up. His shirt and pants dripped with soapy water and blood ran down his leg. He took one tender step and limped away.

A few minutes later, the same man came back with a mop and an armload of dry blankets. His clothes and leg still dripped blood and water onto the floor.

He mopped up the water, removed the wet blankets, and replaced them with dry ones. The lions rearranged themselves on their fresh bedding and the man cleaned up the blood fallen from his own wounded leg. Then he hobbled out of the room and didn't come back.

Most of the human attendants walked around the room completely naked. Others wore loin clothes and some women wore bikini tops and briefs.

Dina got her first chance to examine the helpers up close with their clothes off. For the first time, she noticed that all these people bore the same pattern of scarring around their hips. Deep, straight lines scored their flesh in the shape of an inverted V. The lines formed a point on the lower abdomen and sloped downward on either side of the genital area like a tent.

The lines ran straight and evenly spaced and each person's scars were identical to everyone else's. They couldn't be accidental.

The scar tissue penetrated so deeply into their pelvic structures that it affected their body movements. The lines damaged the tendons and ligaments in their hips so they couldn't stand fully erect. Every helper in the place walked slightly bent over just like Alexander Mathus and the subsidiaries in the village.

A male lion sprawled on his side on the floor while a young woman lay on her back on the blankets at his side. She rested her head on his rear flank with her arms draped back over his body.

She wore a scanty bra barely covering her breasts and no other garments at all. She propped one bare leg against the lion's chest while he licked his paw. Then he moved from licking his paw to licking the girl's leg. He licked up the inside of her thigh to her genitals, licking, licking, licking. Her head lolled back and she moaned in obvious pleasure.

Dina's jaw dropped gaping at them. She might have misinterpreted the interplay between Tom and Elyse, but here was a cat performing a sexual act on a person right in front of Dina's eyes.

Renfroe and Lord Helion must have seen the lion titillating the girl in plain view of the whole room, but neither showed any sign of surprise.

A young lioness crouched on the floor nearby with a man kneeling behind her. He leaned forward and supported his weight with his hands flat on the floor.

Only, perhaps, if Dina had been blind could she mistake the pumping action of the man's hips against the lioness's hindquarters. Dina suddenly wished that she had been blind so she wouldn't see what was happening.

Still, she found it impossible to look away. The man's scars immobilized his hip joints so he couldn't bend all the way forward or backward. When he thrust his pelvis, he had to move his whole body along with it.

Renfroe finished talking to Lord Helion. He padded to the door within inches of the man mating with the lioness, but Renfroe didn't even glance at them. He walked out the door, past Dina, and onto the sidewalk.

Dina didn't see him. She stared at the scene in horror. All over the room, cats and humans engaged in every conceivable combination of sex acts involving both sexes of both species. She couldn't tear her eyes away even as she commanded herself to get out of there.

Renfroe stopped on the sidewalk and looked back. Dina hadn't followed him the way she should have. He came back and his deep rumbling voice snapped her out of her trance. "Come along, Dina."

She staggered after him and left the spectacle of Helion House far behind—but not far enough behind. Her mind whirled over everything she'd seen, but she didn't dare to speak.

They got within a few of blocks of Renfroe's house when he stopped in front of a big house just like his own.

"Listen to me, Dina," he rumbled. "This is Fallon's house. He's benefactor to your friend, Matthew. I have to warn you that Matthew has not fared well here. He has run afoul of Fallon."

"What does that mean?"

"It means he and Fallon don't get along very well. Matthew has suffered for it. Matthew doesn't have a good understanding with Fallon."

Dina opened her mouth and shut it again. "Oh."

"I'm warning you, Dina. Don't open your mouth to say a single word while we're in this house. No matter what you see or think or feel, keep quiet. Fallon doesn't tolerate helpers stepping out of line. Let me do all the talking, and whatever you do, don't interfere between Fallon and Matthew. Do you understand?"

Dina swallowed hard and nodded. "I understand."

"Fallon is a Manx cat. He and his family are the only Manx cats in all of Prideland and they all live here. Do you know anything about Manx cats?"

Dina shook my head.

"They're an aggressive breed. One of Fallon's females just gave birth to a litter of kittens. So whatever you do, don't touch anything. They're a bit touchy right now."

"Will Fallon let me see Matthew?" she asked.

"He might. I think it highly unlikely he'll let you speak to Matthew, though, and I guarantee he won't let you speak to him in private. Fallon doesn't approve of that."

"Why is he so strict?" she asked.

"You'll find, Dina, that most cats in our Pride feel the same way."

Renfroe led the way through the front door into a central corridor exactly like his own except that this house was full of people. Cleaners, gardeners, and butlers scurried everywhere. Like Renfroe's house, this house contained no seating or any other furniture for people.

The Manx cats were much larger than ordinary house cats with only short stubs for tails. Three stately females crossed the corridor together in front of Renfroe and Dina.

Renfroe followed them into a side room. Another female cat lay near a blazing fire with a litter of newborn kittens at her side. A bevy of housemaids fussed around the room and opposite the fire sat a giant orange cat. His head came up to Dina's thigh. He scanned the room with aloof superiority.

Dina stopped in the doorway, but Renfroe approached the fire and sniffed the kittens. Then he retreated and sat down at Dina's side. "Congratulations on this addition to your family."

Fallon blinked and looked away.

Renfroe swiveled his head toward Dina. "As you know, this new helper of mine came to Prideland with three others with the intention of incorporating us into their Coalition of Inhabited Planets."

"Actually," Fallon growled, "five of them landed originally. Hector and Victor reduced one of them just after they landed."

"Of course you're right," Renfroe replied.

"They came here to incorporate the human population. They had no such intention of incorporating the cat population." Fallon sniffed in Dina's direction. "Ask your new helper to clarify that point for you."

"I don't have to clarify it with my helper. I know you're right about that, too."

"So what is it you want from me?" Fallon asked.

"Firstly, I would like to speak to your helper who landed with them. Matthew is his name."

"I know the one you mean."

"And secondly," Renfroe went on, "I would like to discuss with you the possibility of accepting this Coalition's embassy. I would like the Pride to seriously consider joining this Coalition and taking our place in the wider galactic community."

"I don't have to consider it. I oppose such a proposal most strenuously."

Renfroe stiffened. "May I ask why you oppose it?"

"I oppose it because we have a very favorable understanding with the human beings on this planet. Joining this Coalition would put that understanding at risk. Ask your helper there if any of the other planets in their Coalition have races of sentient cats on them."

"I don't have to ask her. I am sure none of them do."

"My point precisely," Fallon replied. "We would be the only race of sentient cats incorporated into a Coalition of planets inhabited and governed by humans. Our present understanding with our human helpers and subsidiaries would dissolve completely. We would find ourselves the subsidiaries with none of the rights and privileges we currently enjoy. Ask your helper. She will tell you the same thing."

"I ask you to consider," Renfroe growled, "the larger benefit of contact with other cultures and species. Surely these benefits outweigh the convenience of maintaining the status quo."

"I disagree. Now, if you don't mind, I don't wish to discuss politics in front of my family. If you wish to see Matthew, you may see him here, but I don't give permission for you to talk to him outside my presence. I also don't give permission for you to discuss with him his mission to incorporate our planet."

Renfroe sighed. "Very well. Your conditions undermine my principal objective in coming here, but I'm sure Dina will appreciate seeing him and satisfying herself of his well-being."

Fallon addressed one of the maids tending the mother cat. "Mary, would you please go get Matthew and bring him here? He's out in the garden digging a trench."

The maid vanished.

"I'm not so sure you will satisfy yourself of his well-being," Fallon remarked after the maid left. "As you may have heard, I've had occasion to correct his behavior since he came here. You may find him slightly the worse for wear."

"So we heard," Renfroe replied.

The maid came back. Fallon licked his lips and showed his teeth. "Here he is."

Dina couldn't stop herself from gasping in shock. "Matthew!" She would have run to his side if Renfroe hadn't warned her not to.

Blood-caked scratches crisscrossed his face, arms, and legs. A nasty gash cut into his upper lip and made it curl up in a hideous snarl. He clutched his right arm across his chest and he limped on his left leg. A dark wet stain soaked his shirt under one arm.

"You see what I mean?" Fallon asked. "He doesn't seem to want to come to an understanding with me or any other cat."

Matthew's eyes darted to Fallon. Then he cast a quick glance at Dina and lowered his eyes to the floor. He understood enough to keep silent.

Fallon sniffed and him and looked away. "So what do you want to talk to him about?"

Dina opened her mouth, but she couldn't make her voice work.

"You can see for yourself the state he's in," Fallon went on. "If that's all you want, I'll thank you to go about your business, Renfroe. I don't want my little ones disturbed."

Renfroe nodded. "We'll bid you good day, then. I appreciate you seeing us. We can discuss business another time."

Matthew mistook this exchange for a dismissal because he turned to walk away. In a flash, Fallon launched himself from his place by the fire and struck Matthew across the back. His weight knocked Matthew flat on his face and Fallon sank his teeth into Matthew's neck.

Matthew screamed and Dina screamed in response. She extended her arm towards him, but Renfroe slipped in front of her and blocked her from moving.

Matthew struggled for his life, but his movements only sparked an aggressive response from Fallon. The cat kicked all four limbs and shredded Matthew's back and thighs with his claws.

The louder and more desperately Matthew screamed, the harder Fallon kicked. Dina covered her mouth with both hands to stuff her own screams down her throat, but they kept coming no matter what she did.

No one else moved a muscle. The cats blinked at the display with distracted indifference. The maids betrayed not a flicker of alarm. They must have seen Fallon do this all the time.

Matthew finally stopped struggling long enough for Fallon the calm down and hop off him. Matthew's shirt and pants hung off his body in blood-soaked rags.

As soon as Fallon jumped off, Matthew hoisted himself up on his hands and knees. He cast one wretched glance over his shoulder to meet Dina's eye and he crawled to the door, dripping blood on the tiles.

A maid wiped up the drops with a rag. Fallon took his seat by the fire and cleaned the blood off his paws and chin. Matthew dragged himself to the door, but just as he reached it, Fallon pounced again. The same sequence of events repeated, with Fallon mauling Matthew to shreds. He only stopped when Matthew lay still and stopped struggling.

The second time Fallon jumped down from Matthew's back, Matthew lay still for several seconds, not daring to move. Fallon sat at Matthew's side, studying him.

Matthew made another attempt to crawl out of the room. The instant he rose up on his knees, Fallon extended one paw and raked his claws into Matthew's leg and drew another piercing scream from Matthew.

"Now get back to work," Fallon ordered.

Matthew boosted himself up onto his hands and knees and bolted out of the room. Fallon strode back to the fire and fixed his eyes on Dina. "So you see he hasn't yet come to an understanding with the Pride. I hope for his sake he figures it out soon." He yawned loudly in Dina's face. The faintest peeping noise came from the nest by the fire.

"Come along, Dina," Renfroe murmured. "Good day, Fallon."

Dina stumbled out of the house. Renfroe didn't stop until they got around the corner out of sight of Fallon's house. He watched her wipe desperate tears off her cheeks. "Are you all right?"

"All right!" she choked. "How could I be all right?"

"What's wrong?"

"Wrong?" she shrieked. "Why, whatever could be wrong? I just watched your good friend Fallon try to kill Matthew."

"Believe me, Dina. Fallon did not try to kill Matthew. If he wanted to kill him, he would have done so with no trouble. He enjoys testing himself. He challenges himself to see how far he can go without killing him."

"That's even worse!" she shot back. "It would be better if he just killed Matthew outright instead of torturing him like this. You just finished telling me how nice it is for people living with their cat benefactors. What a joke!"

"I admit it isn't very nice for Matthew right now, but think how nice it is for Tom living with Elyse. It could be just as nice for Matthew if he came to an understanding with Fallon."

"Understanding?" she bellowed. "I understand the Pride perfectly now. I couldn't fail to understand after what I've just seen and I'm sure Matthew understands, too. I understand you, too. You'll always be part of the Pride. No matter how nice you are to me, we'll always be cat and mouse. That's all we'll ever be."

She crossed her arms over her chest and looked away. Renfroe regarded her for a moment and then sighed. "Let's go home, Dina. I thought seeing your friends might settle your mind and help you understand the Pride better. If I made a mistake, you may lay the blame with me. It's late now and we both need to eat something and go to sleep. Maybe you'll feel better in the morning."

Chapter 25

Dina ate by herself in the kitchen. Darkness hung over the house. Buck and Belinda must have gone to bed hours ago.

The quiet kitchen calmed her. After she ate, she wandered through the house. At the garden portico, Renfroe slipped out of the shadows. "I hoped you would still be awake. I want to talk to you before you go to bed."

"What about?" she asked.

"You seem particularly disturbed by what you saw today. I thought you would want to talk about it."

Dina stared out into the darkness. "Fallon dismissed our mission so casually. He didn't even give it a second thought."

"Most cats of the Pride will feel the same way, but the greatest resistance will come from the human population."

"Why would they resist it? Won't they want to break away from this..." She stopped herself. "This...understanding they have?"

"These people are happy with the understanding exactly as it is. They will reject your proposal even more strenuously than the cats."

"Why would they do that?" she asked.

"Think about it. If they wanted to, these people could break the understanding whenever they wished. Look at the slags. They have no understanding with the Pride."

"I don't know anything about the slags. You said they live in terrible conditions in their cantons."

"They don't live as comfortably as the subsidiaries, but they live much more comfortably than Matthew does." Renfroe chuckled low under his breath.

Dina grimaced and turned away. He pretended not to see her.

"The slags could improve their condition considerably if they wanted to. They could keep livestock. They could cultivate crops. They could have everything the subsidiaries have without the Pride and without the understanding."

He broke off and eyed her while he waited for her to say something. "I'm surprised at you, Dina. I'm surprised you reacted the way you did. Is there anything I should know about it?"

She refused to look at him. "I don't know what you're talking about."

He sat down and sighed. "You don't have anything to hide from me, Dina. I had to stop you from throwing your life away trying to help Matthew. What bothered you so much about Fallon disciplining him?"

"Is it so hard to believe I would want to help another human being in trouble? That only goes to show how far these people have fallen from being truly human."

He watched her in silence. Dina kept her eyes on the treetops beyond the garden. She tugged at her lip until he broke in on her thoughts. "Where did you get that scar on your lip?"

Dina's shoulders sagged and her chin fell onto her chest. "I don't want to talk about it. I don't want to talk about anything."

"As you wish." He turned his head away, but he didn't leave.

Dina let out a heavy sigh. "I might as well tell you."

He said nothing and waited for her to open up of her own accord. "When I was little, my grandmother made me a rag doll for my fourth birthday. It was my favorite toy and I still have it now. It's in my quarters on the *Savannah*.

"My mother and father split up when I was five. Within a year, my mother remarried another guy. He was a real scumbag. He would come home stinking and greasy from the auto repair shop. He would plop down on the couch and drink himself into a stupor. My brother and I hated him."

Renfroe sat down to listen. His ghostly eyes gave Dina the only clue that he was listening.

"He used to get drunk and beat up my mother and my brother and me. He used to come into my room early in the morning and get into my bed. He would climb on top of me and force himself on me. I'll never forget the smell of his breath and he would corner me in the house when my mother wasn't around.

"My brother and I would run away out of the house the minute he came home from work. We built a fort in the long grass in a field behind our house where we would hide.

We hid there for as long as we could, but in the end, we usually came back when we heard our mother screaming. Then, of course, we would get our fair share.

"I always took my doll with me when we ran away. I called her Matilda. Back then, I thought she was a real person. She was real to me. I didn't want to leave her in the house with that creep. I took her with me to protect her from him, and sure enough, I was right.

"One afternoon, I didn't get out of the house fast enough. My stepfather caught me on my way out the door. He snatched my doll away from me.

"I screamed at him, 'That's mine! Give that back!' but he didn't give it back. He held it above his head while I hopped around his legs trying to reach it. He laughed and waved it in my face. Then he yanked it away again.

"He said, 'I hate this thing and I'm gonna get rid of it!' He took it over to the woodstove in the kitchen and opened the door to throw my doll into the firebox. I went wild. I screamed at him and beat him with my fists and kicked him in the shins, but he ignored it all.

"Then, with one swipe of his hand, he sent me sprawling backward and my lip split. When I jumped up, I saw him bending down to throw my doll into the fire. Something snapped inside me. A force came out of me that I never knew was there. I saw myself from a distance like a different person was acting through my body.

"My feet left the ground and I sailed through the air toward him. I tackled him with all my strength. That wasn't much compared to him, but I sent him rolling. He rolled across the kitchen floor, but I held onto him. When he stopped rolling, he was still conscious and he still had my doll in his hand. I bared my teeth like some kind of animal. I grabbed two fistfuls of his hair and smashed his head into the floor as hard as I could. I didn't stop until blood came out from underneath his head.

"When I let go of his hair, his eyes were closed and he didn't move anymore. I grabbed my doll out of his hand and ran out of the house. I hid in our secret fort until after dark. I missed dinner and everything.

"I hid my doll in a secret place in the woods. Not even my brother knew where she was. I snuck back into the house and went straight to my room. I got into bed and went to sleep. The next morning when I got up, I didn't see anybody. I ate breakfast and went to school the way I always did.

"When I got home from school, everything went on as if nothing had happened. My stepfather had to go to the hospital to get his head x-rayed and his scalp stitched up. He took weeks to recover, but no one said a single word to me about it.

"I kept my doll hidden until I went away to college. I made sure to do well in school so I could go to college and get away from home. I loved school where everything was stable and orderly—so different from home. I guess the same thing led me to join the Armada. Even when our landing team had to fight for our lives against hostile populations, I could always count on the rules. No one would dare to break them. I've kept Matilda with me ever since."

Renfroe let the silence settle.

"I guess that's why I'm kind of sensitive to people getting hurt or mistreated," she finished. "I can't stand seeing anyone get abused or exploited."

Renfroe stretched out on the grass at her feet. "Come and sit down next to me. You've had a big day."

She let out a long, shaking breath. If only Tom was here to wrap his arms around her. That's what she really needed right now, but she had to settle for leaning against Renfroe instead.

She sat down on the grass at his side. His cat smell filled her nostrils. In just a few days, that smell had changed in her mind. At first, it set off alarm bells in her head that made her jump and want to run away. Now it soothed her.

What harm could come from resting her head against his shoulder? He wasn't a predator out to catch and kill her like Fallon and Khalid. She could lose herself in him. She could belong to him and enfold herself in him. Everything outside the garden faded into the night and she fell into his intoxicating presence and disappeared.

Chapter 26

"Dina dear," Renfroe said, "I have a job for you."

Dina looked up from her breakfast. "What is it?"

"I want you to go to Elyse's house and talk to your friend, Tom."

Her eyes popped open. "I'd love to."

"This isn't a friendly social call between helpers," he told her. "I want you to talk to him about something specific."

"What do you want me to talk to him about?"

"He's been called before the Senate to answer some questions about your mission. I want you to talk to him about what he plans to say in his address. I want you to prepare him to make an acceptable presentation."

"Don't worry about Tom. You can trust him to make a good case. He's the Coalition representative for our team. He's empowered to carry out all the negotiations."

Renfroe's voice cut the air much more dangerously than she'd ever heard before. "This appointment before the Senate will not be a negotiation. I'm sending you to warn Tom of that fact. He seems reluctant to heed any advice on that point. He is a human being addressing a Senate of cats. The Senate won't tolerate disrespect of any kind."

Dina looked back down at her plate. "I see."

"I'm glad you see my point. If he wants this mission of yours to succeed, he'll have to convince the Senate. He'll have to convince them not only of the merits of your proposal but of your respect and understanding for the Pride. Without that, they won't listen to your proposal at all."

"I understand."

"I'm glad you understand because I want you to go after breakfast."

"Will the rest of our team be there? We're supposed to be carrying out this mission together."

Renfroe kept his tone measured. "I think it highly unlikely that Fallon and Khalid will give permission for Matthew and Tania to attend. Tom will be the first human to address the Senate in its entire history. You have my permission to attend, but other helpers have work to do. They don't usually attend."

"How can this be the first time a human has addressed the Senate?"

"It simply isn't done. Only cats occupy seats in the Senate and only cats address the Senate."

"But there are so many people living in Prideland. They ought to be able to speak on their own behalf."

"Only cats may speak. Cats speak on behalf of the humans when such an occasion arises, but humans do not speak."

"Not even in their own interests?" she asked.

"Not even in their own interests. Humans aren't even allowed on the lower floor of the Senate chamber. On the rare occasion that some human attends the proceedings, they stay in the upper gallery as you will. Now stop arguing and let's go. You'll walk down to the Senate building with me. I'll point out the entrance you'll use to get into the building."

"What's wrong with the front door?"

Renfroe shook his head. "Only cats use the front entrance. People use the side entrance. Once you get into the building, follow the signs to the upper gallery. You can watch the proceedings from there."

After breakfast, Renfroe took Dina to the southern part of the city and showed her the Senate building. They circled around the back where he pointed out a shabby little door in the side wall. Then she went on alone to Elyse's house.

To her relief, Elyse wasn't home. "She's gone down to the Senate already," Tom told her. "I'm supposed to go down there in an hour or two. They're going to send someone to get me when they're ready for me. I guess they want to discuss the situation before I get there."

"Have you thought about what you're going to say?" Dina asked.

"I haven't given it a second thought. I'll figure that out when they ask their questions."

"This could be the break we've been looking for. Our whole mission could turn on this."

He waved that away. "I'm only doing this because Elyse asked me to."

The hair stood up on the back of Dina's neck. "Did she ask you or did she tell you to do it?"

Tom stared out the window. "She said they called me and that she was going. I'm doing this as a favor to her. I don't care about their Senate."

Dina's heart sank. "Please, Tom. Please try to be respectful to the Senate."

"Why should I be respectful to a bunch of cats? We came here to talk to people and we haven't spoken to a single one since we got here. Addressing the Senate won't change that. It won't get us one step closer to achieving our objective."

"We may not like it, but the Senate is their recognized form of government. These are the leaders we've been looking for. We have to make our case to them."

He set his jaw and glared out at the garden. "I'm not making my case to a bunch of cats. I have a mission to fulfill and that mission is negotiating with the human population. I'm not going to let these cats get in the way of that."

"These cats have the power of life and death over us—and not just over us, but over all the other people on this planet."

"You're wrong there. There are a lot more people on this planet than cats and the cats are benign."

"Benign! You should go around and take a look at Matthew—that is, if Elyse lets you. He'll be dead in a few days if Fallon has his way. He toys with Matthew like a mouse. He bites him and tears at him with his claws. He doesn't care if he kills Matthew and I've seen more of the same thing from other cats."

"You're wrong," Tom replied. "The cats are harmless. They might make a mistake now and then, especially the younger ones. Elyse told me all about it. Sometimes when a cub doesn't understand its own strength, it will go after humans and hurt them, but they don't do it deliberately. They don't do it just to be cruel. I'm sure of that."

"How can you be so sure—because Elyse told you so?"

"Leave her out of this," Tom told her. "Elyse has been very good to me. I won't say anything against her. It's because of her that I'm addressing the Senate at all. If she hadn't asked me to, I wouldn't stoop so low."

"Please, Tom, please reconsider. You have to show the Senate that you respect their authority. Please try to be at least a little bit humble. Show them you understand your position as a human in the Pride."

Tom smiled. "You're starting to sound just like them."

Dina lowered her eyes. "I'm sorry. You're right, but you can't accomplish our mission by alienating the Pride. They hold all the power in this society."

"I won't humble myself to them. We don't need to do it to accomplish our mission. I'll stand up to them and put them in their place. We can incorporate the humans and leave the cats in the dust."

"The human population of this planet will never consent to that."

"You don't think so? Whether they will or they won't, all I have to do is threaten that they will and the cats will cave to my demands. They're petrified of a human uprising."

"They have nothing to fear from any humans. The people on this planet wouldn't give an uprising a second thought. Most of them are happy with the understanding they have with the Pride and the ones that are happy with it keep the ones that aren't in line."

Tom shook his head. "We can't bow to the Senate. That's the worst thing we could do. We have to stand up to them. It's our only option."

A footstep rang out on the path and one of Elyse's helpers came to take Tom to the Senate hearing. He kissed Dina's hand and strode away.

She hurried back to the Senate building and entered the building through the side door. Sure enough, signs showed her the way to the upper gallery. She approached the front railing and looked down.

A central stage at the front of the Senate building looked out over an amphitheater. Cats of every size, shape, and color crowded the seats and the stage. They sat and reclined on every surface, groomed themselves on the seats, and strutted up and down the aisles.

Renfroe, Lord Helion, Elyse, and four other cats sat in a row across the stage. They ignored clusters of cats from burly lions down to tiny kittens all around them. A pack of older kittens wrestled and tumbled around the lip of the stage in front of the senators.

After a while, Lord Helion raised his massive head and let out a deafening roar that rattled the windowpanes. Silence descended over the room. The kittens ceased their play and padded down to the seats.

Dina took a seat, too, and Tom entered through a door next to the stage. The Senators stared down at him. Renfroe examined Tom with interest, but Lord Helion barely looked at him at all. Elyse smiled at him and twitched her whiskers.

An ordinary tabby cat addressed Tom first. "You belong to the landing party from the Coalition of Inhabited Planets, do you not?"

Tom's voice rang out over a subtle murmur from the crowd. "That's correct."

"Could you tell us more about this Coalition's intentions toward our people?" the tabby asked.

"They intend to incorporate this planet into the Coalition," Tom replied. "Everyone already knows that."

The senators stiffened at Tom's reply and Dina cringed. So much for showing the Senate respect. "How do you plan to do that?"

"By offering our proposal to the people on this planet," Tom replied. "How else?"

Renfroe and Lord Helion glanced at each other. Elyse sniffed and looked away. Another male lion sitting apart from the rest of the Senate spoke up. "Have you discussed your proposal with the people on this planet?"

"No," Tom replied. "We were in the middle of stating our case to some village people when they sent us to the city. I haven't had the opportunity to discuss it with anyone since."

"The Senate speaks for the Pride and the Pride speaks for the population of this planet, cat and human alike," the tabby told him. "If you want to propose that we incorporate with your Coalition, you should propose it to us."

Tom drew himself up to his full height. "I didn't come here to negotiate with cats."

Lord Helion joined the conversation and every cat hung on his words. "Your experience with the subsidiaries should give you some insight into their feelings on the subject. The people of this planet don't make a move without the approval of the Pride. They won't even talk to you. That's why they sent you to the city."

"We'll see about that," Tom returned.

"Do you have some reason why you refuse to negotiate with cats?" the tabby asked. "We hold the authority to decide political matters in Prideland."

"I came here to negotiate with humans," Tom replied, "not with cats."

"But you come from a Coalition of Inhabited Planets," the tabby pointed out.

"Yes," Tom replied. "Inhabited by humans."

"This planet *is* inhabited by humans," the tabby told him.

"And they are the ones we will incorporate," Tom replied.

"How do you plan to incorporate the humans without incorporating the cats?" Lord Helion rumbled. "You would have to demolish our entire social structure."

Tom's voice echoed through the chamber. "If we have to, we will."

Renfroe and Lord Helion exchanged another glance. "I think we've heard enough," Lord Helion growled. He nodded to a cat near the side door who escorted Tom out of the building.

Dina snuck out of the Senate building and started toward Renfroe's house. That couldn't have gone worse.

She got within a block of the house when she stopped. Doubts nagged her mind and she threw caution to the wind. She had to talk to Tom again. He might not listen to her, but she had to try one more time even if it didn't work.

Besides, she had to get close to him. She needed some human contact to counteract Renfroe's influence. The more she thought about it, the faster she walked.

When she got to Elyse's house, she crept through the hole in the hedge. She had to see Tom alone. She found the garden deserted and she tiptoed up the path to the doorway.

None of Elyse's other helpers moved around inside. Dina didn't dare to enter the house uninvited, so she skirted around to the left. She peeked through a window and spotted two female helpers cooking in the kitchen.

She ducked below the windowsill and slunk farther around the building. Another window gave her a view into an empty hall. The third window gave her a view of the sitting room where Renfroe and Dina met Tom and Elyse.

Tom sprawled on a divan completely naked. He clenched his jaw and glared at Elyse who stood on the divan between his spread thighs. She arched her fluffy white back to throw up her fur in a halo of downy puffs. She purred and rubbed her head through Tom's wiry pubic hair.

His penis lay languid and asleep against his thigh. Elyse rubbed her head and then her furry body against his thighs, his scrotum, and his penis. She purred so loudly Dina could hear Elyse purring through the glass.

Elyse massaged her cheek and chin into Tom's thighs and then rubbed her neck and chest against him. She worked up into the hollow between his legs.

She slithered her whole body along his genitals all the way to her tail. She licked her rough tongue along the underside ridge of his penis.

His shaft swelled and flexed. He closed his eyes and his head fell back against the couch. She licked his shaft until it stood to attention.

She brought him to full rigidity and then walked up to his rib cage and back down to his thighs. She massaged his abdomen and hips with her paws. Tom glared at her in a fever of passion.

She stepped off of him onto the divan. She turned her rear end to him, flicked her tail, and arched her back. Her purring changed to excited peeps and chirps. She strutted in circles in front of him with her tail whisking back and forth and her hind end pointing up at him.

Tom gritted his teeth and snarled at her. He shoved Elyse around so her hindquarters faced him. She stopped circling and stood still. Only her magnificent plume of tail swished back and forth. Her chirps escalated to a faint yowl.

Dina hardly dared to blink her eyes. She almost vomited there under the window. Tom—her own Tom—climbed up onto his knees on the divan and thrust his rigid spike into the hole under Elyse's tail.

How he got it in there, Dina couldn't imagine. Maybe Elyse had so many human helpers she was used to their anatomy. Dina couldn't think about it without this sick feeling welling up in the pit of her stomach.

Somehow, he managed to get it in. He grabbed two fistfuls of her glorious white fur, one on either side of her body. He pumped his rigid cock in and out of Elyse as steadily and precisely as he ever pumped it in and out of Dina.

He bared his teeth as he wound up to his climax. Elyse squealed at him over her shoulder. Dina didn't wait around to see anymore. She bolted out to the garden with that last image forever scorched into her brain. She staggered into the sanctuary of the hedge and wretched into the bushes.

Chapter 27

Dina burst through the door and slammed it behind her before she noticed Renfroe sitting across the foyer. "What's all the noise about?"

She plastered her spine against the door and glanced around with wild eyes. "I don't want to talk about it. I just want to go to my room and sit down."

"Come and talk to me. I want to discuss the Senate hearing with you." Renfroe strolled out to his favorite spot by the fountain. "Tom didn't make a very good impression on the Senators."

Dina snorted. "That's putting it mildly."

"Why did he behave so rudely to them? Doesn't he understand this was his only chance to persuade them?"

Dina shrugged. She still couldn't relax after what she just saw at Elyse's house. "I shouldn't have tried to convince him to submit to the Senate's authority. That was the worst thing I could have done. It only made him more determined to throw the Senate's authority back in their faces. He was determined before, but my trying to convince him only made it worse."

"He must see the need to respect the Pride's authority. Any sensible person would see that."

Dina shook her head, but that didn't clear her thoughts. "He only agreed to address the Senate because Elyse asked him to—or told him to. I'm not sure which, but if she hadn't asked, he wouldn't have gone at all. He won't negotiate with cats."

"That's what he said. It was a very foolish thing to say."

Dina stared at the evening sunlight shining on the leaves and listened to the tree lizards croak in the trees, but the world didn't make sense anymore. Nothing she knew a few minutes ago could possibly be true. Nothing could ever be the same.

"Maybe if you tried again, you could convince him," Renfroe went on.

Dina didn't hear him. Her mind drifted a thousand miles away to Tom, her Tom, the Tom she knew on board the *Savannah*, the Tom she was going to marry just as soon as they got back from this mission. Now she didn't know him at all.

Renfroe's voice shattered her vision. "Dina, I'm talking to you."

Her head shot around. "Huh? I'm sorry. What did you say?"

"I said," he repeated, "that you might convince him if you tried again. You could go to Elyse's house and talk to him again. Maybe he'll listen to you, now that the Senate hearing is over."

Dina shuddered. "I won't go back to Elyse's house."

Renfroe blinked. "Why not? Don't you want to see Tom again? I thought he was your mate."

"Maybe he is and maybe he isn't. Either way, I won't try to convince him again."

Renfroe stretched his head toward her and took a deep breath. "Are you angry over his behavior at the Senate hearing?"

Dina hesitated, but she had no one else to talk to. It was Renfroe or no one. "Do very many people have sex with the cats?"

He stared at her for a moment. Then he burst out laughing.

His laughter turned her confusion to rage. "What's so funny?"

He finished chuckling. "Is that what's bothering you? Did you just discover that, just now? I thought you were more perceptive."

"I saw it at Helion House and I was shocked, but that was nothing compared to...." She stopped and shuddered again. She wanted to throw up, but she didn't think she could.

He waited for her to say something and then he laughed again. "There's only one explanation. You just discovered what's going on between Tom and Elyse. Is that it?"

Her cheeks and ears burned. She turned her head away and nodded.

He laughed deep in his chest. "What's so strange about that? Everybody does it."

"Everybody?" she asked. "We aren't doing it."

He shrugged. "So what happened? You saw them together."

Dina nodded down at her shoes. "They were.... doing it."

"He is her helper, after all."

"What's that got to do with it?"

"He's her helper. He's helping her." He laughed again. "Is he ever helping her!"

"What are you talking about? How can being her helper mean poking her in the rear with his...." She broke off again.

Renfroe roared with laughter. "That's what being a helper means. Don't you understand? He's helping her. She's helping him. That's what it means."

Dina shook her head in confusion. "Helping means.... having sex with her? Is that what you're saying?"

He narrowed his eyes at her. "Dina, you're an intelligent woman. The cats and humans get a lot of mutual benefit from each other. This is just one more dimension to their understanding."

She could barely form words to answer him. "Are you saying.... that the understanding you have...... is sexual? Is that the understanding I'm supposed to come to with you? Is that where this is all leading?"

"Of course not. You and I don't have a sexual relationship. You can come to an understanding with the Pride even if we never do. Lots of people never have sex with cats. Most of the subsidiaries never do, but the helpers do. That's what being a helper means."

"So......do you have sex with Belinda? She's your helper."

"Of course not. I've never had sex with any helper—certainly not with Belinda."

"Then how can being a helper mean.... what shall we call it? Being a helper means being a sex toy. How can being a helper mean being a sex toy if you don't have sex with helpers?"

"You know what I mean. It has a double meaning. At least, it has a double meaning to us—us cats. I'm not so sure it has a double meaning to the helpers, but that's what helping means to us. It means sex."

"So what does that mean for me? I'm your helper, but we aren't doing it. Maybe it means that you intend for our relationship to go in that direction. Is that what it means?"

He turned away and didn't answer.

"Okay, I get it," she told him. "And I suppose, when Fallon and the Helions and Khalid and all the other cats see us together, they assume we are doing it. That's what they mean when they call me your helper. Is that it?"

His whiskers twitched.

Dina got to her feet and started to walk away. "And that's what Tom and Elyse think, too. When we visited Elyse's house, they assumed you and I are doing it the same way they are." Her voice cracked with pent-up emotion. Her Tom, her own Tom, her fiancé—he thought she was having sex with Renfroe. He thought Renfroe was sticking her the same way he was sticking Elyse.

She clamped her eyes closed and ran to the portico. She had to get as far away from Renfroe as she could, but in one leap, he sprang in front of her and blocked her path.

"Wait, Dina. Don't go, not like this. Would it really be so bad if there was something more between us? Don't turn your back on me like this."

She kept her eyes closed and shook her head. She couldn't look at him. If only she could get those terrible images out of her head. "I can't. Don't you see? It isn't natural. Cats and humans—doing *that*! It goes against every natural law I can think of. It's sick. It's disgusting. I would rather drown myself in the river than dirty myself like that."

"Am I so disgusting to you? I thought you cared about me as much as I care about you. What could be so bad about us being together?"

"You never said anything about sex! You said sitting together and leaning against you like an ox in a field. You didn't see a man poking himself into an ox—or maybe you did." She exploded in hysterical laughter. "That would be just like this crazy planet if that was going on, too."

"Come on, Dina," Renfroe chided. "Of course I didn't see a man poking himself into an ox. That would be protected."

"Protected!" she shrieked. "Can't you talk straight for once? It's no more protected for a man to poke himself into an ox than into a cat. What's the difference?"

"Pull yourself together before you break down completely. Of course these people don't stick themselves into oxen or any other animals, but these people live with cats in their houses. They spend their lives intimately involved with cats. Of course it would come to that eventually."

She collapsed onto the stone bench by the fountain. "I saw it happening all over the place at Helion House. Men were doing it with lionesses and male lions were doing it to women, but this was different." She couldn't say the words out loud. That would make it all too real.

He said the words for her. "This was Tom. This was your mate."

She couldn't hold herself together any longer. She covered her face and broke into loud sobs. "We were going to get married as soon as this mission was over and we went back to the ship."

"He's still your mate. A lot of helpers have human mates. Being helpers shouldn't stop you from being mates to each other."

She shook her head. "I couldn't. I couldn't go near him again without seeing him.... with her. I'll never get that image out of my mind."

She rocked back and forth and sobbing into her hands. She couldn't talk anymore. The image of Tom and Elyse together burned in her mind's eye. Nothing would ever comfort her again.

Renfroe didn't move. Did he even know how to love? He was just an animal.

After a few minutes of silence, he flicked his tail and sidled over to the bench. He jumped up on it and sat down next to her, just close enough for his shoulder to touch hers. He wanted to comfort her. He knew enough to want to ease her pain. Having him near her opened the floodgates of her heart and her tears poured out of her.

She leaned against his shoulder and he braced his legs to hold her up. She didn't try to hold back anymore. She turned her face into his coat and let her tears wash her pain away.

Chapter 28

Renfroe stretched out on the ground with Dina by his side. She rested her head on his shoulder and gazed up into the night sky.

"Are you awake?" he purred.

"Yes. I guess it's pretty late."

"We've been out here half the night," he told her.

"We should go in," she suggested.

"Why should we?"

"Buck and Belinda will be awake soon. It will be breakfast time and we'll be starting another day." She sighed. "I don't know what this day will hold, but I'm sure it will be just as horrific as the last ones. The longer I spend on this planet, the more horrible it gets."

"It isn't as bad as that. Prideland has a lot of good things in it, too."

"Like what?"

He snorted through his nose. "Let's not start all that again. You were caught off guard when you saw Tom and Elyse together, but now you know the truth about Prideland. You know now that helpers have sex with their cat benefactors. That's one of the services they perform. You'll get used to that and then it won't disturb you so much."

"I'll never get used to it," she muttered.

"Sure you will. Everyone does. That's the way it is. We've been doing it this way for centuries."

"Centuries? Really? Have people been living with the Pride as long as that?"

"Of course. That's how we know it's as natural as anything else. If it wasn't natural, it wouldn't be going on so long."

"I didn't know you'd been on this planet so long," she remarked. "I thought cats only just crashed here recently."

"Cats have been living on this planet for millennia. Cats have been here much longer than humans."

"If that's true, then who built these cities? You have metal and glass and advanced architecture. Human beings must have built these cities. Cats couldn't have done it."

He cocked his head to one side. "I can't answer that, but we know for certain that cats came to this planet first."

"How do you know?"

"We have histories. Every advanced culture has them."

Dina blushed. "I'm sorry. I should have assumed you had them, too. I didn't think you had written historical records. I haven't seen anyone writing here."

"The histories aren't written down. They're more like long stories and they tell us all about how cats came to this planet."

"How did they come?" she asked.

"They crashed in a starship. The histories don't tell us why the ship carried so many cats of all varieties, but they crashed here."

"Were you sentient then or did that evolve later?"

"I would assume that we were sentient when we landed. How else could we have kept our own history?"

Dina nodded. "That makes sense. Do you know when humans arrived?"

"I don't know the whole history by heart, but you could find out from the Senate archives. At least, *I* could find out and tell you. Helpers don't have access to the archives."

"The subsidiaries must keep genealogies of humans on this planet. They probably know."

"I wouldn't count on that," he told her.

"Why not?" she asked. "They must keep track of their own people. They must have genealogies of who marries whom and which children get born to which parents. It's part of living in a society with other people. I've never heard of any people that didn't keep track of that sort of thing."

"Then you don't know the subsidiaries. They don't keep track of it. The Pride keeps the histories in order, but we keep track of the cats, not the humans."

"But the people are part of your society," Dina argued. "It's your duty to record their social relationships along with your own."

"The Pride is the society. The people—well, they're really just adjuncts."

"Adjuncts?" Dina shot bolt upright. "How can you call them that? They're human beings and they're just as much a part of your society as the cats."

He turned away. "That's the way it is."

Dina settled back against his shoulder with a sigh. What was the point of arguing anymore? "I'd like to question the subsidiaries about it sometime."

He ignored her. "Our history contains several references to cats and humans mating. They've been doing it throughout their history together."

"I guess there's no chance of the two species producing any offspring," she remarked.

"They never have. They're too far apart biologically."

Dina snorted. "That leaves everyone free to play with each other as much as they want."

Renfroe rubbed his chin against the top of her head. Then he ran the side of his cheek down along her forehead. "You're coming much closer to a true understanding with the Pride than you ever did before. That's the way it should be."

She stiffened at his touch, but then she let herself relax into it. Where was the harm in it if it made them both feel good? It was only an innocent touch—nothing more. "As long as you understand I won't be your helper like that, we'll be okay."

"You don't have to do anything you don't want to do. If you don't want to do it, we won't."

"You said we would be companions. Now you're saying you want us to be more than that."

"I told you from the beginning," he replied. "You're like no one I've ever met. I've never felt this way about anyone. You're special. I don't want to lose you, but I want to have you as much to myself as I can. Of course I would love to have you as a helper—*that* kind of helper—but I would be happy just to be your companion. If we never do any more than just lie here together, talking and comforting each other and keeping each other company, I'll be happy."

"I can never be anything more than that to you. I can't stand the idea of crossing the boundaries with you that way. I hope that doesn't offend you. I care for you and I'm grateful for your kindness, but I'll never be anything more to you. Please understand that."

"I understand it perfectly and it doesn't offend me at all. In fact, I'm delighted we can continue the way we are now. You'll never know how happy I am right now, being here with you."

Dina smiled and struggled to swallow a lump in her throat. "I'm happy here with you, too. I wish we could stay like this forever."

"We can. There's nothing stopping us. You're my helper. You'll be living here from now on."

"I mean I wish I didn't know what went on outside this house. I wish that what's going on between us right now was all I ever had to think about. I wish the rest of it would just disappear."

"Make it disappear," he rumbled. "Don't think about anything else. Make this the only reality—you and me."

She shook her head in the darkness.

He nuzzled his chin against her neck. "Let me take it off your mind. Pay attention to me."

Warm, sleepy comfort spread through her body and she sank into him. Her eyes drifted closed and she almost slipped into blissful sleep.

Just as her mind floated away, the image of the lion licking the young woman between the legs flashed before her eyes. Would Renfroe lick her the same way? Would her eyes close and her head fall back in the same languid ecstasy?

She stiffened against the softness washing through her. She couldn't let it happen. She had to keep her eyes open and her guard up, no matter what.

Renfroe sensed the change in her. "What's wrong?"

Dina struggled to collect herself. She couldn't give herself to him, but she couldn't pull away, either. He wasn't her enemy. Her life would be so much easier if only she could give herself to him. Everything would make so much more sense if she did.

She rolled over on her side to face him. "Don't ask me. I can't do it, so don't ask me."

He sniffed at her hair and his whiskers tickled her face. "I thought we understood each other."

"We do." She put her arm around his body over his shoulder. "Just let it be the way it is now. Don't ask me for anything more. Let this be enough."

He put his head back down on the ground and settled into the fold of her arm. "All right."

Chapter 29

Dina twirled her spoon between her fingers and watched tree lizards catching moths in the branches outside the open window. Renfroe munched the calf carcass on the other side of the room. He sneezed a bunch of fur off the end of his nose.

She put her spoon down. She couldn't eat. No matter what she said, he would know she was lying. "I was wondering if you would give me permission to go into the city today—by myself, I mean."

He stared at her. She couldn't look at him. She had to look at something, so she forced herself to stare out the window.

"What do you want to go alone for? If you want to go into the city, I'll take you there myself. Some cats don't look kindly on a helper alone. I can protect you."

"You don't have to do that," Dina stammered. "I have to learn my way around sooner or later and I want to see the market again. Let me go by myself."

He went back to his meal. "Very well, but if you get into trouble, be sure to tell them you belong to me. No one will harm you then."

"I'm sure I'll be just fine."

He dropped the calf's leg and licked his lips. "I'm glad to see you reaching out for your place here. I didn't think you would do it so soon. I thought you would stay indoors more or go out with me. I'm relieved."

Dina did her best to smile at him. "I'm getting used to it. Maybe I'm finally coming to an understanding with the Pride."

"I'm delighted."

"I'll leave as soon as I finish breakfast."

"Oh, no," he replied. "You can't."

Her head shot up. "Why not?"

"I want you to come with me and do something else first—something more important. You can go out after that. The market will still be on this afternoon. You'll have plenty of time. This morning you're coming with me."

"What are we doing?"

"There's something I want you to see—something we do in Prideland to strengthen our understanding with the humans on this planet."

"What's that?"

"We're going hunting in the jungle."

Her eyes widened. "We are?"

"I mean *I'm* going hunting in the jungle with some other cats. You won't be hunting. You're just coming along for the ride."

"What are you hunting?"

"Slags."

Goosebumps erupted on her skin. "You're hunting slags? But the slags are people."

"Slags are not people. They're vermin. They breed out of control and they serve no social function whatever. They infect the subsidiaries and the helpers with their noxious poison. It's our duty to clear them away whenever we find them. We heard about an infestation of them in the jungle near the village where the subsidiaries found you. We're going to reduce the infestation."

"If there's an infestation somewhere," she murmured, "it's the festivals. If you want to perform a public service, why don't you reduce them?"

"You know we couldn't reduce the festivals. The festivals are for helpers. The slags don't have an understanding with the Pride. That's exactly why we have to reduce them when we get the chance."

"I don't want to be there when you hunt them down and kill them. They're people."

"Slags are not people," he repeated. "We wouldn't hunt them if they were."

She looked away. "You would find someone to hunt, whether they had an understanding with the Pride or not."

He sat up and cleaned his face. "We only hunt them because they're a menace to our society. If they weren't slags, we would find a way to include them in the Pride the same way we include the subsidiaries and the helpers. We would bring them to an understanding with the Pride so they could live in harmony with us."

"Are you sure?" she asked.

"Of course. Look what we did with you and your friends. We didn't reduce you. We brought you to this city and placed you with the cats who could best bring you to an understanding with the Pride. Everyone gets the same chance to come to an understanding with the Pride. We make sure of that. No one has to be a slag if they don't want to be."

Dina nodded into her bowl and didn't answer. If going on this hunt gave her permission to get out into the city alone, she would go along.

"A wagon will pick you up after breakfast."

"I thought I was going with you," she countered.

"I'm going with Khalid. You will go in the wagon with the other helpers. That's the way it works."

Dina stiffened. "Khalid? What are you going with him for?"

Renfroe cocked his head to the side. "He's my friend. Besides, he's a powerful hunter. He's the best there is, in fact, except for maybe Hector....and Fallon. They're the best hunters we've got. I would be a fool not to hunt with them."

"They probably think the same thing about you."

He shook his head. "Not like them. I'm too big and heavy. I'm better at bringing down water oxen, but that's all. They have all the speed and agility and they're just as strong as I am. Besides, they're ruthless. They don't think about the animal they're killing, They're consummate predators. I think too much to be much good at hunting."

"I can't wait," she muttered.

"Good." He shook himself and stood up. "You'll leave first, so you and the other helpers get to your places before us. Then you'll be able to see everything. We come after."

"Do you do this sort of thing a lot?"

He nodded. "All the time."

"How often do you do it?"

He calculated in his mind. "At least as often as the festivals. We have to do it on a regular basis to maintain our understanding with the people."

"I'm sure they wouldn't think twice if you stopped hunting people down in the jungle. They might appreciate it."

"As a matter of fact, the village factors find the infestations for us. They demand we go out and reduce the slags. We wouldn't do it if they didn't demand it. You can ask them if you don't believe me. They'll tell you the same thing."

"I won't ask them. I won't talk to them at all."

Belinda approached the portico where Dina and Renfroe were eating breakfast and he took Belinda's presence as silent communication. "The wagon is here, Dina dear. You can go out through the kitchen and I'll see you later."

She found a wagon drawn by two water oxen waiting for her on the street outside the kitchen. So many people packed the wagon bed that no one had room to sit down. Men and women hung over the sides and clung to each other to keep from falling out.

Dina recognized the driver as Harmon Farley, the speaker from the festival. He waved his whip at the helpers in the wagon box. "Make room for Senator Renfroe's helper. Come on, you worthless slags! Make room. We can't stand here all day. Let her sit in the corner. She won't stand like the rest of you."

Someone grumbled from the back of the wagon. "Who are you calling slags? We're all good helpers here."

"You're Senator Renfroe's helper," Farley told Dina. "You sit down there."

The others crowded in around her, jostling and shoving. Farley climbed back into the driver's seat and started the wagon forward.

Before they left the city, Dina wished she could stand up with the other passengers. Legs and knees bumped her head and shoulders and no one could talk to her down on the floor, but she was Senator Renfroe's helper. She had to sit in the place of honor.

The wagon rumbled along the same road the landing team traveled to get to the city. The wagon passed through the same village with the flower bed in the middle of the road. The subsidiaries lined their fences to watch the wagon pass.

Every now and then, someone tumbled out of the wagon onto the road. They had to run to catch up and the others hauled them back on board, but the wagon never stopped moving.

Dina's hips and legs ached from the constant vibration of the boards she was sitting on. She longed to get out and walk, but she didn't dare to move. The road went on into the jungle with no houses, farms, villages, or anything else as far as the eye could see.

"I haven't been on a hunt in a long time," a young girl near Dina remarked and Dina recognized Maddy, Khalid's helper.

"It's the best entertainment in all of Prideland," Farley exclaimed. "I wouldn't miss it."

"Well, some of us have work to do," Maddy shot back. "Not everyone has a benefactor who lets them run all over the place."

"I do have a very kind benefactor," Farley replied. "I haven't missed a hunt in years."

"I hear Khalid and Renfroe are hunting together with Hector," Maddy went on. "That should be a sight."

"I should say so. Anytime Hector or Khalid goes out to hunt, it's a sight worth seeing, even when they go alone. Just imagine how it will be with the three of them together!"

"I can't wait!" Maddy clapped her hands. "I love to see cats in action. They're so beautiful and powerful. It makes you proud to be a part of the Pride, even if only a very small part."

"We all feel the same way. Admiring them and watching them hunt makes you appreciate how fortunate we are. Everyone should be required to watch the hunt at least once a year. It should be part of the children's education, the same as the festivals and classes. It would go a long way to building the understanding we have with the Pride. It would do us all a world of good."

Chapter 30

T he wagon pulled to a stop on a hill overlooking a valley with a stream running through the bottom. The helpers piled out with groans and sighs of relief. Dina stretched her legs and climbed down, too.

"I thought we'd never get here," Maddy exclaimed. "I don't remember the trip taking so long."

Farley laughed at her. "It's the same trip it always was."

"Do the cats hunt in the same place every time?" Dina asked.

Farley raised his eyebrows. "Of course! How could we watch if it wasn't here?"

Dina blushed. "This is my first time. I didn't know they came to the same spot."

Farley frowned at her. "I didn't think there was anybody left in Prideland who hadn't been to the hunt."

"How can they hunt in the same place every time if they're going after slags?" Dina asked. "Don't they have to track them down in the jungle?"

"They flush the slags out of their hiding places and drive them here so we can watch the cats reduce them." Farley raised his eyes to heaven. "Watching the cats reduce slags is the most inspiring thing I can think of. When I feel hopeless and glum, I come out here and watch a hunt. Then I feel better than ever. It lets me know everything is right with the world. I can't think of anything I'd rather do." His head swung around. "Look! Here they come."

Everyone strained to catch a glimpse of movement between the trees. A flash of light caught Dina's eye and Maddy gave a cry of excitement. The tree branches waved and parted.

A gasp went through the helpers as two men and a woman broke out of the trees and ran up the stream into a clearing at the base of the hill.

So these were the dreaded slags. Their hair hung greasy and ropy down their backs. Grime stained their skin and hands and they wore ragged animal skins for clothes. They searched the surrounding forest with wild eyes for some shelter or escape.

Maddy growled through gritted teeth. "Oh, they're bad ones! You can just tell. Thank goodness we have the cats to deal with the likes of them."

"Just look at them!" Farley murmured. "They're animals. If the cats didn't reduce them, we would have to soil ourselves by doing it. The cats do it to protect us from them."

The three people on the valley floor ran into the open and Dina bit her lip. She knew what would happen and she couldn't stop it. The woman glanced over her shoulder, and one man shouted to the others. The trees swayed again and a watery shape slithered into view. It was Renfroe.

He galloped into the clearing with Hector right behind him. The helpers cheered and Maddy clasped her hands over her heart. Harmon Farley closed his eyes and laughed in transported ecstasy.

Khalid's black shadow glided into the clearing. The slags quickened their pace, but it did no good. Khalid slid over the ground faster than thought and Hector charged the slags with his mouth open and his ears flattened against his head.

Renfroe ran at his top speed. Every muscle strained to its limit, but he couldn't keep pace with Hector and Khalid. They left him behind and closed in on their prey.

The three people stumbled over the rough ground to get away from the cats, but the cats gained on them at every stumble. The woman gasped for breath and the men gnashed their teeth. They knew exactly what was about to happen.

Dina knit her fingers until her knuckles ached. Hector and Khalid leapt fallen tree trunks and clumps of grass. The men separated to keep the woman between them, but the man in the rear kept glancing over his shoulder to see how far away the cats were.

He finally tripped and lost his footing. He toppled forward with a cry and landed full length on his chest in the grass. In an instant, Khalid pounced and his jaws closed on the man's neck.

The woman looked back and saw Khalid finishing the man off. She stumbled and Hector sprang at her with his claws flexed.

Like lightning, the second man leapt between his companion and the attacking cat. His arms swung around and Dina saw for the first time that he held a long pole in his hands. The pole wheeled over his head and knocked Hector off. The jaguar landed on his feet a few paces away.

The man shouted something over his shoulder to the woman. She broke and ran on and the man remained behind to cover her retreat.

He shifted his pole to one hand and drew a twisted leather rope from his belt. Two stones hung from each end and he swung them through the air. He planted his feet wide and faced his enemies with his weapons in his hands.

Renfroe caught up with his friends. Hector landed behind Renfroe and spun around to make another spring, but when he saw Renfroe moving in, he held back.

Renfroe never stopped running. He charged the man with all his might taking no heed of the man's weapons. The man brandished his weapons before him and bellowed as Renfroe sailed through the air to attack.

Renfroe bared his teeth and his fangs flashed in the sun. The man waited until the last possible moment and then his pole whistled through the air.

It cracked the side of Renfroe's head so hard the tiger never made a squeak of pain. He landed unconscious on top of the man and Renfroe's teeth and claws did him no harm at all.

"Oh, those slags!" Farley muttered under his breath. "They're pure evil. They should all be reduced for what they've done."

"They can't win!" Maddy exclaimed. "They can't! It wouldn't be right."

Farley put his arm around her shoulders to comfort her. "Don't worry. They won't win. Just wait. Something will happen. It has to!"

Renfroe's weight almost knocked the man to his knees. He staggered and only just flung the tiger off before Hector charged. Renfroe landed at the base of a tree and lay motionless on his side.

Hector trotted a few paces and then broke into a run. The man brought up his weighted thong and twirled it over his head. Saliva flew from his mouth and his breath rasped between his teeth.

Had any of the cats been hunting alone, the man would have won and escaped with his life. He would have rescued his female companion and they would have disappeared together into the jungle.

Three against one left him no chance at victory. Hector bared his teeth and snarled. The weapon sang around the man's head so all the helpers heard it on the hilltop.

Hector came close enough to spring, but at the last instant, he hesitated. He only had to wait until Khalid finished with the first man and joined him.

The panther trotted to Hector's side licking the blood from his chops and surveying the scene. He slipped along the ground to circle to the man's opposite side. The helpers erupted in wild cheers of delight.

"Get him, Hector, get him!" Farley screamed. "Tear him to pieces! Rip him limb from limb and leave him for the maggots!" Maddy laughed and sobbed in pure rapture.

Hector stopped growling and snarling when Khalid arrived. The two cats circled the man and waited for an opening.

The man rotated his pole in one hand and his weighted thong in the other to drive the cats back on either side, but he couldn't keep it up for long. He couldn't face both cats at once.

He turned back and forth to keep both cats in sight. The instant he turned his head, Khalid darted under his arm and hooked his claws into the man's clothes. The weighted thong thunked against Khalid's soft abdomen and didn't harm him.

Khalid reared on his hind legs and closed his jaws on the man's armpit. The man shrieked in pain and his pole fell out of his hand. Then Hector closed in. The man disappeared under the two cats, and that was the last Dina saw of him.

She stared down from the hilltop. She didn't realize until the man went down that she hadn't been breathing until now.

She started breathing again and her shoulders slumped. It was over. She watched the cats kill the man with no more feeling than when she watched cubs killing lizards in the market.

What difference did it make? One prey species was the same as another. Large cats needed something to chase, something that would fight back.

So this was true understanding. This and only this was the understanding she was supposed to come to with the Pride.

She was no different from those people down there. If she was Renfroe's helper, she was just one step away from being his next meal. If she didn't give herself to him, if she didn't please him, this is where she would end up. This was the fate of all slags.

She couldn't stay here. She had to find a way to get off this planet even if it cost her life. She couldn't live her life as a slave, not even as Renfroe pampered sex slave. She had to find a way to escape.

The excitement died for the other helpers, too. They clapped and cheered and called down praise for the cats, but the drama was over. Hector jumped off the fallen man and ran up the hill toward the helpers. All noise stopped and they waited in silence for him to reach them.

"You helpers get your wagon down into the valley," he ordered. "Load up Renfroe and take him back to the city."

"Yes, sir!" Farley replied.

The next moment, Hector wheeled around and charged back down the hill. He ran to catch up with Khalid who was already moving off onto the trail of the fleeing woman.

From the hilltop, Dina stared down at the motionless corpse with his throat torn out and half his face gone. Farley called out, "You heard him! We have to get down there and help Renfroe. He could be hurt."

Farley steered the wagon around the hill and up the stream bed to the clearing. He jumped down and laid his hand on Renfroe's side. "He's breathing. He doesn't look hurt. He probably just took a knock on the head."

"It will take all of us working together to lift him into the wagon," Maddy remarked. "He's probably the heaviest cat in the whole Pride."

"Except for Lord Helion, maybe," Farley agreed. "I'll bring the wagon closer."

Dina glanced over her shoulder at the man stretched out under the trees. "What about him? What should we do about him?"

Farley sneered at the corpse. "Him? Nothing."

"We can't just leave him there. We ought to at least bury him."

"Bury him!" Farley spat. "That's the last thing he deserves. Let him rot there in the sun. That's all a slag is good for. Our job is to take care of Senator Renfroe. You're his helper, aren't you? What do you care about that piece of trash? That slag is the one who injured him."

All eyes came to rest on Renfroe. He breathed gently and not a whisker or paw twitched. If his eyes weren't glazed over, he could have been asleep. The helpers surrounded him, and at a word from Farley, they heaved him into the wagon. An awed hush fell over the group.

"That slag deserved to die a thousand deaths for what he did," Farley growled. "I wish he was still alive so I could kill him all over again."

Maddy sniffed back tears.

Farley scowled at the other helpers. "You fellows will have to walk back. There isn't room in the wagon for you with Renfroe here. You!" He jerked his head at Dina. "You can sit next to him and tend him on the way home."

He climbed into the driver's seat and got the oxen moving. Dina took her place in the wagon bed next to Renfroe. Maddy sat next to her and two other women across from them. None of them looked each other in the eye and the trip back to the city passed in silence.

The sun glistened on the jungle and the tree lizards sparkled in the tree branches. The air throbbed with life. Renfroe breathed at Dina's side and he groaned in his sleep.

Her heart went out to him and she ran her fingers through his fur. Tears ran down her cheeks. He hadn't killed anyone in that hunt. Could she still rest her head on his shoulder? Could he shelter her from himself?

Maddy saw her tears and patted her knee. "Don't worry, dear. He's going to be just fine. That slag didn't hit him all that hard and the bastard is dead now. We're going to get you home and you'll take care of Senator Renfroe. You'll nurse him back to health and then you can go on with your lives together."

Chapter 31

Belinda put a basin of water on the floor next to Renfroe. He raised his head and growled. "Leave me alone. I don't want all this attention. I need rest. My head is killing me."

Belinda turned to the helpers standing around. "You heard him. He wants to be alone. Thank you for bringing him in. He'll be fine now. You all go home."

She herded them out of the room and Dina gazed down at Renfroe. "Do you want me to go, too?"

"You go, too," he growled. "I need to sleep. Go out to the market the way you planned. I'll see you for dinner tonight when I'm feeling better."

Dina's heart soared. He closed his eyes and she slipped out of the house. The wagon trundled away around a corner and the other helpers waved to her. Dina strode after it until it disappeared and quiet descended on the street.

Her nearest teammate was Matthew. He would be the most dangerous to visit, but she had to try.

She found Fallon's house with no trouble, but she paused on the street and surveyed the high garden walls while she mulled over how to get inside.

She still hadn't made up her mind about how she was going to see Matthew when a group of Fallon's helpers came out through a door in the wall. Dina recognized the housemaids and a handful of men came with them. Matthew came last of all.

His injuries had aged and new ones stood out on his face and arms. He wore the same blood-stained clothes and fresh blood discolored them in new places. He swayed and staggered behind the others and he barely raised his eyes from the ground.

The helpers carried sacks and pushed wheelbarrows of garden clippings and household waste to a ditch behind the house. They dumped everything into the ditch and went back into the garden one after another.

The women recognized Dina and smiled at her, but they didn't speak to her. They went about their business until they vanished through the door. Their companions queued for their turn to dump their containers.

Matthew brought up the end of the line. He happened to glance up, and he noticed Dina across the street. He stared at her, but he didn't smile. Did he even recognize her? Then he inclined his head toward the ditch and nodded.

All the other helpers went first. By the time his turn came, he was the only one still outside the wall. He emptied his sack and followed the others inside, but he left the door standing open.

Dina got halfway across the street when Matthew came back out—alone this time. He carried another sack and he walked along the wall same the way he did before.

He looked up and saw her, but he didn't stop. He walked to the ditch and tipped up his sack to empty it, but after he finished, he ducked aside. The ditch cut back under some low-hanging trees and the branches hung over to make a sheltered place against the wall.

He hid behind the wall and Dina darted in after him. "You shouldn't have come. You could get visited for this or worse."

"I had to see you," she whispered. "I'm going to see Tania and Tom after this. I had to find out if you were all right." She scanned him up and down. "*Are* you all right?"

He dropped his eyes. "You shouldn't have come. It's too dangerous."

She touched his arm. "You're hurt. Fallon's been at you again, hasn't he?"

Matthew's set his jaw and shook his hair out of his face. Discolored patches of skin showed along his hairline.

"What made him hate you so much?" Dina asked. "He doesn't seem to go after his other helpers this way. I don't see them limping around torn to pieces."

"That's because all the helpers he does go after wind up dead. He doesn't hate me. He goes after me because he can, because I'm here. I've been watching him. He does it for fun. He's bored and he needs something to do."

"Did his other helpers tell you that?"

"They don't tell me anything. No one in Fallon's house talks to each other about anything but following his orders and serving his family. I can tell by watching him and by the comments he makes when he attacks me. He doesn't hate me or any other person. We're toys to him. That's all."

"You can't stay here," she began. "You'll be dead in a few days if you stay here. We have to escape. If we all break out together, we can get back to the pod and leave. We can get off this planet and never come back. We can tell the Coalition what's going on down here and no one else ever has to come here again."

Matthew gave her a sad smile. "I can't leave. I can't risk Fallon catching me. If he did, he would kill me for certain. He watches me to see if I'll do it. He thinks he can drive me to desperation and force me to try it."

"He'll kill you either way. You just said yourself the helpers he goes after wind up dead. You'll be next."

He shook his head. "I have to wait it out until he loses interest in me. Once he sees I'm not going to escape or fight back, he'll find another toy to play with. He'll get bored with me and leave me alone."

"Don't you want to get off this planet? I'm going to see Tania after this. You have the rest of your lives together back on the *Savannah*. Think of that."

"I think about it all the time, but I have to focus on the present. I have to stay calm and focused until he stops toying with me."

Dina's heart sank. "When he stops toying with you, he'll get rid of you."

"I'm only one person, just like Marcus. Tom didn't abort the mission when Hector killed Marcus and we shouldn't abandon it now because I'm hurt."

"Are you ready to die for this mission?"

He did his best to draw himself up against the pain. "I can't give in to fear and despair. If I lose my focus, I'm lost."

"This isn't the *Savannah*, Matthew. Staying focused and waiting it out won't work here."

Matthew started to turn away. "Your plan to escape will never succeed. You said you were going to see Tom. He'll never agree to leave this planet."

"If I can convince him this mission is hopeless, he might back out."

"You know he won't do that, Accomplishing the mission is everything to him. He won't turn his back on it."

"This mission is a failure. We aren't going to make any progress with these people. They're too stuck on their cats. Once Tom realizes that, he'll abort the mission and we can get out."

"None of us can leave against his orders. We're stuck here until he decides to leave."

She hurried after him. "You don't have time to wait for Tom to decide to leave. You have to get out now. Forget leaving as a group. If Tom wants to stay behind, let him. The rest of us can go and report to Captain Doyle."

He cocked his head to study her. "Would you really leave Tom behind? I'm surprised to hear you say that."

"I don't want to leave him. I don't know how I could go back to my life on board ship without him, but I don't want to live the rest of my life waiting for him to come to his senses. He doesn't understand how dangerous these cats are. He's living a pampered life with his benefactor."

Matthew lowered his eyes. "I heard about it."

Dina's cheeks burned remembering.

"I heard about you, too, Dina," Matthew murmured.

Dina's blood ran cold. "You heard...what?"

"You don't have to deny it. I know your benefactor gives you special treatment. It must be nice to have a benefactor who's agreeable to that sort of arrangement."

"But I never...." Dina stammered. "I don't.... I would never.... You can't think I would do something like that."

"Tom's doing it. Why shouldn't you do it, too? Maybe even Tania's doing it. I don't know."

Dina pursed her lips and took a step toward him. "Listen to me, Matthew. I'm not doing anything with Renfroe. He's been very kind to me, but he's a cat and I'm a human being just like everyone else on this planet. Every one of us is in the same danger."

"Do you have a plan for how to escape?"

She shuffled her feet. "Not exactly."

"That's what I thought." He headed for the corner.

She took one last step. "Don't go, Matthew. Don't give up just yet."

"Do you really want to explain to Dr. Galvin about Tom and Elyse....and about you and Renfroe?"

She opened her mouth and closed it again without saying anything. She could never explain Tom and Elyse to anyone, especially not Dr. Galvin.

"We couldn't escape even if you did have a plan. We have to wait for Tom's order. The captain and Dr. Galvin will only accept our story if we all go back together and tell them the same thing. If one or two of us go back without Tom, we'll be treated as hostile. That's Armada protocol. You know that. We'd be thrown in the brig and interrogated to find out what went wrong and who betrayed the mission to leave our commanding officer behind. I don't want to face Dr. Galvin any more than you do." He shuddered. "I can't stand her questioning and analyzing me like some kind of patient and she would never believe us about what's going on down here. I wouldn't believe it if I hadn't seen it myself."

"We'll make them understand."

"I respect you as my teammate and a fellow officer, Dina. I trust you with my life when it comes to combat, but you aren't qualified to take over command from Tom. You can't make decisions for the team against his orders. I'm sorry to have to tell you this, but if someone's going to take over from Tom, it should be me and I would make the same decision to stay and complete this mission. I wouldn't change my mind just because one person was in danger."

"How would you complete our mission?" she asked. "These people won't listen to us and the cats control the planet."

He didn't listen. He limped to the corner and called back over his shoulder. "I better go. I can't risk anyone finding out I'm gone."

Dina watched him walk away feeling worse than if she'd never seen him at all. He dragged one leg and he didn't put his full weight on the other. He could barely walk.

As soon as he passed out of sight, she left the hiding place. She couldn't stay here and risk one of Fallon's helpers finding her.

She paused at the corner to glance right and left, but the street was empty. The door latch clicked behind Matthew. He was gone. She had no more reason to stay here.

She stepped into the street and hurried away toward the city center. She had to find Tania. If anyone could convince Matthew to escape, Tania could.

Chapter 32

Dina gazed up the hill toward Khalid's house. Khalid was up there somewhere. She couldn't see him, but she sensed his presence.

He slunk through the tree branches up there. He could drop on her at any moment, but she had to risk it. She couldn't leave without seeing Tania.

She sighed and started forward. She hadn't gone more than two steps when she met Tania and Maddy coming back from the market together.

"Tania!" Dina exclaimed. "I was just coming to find you."

Tania glanced at Maddy. "You didn't have to do that."

"I wanted to. How are you? Are you okay?"

Tania's eyes darted back and forth and her head jerked to look over her shoulder again and again in a nervous twitch. "I'm just fine, Dina. You can see that for yourself. I have plenty to eat and a roof over my head and nice people looking after me."

"I can see you're all right physically," Dina replied, "but you don't look happy."

Tania's voice shook when she spoke. "I'm just fine. Khalid is a good benefactor. He's not like some of the others who let their helpers go hungry and make them sleep out in the cold. All his helpers have nice quarters and the cooks make us good food and he keeps the house warm for us, even though he's hardly ever there himself." She glanced at Maddy again.

Maddy smiled. The sunshine glowed on her forehead and her golden hair. She definitely looked happy and not nervous at all. "Khalid is the best benefactor a helper could ask for. He's generous and caring. He keeps a lot more helpers than he needs just so he can give them a nice place to live where they're taken care of. That's the kind of benefactor he is."

Tania stared down at the ground and didn't add anything to this.

"Have you been Khalid's helper for long?" Dina asked.

Maddy laughed and the sound startled Dina. Laughter didn't sound right with Khalid lurking around. "I've only been in this city for about a year. I was too young to be a helper before that. I'm only seventeen."

Dina's eyes widened. "Really? I thought you were much older."

Maddy tossed her head and beamed in triumph. "I look older than I am, but I wanted to come to the city to be a helper even when I was a little girl. My mother told me to behave or they wouldn't send me." She laughed again.

Dina's stared at her in shock. "Your parents sent you to be a helper?"

"Sure, they did. Everyone wants to be a helper, especially the young women. They get the best benefactors and the best treatment. Everyone I know back in my home village wanted to be a helper. I was lucky. I had the looks and I made sure I did everything the factors and my parents wanted me to. I made sure I got sent and here I am."

"You came from a village? Which one?"

Maddy pointed to the west. "It's the same village we passed through yesterday on our way to the hunt."

"That's the same village we came from," Dina remarked.

"I was born and raised there and now I'm a helper to Khalid. Who would have believed it?"

"Are you happy with Khalid?" Dina asked. "Are you afraid of him?"

"Why would I be afraid of Khalid?"

"After seeing him kill.... I mean, after seeing him reduce those slags yesterday, I wouldn't want to do something wrong around him. Renfroe says he's the deadliest cat in the whole Pride. Even Renfroe is afraid of him."

Maddy threw back her head and laughed even louder. "That's wonderful! I knew Khalid was a powerful cat, but I didn't know he was that powerful. Don't you see what this means? He's the most powerful cat in the whole Pride. It means he could be in the Senate himself—not that he wants to. He likes to keep to himself."

"I'm surprised you aren't afraid of him, too."

"Khalid thinks I'm special. We have a special relationship. I'm his special helper."

"Oh," Dina muttered. "I see."

"I don't have any reason to be afraid of him. I get special treatment and all the other helpers have to do what I say. I get the best food and I have Khalid all to myself when he comes into the house after he's been out hunting. I'm probably the most important helper in the whole house."

Tania listened in silence and kept her eyes fixed on the ground. "I understand," Dina replied. "That's a pretty good arrangement. I'm happy for you."

"You bet it's a good arrangement. I wouldn't trade places with any other helper. I'm proud to be Khalid's helper and I'd do anything to stay where I am."

Dina nodded. "Good for you. Would you mind if I have a word with Tania? I know helpers aren't supposed to, but we only just got here. You don't mind, do you?"

"I don't mind. I know you two came together and you'll probably come to an understanding with the Pride a lot faster if you do talk." She turned to Tania. "I'll see you back at the house....and don't worry. I won't tell Khalid or anyone else that you talked."

"Thank you, Maddy," Dina exclaimed.

Maddy tossed her head again and strode off up the hill toward Khalid's house. Dina turned back to Tania and the two women stared at each other for a long moment. "You're afraid of Khalid, aren't you?"

Tania's head gave a violent jerk. Her whole body shook and she wrung her hands. Her teeth started chattering and her eyes darted downhill toward the market. "I'm in big trouble here, Dina. I can't take much more of this."

Dina squeezed her arm. "It's okay. You're going to be okay. We're going to find a way to get back to the *Savannah* and everything will be okay."

Tania stared at her with wild eyes. "This mission is a failure. You're the only one with the sense to see that."

"Take it easy," Dina murmured. "You're hysterical. I've been thinking about escaping, but I don't have a plan yet. I have to talk to Tom and he still wants to convince these people to join the Coalition."

Tania glared up at the Khalid's house, but she didn't see any of the people passing by. "These people will never join the Coalition. Khalid told me so. He said the same thing those village subsidiaries told us. We were lucky not to get reduced on the spot the moment we landed. Some of these subsidiaries wait their whole lives to come to the city to work as helpers. It's the greatest thing they can achieve in their lives."

"I've heard the same thing. I just have to convince Tom the mission is hopeless."

Tania cocked an eyebrow at her. "So Tom didn't order you to find a way to escape?"

"I haven't talked to him yet. I'll go see him after I talk to you."

"If he didn't order you to escape, you have to stay where you are until he does give the order. You can't go against him. I'm surprised you would even suggest it." Dina started to reply, but Tania interrupted her. "Khalid is a devil! Have you seen him? He's a black panther."

"I've seen him."

"I can't stand the sight of him!" Tania hissed. "I can't stand it if he even looks at me. I hide from him whenever he comes into the house, and if I can't get away, I try to make myself invisible."

"I didn't realize it was that bad."

"Khalid has a dangerous reputation among his helpers. Maddy says he kills people whenever the mood strikes him. He kills anyone who displeases him. I can barely sleep at night. He might sneak into my room and eat me."

"He isn't going to eat you, Tania," Dina chided. "These cats don't eat people."

Tania gaped at her. "Who told you that? Who told you they don't eat people?"

"No one told me, but it only makes sense. These are sentient creatures, Tania. They're intelligent and reasonable."

"They're cats, Dina!" Tania shot back. "They hunt and eat people all the time. Why do you think they keep all these people around? What do you think those jaguars did to Marcus Harte?"

"They didn't eat him. They attacked him and killed him, but they didn't eat him."

"Yes, they did. Khalid said so. He didn't say how he knew, but if you ask me, Hector and Victor invited him to share the spoils. Of course they eat people. Wake up, Dina!"

"Come on, Tania. You're blowing this way out of proportion. An intelligent, level-headed individual like Renfroe wouldn't resort to eating human beings. It's not in his nature."

Tania shook her head. "You're going to wake up one morning to a very rude understanding of what these cats are capable of. I'm not taking any chances. I'm going to make myself more valuable to Khalid so he won't kill me."

"What are you going to do?"

"Maddy told me to seduce him."

Dina gasped. "What!?"

"I'm going to offer myself to him as a helper—*that* kind of helper. You know what I mean."

Dina's chin collapsed to her chest and she groaned in despair. "Tania, you can't do this. Just imagine how you'll feel selling yourself like that—to a cat!"

"I'm doing it! Don't ask me how I'll do it because I'm as scared to do it as I am *not* to do it, but it's the only way to gain any advantage."

"What about Matthew?" Dina asked. "He's having a hard time. His benefactor isn't as nice as.... well, he's just not nice. Matthew doesn't look good at all. What will he say if you give yourself to Khalid?"

"If that's the case, then I really have to do it. Matthew would be shocked if he knew, but maybe I can gain some favors for him."

"You don't have to do this," Dina told her. "We're going to escape. I just have to figure out how."

Tania's features hardened. "You can't escape. None of us can. The only way to survive is to come to an understanding with the Pride. That's the only way to get some advantage and that's what I'm going to do. You should do the same thing, Dina."

"Tania, please don't do this," Dina moaned. "You don't know what you're getting into. Trust me. I know what I'm talking about."

Tania wouldn't listen. "I haven't been able to do it yet, but I'm going to do it. I've made up my mind."

"Don't lose heart. You've taught me more about combat than anyone. There must be a way out of this."

"All my combat experience has been in open confrontations. This is different. If Tom didn't order you to escape, then the only way to deal with this is to go along with the rest of Prideland and come to an understanding with the cats as soon as possible."

"I will never come to an understanding with the Pride," Dina snapped. "I'm getting out of here."

Tania shook her head. "I could never leave without Tom's order. I could never face my parents or Captain Doyle or Dr. Galvin if I disobeyed orders."

"Do you really want to stay here? Do you want to die here like Marcus did?"

Tania's locked her eyes on Dina. "I didn't want to tell you this, but after Maddy took me to Khalid's house, three men took me into a back room and beat me black and blue. They said Khalid owned me now and if I tried to run away, they would do the same again or worse."

Dina groaned. "Oh, Tania!"

"I thought like you at first. I thought I could lie low and find a way to escape, but after a while, I realized how hopeless it really was. Khalid has loyal helpers swarming all over his house and I'm alone and unarmed. Khalid's always lurking around somewhere. He never confronts you openly. You never know when he's watching you or when he's miles away."

"Don't give in just yet. We'll get you out of here."

Tania shook her head. "We could never escape. We would be unarmed and our training won't help us against these cats. They're too strong and fast and they've got eyes everywhere. I would never want to face Khalid in a fight. Besides, no one would believe us even if we did get back to the ship."

"We could corroborate each other's stories. If more than one of us tells the same story, they would have to believe us."

"We won't corroborate each other's stories because we would never escape alive. We would have to fight our way out and we could never win. You would have to fight Renfroe. Are you prepared for that?"

Dina lowered her eyes.

"I'm not, either. Maddy helps Khalid—I mean, she helps him in *that* way. She says you imagine it to be a lot worse than it is. She says once you get used to it, it's a piece of cake. She does a fraction of the work the rest of us do and she doesn't have to run and hide when Khalid walks in the door. I'm going to do the same thing. Then maybe I won't have to run and hide, either, and I won't have to keep looking over my shoulder all the time, waiting for him to pounce."

"Please don't do this." Even as she said the words, Dina's last hope died away. It was already too late.

Tania didn't bother to argue anymore. "Walk me home, Dina. I can't be late."

Tania put her arm around Dina's shoulder as if she was the one comforting Dina instead of the other way around.

The sun sank behind the buildings and people scurried in all directions to get indoors before the curfew bell. Dina would be late after walking Tania home. Hopefully, Renfroe wouldn't be too mad. She didn't have time now to go see Tom.

Chapter 33

K halid's villa perched at top of the hill overlooking the city. Before they reached it, Tania broke away from Dina and vanished through a side door. Human voices inside reached Dina's ear and Maddy leaned out of a top-floor window. She spoke over her shoulder to someone inside the house.

Dina spotted a black shadow prowling along the roof parapet. Khalid was home.

She bolted away at a fast walk, but the sun was already disappearing behind the buildings. She raced through the deserted square just as the curfew bell rang out in the distance.

Dina quickened her stride, but the instant the curfew bell stopped ringing, dozens of cats slithered out of windows and doorways and crevices. Dina had never seen so many cats in one place. Not even the market could compare with this.

They were all house-sized cats from mongrel tabbies to Mexican hairless to blue-point Siamese. They swarmed over walls and roofs, padded silently along the sidewalks, and tiptoed through flowerbeds.

Their silken bodies clustered thicker at the intersections. A hushed murmur ran through the river of bodies. She tried to keep her pace steady, but fear gripped her as more and more cats poured out of every corner.

She hurried as fast as she dared toward Renfroe's house. At the last corner, she cast a quick glimpse over her shoulder. A fluid wave of legs and tails flowed toward her. Marcus Harte flashed through her mind and she told herself again and again, *Walk. Walk slowly. Do not run.*

In the end, her terror overcame her and she burst into a run. She didn't have to hide her fear. These cats already knew she was running for her life.

At all costs, she had to avoid anything in her path that could trip her up. She had to run and keep on running until she reached Renfroe. At least she had Renfroe to run to. Only he could protect her.

Cats pranced along tree branches at her side, over the pavement at her heels, and over garden walls. None of them ran at top speed. They were toying with her.

She noticed a particular big cat and she recognized Fallon. He trotted at her side even when she ran as fast as she could. Was he waiting until she tripped and fell in panic? Then all of them would pounce in a single mass. She would die in their jaws just like that man in the jungle.

She ran until her chest exploded, but she didn't stumble or fall. She ran into Renfroe's courtyard, forced open the kitchen door, staggered inside, and slammed the door behind her. Belinda scowled at her across the kitchen. "You're late."

Dina caught her breath and brushed her hair out of her face. "I know."

"Renfroe wants you. He's been asking for you."

"I didn't know he was awake."

"How could you know? You've been traipsing around doing who knows what. It's long past curfew. You could get visited for this, you know."

Dina let out a shaky breath. "I almost did."

Belinda's head shot up from her work. "What's that supposed to mean?"

Dina turned away. "Nothing. Renfroe told me he didn't want to see me before dinner and he told me I could go out by myself. I'm sure he won't mind that I wasn't here when he woke up and wanted me before then."

Belinda shook her head and went back to what she was doing. "You better be careful. You're flirting with disaster. Don't say I didn't warn you."

"You've warned me many times," Dina muttered.

She pushed the kitchen door open and went straight to the parlor where she found Renfroe stretched out in his usual place by the fire. "There you are. Where were you?"

"I told you I was going out into the city. I ran into Tania at the market and we got talking. That's why I'm late."

He didn't raise his head. "You should be more careful. There are cats who patrol the city for curfew-breakers."

Dina sat down on the floor near him. "I know. I saw them."

"If they caught you, they would kill you without asking any questions. Nothing could save you."

She nodded and folded her legs under her.

"That's why you should only go out with me. If we were together, you wouldn't have to worry about staying out after curfew. I could protect you. They only go after helpers caught out alone."

"I have to go out alone sometimes. I can't stay cooped up in this house for the rest of my life."

"You don't have to stay cooped up. I just said I would go with you."

"I have to be able to go out on my own. If I don't, I'm no better than a prisoner." She cocked her head. "I'm not a prisoner, am I?"

"Of course not. No helpers are prisoners."

"What about Matthew? Are you telling me he's not a prisoner and that he can leave Fallon's house whenever he wants?"

Renfroe raised his head and his eyes gleamed in the firelight. "Why do you mention him?"

Dina turned her eyes away and stared into the fire. There was no point in lying about it. "I saw him today, too. He hasn't got long to live the way he's going."

He put his head back down. "You shouldn't have gone to see him. You would only make it worse for him."

"No one saw me. I had to know how bad it was."

"I didn't want you to know how bad it was."

"Why not? What could you hope to gain by keeping it from me?"

"I didn't hope to gain anything. I just didn't want you to know how much danger he was in. I wanted you to understand that you weren't in any danger here. You were already scared enough of me. I didn't want to make it worse."

"Then why did you take me to see the hunt?" she asked. "If I was scared of you before, that only made me more scared. If you wanted to set my mind at ease, you should have left me at home."

"You have nothing to fear from me. You should know that, even after seeing the hunt. I didn't kill any of those people. Khalid and Hector did."

"You would have. You would have killed that man if he hadn't knocked you out. You would have helped your friends the same way Khalid helped Hector and you would have crushed his throat the same way he did."

He looked away and blinked into the flames. "Maybe I would have, but your situation is different from Matthew's. You must see that."

"It's different, all right! You want me for a sex playmate—or whatever you want to call it. You want me to cross the boundary with you so we can be physically intimate. Isn't that right? You want me to be a different kind of slave, but still a slave. I couldn't be anything other than a slave in Prideland. The only other choice is to be a slag and I know what you do with slags."

Renfroe closed his eyes. "When are you going to realize that I don't think of you that way? I don't want you for a sex toy or a slave or any of your other dirty words for it. I want you for you. I want to care for you, to elevate you, to set you above the common helpers I'm so tired of."

"That sounds like Maddy's relationship with Khalid. She's his special helper. She doesn't have to work and she doesn't have to fear him the way his other helpers do. She has special privileges and advantages. That's what you have in mind for me, isn't it?"

"Of course not! I know how Khalid treats his helpers. He gives them favors in exchange for their bodies. I won't deny that, but it's strictly business with him. He doesn't care any more for Maddy or whatever you said her name was than he does for anyone else. He'll have a new special helper before very long and Maddy will be back in the scullery with everyone else."

"And you want me to believe it will be different with you?" Dina asked.

"It will be different," he told her. "I've never had a helper before—not that kind of helper. Ask anyone. Buck and Belinda are the only helpers I've ever had and I've never been intimate with either of them. You've seen how it is. We barely speak to each other."

"I'm sure Khalid doesn't speak to Maddy, either."

"Dina," Renfroe exclaimed, "you are the only helper I have ever wanted. If you become my helper, you will be the only helper I will ever have. We will be lifelong companions."

"That's what you say."

"Why would it be any different? Do you really think I would make all this up just to deceive you? What could I possibly hope to gain?"

She shrugged. "I don't know. Maybe a helper."

"I don't need a helper. I can have any helper I want. If I want a slave or a toy, I have all of Prideland to choose from, but I don't want that. I want you. You're one of a kind and there isn't another helper like you. I don't want you for your body and I don't want you to submit to me like a slave. I want you for your mind and your heart and your spirit. Is that so bad?"

"How can it be different for us?"

"Why shouldn't it be? You and I are different from the rest of Prideland. You're a starship officer and I'm the only cat in the Pride who thinks we ought to contact other races on other planets. We're matched in our thinking and our desire for more than Prideland can offer. Why shouldn't we be together? It only makes sense."

She shook her head and stared into the fire. "I really wish I could. My life would be so much easier if I did, but it's impossible."

"Why?"

"Because I'm a woman and you're a cat. We aren't supposed to be together. We're two different species. I should be with a human man and you should be with a female tiger. That's the way nature works."

"We're here together right now, Dina. There is no human man and there is no female tiger. What's so wrong about us being here together right now?"

"Tom is a human man. He's the one I'm supposed to be with."

"He isn't here now. I am. I am the male that is here with you right now. I am the one you should be with."

"Are you telling me there isn't a female tiger in this Pride who could be your mate? Wouldn't you be happier being mated to one of your own kind?"

Renfroe laid his big head on the floor and breathed a loud sigh. "I don't want them. I want you."

"Don't you want offspring? Don't you want to father cubs of your own? You can't do that with me."

"I already have fathered cubs. I've mated with female tigers in this Pride and I've had cubs. I don't need to do that again."

"You have?" she asked. "Where are they?"

"They live closer to their mothers than they do to me. I'm not as young as I once was and the cubs are all grown. They don't need me in their lives anymore unless they come to visit or they have some business with the Senate. I don't need to worry anymore about fathering cubs. All I have to worry about right now is finding a companion to spend my time with."

"You should want the companionship of an equal. You shouldn't be looking for a companion among the helpers."

"First of all," he began. "I'll be the one to decide where I find companionship. If I find it one place and not another, no one can blame me. Companionship is companionship, no matter where I find it. Second of all, no one ever said finding companionship among the helpers was protected. What do you think the Helions are doing with all their hundreds of helpers? Not all of them clean the floors and slaughter their meat for them. They have their special companions and some have had the same companions for years."

Dina glanced up. "I didn't know that."

"And since you bring it up," he went on, "I *am* getting the companionship of an equal. You are my equal in every way that counts. You have the intelligence, the strength of character, and the determination to be my companion. I've never met anyone else who had all that."

"But I'm a helper. That on its own proves I'm not your equal."

"Maybe not in the eyes of the Pride," he admitted, "but to me you are my equal. Let the other cats think you're an ordinary helper. Let them think you're my sex toy and my resident ear-scratcher. What do we care what they think? You and I will know it isn't like that when we get behind closed doors."

"In the eyes of the Pride, I'm a slave. You might not want it to be that way, but it is. You're one individual. You can't change the laws of a whole society, no matter how much you want it to be different."

"If I say it's different, then it is different."

"You can't stop those cats from killing me if I go out of the house by myself," she pointed out. "You couldn't stop Khalid or Fallon from killing me if I wanted to talk to my teammates without their permission. I'm human and that means I have a certain status in this society. I'm a helper. I'll never be anything else and there's nothing you can do to change that."

He raised himself up on his side. Even that caused him pain, but he pushed through it until he brought his head around and laid it in her lap.

Before she thought to stop herself, she let her hand rest on his head, stroked his bristly cheeks, and petted his forehead. It seemed like the natural thing to do.

"Let our attachment to each other be enough, Dina," he breathed. "Let this moment be enough."

"It isn't enough," she whispered.

"It is. You know it is."

They didn't speak anymore. She stroked him and their breath joined together into one steady tide. The fire crackled in the deepening night and they still sat together.

She tried to think about her plan to escape, but she couldn't. He was right. Simply being together and occupying the same space was all she needed in the world. It was enough.

Chapter 34

The morning sun woke Dina up. Her limbs hurt from sleeping on the parlor floor and she was cold. She sat up and looked around. Renfroe was gone and the fire was out.

Belinda usually had an uncanny knack for showing up with food the moment Dina opened her eyes, but this morning, Belinda was nowhere in sight, either. Dina got to her feet and stretched her legs. She walked through the deserted house searching for anyone at all but finding no one.

The eerie silence made her nerves prickle. She hadn't been alone like this, completely unsupervised, for so long. She wasn't quite sure what to do with herself. She wanted to get out into the city to track down Tom, but she didn't dare to leave without checking with Renfroe first.

Then she realized how stupid that was. She was a grown woman with a mind of her own. Renfroe and Belinda and everyone else kept insisting that she wasn't a slave and there was no slavery in Prideland, so she must be free to come and go as she wished. She could leave the house at any time and talk to whomever she wanted.

She still hesitated to just walk out the door. What if someone found out? She could get visited, whatever that meant. Then she shrugged off her doubts, grasped the door handle, and pushed it open. She would never get a better chance to talk to Tom. If she got visited, at least she would find out once and for all what that word meant. She probably wouldn't find out any other way.

She closed the door softly and hurried away before anyone spotted her. She kept to the back streets and avoided the market. The less notice she attracted, the better.

She got to Elyse's house and snuck through the hole in the hedge. Elyse wouldn't mind Dina talking to Tom, but Dina wasn't sure how to approach the house. She couldn't just knock on the front door.

Just then, the double doors opened, and Tom and Elyse came out into the garden together. Tom strolled through the avenues of shrubbery and Elyse tripped over the grass at his heels. She stopped every few steps to shake the dew off her paws. She looked up to speak to him and he murmured back down to her.

Dina walked right up to them and smiled at Tom.

"Good morning, Dina," Elyse exclaimed. "What brings you here so early in the morning?"

Dina waved her hand and looked away toward the hedge. "I just wanted to take a walk in the city."

"Does Renfroe know you're here?" Elyse asked.

"I asked him if I could get out and explore the city so I could learn my way around. I have to find my own way eventually. I found my way here, anyway, so I must be getting my bearings. I thought I'd stop in and see Tom....and you."

"We were just out for a walk ourselves," Elyse remarked. "It's a perfect day."

Dina looked up at the sun. "Prideland has such mild weather. Most planets with jungle vegetation are much hotter and more humid."

Elyse sneezed. "You sound like you know all about it."

"Dina's our xenobiologist," Tom told her. "That's the study of biology on planets other than our home world."

"How interesting!" Elyse exclaimed. "What else have you discovered about this planet that strikes you as unusual?"

"Everything related to the relationship between the human population and the cat population is unusual," Dina replied. "I would be surprised if that was repeated anywhere in this galaxy or any other."

"Do you really think so?" Elyse twittered. "I suppose we get used to it. We think of it as normal."

Dina nodded. "I can understand that. Even in the short time I've been here, I've started to get used to it, too."

One of Elyse's other helpers came out of the house at that moment and headed straight for Elyse. She turned away before the guy had a chance to say anything. "Will you excuse me, Dina dear? One of my helpers is giving birth and I must look after her. I'll leave you to catch up with Tom. I hope I'll see you later."

"Thank you," Dina called after her.

Elyse and the man disappeared into the house.

Tom smiled after her. "She really is a caring soul. She treats all her helpers like one big family. Did you know some of them have been with her all their lives? She keeps their children on as helpers, too, so the families can stay together. Isn't that amazing?"

Dina faced him. "It's amazing because she doesn't have to. It's amazing that she does it at all when most of the cats in this city don't bother. They treat their helpers like the slaves they are. They don't think twice about separating families or even killing them off when they outlive their usefulness."

Tom shook his head. "I can see you haven't yet come to an understanding with the Pride."

Dina froze staring at him. "What did you say?"

"You should try a little harder. The Pride isn't out to destroy its people. It has a place for everyone. All we have to do is understand it and we can find a place in it that benefits us as much as it benefits the cats."

"I can't believe I'm hearing this from you! Just the other day, you said you weren't here to negotiate with cats. What happened?"

Tom shrugged. "I'm not here to negotiate with them. I'm just trying to make my time here as pleasant as it can be. I have Elyse to thank for making it that way and for helping me come to an understanding with the Pride."

Dina snorted. "I'll bet she has."

"I'm sure Renfroe has done everything he can to make your stay here pleasant. You can't blame me for doing the same thing with Elyse."

Dina stiffened and faced him down. "If that's what you mean, then, no, I haven't. Renfroe has been very good to me and if I was going to come to an understanding with the Pride, it would be because Renfroe wants me to. I have an understanding with him, even if I don't have one with the Pride itself."

"There you go. So you know how it is with me. I don't have to explain it to you."

"I don't have an understanding with the Pride and I'm not going to have one. I'm going to get out of here. I'm going to get back to the pod and get off this planet. When Captain Doyle finds out what's going on here, he'll understand why we didn't complete our mission. He can explain it to Chancellor Mathus."

"I'm not leaving until this mission is completed," Tom replied, "and neither are you. I'm in command of this landing party. You can't leave against my orders, and if you try, you'll be disciplined for gross insubordination. You know that."

Dina squared her shoulders at him. She had prepared herself for this. "Our lives are in danger here. We have every reason to abandon the mission. Our mission never called for us to endanger our lives. It's not insubordination to say so. We're being held here under duress. We have to break out and get back to the ship."

"I'll be the judge of how much danger we're in."

"You should see Matthew. Renfroe wanted to hide the danger that Matthew is in so I wouldn't be afraid of him. Maybe Elyse is doing the same thing with you. If you saw him, you would understand the danger. You would agree to leave this planet while we can."

"Elyse isn't hiding anything from me. She's the one who arranged my appointment with the Senate, remember?"

"The Senate turned down your proposal for incorporation. Our mission is dead in the water."

"I never made any proposal for incorporation to the Senate. I never had any intention of incorporating these cats. All I care about is the people and we still have a chance with them."

"We're prisoners here, Tom," Dina insisted, "and that's because these people serve the cats. They're the ones who turned us over to the Pride in the first place and they're the ones who will keep us here."

"You're wrong. These people want to incorporate. They just need to get rid of the cats."

"How can they get rid of them? The cats are stronger and faster and more powerful. Anyone who fights back gets killed."

Tom shook his head. "These cats are pets. They're lazy and harmless. They couldn't keep up this facade of society if they didn't have people cleaning up after them and brushing their fur."

"Maybe you have it too easy with Elyse. I've seen enough to make me realize the danger we're in. You can't put the team in danger any longer."

He waved his hand around at the garden. "Does it look like we're in danger here? I don't know about you, but I've never been so far out of danger in my life. Even my life on the *Savannah* was less dangerous than this."

"You haven't seen Matthew. He's in danger."

"Then he should come to an understanding with the Pride."

"And then there's Tania," Dina went on. "She's in a terrible state. She's petrified of her benefactor and she plans to give herself to him as a helper—*that* kind of helper—just to stay alive."

"That's no more than the rest of us have done. She should do it and get it over with. She'll be happier that way."

Dina's jaw dropped in horrified shock. "How can you say that? How can you expect her to degrade herself that way when all we have to do is get back to the pod and leave?"

"We aren't leaving."

Dina shook her head sensing the last shred of hope slip through her fingers. "Elyse really has got her grip on you."

"Leave Elyse out of this. She's the best thing that's happened to me on this planet. You're jealous of her."

Dina pulled her head down between her shoulders. "I won't say I'm not. I can't stand the idea of you messing around with her."

"I'm just doing my job. I have to come to an understanding with Elyse and the rest of the Pride if we're going to accomplish this mission. You shouldn't be jealous of a cat." He laughed at the idea.

Dina wasn't laughing, though. "I think you're doing a little more than your job."

"You have nothing to complain about. I saw you with Renfroe the other day. You're doing the same thing. I'm the one who should be angry. How could I ever touch you again after that?"

"Tom!" Dina gasped. "I haven't done anything with Renfroe. I would never give myself to anyone but you."

"I wish I could believe that. Everyone belongs to some cat here. It only makes sense that you would give yourself to him."

She pointed at him. "This is what I'm talking about. None of us can think straight anymore. We have to get out of here while we still can. If we stay, we'll lose our will to resist. We'll be no better than these other helpers who think coming to an understanding with the Pride is the best thing for them."

"I won't leave the mission undone and I couldn't walk out on Elyse after everything she's done for me. I owe her that much."

"Elyse is not your friend, Tom," she told him. "She's not interested in protecting you or furthering this mission. You have no reason to be loyal to her."

"She got me that Senate hearing. I owe her loyalty for that alone."

"It wasn't Elyse. It was Renfroe. He's the only cat in the whole Pride that wants contact with the wider interplanetary community. Elyse doesn't want that. She only went along with the Senate hearing to pacify you."

"That's a lie!" he snapped.

"If she wanted to help our mission, why didn't she speak up before the Senate? Why didn't she support Renfroe's suggestion that they accept our embassy and incorporate with the Coalition? She didn't. She sat there in silence. She has never supported incorporation. She wants our mission to fail, but she wants you to think she cares about you so you'll stay here with her. Can't you see that?"

Tom gritted his teeth. "You take that back right now. I won't stand here and listen to you say anything against Elyse."

"Elyse is a cat of the Pride, Tom. She will never be anything else. She holds the power of life and death over you. She could force you to submit to her any time she chooses."

"She would never do that. She cares for me. I can see from what you're saying that she cares for me a lot more than you ever did."

"I know Elyse has been good to you, but not all the cats of the Pride are like Elyse. Some of them don't give a fig for human life and others are downright vicious. Have you forgotten what Hector did to Marcus?"

He looked away. "I haven't forgotten."

Dina started talking faster. She was almost out of options here. "I know you're my commanding officer and I'm just a biologist. I know you've got a lot more command experience than I have, but just listen to what I have to say."

"I'm listening. Say what you have to say."

Dina took a deep breath. This was her last chance to convince him. "We didn't know what was happening on this planet. We knew there were humans here and we knew there were cats, but we didn't know the two species lived together. We didn't know until after we landed. Now we know."

"Is that what this is about? Did you come all the way down here to say, 'I told you so'? You tried to tell us at the briefing there was something strange about the cats and people living so close together. Well, I'll be the first to admit you were right."

"I didn't come here to say, 'I told you so'. I'm only saying we made our plan for incorporating this planet based on incomplete and incorrect information. Now we have the correct information. We need to revise our strategy to account for all the facts."

"I'm not revising our strategy," he repeated. "We have a good chance of incorporating these people and that's what I'm going to do."

"These people will never throw off the cats. They will never break out of their understanding with the Pride. It doesn't matter how many people or how many cats actually live on this planet. We have no chance of overthrowing this social structure the way it is now. No one will step out of line."

"The Coalition won't turn its back on this planet. I'm surprised you let petty fears get you down. Stick it out and we can accomplish our mission."

Dina shook her head. "We only have two choices. We can bring the whole Armada in here with guns blazing. We can raze Prideland to the ground and rebuild it with the human beings in charge, but they'll need all the Armada's firepower to back them up. The only other option is for the four of us to get out of here with our lives and leave Prideland the way we found it."

She might as well have been talking to the wall. He didn't even look at her anymore. "We can't leave. We have to accomplish our mission."

"We have less than two weeks left before the Pod's power packs run down. We won't be able to lift off after that and we won't be able to contact the *Savannah*, either. Whatever we're going to do, we have to do it before then."

"Then we have plenty of time. Even if we're a little bit late, we can always use the autostart to charge the power packs."

"You know as well as I do that the autostart needs a residual trickle of power to charge it up. If we miss the deadline, even the autostart won't work. We should go now. We should at least start to plan now. It could take us that long to break out. Cats patrol the streets after curfew, and if we get caught, we won't get another chance. We'll be lucky if they bring us back alive."

Tom gazed toward the house and didn't answer. Whatever was going on in there mattered a lot more to him than anything she said.

He took a step toward the door. He might as well have been asleep. She touched his arm. "Tom? Did you hear what I said?"

He nodded, but he didn't look at her. She could have been touching the tree branch for all his flesh gave under her hand. He didn't even blink. "We have plenty of time. Elyse will help me convince the human population, but we have to give it time. The first step is to come to an understanding with the Pride—all of us. No one will trust us or give our mission the time of day if we don't."

Dina stared after him as he strolled back to the house. He hadn't heard a word she said.

Chapter 35

Dina returned to Renfroe's house, but he still wasn't there.

Belinda was. She glared at Dina, but she didn't scold and Dina went straight to her room. She had too much to think about. She had to come up with a plan to get back to the pod. She had almost two weeks left to come up with a plan and none of the others would go with her.

Dina sat down on her divan bed and gazed out the window. The afternoon sun streamed through the leaves and tree lizards jumped from tree to tree outside. The garden looked so beautiful that she stood up and took a walk in the garden to clear her head. She strolled past the fountain and admired the flowers. She was really starting to love this garden. She would be sorry to leave it.

She could get used to being Renfroe's lifelong companion. She would never go hungry or be cold and he would protect her from other cats. She just had to follow the rules. Was that really so bad?

Belinda would light the fire in the parlor when night came and bring Dina's dinner on a tray. She would eat with Renfroe and they would talk things over. Then they would fall asleep side by side.

Dina would drape her arm over Renfroe's big chest and snuggle into the fur between his forelegs. His smell sent her into a hypnotic trance and she would fall asleep in the shelter of his protection.

Was it really so different from leaning against the side of an ox in a field or a housecat keeping a person's lap warm? That was a nice understanding to come to with the Pride. If that's what coming to an understanding with the Pride meant, she could be satisfied with it.

In answer to her thoughts, Renfroe slid out from behind a tree and padded toward her. "Did you have a nice day?"

Dina nodded. "What about you?"

He sat down next to the bench and laid his head on her lap. "Not as nice as seeing you again. I enjoy coming home, now that I know you're going to be here. I never used to want to come back home."

"What did you do instead?"

"I went hunting. I hunted deer and oxen along the river or I would get animals from the market and release them in the parks so I could hunt them down. Sometimes I would visit my friends. I rarely spent any time here at the house. It was too quiet."

"I thought you liked the quiet. Tigers are supposed to be solitary animals."

"We are and I am, but I didn't like being behind walls. I wanted to be out in the world. Now all I want to do is come back here and see you."

"After a while, you'll get tired of me and want to get out again."

He rubbed his chin against her leg. "What did you do today?"

"I went out into the city again."

He stiffened, but he didn't raise his head. "You shouldn't have done that. It's dangerous."

"I wasn't in danger walking around the city in the middle of the day."

"I don't like it," he replied. "I wouldn't want anything to happen to you."

"I went to see Tom."

He raised his head this time. "How is he doing?"

"He's fine. He's as happy as a clam with Elyse. I think he'll stay with her forever."

"I'm sure she would like that."

"I can't blame him," she went on. "He has a pretty good life there—much better than most helpers."

"And you have a very good life here, too. Not many helpers live the way you do."

"I know. That's why I can't blame him for wanting to stay. I wouldn't mind staying myself."

He turned away. "You're going to stay one way or the other. You might as well have a good life while you're at it."

"Tom still thinks he's going to convince the human population to incorporate. He still thinks we can accomplish our mission."

"If that's what the thinks, then he's not the man I thought he was. I thought he was smarter than that."

"Elyse must have dropped a few choice words in his ear. She lets him believe what he wants to believe to keep him happy in her house."

Renfroe nodded. "That makes more sense. It makes sense he would let himself believe it. It beats believing the truth."

"Which is that the Pride will never let us leave. We're stuck here."

He sighed. "If you come to an understanding with the Pride, you'll be happy to stay. You'll realize you're part of the Pride."

"Can we talk about something else?"

"Come inside. It will be dark soon." He started toward the house.

The house was much darker than the garden. They found their food in the parlor and the fire blazing. Renfroe sat in his usual place by the fire and sniffed the platter of raw meat set out for him.

Dina sat across from him and lifted her bowl of vegetable stew into her lap. She pushed it around with her spoon, but she didn't eat it.

"Aren't you hungry?" he asked.

She shrugged and put the bowl down again. "I'm hungry, but I don't want to eat."

"What do you want to do?"

"I just want to talk to you and enjoy your company. That's all I want to do."

He moved across the space between them and laid himself down at her side. He put his head in her lap and her hands moved over his neck and side. He twisted his head around to press his head into her legs and scooted his body over the floor so the whole long line of his body contacted hers.

His pungent scent filled her mind. She rested her hand on his head in perfect safety. Nothing could represent safety the way he did.

She lay down by his side and wrapped herself in a nest of comfort more secure than any feather bed. He flipped himself over and slid his spine along her back. She sank into a bubble of rest unlike any she had ever known before.

She dissolved in the heat of his skin and fur. Nothing disturbed her peace of mind. She knew nothing but bliss and comfort and the happiness of finding her own place in the Pride.

She woke up in the middle of the night. Half-dead embers gave the only light in the room. The rest of the house and the rest of Prideland slept in silence.... or maybe they didn't. No one could ever know who was out hunting in the middle of the night, but that didn't matter. Renfroe was by her side. She was safe.

She rolled over onto her other side and snuggled her back between his legs. He growled in his sleep and his foreleg flexed to hug her closer to him. She closed her eyes. His heat kept her warm. Their breathing synchronized and she dozed off.

Her eyes popped open in a flash when Renfroe's breathing changed. He wasn't asleep.

She tried to go back to sleep, but something stopped her. She slept with him like this all the time now and Renfroe would never hurt her. Sometimes she even played with his toes and scratched her fingertips over the points of his claws, but something didn't feel right.

Her instincts told her to sit up, but she didn't. She gazed into the embers and drifted with her thoughts. All at once, he arched his back and brought his hips hard against the small of her back. She froze, but not from fear. He wanted her. He wanted to mate with her.

She had to stop this before it started, but her body refused to move. A charge of sexual tension shot through her.

Everything they said and did together, all their touching and cuddling—it all led to this moment. What else could they have been doing all these nights together but preparing to consummate their relationship?

Her mind just wouldn't believe it. She couldn't do it with a cat. How did she know what his anatomy would do to her? His bodily fluids could give her a deadly disease, but that wasn't true, either.

Tom did it with Elyse without any trouble. The Helions did it with their helpers—who knew how many times a day, for centuries. Renfroe said everyone was doing it. That's what the term 'helper' meant.

At least he wasn't doing it to degrade her. This was normal to him. Cats and people coupled all around him. He could mate with a woman if he wanted to.

He had no reason not to and what about her? What reason did she really have to resist him? The rules separating humans from animals came from Earth and Earth was a million miles away.

A wave of excitement rippled down his body and he pressed closer to her. She tucked her head into her chest. Tension stretched her taut until she could barely stand it. He dug his chin into her shoulder and growled.

Another jolt of electric energy rolled down his belly to the thick shaft of tissue tucked under his skin. He extended his claws, but he didn't grab her with them. He clutched her with his forelegs and burrowed his face into her neck. All at once, he let out a yowl that stood her hair on end. She couldn't move an inch one way or the other.

The next instant, he locked his jaws on the back of her neck. His teeth stabbed into her skin. He didn't have to hold her still. She wouldn't have moved for anything. He could snap her neck with a slight pressure of his jaws and then ravage her dead body.

Her breath caught in her throat and her blood pounded behind her eyes. His voice whined and rasped against the back of her neck. With a powerful wrench of his muscles, Renfroe flipped her over onto her stomach. He tightened his grip on her neck and she went limp. He could do what he wanted with her.

He rolled on top of her and his hips and belly flexed again. He planted both forepaws flat on either side of her shoulders and his hind legs squatted on either side of her hips. His long bulk crushed her to the floor and she fought to breathe. She couldn't do anything but stare at the embers and brace herself for the inevitable.

Renfroe's breathing quickened and his voice rose almost to a screech. His tail snapped back and forth. The movement translated through his body and into hers. His hips moved against her in a simulation of thrusting. He would push into her any second now.

Her mind refused to function. She watched the scene unfold from somewhere removed from herself. Renfroe brought his hips down hard onto her back.

The rigid shaft of his penis dug into the furrow between her buttocks and pushed her hips into the air, but some force inside her had other ideas.

In a flash, she launched herself up and away from him. How she got out of his grip without hurting herself, she would never be able to figure out. She bolted out from under him and scuttled across the floor.

She couldn't see him in the dim light, but she shuddered when she thought about what she'd just done. What would he do to her for rejecting him? Had she thrown away her last chance at peace and contentment?

Her teeth chattered, but every muscle tensed ready to run from him. "I'm sorry. I didn't mean to...."

He got to his feet with a growl. "Of course you didn't. You told me before you didn't want to."

"That's just the thing. I do want to. I just.... I don't know what came over me. I guess I was just caught off guard."

He nodded, but he didn't answer.

"Can you forgive me?" she asked.

"I don't have to forgive you. You already told me you didn't want to. I thought from the way you were rubbing against me that you wanted to. I must have misunderstood."

She swallowed hard. "You won't send me away, will you?"

"I won't send you away, but I won't approach you that way again, not unless I know for certain that you want me to."

"Why can't we go back to the way we were before? Why can't we hold each other and sleep next to each other and spend time together? Why do we have to throw all that away?"

"We don't have to throw it away. You say you want to do it, but you don't do it. You don't know what you want from me the same way you don't know what you want from the Pride. You should make up your mind one way or the other. If you want me the way you say you do, you have no reason to run away from me. If you don't want me, you don't have to stay here. You can go somewhere else where you have an understanding with the Pride that satisfies you." He started for the door.

She started to get up, but she didn't move toward him. A tornado of emotion tore her apart. "Wait, Renfroe. Don't leave."

He paid no attention. He vanished into the night. She couldn't even see which direction he went.

"Renfroe!" she cried. "Renfroe!"

Chapter 36

D ina waited all the next day for Renfroe to come back, but he didn't. Belinda left her meals outside her room and tiptoed away before Dina knew Belinda was there. Dina sat in all their favorite places while her mind tumbled over itself in a chaotic jumble of loyalties, expectations, and desires.

What was she going to write in her report? Was she really going to tell Dr. Galvin that three of the four landing party members engaged in bestial acts with cats? Was she going to tell Captain Doyle that three of his most trusted officers threw over their responsibility to their crew and country to belong to a slave class on this planet?

She buried her face in her hands at the thought. She would rather stay on this planet forever rather than try to explain to anyone what happened here. What had she come to? She had to do something drastic to cleanse herself of the very thought of giving herself to Renfroe.

She hadn't even done anything yet. She was still human enough to get away from Renfroe before he actually did anything to her.

If only she could talk to someone she trusted about this—but who? The only person she could think of was Captain Doyle. If she could get out of the city, she could fire up the pod's engines and get off this planet and never come back.

Then the Armada would treat her as hostile exactly the way Tania said. The captain would throw her in the brig. The Armada would interrogate her and treat everything she said as a lie. Could she really face that?

Thick black clouds gathered on the horizon. Forked lightning rocketed down to the ground on the distant hills and thunder rumbled toward the city. The storm would overtake the city by nightfall.

Would Renfroe ever come back? She had to be ready for him when he did. She had to make up her mind about what she was going to do so she could give him her answer the very next time she saw him.

Was she going to stay here as his helper? If she didn't give herself to him willingly, he would get rid of her one way or the other.

She paced empty rooms and out into the garden, but no escape plan came to her. She didn't know the city well enough to get past the sentinel cats and out into the countryside, but she couldn't wait for Renfroe to come back.

She had to get away. With any luck, she would be in orbit before anyone knew she was gone. Every eye in Prideland would be on her and every hand and paw would turn against her if she got caught.

The wind whipped the trees and the storm came with it. The sky darkened early. The first rain spattered roofs and paving stones and the sky crackled with electricity. Branches thrashed in the wind.

The first spray splashed her face. Lightning cracked out of the sky and struck somewhere nearby. The concussion rattled the windowpanes and the tree lizards screeched and scurried out of sight.

Dina turned back toward the house to find Renfroe watching her from the doorway. She smiled at him in spite of herself. "How long have you been standing there? I didn't even know you were home."

"I wasn't. I just got back from the Senate."

She stepped to his side, but he kept his distance. "Are you coming in for dinner?"

He nodded and moved down the corridor. He walked slowly so she could match his stride. "Have you been home all day? You didn't go out again, did you?"

"No, I was waiting for you."

"You didn't have to do that. You could have done something else to occupy yourself."

"It's all right. I wanted to see you the moment you got back."

"Did you come to any conclusions?"

Dina looked down at the ground. "I came to the conclusion that I'm grateful to you for your kindness. I wouldn't want any other cat as a benefactor."

"No other benefactor would give you a choice about being his helper. You would be whether you wanted to or not."

She blushed. "I realize that and I'm grateful."

He shrugged and sat down by the fire. "I gave you the choice because I care about you and I want you to care about me. If I didn't care about you and only wanted your body to myself, I wouldn't bother talking to you. I would just take you by force."

"I know," she murmured.

"I don't want your gratitude. I want you to return my feelings for you."

"I do return them. Don't you see? I care for you just as much as you care for me. I just can't do anything physical with you."

"We sleep in one another's arms. That's physical. You haven't had any trouble doing that."

"I don't mean that. I mean anything sexual. We can be companions, but I can't mate with you. It isn't natural. It's obscene."

"Obscene?" he repeated. "So I'm obscene, am I?"

"Not you. You're not obscene, but a woman and a tiger having sex together is. You should realize that. It's contrary to everything natural. I couldn't do it."

"You said before that you wanted to."

"I can't do it whether I want to or not. I'm human. You're a cat. I wouldn't be human if I did it with you."

"None of the other helpers have any trouble with it. They're all perfectly human."

"That's them. If they want to do it, they can go ahead. I'm not them."

"I know you're not them. That's exactly why I want you and not them." He paced across the room to the door.

"Where are you going?"

"I'm going to Elyse's house."

She stiffened. "What for?"

"I have Senate business to discuss with her. We have a hearing tomorrow and I want to go over the issues beforehand."

"What about dinner? Aren't we going to eat together like we usually do?"

"I'll eat there."

"When will you be back?"

He didn't turn around. His nostrils flared at the pungent air outside. He wanted to be out in the open. Her presence in this house no longer appealed to him. "I don't know. I was planning to go out hunting, but with this weather blowing in, I guess I'll skip it. None of the others will want to hunt, either. The sentinel cats won't be out tonight, either. They don't like to get their little feet wet." He chuckled under his breath. He wasn't talking to her anymore.

He moved away into the dark. She didn't try to call him back, and in an instant, he was gone.

Her heart ached at losing him, without a word of goodbye, but only one thing he said stuck in her mind. The sentinel cats would be hiding indoors tonight. She wouldn't get another chance like this.

She strained her ears to listen. Belinda brought her meal and Dina smiled at her. The smell of food tightened her stomach into knots, but who knew when she would get a chance to eat? She forced herself to eat as much as she could hold.

The storm blew up a torrent of thunder and lashing rain. Dina stared into the fire and ran through her escape over and over in her mind. She could find her way to the open road if only she could get there unmolested. From there, she had a straight run to the village and then into the jungle.

She twisted her shaking fingers together and buried them in her lap. If Belinda suspected anything, Dina would lose her chance.

She had to behave normally, but nothing was normal now. Belinda went through the house to close the windows and doors. She came back through the parlor to collect Dina's tray. Belinda would spend an hour or two in the kitchen cleaning up. She wouldn't go to bed for hours.

Lightning beat the garden walls. Rain soaked the grass and the tree branches sagged and tossed. What time was it? Dina had to get out of the house and moving if she wanted to reach the jungle before dawn. Every minute dragged and she still didn't dare make her move. The storm didn't ease off in the slightest.

Belinda would certainly be in bed by now. Solid darkness enveloped the house. She padded along the corridor and rolled on the outsides of her feet to silence her footsteps. Her heart twisted at the slightest sound.

At last, she grasped the front doorknob with trembling hands, swung the door open, and hesitated on the threshold. The wind tore the shrubs and branches.

How far would she have to travel before she found shelter? She couldn't stay in this house a second longer. She stepped through the door and reached back to pull it closed behind her.

"Who's there?" a voice barked from the darkness.

Dina jumped out of her skin and fought the urge to panic. "It's me, Belinda. It's Dina."

"What are you doing out at this time of night?" Belinda snapped.

"I just wanted to see the storm. I haven't seen this kind of weather since I came to Prideland. I am a scientist, you know."

Belinda hesitated. She might not even know what a scientist was. "This is no night to be outdoors. Come inside before you get sick. You can watch the storm from the window."

"I'll come in a minute. I just want to see this for myself. I promise I won't be long."

"You're crazy to be out in this weather," Belinda grumbled.

"It's only for a minute. I'll be back inside soon. I won't get sick."

Belinda vanished into the dark with a wordless grunt. Dina held her breath listening to Belinda's footsteps die away. Dina finally pulled the door closed behind her and walked away as fast as she dared.

She retraced the route she followed to Elyse's house without seeing a single cat. The rain was pelting down in torrents by the time she found the river. The rain soaked her clothes and chilled her to the bone.

She wrapped her arms around her and strode along the river as fast as she could without breaking into a run. She walked all night. The rain slackened when she entered the village, but her wet clothes chilled her until her teeth chattered.

She longed for shelter, but she had to get through the village unnoticed. She hurried toward the jungle. Light spread through the sky and she quickened her pace to leave the village behind. She had to find a place to hide before day came and she had to find some way to warm herself and dry her clothes.

She clenched her teeth to stop them from chattering, but she couldn't feel her lips from the cold. She hugged her arms around her chest until her fingers went numb, too. Every step squeezed water out of her shoes and she couldn't feel her legs. She couldn't go much further.

She stumbled past the flowerbed. Just enough light gleamed in the sky to see the other side of the village. Fields and pastures stretched empty and welcoming all the way to the jungle.

She almost laughed out loud in pure relief at the sight, but at that moment, a hand clapped her hard on the shoulder and spun her around. A terrible voice shattered the stillness. "You!"

Dina gasped at the face staring down at her. It was Alexander Mathus.

Chapter 37

A lexander hauled her back to the house where she got her first taste of Prideland. He shoved her inside and latched the door behind him, but no other villagers stood around waiting to pounce on her.

A fire flickered in the center of the room, and a thin, pinched woman sat next to it with two children at her side. A boy and a girl looked up at Dina with the same blank expression she remembered from her first day on the planet.

Alexander pointed to the fire. "Sit down."

Dina obeyed. She knew what would happen next. She wasn't Renfroe's pampered pet anymore. She'd squandered his protection. Alexander would get his henchmen to give her another class or whatever. Then he would send for the cats to come and get her.

Minutes passed, but he didn't leave. He sat down next to the boy. "This is my wife, Darcy, and these are my children, Sonya and Christian."

Dina stole a glance at the woman who poured a cup of steaming tea and handed it to Dina. It burned her frozen hands, but the smell drifted into her nostrils and started to thaw her numbed brain. "You must have had a long journey."

Dina bent her head over the cup. She couldn't hold eye contact with this woman, not after everything that happened. "I came out from the city."

The woman gasped out loud. "In this storm? You must be crazy!"

Steam penetrated Dina's body, and her hands shook. "I didn't expect...." She stopped.

"Isn't it obvious what she's done?" Alexander roared. "I just caught her trying to sneak through the village without getting caught. She ran away from her benefactor."

Darcy's smile evaporated. "Oh. Who is your benefactor?"

"Renfroe."

"The senator? Is he a good benefactor?"

"He's been very kind to me."

"Why did you run away, then?" Alexander snapped.

Dina stared down into her cup. "I didn't run away from Renfroe. I just want to go home."

"Prideland is your home," Alexander boomed. "You aren't going anywhere. You should be grateful to be part of the Pride, but you aren't. You're a slag. You'll never be anything but a slag. You ran away and you'll get what all the slags get."

Darcy touched his sleeve. "Please, darling. Can't you see she's half frozen? Don't jump to conclusions. Renfroe might want her back. You have to find out what the Pride wants to do with her. They might want to make an example out of her or they might want to bring her to a different understanding with the Pride."

"You're right. We can't do anything until we tell the Pride you're here."

Dina's heart sank. She was so close to escaping. Maybe she still had a chance if she played her cards right.

Alexander shook his finger at her. "I remember you. Hector told us you have your craft hidden somewhere near here. You're probably on your way there right now."

Dina searched his face for any hint of compassion, but her eyes kept moving back to Darcy. "Isn't there any way you can let me go? I have to get back to my ship and tell them what's going on down here. I left my three teammates in the city and I have to get them out. Them—and you, too. You don't have to stay here. You can come back to the Coalition. We came here to find you and bring take you home."

Alexander shook his head, but Dina caught a different reaction from his wife. Her eyes widened and she opened her mouth to answer, but then she glanced at her husband and closed it again.

"We aren't going anywhere," Alexander countered. "We belong here now. We have an understanding with the Pride that's better than anything we ever had with the Coalition."

Dina answered him, but she kept her eyes on Darcy. "What about your families? Your father, Chancellor Mathus, wants you back badly enough to send us here to find you. He must be worried about you and your children. Don't you want to see him again?"

Darcy covered her mouth with her hand, but she didn't interrupt when Alexander answered. "We might miss our families, but we have a new family here. Maybe your friends understand that better than you do."

"Maybe they do."

"Why didn't they come with you?" Darcy asked.

"They wouldn't leave. Tom—he was the very tall man with curly hair. He's First Officer of our ship and he doesn't want to abandon our mission. Besides, his benefactor treats him well enough that he doesn't understand the danger of staying."

"You wouldn't be in any danger if you came to an understanding with the Pride," Alexander told her. "No one is."

"That may be true, but our other teammate, Matthew, *is* in danger. Maybe you remember him. He's the short man with straight black hair and the round face. He'll be dead if he stays here much longer."

"What's wrong with him?" Darcy asked.

Dina chose her words carefully. "You could say he never came to a satisfactory understanding with his benefactor."

"Who's his benefactor?" Alexander asked.

"His name is Fallon."

"Everybody knows Fallon," he replied. "If your friend can't come to an understanding with the Pride, then he's as good as dead already. The best any of us can do is to come to an understanding with them and learn to live in peace. If your friend can't do that, he might as well dig his own grave and stop taking up the space another helper could fill."

"That's a heartless thing to say about another human being," Dina fired back. "The last time I saw Matthew, he could barely walk and he'd lost the use of one of his arms. He never did anything to Fallon. Fallon toys with him for amusement. He won't last much longer."

Alexander turned away. "Then he's a hopeless case. He should be reduced and put out of his misery. I know Fallon's other helpers. He's very kind and considerate to those who make an effort to come to an understanding with him."

Darcy spoke up. "You said there were four of you. You've mentioned two others. What about the fourth one?"

"Tania. She's Khalid's helper."

Darcy and Alexander exchanged another glance. "Oh."

"Why do you say that?" Dina asked.

Darcy looked down at her hands. "We know about Khalid, too. He and Fallon are the deadliest cats in the Pride."

"That's what Renfroe says. Tania is terrified of Khalid. She plans to give herself to him as a helper, just to get some safety from him. She lives in constant fear when he comes into the same room with her."

They stared at her. "What do you mean, she's going to give herself to him as a helper? She's already his helper."

"You know what I mean. She's going to offer herself to him, to be used as a helper. You know what that means."

Alexander frowned. "No, I don't know what that means. You said she's living with him. That makes her his helper. She doesn't have to offer herself to him."

"I mean she's going to offer herself to him in a sexual way," Dina explained. "She's going to be *that* kind of helper."

Alexander shook his head. "You're mistaken. That kind of thing doesn't happen in Prideland. Mixing the species is definitely protected."

"According to Renfroe, it happens all the time. He said everybody's doing it and he ought to know."

"I won't contradict Senator Renfroe," Alexander replied, "but we have rules against that kind of thing. A helper could get visited for doing anything like that. We have a strict code of conduct when it comes to helping the cats."

"I've seen it with my own eyes," Dina told him. "I saw dozens of people and cats doing it at Helion House and no one seemed at all concerned with getting visited. They did it like it was expected of them. That's why the word 'helper' has two meanings. It means living and serving the cats, but it also means being sexual with them."

Alexander shook his head again. "That's not possible. Crossing the line between the species is our most protected taboo. No one would dare to do it."

"Do you know Maddy?" Dina asked. "She's one of Khalid's helpers and she said she came from this village. Maybe she went to the city before you came here, but her family must be here."

"I know who you mean," Darcy told her. "I know her mother. What about her?"

"She helps Khalid. She helps Khalid—in *that* way, in a sexual way. She's his special helper, which means he uses her for sex. She's the one who told Tania she ought to offer herself to Khalid to gain advantages and maybe do some good for Matthew, too."

"We have an understanding with the Pride," Alexander repeated. "No helper would cross the barrier between the species. The cats are too good for that. They're superior to us in every way. Even if a person wanted to degrade themselves with a cat, the cat would stop it."

"I'm telling you I've seen it with my own eyes," Dina argued. "Tom does it with Elyse, and from the comments she made, she does it with her other helpers, too. It's a form of recreation for her."

Alexander threw back his shoulders. "You're making this up to slander the Pride. You've been against the Pride from the beginning and this is your way of ruining our understanding with the cats."

"Why would I do that? Why would I lie about it?"

"Even if a few bad apples did something like that with the cats, it's the people who contaminate the understanding. Maybe that's what happened with your friends. You're outsiders which means you're nothing more than slags anyway, but our people would never do anything like that. We know better and we have an understanding with the Pride."

Dina changed the subject. "You've only been on this planet for six months. How did you come to an understanding with them? Didn't you struggle with it in the beginning? You couldn't just drop the Coalition and everything it stands for, just like that."

"When our shuttle crashed here," Alexander told her, "the whole complement of our crew and passengers integrated into this village as best we could. We didn't know the Coalition would send anyone to rescue us. We thought we might be here forever. The only way we could live here was to come to an understanding with the Pride."

"But you're a factor now. I thought only the most trusted subsidiaries got to hold that position."

"When we landed, I told the subsidiaries about my father and about the Coalition. I offered myself as a representative of the Coalition and they accepted me. So in a sense, this planet is already part of the Coalition and I'm governor."

"You can't be governor," Dina argued. "The Coalition is a representative democracy and you haven't been elected by a majority vote. Besides, the Pride controls this planet through the Senate. They aren't a representative democracy, either, since the human population isn't represented."

"You're splitting hairs," Mathus countered. "Those are all minor details."

"You might have a small degree of power over the people in this village, but you certainly aren't the governor of a Coalition planet. That's what we're here for. We're here to incorporate this planet—and to rescue you."

Alexander Mathus shook his head. "This planet will never incorporate, not as long as I have anything to say about it."

Dina refused to back down. "Your father is Chancellor of the Coalition. The order to incorporate came directly from him."

"My father's wishes can't interfere with our understanding. I love and respect my father, but the Pride comes first."

"They're cats," Dina returned. "The Coalition is human. You should support your own species first."

"We serve them because they *are* cats. We can do our best work and live our best lives by taking our rightful places in the Pride. These cats have every advantage over us. We wouldn't survive on this planet without them."

"The slags live in the jungle with no connection to the cats. They're surviving without the Pride."

Mathus wrinkled his nose. "You can hardly call the slags' existence 'survival'. They scratch a living out of the mud. They're worse than animals. They would be better off if the Pride reduced them from the surface of the planet."

"How can you talk about your own people like that?"

"The slags aren't people," he spat. "They're worms. They're bacteria. They're filth."

"They're human beings. The Coalition will have something to say about how they're treated. The Coalition will expect them to have the same representation in government as everyone else. The Coalition will expect the Pride to respect the slags' right to self-determination as equal to the subsidiaries in the village and the helpers in the cities."

"That's why we and the Pride and the rest of this planet, will never join the Coalition. We're here and we'll stay here. We belong to the Pride now. We'll never go back."

"That's for the people to decide for themselves," Dina told him. "The Coalition won't accept that answer coming from you."

"You won't get any answer *except* from me. I speak for these people and I say we will have nothing to do with the Coalition."

"As a matter of fact," Dina pointed out, "the Senate speaks for these people. The Senate speaks for you, too. Not even you can speak for yourself in this Pride. How do you feel about that?"

"I feel wonderful about it. The Senate has my best interest at heart. I don't need representation. The Senate can decide what's best for us."

"So you're perfectly happy to be a slave, and for your wife and children to be slaves, and the rest of the people on this planet to be slaves, with no hope of freedom?"

"We have an understanding with the Pride. That understanding gives us the best life we could possibly hope for."

Dina gazed back down into her teacup. What was the point of going around in circles? The fire warmed her through her wet clothes. Alexander went out and Darcy pulled her children away.

Dina relaxed by the fire. The hot tea comforted her, but her mind wouldn't settle down. She had to get out of this village before they sent her back to the city. She made it this far. One more push into the jungle would bring her to the pod. Then she would be home free.

Alexander came back with an armload of firewood. Daylight streamed through the door and through the hole in the roof. Dina didn't need the fire to see.

"I'll go get the other factors," Alexander told her. "We'll decide what to do with you."

"You said you would turn me over to the Pride. Have you changed your mind?"

"We have to discuss it. The Pride might want you to stay here. They might want us to deal with you ourselves. We have procedures to follow. You'll stay here in my house until we come to a decision."

Chapter 38

D arcy smiled at Dina. "Let's get you out of those clothes. You'll never get warm if you keep them on. Here. I have some extra clothes you can change into. Then we'll get you a meal. You must be half dead. Then you can get some sleep. We have a festival later and you won't want to miss it."

Dina groaned. "Not another festival!"

"You're thinking of the helpers' festivals in the city, with all that talking and talking and talking for hours. This isn't like that at all. It's a Children's Festival."

Dina perked up her ears. "Children's Festival? I never heard of that."

"It's a special festival for the children. It brings them to an understanding with the Pride and it teaches them to value their place in it."

Dina's heart sank. "Oh. Great."

Darcy smiled again, but Dina still noticed a trace of doubt in Darcy's eyes. "Don't worry. It's good for them."

"Don't tell me you agree with this," Dina countered. "You can't want your children sold into slavery to the Pride. I don't know how any parent could let that happen."

The door opened just then and another woman came in. She wasn't much taller than the children and her stout form waddled from side to side when she walked. The characteristic hunch made her look even shorter.

Darcy brightened up and took the woman's arrival as an opportunity not to answer Dina. "This is my friend, Berys. She can explain everything much better than I can."

"What can I explain?" Berys asked.

"The Children's Festival," Darcy told her. "This is.... what did you say your name was?"

"Dina," she replied. "Dina Dyer."

"Dina just came from the city," Darcy went on.

"If she just came from the city," Berys returned, "she should know all about the Children's Festival."

"She just came to Prideland," Darcy explained. "She landed here with some of her friends."

Berys turned to Dina. "Did you crash the way Darcy and Alexander did?"

Dina fidgeted. "Not exactly,"

"I was just starting to explain about the Children's Festival," Darcy told her, "but you can do a better job than I can."

"I'd be happy to explain it, but it will make much more sense if you see it for yourself." Berys sat down next to Dina. "That's why we do it—to show the children how to come to an understanding with the Pride. They can understand much better by being shown than by being told."

"What do you show them?" Dina asked. "Why do you have to show them when you could just tell them?"

"They've been told a million times all their lives. They've been to classes like everyone else and their parents tell them every day how important it is to come to an understanding with the Pride. That's the problem. They've heard it too many times. After a while, it just goes in one ear and out the other. They have to see it to really understand it. You will, too."

"I don't want to see it and I don't want to hear it," Dina growled. "I don't want to come to an understanding with the Pride. If I did, I would be back in the city where I came from."

"Then you're a slag," Berys snapped. "People who don't come to an understanding with the Pride are slags. You don't want to be one of them. You should do anything you can to make sure you don't turn into one."

"So I've been told."

"Then you really need to see the Children's Festival. That will convince you if nothing else will."

A commotion rose outside and Darcy and Berys strode past Dina into the yard. "Come on! It's starting!" Darcy's children hurried to catch up with them and Dina followed. Anything was better than sitting in the house all day and waiting for Alexander to come back with his decision.

Sing-song voices and the buzz of activity filled the village. Everyone in the village flooded into the road and headed out into the fields.

The village people wore their best clothes, especially the children who had all been bathed and combed for the occasion. None of the children ran or skipped or laughed. Some held their mothers' hands and most stayed close to their parents' legs.

The crowd marched out to a newly mown field where they gathered around a platform like the one at Helion House. The Children's Festival started off with the same speeches and stories. Alexander Mathus got up on the stage and told how he and his people crashed on the planet and now loved Prideland too much to leave.

Another man Dina didn't recognize took the stage after him. "It's Porter Wainright," Berys whispered. "His son Alger is getting the House of Man today along with Sonya."

"What's that?" Dina whispered back.

Berys nodded toward the platform and didn't answer. The man fidgeted on the stage with his eyes on the ground and the crowd fell silent to hear his words.

"I remember the day I received the House of Man," he began. "I was afraid of the cats and I told my father I didn't want to go. He said I had to get it no matter what. He wasn't going to let me humiliate my family in front of the whole village."

He knitted his fingers together. "I cried and ran to my mother. She talked to me until I calmed down. She told me the House of Man stands for the Pride's protection. She told me how it showed I had an understanding with the Pride and I wanted to have an understanding with the Pride."

He glanced up at the crowd and scanned the wall of faces until he found his son. The father smiled at his son but the boy hid his face in his mother's skirts.

"She told me I had to have the House of Man if I ever wanted to become a helper or a factor, or if any of my children wanted to become helpers or factors. If I didn't get the House of Man, I would be hounded out of the village to rot in the cantons with the slags."

A murmur of approval ran through his listeners.

"And now here I am," he went on. "I'm a father now and I've brought my son and my nephew to the Children's Festival. I've brought them the same way I was brought and my parents and grandparents and all the rest of you were brought. So let them receive the House of Man and let us all give thanks to the Pride which has done all of us so much good."

He finished his speech in a rush to get off the stage. Three more men made identical speeches after him. They all brought their children to the Children's Festival to receive the House of Man along with Sonya and Alger.

Then Alexander lectured on the virtues of the Pride and the hatefulness of the slags. He spoke for about an hour and was just getting ready to launch into hour number two. Dina glanced around for a place to sit down. None of these people would last long standing out in the sun and the festival organizers didn't plan any seating for anyone.

Alexander warmed to his subject, but just as he really got going, he spotted something at the back of the crowd. He swallowed the rest of his speech and left the platform. A commotion broke out at the back of the crowd. The village people parted and Lord Helion strode up to the platform along with Hector and Victor.

Dina's blood ran cold at the sight of them. "What are they doing here?"

Berys whispered back, a hush of awe in her voice. "They're here to perform the House of Man."

"What is it?" Dina asked again.

"All the children get it at the age of eight," Berys explained. "It shows their understanding with the Pride. Sonya's getting it today and so is her cousin Alger and four others."

Dina swallowed hard. "What are the cats going to do to them?" She didn't want to know.

"They're going to mark them with the House of Man. You must have seen it. It's a symbol of protection in the shape of a roof over the person's hips. All the children get it."

Dina's jaw dropped and her spine chilled. So this was where those scars came from. The cats scratched those lines into their slaves' bodies. They branded them like cattle and now they were going to do it to Sonya.

The little girl cowered behind her mother and turned her face away so she wouldn't see the cats walking right past her.

Lord Helion and the twin jaguars climbed the platform and sat down in a row. The sight of them drove Dina out of her mind. She grabbed Darcy by the arm. "Please, Darcy, don't do this. Don't let them make your daughter into a slave."

"No one is making her a slave," Berys snapped.

"Don't you see?" Dina almost yelled. "Don't you see they're using your children against you? They're making you harm your children to prove your loyalty. Don't sacrifice your children to them!"

Berys stared at her in horror, but not in horror at the appalling act these cats were about to perform on defenseless little Sonya. It was the horror of confronting an insane person, a person outside her world. Dina had no understanding with the Pride and she never would. A bottomless gulf separated her from these people and she would never cross that gulf until she submitted to the Pride.

Her voice attracted the cats' attention. Lord Helion looked down toward the noise. His eyes met Dina's and he recognized her. She shut her mouth, but the damage was done.

Darcy listened with the same pinched expression. In the end, she lowered her gaze to the ground. She couldn't exactly turn against the Pride there and then, with those cats sitting on the platform and the whole village standing around. She had to stay in line.

"I *am* loyal," she murmured.

The children's mothers brought them to the platform. They formed a line with Darcy and Sonya in the front. Sonya shook all over as her mother led her onto the platform.

Alexander and Darcy each took hold of their daughter's arms. The girl turned white as chalk. Her mother whispered reassurances in her ear, but she didn't respond. A deathly hush fell over the crowd. They laid her on her back on the hard wooden boards.

Alexander threw Sonya's skirt up over her hips and Darcy pulled the girl's leggings down to expose her delicate young skin to the light of day. She slid the leggings all the way down to Sonya's ankles, along with her white underwear. Sonya gasped and sobbed in terror. No other sound disturbed the morning stillness.

Dina fought to breathe. Her teeth chattered no matter how hard she clenched them shut. She wrung her hands in despair and her panting breath threatened to break out in wracking sobs.

She shifted from one foot to the other and glanced right and left in search of anyone or anything she could call on for help. She should snatch Sonya away from her parents and carry the girl far, far away, but there was nothing Dina could do.

Alexander rolled up a ball of cloth and stuffed it into his daughter's mouth. She let out a faint cry when he lashed the gag in place with a rag tied around the back of her head. He and Darcy held the girl's arms down and two other factors pinned her legs to the platform.

Victor approached her and loomed over Sonya's prostrate body.

"And now," Lord Helion boomed out over the crowd, "enter the House of Man."

At his word, Victor raised his paw, extended his razor claws, and raked them across Sonya's tender flanks. Her scream ripped across the field even with the gag in her mouth. The whole crowd shuddered and some of the younger children started to cry.

Dina knew better than to scream in horror or to try to intervene. She couldn't do anything but cover her face with her hands and weep.

Chapter 39

S onya lay on a bed by the fire. Berys sat between her and Dina and prepared a meal for the family. Darcy hung back in the shadows. She entered the firelight to check on Sonya, but she left everything else to Berys.

"I hope you learned your lesson today," Berys snapped.

Dina's head shot up. "What do you mean?"

"Lord Helion saw you at the festival today. He recognized you. He'll tell your benefactor where you are. They'll take you back to the city."

Dina went back to staring into the fire. She couldn't get the children's screams out of her mind. "Did the factors decide what to do with me?"

"It doesn't matter what they decide. We can't let the Pride think we helped you escape. If we didn't send you back, we could get visited for helping you. We have to enforce the understanding with the Pride."

Dina blinked into the firelight, but no more tears would come. Nothing could be worse than what she witnessed today. "I still can't believe you let them do that to your own children."

"Do what?"

"The House of Man. How could you let them do that? She's just a little girl."

Berys smacked her lips. "The House of Man doesn't hurt them."

"Doesn't hurt them?" Dina shot back. "How can you say it doesn't hurt them? Look at her lying there. Are you telling me she isn't in pain right now? Ask her if it hurts. Maybe she knows better than to say so. These children know how to keep their mouths shut, but I can tell you what hurts the worst. It's that her own parents did it to her. They held her down while the cats did it. You fill their heads full of nonsense about how good and special and wonderful it is to have an understanding with the Pride. That's what hurts. She would tell you if she only dared."

Berys waved her hand. "The House of Man doesn't hurt. I had it done when I was that age. We've all had it done. It didn't do us any harm. It might hurt when you first get it done, but the pain goes away. I understand now why my parents did it. I appreciate that they did it for me because I love being a subsidiary to the Pride and the House of Man makes me that. The Pride is my life. It's all our lives. We all feel that way."

"You're all suffering from the same insanity. That's the understanding you have with the Pride."

Berys shook her head. "You obviously don't have an understanding with the Pride yet, but you will. Even if you have to get visited to get it, you will get it. No one can live in Prideland without that understanding. If you know what's good for you, you'll go back to your benefactor and be grateful for the understanding you have with him. That's the best life you can hope for in Prideland. That's why we give our children the House of Man, so they can become helpers. That's the only way we can be sure they have a better life."

Dina went back to staring at the fire. "When your children become helpers to the Pride, do they help in every other way the adult helpers do?"

"Of course. They help in any way that's needed. Why do you ask?"

"Do you bother to check to make sure they aren't doing anything...you know...protected?"

"If it's protected, they won't do it. That only makes sense."

"Are you sure?" Dina asked.

"Of course, I'm sure. The cats would never do any such thing and the other helpers would make sure our children never did anything protected. Of course they wouldn't."

"How can you be absolutely sure that what is protected to you is protected to the cats? Maybe the cats don't see it as protected at all."

Berys stared at her. Then she let out a gasp of exasperation, got up, and went about her work without answering. Dina waited, but Berys never came back to finish the conversation. She and Darcy kept away from her for the rest of the evening.

Dina turned her attention to Sonya. She was the only person left to talk to, but when Dina met the girl's eyes, she lost her nerve. What could you say to a child who'd been treated so brutally?

Now Dina knew why the children didn't run around and laugh. Sonya looked like she would never smile again. Her situation was nothing to smile about. No one understood better than she did.

Dina went for a walk outside to clear her head. No one tried to stop her. Darcy and Berys wouldn't have anything to do with her. Sunset colors streaked the sky and the night chill fell over the village. Dina wandered around until she found herself in the same field where the Children's Festival took place.

What a heartless joke that name was! She could joke about the treasure hunters and their Museum of Antiquities, but not this. Village men were hard at work dismantling the platform, but Dina couldn't erase the sight of Sonya's petrified face from her mind.

The sky outlined the trees' black silhouettes. She would do anything for Sonya. Dina had to do something to show her that at least one person on this crazy planet cared about her.

Dina couldn't tell her with her parents in the room. She wanted to give Sonya a gift, something to brighten up her days while she recovered—but what could Dina give her?

Dina had nothing but the clothes on her back. Memories of the day mingled with older memories of herself as a girl and that gave her the idea to give Sonya a doll.

She picked up a handful of dried grass from the edge of the field and twisted it into the crude shape of a person. It wasn't any great piece of workmanship, but it looked enough like a human shape to serve the purpose. She hurried back to the house and took her seat by the fire.

Berys smiled at her but continued her work without speaking before she vanished into the darkness. Dina slid over to Sonya's bed. "How are you feeling?"

Sonya sniffed and stared up at the rafters. "I'm okay."

"I brought you something." Dina held out the doll.

Sonya examined the doll with a blank expression. "What is it?"

Dina blushed, but she couldn't take the doll back now. "It's a doll. Where I come from, they call these dolls made out of grass 'corn dollies', but it's a doll. It's supposed to represent a person."

Sonya looked at the thing from every angle. "What is it for?"

The smile melted off Dina's face. She would have yanked the doll out of Sonya's hand and tossed it in the fire if she hadn't just given it to her as a gift. "Just to play with."

Sonya turned it over in her hand. "What am I supposed to do with it?"

"You can play house with it.... or you can pretend it's a baby."

"What does 'pretend' mean?" Sonya asked.

"You imagine it's your baby and you're its mother. You can pretend to feed it or put it to bed. You can carry it around and talk to it."

"What for?" Sonya asked.

"Just to have fun."

Sonya studied the doll again and Dina watched her. Somewhere far away, Matilda sat alone on a shelf in Dina's quarters on the *Savannah*. She sat perfectly still and waited for Dina to come back.

Dina had to get back to her. She had to get out of here and get back to the ship. She had to see Matilda again if it was the last thing she ever did.

Sonya turned her eyes back to the ceiling. The doll hung limp in her hand and Dina retreated into the shadows. She never spoke to Sonya again. Maybe Sonya did throw the doll in the fire after Dina left. Dina wouldn't have blamed her.

Chapter 40

Alexander and Darcy Mathus sat by the fire talking in low tones, but Sonya didn't join in the conversation. She stared straight up at the ceiling throughout the evening meal. Darcy kept trying to catch Sonya's eye, but the girl didn't look at anyone. Dina looked down into her dish and kept silent, too.

Darcy collected the dirty dishes. Alexander got to his feet and turned to Dina. "You'll go back to Renfroe in the morning. He's sending a wagon from the city to pick you up."

Dina looked up at him. "Just like that? No visits or classes or public humiliation?"

"Renfroe must think an awful lot of you. He wants you back. That's all. You better come to an understanding with the Pride soon and keep your place. He won't be so generous next time."

He walked out of the house and Dina went back to staring into the fire. She wouldn't go back to Renfroe no matter how much he cared for her. She had to leave this village tonight and get back to the pod. The thought consumed her so she didn't see Darcy lurking just outside the ring of firelight.

Dina started out of her reverie when Darcy sat down at her side. "I can't talk long," she breathed. "Alexander could come back any time, and if he caught me talking to you, I could get visited."

"Why doesn't he want you talking to me?"

"You know you're protected," Darcy told her.

"Protected!" Dina repeated.

"You ran away. You're practically a slag already after the things you said. No one will talk to you now and Alexander knows I wouldn't be able to stand up to the things you say. I'm not as strong as he is."

"What makes you think you aren't strong?"

Darcy shook her head. "I can't talk long, but not all of us feel the way he does. Some of us want to get out of here."

Dina's mouth fell open. "You do? I thought you all believed in Prideland just as much as he does."

"We have to act that way. We could get visited if we didn't."

"How many people feel this way?" Dina asked.

"I don't really know. I whisper in secret with some of the other women—you know, to keep anyone from finding out—but there must be others—not only here, but in the other villages. There must be helpers that want to get out, too."

"Does Alexander know you feel this way?"

"Oh, no! I could never tell him. He'd have me visited for sure."

Dina gasped. "Your own husband would have you visited? How could he?"

"He's a factor. He would have me visited faster than anyone, but I've mentioned it to two of my children that are old enough to understand."

Dina glanced around. Sonya's eyes gleamed across the fire. She could hear every word. "How many children do you have? I only saw two."

"I have five. They're staying in other houses until Sonya recovers. My older boy loves his father so much I would never breathe a word to him. My youngest daughter repeats everything everybody says, so you have to watch what you say around her, but my younger boy and my older daughter know enough. They understand."

"What have you told them?" Dina asked.

"Alexander wants them sent to the city as helpers. They don't want to go, of course, and they have to get the House of Man to become helpers."

Dina glanced over at Sonya again. "I don't blame them for wanting to get out of it."

Darcy lowered her eyes. "Sonya is my oldest child. I put it off as long as I could, but Alexander insisted on it. The children see their friends getting it done. They talk more freely among themselves than around adults. They know more about what's going on here than I do."

"If people aren't willing to stand up to the factors and the Pride, there isn't much I can do. Knowing you want to get away isn't enough. People actually have to do something about it."

"Everyone's too frightened. No one wants to get visited."

"Do you know what that word means? I can't get anyone to explain it to me."

Darcy shook her head and cast a glance over her shoulder. "I don't know what it means. I don't understand half the words they use, but at the same time, I know what they mean. That probably doesn't make much sense."

"Actually, it does."

Darcy sighed. "You're right. There's nothing you can do if people aren't willing to step out of line and stand up for themselves. I just wanted you to know there are people here who want to do something. They're just waiting for someone like you to tell them what to do."

"I can't do that. I'm not even supposed to negotiate with you. Our representative is supposed to carry out all the negotiations on behalf of the Coalition, but Alexander is dead set against it."

"He's one of the factors and the factors control the villages," Darcy replied. "If he tells the people to oppose the incorporation, everyone will obey him."

"How many factors are there?" Dina asked.

"Every village has ten factors. Alexander is head factor here. He's the most powerful of all the factors. Even the other factors obey him."

"How did he become a factor so fast when you only landed six months ago?" Dina asked.

Darcy shrugged. "It wasn't hard. Anyone who develops a clear understanding with the Pride and is willing to enforce it can become a factor."

"If they have to enforce it, it isn't really an understanding, is it?"

Darcy smiled. "You know what I mean."

"Yes, I do." Dina patted her arm. "I appreciate you telling me that you want to get out. I'll let you know if anything changes and we can do something. In the meantime, don't put yourself or your children in danger. As long as there's nothing to do, you might as well take advantage of your husband's position. That must give you a certain amount of security."

"That's what I thought at first. That's what he thought, too. That's why he became a factor. Now I'm not so sure. Now I think it puts us in more danger than before. I certainly don't want my children staying here."

"Have you thought about going out to the jungle? You could go find the slags. They don't have the same loyalty to the Pride. You might be safer there."

"I couldn't do that. We could never live like that."

"You never know until you try it. The factors could be making the slags out to be worse than they are to stop people from running away. If you really want to get away, you could at least consider it."

"No," Darcy returned. "We won't go to the slags."

"Then you have your own understanding with the Pride, don't you? Even if you don't agree with everything they do, even if you're living in fear all the time, you have your own place here. If you won't break it, you can't expect anyone else to do it for you."

"We will break it," Darcy breathed. "We just need someone like you to show us how. Once you do that, we'll be happy to leave the Pride."

Dina sighed. "I'll let you know as soon as I figure it out for myself."

Chapter 41

Alexander Mathus tied Dina to a house support post. He tied her sitting up with her hands behind her back so she couldn't fall asleep. She stared straight ahead of her in the dark and listened to the steady breathing of the family around her.

Berys lay across the fire to guard her. Sonya slept on a makeshift mattress nearby the fire. Dina closed her eyes in a hopeless effort to doze off. The embers cast the only light in the room and she shivered from the cold.

All at once, a rustling sound and a flash of movement across the fire caught her eye. Two eyes gleamed in the dark and Dina stared at Sonya. The girl regarded her in silence across the fire. Then, with a flick of her wrist, Sonya flipped her blanket off her bed. It landed at Dina's feet.

Dina's stared at the blanket in amazement. It was close enough for her to reach.... if only her hands weren't tied.

Sonya couldn't move her legs, but she could move her arms. She pulled something out from under her legs and pitched it across the fire. It landed next to the post. Dina stared down at a knife blade glittering in the firelight. It was close enough for Dina to reach, too.

Dina raised her eyes and found Sonya staring at her with dead eyes. Then Sonya rolled away and turned her vacant gaze back to the ceiling.

Dina didn't wait for any further invitation. She swung her leg wide and hooked her heel over the knife. She nudged it closer to her hand and into her waiting fingertips. She glanced at Sonya while she worked the blade against the rope, but Sonya didn't look at her again.

The rope parted and Dina rocketed to her feet. She set the knife back on the hearth near Sonya. No one would ever know that Sonya helped her escape.

Dina snatched the blanket and ran for the door. She wrapped one finger at a time over the latch and froze on the threshold to listen.

The cloudy sky blocked out all light from the moon and stars. She had to find some kind of light. Did the village have a night watchman? Did cats patrol the roads this far away from the city?

She should have asked more questions about their night procedures, but it was too late now. She tightened the blanket around her shoulders against the cold.

While she stood listening, a jingling sound and a faint pinpoint of light came bobbing along the road. A watchman strolled past swinging swung a lighted lantern in his hand and scanning the village on either side. He didn't search very carefully. His people stayed in their beds at night. Only Dina could afford to lose sleep.

The watchman's lantern and his step told her which direction to go. She ducked from one building corner to a fence and onward to a woodshed. She followed the watchman up the road all the way to the edge of the village.

She never knew what she did to tip him off, but something must have caught his attention. He stopped on the road and raised his lantern. He swept his ears back and forth to catch any stray sound.

Dina hid behind the woodshed hardly daring to breathe. The watchman turned back on his beat, but he didn't lower his lantern.

She could only hold her breath for so long. He must have heard her and he stopped opposite the shed. Then he veered to one side and headed straight for her. She broke from her hiding place and tore out of the village, but she waited too long. He overtook her in a few steps and grabbed her by the blanket.

He yanked her off her feet with one tug. Her feet flew out from under her and she toppled onto her back staring up at the starless sky. She could be sleeping in Renfroe's warm house right now instead of lying in the chilly dirt.

The watchman's voice snapped her back to her senses. "So you tried to run after all." She didn't recognize his voice. Alexander must have told him to keep an eye out for her. He set his lantern on the ground and stood over her. His black shadow loomed against the sky, but she couldn't make out his face.

His voice boomed in her face. "Well, come on. We'll make sure this doesn't happen again."

He grabbed two handfuls of her blanket and heaved. Her last chance at freedom slipped away and she jolted out of her stupor. She swung her arms up and threw her blanket off. His grip broke and she kicked him in the knee.

He staggered away still clutching the empty blanket. She would have liked to make a clean break then and there, but she couldn't get out of the village in total darkness.

She jumped on top of him. He stumbled away from her in a wild effort to free his hands from the blanket. Dina pummeled his face and body with blows. He tripped and fell, and in a flash, Dina snatched the blanket out of his hands.

He gave it up willingly to fend her off. The next instant, she jumped clear and tossed the blanket over the lantern. Pitch darkness fell over the village. She scooped up the blanket-wrapped lantern and ran.

The watchman couldn't follow her without the light. All she had to do was stay quiet and hidden. He looked around as best he could, but she hid under a bench, and eventually, he had to leave.

She kept the lantern covered until she felt the heat radiating through the blanket. She unwrapped it enough to keep the blanket from catching fire and to stop any ray of light from escaping.

She waited an hour or two to make certain no one followed her out of the village. Male voices rang out of the houses and running feet pounded down the road, but as long as she sat still, they'd never find her.

The village settled into silence again and she snuck out of her hiding place. She uncovered the lantern just enough to see where she was going and she slipped out of the village.

She found the path leading into the jungle and buried herself and her lantern under the canopy. Once she got out of danger, she hurried on her way without worrying anymore about making any noise.

She broke tree branches and waded through dried leaves. She didn't care about anything but getting far away from Prideland.

She couldn't find the pod at night even with the lantern. She planned to hole up somewhere until daylight, but she changed her plans. She kept moving until dawn and beyond. She followed the path, but by daybreak, she no longer knew where she was.

She blew out the lantern and kept walking all day. Jungle surrounded her on all sides. She drank water from dripping leaves, but she refused to acknowledge the hunger gnawing at her guts. She forced the pain down into her legs and drove herself onward.

The sun slipped down toward the horizon and the jungle chilled. She wrapped the blanket around her shoulders, but she couldn't relight the lantern. She'd have to stop for the night, but she couldn't sleep on the ground with cats prowling around.

She almost collapsed at dusk, but just as all hope left her, she came in sight of a tall fence built of logs lashed together. The fence surrounded a timber stockade and a man stood outside it. His hand rested on the frame of the only gate in the fence. This must be a canton where the slags lived. Horrible images flooded her mind of hollow-eyed skeletons gnawing human bones.

The man examined her and he noticed the blanket and the dark, cold lantern. He wore leather leggings and a leather jacket tied with a leather strap for a belt.

Leather boots covered his feet with leather laces winding up his calves. What could she possibly say to him? To her relief, he spoke first. "Did you come from the village?"

Dina nodded. "From the city."

"That's a long way," he remarked.

She glanced at the log fence. Thatched roofs jutted over it. "What is this place?"

He followed her gaze to the houses beyond the fence. "This is Daustina."

Chapter 42

Dina gasped out loud. "How do you know that name?"

The man at the canton gate eyed her more closely and frowned. "Who are you?"

"My name is Dina Dyer," she told him. "I'm a biologist from the Coalition Destroyer *Savannah*. I landed on this planet with a team to negotiate incorporating the population into our Coalition. We've been prisoners of the Pride ever since."

"The Coalition, huh?" The man snorted. "Well, what do you know about that? I thought the Coalition left us for dead."

Dina stared at him. "What are you talking about?"

"I'm Frank Mathus. Peter Mathus is my father."

She could barely get her voice to work. "What?!"

"Do you know who Peter Mathus is?"

"Of course, I do. He's High Chancellor of the Coalition. He's the one who sent us here, but he sent us here to bring back Alexander Mathus. No one said anything about Frank Mathus."

Frank humphed. "I'll bet he didn't. He thinks Alex will take over for him when he retires as Chancellor. He won't believe that Alex isn't interested in politics."

"Alexander is factor of the village I just came from."

"I know, but he became a factor because he was afraid not to. He thought he could protect his family better as a factor. He pretended to go along with all the rules and to speak the way everyone in the village expected him to speak. After a while, he started to believe his own act."

Dina stared at him. "How do you know all this?"

"How do you think I got here? I was on the shuttle with him when it crashed. We were together in the village for almost three months. After he became factor and started leaning on the rest of us to cooperate—to come to an understanding with the Pride, as they put it—I left and came here."

"But what is this place? Is it another village?"

Frank nodded. "It's a village, but it isn't part of the Pride. We don't pay them tribute and we don't send people to work in their cities. We keep separate from them."

"You don't have an understanding with the Pride. You must be slags."

Frank smiled. "That's the word they use for us."

Dina pointed to the fence. "This must be a canton. I thought…" She didn't finish her sentence.

"I know what you thought. I've heard the same stories about the cantons. Of course the Pride has to make our life out to be as unpleasant as possible to stop people from leaving."

"Do many people leave Prideland?"

"Not many. I think I'm the last one to come out." He glanced at her. "Besides you, I mean."

"They do seem to have everybody locked up pretty tight."

Frank tugged the gate to close it. "I tried to convince Darcy, Alex's wife, to come out here with me. I tried to convince her that she owed it to her children, but it was because of the children that she chose to stay. She thought they needed their father."

"Do you know about the House of Man?"

He nodded. "We all saw it done. I don't know how any parent could subject their child to that barbaric piece of torture."

"She told me she had to go along with it. She said she would get visited if she didn't."

"Who did?" he asked.

"Alexander Mathus's wife."

His eyes widened. "You spoke to her?"

"Alexander caught me sneaking through their village. I stayed with them until they decided to send me back to the city. Their daughter, Sonya, got the House of Man while I was there."

Frank gasped. "What? She didn't!"

Dina nodded. "I had to stand there and watch."

He groaned and turned away. "I can't believe it! I can't believe even Alex would fall so far."

"They called it a Children's Festival if you can believe that."

He growled under his breath. "So you must have heard Alex's talk about how wonderful the cats are. He never lets anyone out of his sight without telling them all about it."

Dina had to smile. Her heart soared talking to him. She wasn't losing her mind after all. "He blew a bunch of sunshine up the leg of my pants about how he was governor of a Coalition planet and how the Senate had been endowed with messianic powers to decide the best interests of everyone on the planet."

"It's the same old story. He'll never change. He *can't* change, now that he's factor."

Dina stared at him. Then she burst out laughing from sheer relief and exhaustion. "I can't tell you how delighted I am to meet someone who understands. He said this planet will never join the Coalition since no one can do any better than to take their place in the Pride. It was the same nonsense they told us at the festivals. You must have heard it a thousand times."

"I've heard it all. When did you talk to Darcy? When did she tell you she only gave Sonya the House of Man to pacify Alex?"

"He must know she doesn't agree with everything because he told her not to talk to me at all. They got some other woman who is loyal to the Pride to come in and explain the whole thing."

"The House of Man, you mean?"

Dina nodded. "This woman spouted a bunch of gibberish about how it doesn't hurt the children and it actually helps them because it allows them to become helpers in the city."

"You still haven't explained about Darcy."

"After Alexander left, Darcy came over to talk to me by herself. She said she and some of the other villagers wanted to get out. She doesn't think her children are safe in the village anymore."

"She doesn't want to get out," Frank countered. "I went back about six weeks ago. I snuck into the village and offered to get her out, but she turned me down. When I told her I planned to bring her here, she refused. She said she couldn't make her children live like this."

"She did say she wouldn't go to the cantons. She said they were horrible places."

Frank shook his head. "She's never seen one. She doesn't know how good or bad it is."

"She said she didn't want her children to get the House of Man."

"She's lying," Frank replied. "She had it done to Sonya, so she must agree with it."

"She said she only did it because Alexander insisted. She doesn't agree with it herself."

"It doesn't matter if she agrees with it or not. She had it done. That's all that matters. She can say whatever she wants. If she had it done, she agrees with it."

"What could she do?" Dina asked. "She couldn't go against her husband. He's the village factor."

"She could come here. Don't tell me no one in Prideland has a choice. They all have a choice. That's what we're here for—to give them a choice."

Dina stared into the dark jungle. "I still can't get the House of Man out of my mind. It was horrific."

Frank looked down at the ground. "The first time I saw it done, I made up my mind to get away. I hiked out to the jungle to try to repair our shuttle, but it was completely destroyed. Then I came here."

Dina brightened up. "Did you name this canton—sorry, I mean village. Did you name it Daustina?"

"Yes. The people here didn't have a name for it before I came. They called it a canton and they called themselves slags. I convinced them to stop using Prideland words against themselves."

"You must have known something about the planet before you crashed. That name exists in the Coalition records. Scanning crews gave the planet that name."

"When our shuttle broke the atmosphere and crashed in the jungle, I skimmed the records to find out all I could before our onboard computer blinked out. I just had time to read the name and not much else."

She stared at him. "I can't believe neither the Chancellor nor Captain Doyle mentioned you. If I hadn't met you here, I never would have known you existed."

"Believe it," he snapped.

"If we accomplished our mission of rescuing Alexander and bringing him and his family back to the Coalition, we would have left you behind. You could have spent your whole life here and never known we were here and taken your brother away."

Frank smiled sadly. "That's what happens when a father worships his first-born son but doesn't care much about his second son."

"That's not right!"

Frank shrugged. "Come inside. It's long past time we locked up for the night. You can stay at my house tonight until we figure out what to do with you."

He held the gate open for her, but she hung back. "You're not going to send me back, are you?"

"We don't send people back. If anyone takes the trouble to come all this way to get away from the Pride, they're more than welcome here. I only meant you can stay at my house until *you* decide what you want to do."

"What else is there to do but stay?"

Frank lashed the gate closed with a leather thong and led her into the canton. "You'd be surprised. A few young people come out from the villages. They usually come right around the time they get the House of Man or else just before their families send them to the cities as helpers. They stay for a while. Then they go back."

"How could they go back knowing what's waiting for them?"

"When they grow up with it from birth, they can't shake it off so easily. You and I have it easy. We grew up with freedom. This way of life violates everything we know about human life. These people have no concept of that."

"Still," she replied, "you would think they would know better. If they know enough to come here in the first place, they must realize the Pride is their enemy."

"The Pride is their enemy," he agreed. "The Pride is also their family. Their fathers are factors. Their mothers hold them down to get the House of Man. They're told all their lives, from the moment they learn to talk, that their lives are dedicated to the Pride. They don't know anything else."

"But they come here. You must tell them the truth."

"We tell them, but it doesn't work very often. We can't undo decades of learning. If they stay here, they'll never see their parents or families or friends again. They want to share their families' lives. The only way to do that is to come to an understanding with the Pride—I mean, to come to the understanding the Pride wants them to have."

"The understanding that you're a slave."

"That's right. Most people would rather be slaves than be alone. We're a social species. We want families, friends, and a place in society. On this planet, that place is in the Pride. No one wants to be a slag."

Chapter 43

F rank led Dina to the main cluster of buildings in the middle of the canton. The houses stood on stilts off the ground. Stick ladders lashed together with leather thongs rose from the ground to the doorways. A welcoming rectangle of light shone out of every doorway.

"This is my house." Frank took the lantern out of Dina's hand, shimmied up the ladder, and disappeared inside.

Dina climbed up after him and found herself in a room exactly like any room back on Earth except that everything had been handmade.

A sturdy table sat in the center of the room surrounded by straight-backed chairs. One long counter ran along one wall where a woman chopped vegetables and gourds with stone tools. A pot steamed over a bed of glowing embers in a stone tray set into her workspace.

A boy and a girl tumbled over the furniture across the room. Every piece of furniture had been built of bent wooden frames stretched with animal skins. Lanterns hung from the rafters and filled the house with light. The light glowed on the leather chairs and the spotless wooden plank floor.

Frank chuckled in Dina's ear. "Not what you expected, is it?"

Dina shook her head in amazement.

"They sit on the floor over pits in the ground back in the village and they say we live like animals. They have to say that. Who would stay in the village if they knew the truth? Who wouldn't run away?"

He went over to the counter. The woman listened to their conversation over her shoulder while she worked. "This is Elana and this is...." He turned to Dina and faltered.

She smiled. "I'm Dina."

"That's right." Frank slapped his thigh. "Dina Dyer from the Coalition Destroyer *Savannah*. How could I forget? She's just come from the city. She's going to stay with us until she figures herself out."

He strolled across the room and threw himself into a chair. "Have a seat. We'll eat in a minute."

Dina took the chair opposite him, but she couldn't stop staring at everything in astonishment. She'd never seen such a beautiful home. She couldn't ask for a more welcoming place to spend the night.

The children kept tussling and scrapping, but their eyes gravitated toward Dina. The girl worked her way from seat to seat, closer and closer to Dina, but the girl still didn't dare to speak. Her brother jumped and bounced around the room and made no end of noise.

"Settle down, Jule," his mother called from the kitchen counter. "You'll frighten our guest away."

Jule laughed. He flipped over a chair and crashed onto the floor. When he sat up, he grinned at Dina, more pleased with himself than ever.

"You'll break your neck one of these days," Frank told him.

"It's wonderful to see children acting like children," Dina said. "I didn't think there were any children on this planet who knew how to play anymore....and it's so beautiful to see children who haven't had the House of Man."

Frank pointed to the girl. "This is Finlie. We have to lock the children up at night to protect them from the cats, but other than that, it does them good to run wild."

"What's the House of Man?" the girl asked.

Frank smiled at her. She was too old to be his daughter. "It's something you don't ever have to worry about."

The girl glanced at Dina. "Did you really come from the city?"

"Yes."

Finlie's eyes flew open. "What's it like?"

Dina glanced at Frank. Elana watched them from the kitchen. "It's nowhere near as nice as here."

Finlie wrinkled up her nose. She'd heard that a thousand times. She'd seen people escape from Prideland, only to return to it.

Elana put the food on the table and Frank climbed out of his chair. "Come and eat."

The children left their play and joined the adults at the table. Elana served each person a dish before sitting down.

"You said you lock everything up against prowling cats," Dina said to Frank. "Are there many cats out in the jungle at night?"

"I don't know how many there are, but it only takes one to wreak havoc. That's why we build our houses off the ground. We lock the gate and pull up the ladders at night. It's not enough to stop them if they do come, but it will slow them down. The noise of a cat climbing the fence and up the leg of a house might give us enough warning to get away."

"Can't you fight back?"

"With what? We've got no weapons other than bows and arrows, spears, and stone knives."

"Can't you get weapons from the villages?"

Frank shook his head. "If they had weapons in the village—which they don't—the Pride strictly prohibits the village people from having anything to do with us. Give us weapons—are you kidding? They could be killed for that."

"Do you mean 'visited'?"

"I mean killed. A person who gets visited doesn't get killed."

"What does 'visited' mean?" she asked. "I can't get anyone to tell me."

"I don't know what it means. All I know is it's a punishment for stepping out of line."

"I guessed that and it's not the cats who do the visiting. Renfroe—that's my benefactor—I mean, that's the tiger I used to live with."

Frank interrupted. "You mean your master?"

Dina blushed down at her soup. "Yeah. My master."

"What did he tell you?"

"He told me the cats don't do the visiting. He insisted on it most emphatically."

"No, the factors do it. That's the only real qualification for becoming a factor. You have to be willing to visit anyone who breaks the rules."

"Did your brother visit anyone?"

Frank pushed his food around in the bowl with his spoon and nodded.

Dina glanced across the table and caught Jule and Finlie listening to the conversation with wide eyes. "I'm sorry," she muttered. "We shouldn't talk about this in front of the children."

"That's all right." Frank's eyes slid across to Finlie. "They need to know the truth about Prideland."

Despite his assurance, her comment ended the conversation. No one mentioned Prideland throughout the rest of the meal. Frank and Dina relaxed in the sitting area afterward while Elana cleaned up. Jule and Finlie entertained them with their acrobatics.

Frank glanced over and caught Dina rubbing her eyes. "You look like you haven't slept in days."

She did her best to smile. "I haven't, not since I left the city."

"Follow me. I'll show you to your bed."

Frank climbed up another ladder rising through a hole in the ceiling. At the top, a tiny chamber opened into three bedrooms tucked under the roof.

"You'll stay here." Frank pointed to one of the rooms. "We don't get many guests, but no one's using this room at the moment, so it's yours until you decide what to do."

"Thank you."

Frank nodded. "I stayed in this room when I first came out from the village. It's a very nice room. Very comforting to the disturbed soul."

"That's just what I need."

"Get some sleep. You look like something out of the graveyard."

She laughed. "Thanks."

He hopped down the ladder out of sight.

A faint glimmer shone up through the ladder hole and brightened the little bedroom. Silvery moonlight streamed through gaps in the wall. A tanned skin covered the bed with the hair facing down. Underneath it, another tanned hide covered a lattice of leather straps tied to the bed frame.

Dina sat down and ran her hand over the hide brushed and buffed to downy softness. The woven lattice underneath swayed and supported her like a hammock.

She lay down and pulled the fur over her. The head of the bed looked out through the gap in the wall and gave her a glorious view of the night sky. The moon sailed overhead in a sea of stars. The fur trapped her body heat and that was the last thing she remembered before she fell asleep.

Chapter 44

Tree lizards leapt from one tree to another in the first light of dawn. Dina listened to them screeching back and forth in the upper canopy and watched them through the crack between the boards.

Every detail of her escape from Prideland came back to her in the tiny bedroom. Frank was right about that. The room really was balm for the troubled soul.

She finally crept down the ladder and found the house door open and the ladder in place down to the ground. She went down it and found Frank lacing up his boots.

"What are you doing awake?" he asked. "I told you to sleep."

"I slept better in that room than I've slept since I landed on this crazy planet."

He smiled. "I told you that room is special. Everyone who leaves Prideland should spend their first night there. It does something to your mind."

"What does it do?"

"I don't know. Maybe it restores your belief in beauty. It shows you a life outside of Prideland. Even if you only see it for one night, at least you've seen it. You can take that knowledge with you, even if you go back to Prideland." He stamped his feet down into his boots. "I'm going hunting. We can talk some more when I get back tonight."

"I want to find my pod if I can. Maybe you could help me."

He nodded. "I know the jungle around here pretty well, but others know it better. Some of them may already know where your pod is. Will you go back to your ship?"

"I hope so. Will you come?"

"I'll have to think it over. I have a pretty good life here. I'm happy with Elana and the kids."

"Whose kids are they?"

"Their father died a few years ago. I stayed with them when I first left the village. I enjoyed it so much that I stayed. I'll talk it over with Elana. Maybe she and the kids will want to leave, too. Then we can all go together."

"What about Darcy and the others from your shuttle?" she asked. "Your brother made it pretty clear he wasn't interested in leaving. He also gave me to understand that none of the others would be leaving, either. We'd have to sneak them out without letting the factors know."

"I can do that. I've been back to the village twice already to talk to Darcy. I don't know if she will come even with a clear way back to the Coalition, but we can try. How many people will your pod carry?"

"No more than ten, but we can use the Pod's communications system to contact the *Savannah*. They can send another shuttle to lift more people off the planet. We won't leave anyone behind who wants to leave."

"What about your people in the city? Will you go back for them?"

Dina winced. "Tom doesn't want to leave. He still wants to try to salvage our mission and he's pretty attached to his benefactor—I mean, his master."

"And the others?"

"I'm sure Tania will go. She's out of her mind with fear and Matthew was in pretty bad shape the last time I saw him. He doesn't get along so well with his.... with Fallon."

Frank narrowed his eyes. "I know that name. That's the Manx, isn't it?"

"Yes. He's pretty fierce."

Frank shrugged. "No fiercer than the other cats of the Pride. You got lucky with your tiger or maybe you just haven't gotten to know the cats well enough to believe what they are capable of."

"I don't plan to stick around long enough to find out. I'm going back to the *Savannah*. You should come, too."

"I'll think about it." Frank slung a quiver of arrows across his back. stuck a chipped stone knife into his belt, and picked up a bow. "I'll see you later. Try to take it easy today. You have a lot of work to do before you leave."

The canton came to life with morning activity. Women climbed down their ladders and carried buckets to a well in the center of the village. Hordes of boisterous children barreled around the stilts of the houses, shouting and tackling each other.

Jule and Finlie ran with the crowd and they must have told their friends about Dina. Several children came right up to her and questioned her about the Pride and the village and the city. They wanted to know all about the helpers, especially children sent by their parents to serve the cats.

Dina evaded their questions at first. After a while, though, she started to understand Frank's point. The only way to counteract the Pride's influence on these children was to tell them the truth.

She sat down on a stump and told them more than they wanted to hear about the hunt, the House of Man, the festivals, the classes, and the helpers.

They listened with wide eyes and their mouths hanging open. Dina told them how Sonya's parents planned to pack her off to the city as soon as she recovered from the House of Man.

Then Dina told them what she'd seen of Fallon and the Helions attacking people and injuring them. The children hung on every word. Maybe they didn't believe it, but they had to hear it.

When she finished, they stared at her in silence for several minutes. Then, with a shout and a skip, they disappeared back to their games.

The canton subsisted entirely on hunting. Food production consisted of skinning, butchering, and preserving the carcasses of animals hunted in the jungle. Groups of hunters trickled into the village throughout the day bringing everything from tree lizards to water oxen.

The moment someone appeared at the gate with a dead animal, people of all ages gathered around to help process it. The younger children helped mostly by bombarding the hunter with questions and getting in the way. The adults gave older children simple jobs like bringing water and cleaning up.

Dina watched the skinning and butchering for a while. Then she explored the canton. She found her way to a covered work area with no walls that served as a communal tannery. Fresh skins arrived from the butchering operations and she watched the tanning process from start to finish.

Dina hung around the tannery until late afternoon. Just as she got ready to return to Frank's house, she caught sight of a bin full of leather scraps in the corner. Elana noticed her fondling the mellow leather and came over to talk to her.

"I've never seen leather this fine," Dina told her. "Nothing on Earth can compare with this."

"Help yourself. The scraps in that bin are free for anyone to take."

Dina rubbed one piece between her fingers. "I'd like to make you and your family a gift to show my appreciation for taking me in."

Elana shrugged, but her face glowed. "We don't need anything, but I appreciate you thinking of us."

"Maybe I could make something for the kids."

"That would be nice. Finlie's developed quite a fascination for you."

"She has?" Dina asked. "Did she tell you that?"

"She didn't have to tell me. She's fascinated with anything having to do with Prideland."

Dina cringed. "I'm sorry to hear that."

"I worry about her. A little while ago, she came up to me and repeated everything you told her about the House of Man and the helpers in the city. She asked me if it was true. When I told her it was, she really had to think hard about Prideland. She realized it's not the fairyland she thinks it is."

"Do young people leave Daustina for Prideland?"

"Sometimes. They're just curious to see what it's like. Sometimes they come back as soon as they realize what it's all about. Sometimes they come back injured. Sometimes they come back on the verge of death and sometimes they don't come back at all."

"I didn't think the Pride would accept a slag from the cantons. They say they won't have anything to do with a slag."

"Oh, they're more than happy when someone comes to Prideland. It's a victory for them. Of course, they're extra hard on any reclaimed slags they get their hands on. The very first thing they do is give them the House of Man. If they survive that and still want to be part of the Pride, they can earn their place there, but they'll never be more than an ordinary slave just like everyone else."

"Some reward," Dina exclaimed.

"By the time they know enough to understand, they've been fully integrated into the Pride. They've been threatened and cajoled and lied to until they come to the understanding the Pride wants them to come to. After that, it's very hard for them to leave. Sometimes they do it. Sometimes they get caught trying to escape and punished or killed. You know how it is."

"I know. My friend Tom has only been here a few weeks and he already believes he's found his rightful place in the universe. It doesn't matter to him that he's First Officer of an Armada ship on the way to being a captain or even an admiral. He's happy to stay here and be a cat's house pet."

Frank strolled up to them.

"Did you get anything?" Elana asked him.

He nodded. "I got a couple of tree lizards. Jule and his friends are cleaning them up." He turned to Dina. "I found someone who knows where your pod is. He'll show you where it is and how to find it on your own."

"Great!" Dina exclaimed.

Frank and Dina went back to the main gate. "Several other people have told me they want to leave this planet when you go."

"How many?"

"Three families. That's fifteen people, including children and babies."

"In that case, we should contact the *Savannah* to send us another craft. We can't lift off all those people with the Pod."

"The whole operation could wind up taking a lot longer than you think," he replied. "You're welcome to stay here or you could return to your ship and make the arrangements."

"Have you thought any more about what you'll do?"

"I'll talk to Elana about it. I still want to go back to the village to try to get Darcy and her children out. There are a few other people from the shuttle that I think will want to go. It could take time."

"We have a little over a week before the Pod's power packs run down. We should conserve power and only contact the *Savannah* when we're ready for them to do something. I still have to figure out how to get in touch with my teammates in the city. I don't want to go back to the *Savannah* without them."

"How will you get them out?" Frank asked.

Dina gazed off into the jungle. "I don't know. I might ask Captain Doyle to send us a squad of security officers armed with proton cannons. That will make the cats stand back if nothing else will."

"But you said your First Officer won't want to leave. What will you do about him?"

Dina turned away. "I don't know."

Chapter 45

An elderly man appeared at the gate. He wore the same hunting clothes and paid keen attention to everything around him. He led Frank and Dina into the jungle until, sure enough, the old man guided them to the pod.

The jungle covered it so completely they probably wouldn't have been able to get the door open. "Will you open it up?" Frank asked.

She shook her head. "I'll use the communication system to call the ship when we know how many people we need to transport. The way we're going, we might need two shuttles instead of one."

Their guide took Dina on a tour of the jungle paths so she could find her way to the Pod by herself. He also showed her the path back to the village and the city. She told him she would never go back there, but he only shrugged and walked away.

Frank and Dina returned to the house. Dina worked on her gift for Finlie while Elana made the evening meal.

Dina used a bone needle borrowed from Elana and sinew to stitch the leather. After hours of work, she succeeded in cobbling together something distantly resembling a shape.

Finlie came up to her after dinner. "What are you making?"

Dina held it out to her. "It's for you. It's a doll."

She burst into a radiant smile. "For me?"

"I know it isn't much to look at, but you could play with it and pretend. I understand if you don't want it. I just wanted to give you something."

Finlie immediately tucked the doll into the crook of her elbow and swung it back and forth in a pantomime of rocking a baby. "Go to sleep, little darling," she sang and giggled at herself. "Thank you. I always wanted one."

"Don't you have any of your own?"

She tossed her head. "I've had lots, but I don't play with them anymore. This one is special because it came from you. I've never had a gift from anyone who came from the city."

Dina flinched again. "Finlie, promise me you'll never go to Prideland."

The girl's eyes flew open. "Why not?"

"It's a bad place with a lot of bad people. I wouldn't want anything to happen to you."

Even as she spoke those words, Dina knew Finlie didn't care about anything Dina said. Finlie made up her mind a long time ago to see Prideland for herself. Nothing would stop her.

Frank and Elana watched them with sad eyes. Finlie had passed out of their reach.

The next morning, Dina met Frank in the same place at the bottom of the ladder. "I just met a whole group of people outside," he told her. "They all came here to talk to you. I told them you were still asleep. If I hadn't stopped them, they would have woken you up."

"What do they want to talk to me about? I hope I didn't offend them. Maybe I shouldn't have told the children about Prideland."

"It isn't that. They all want to leave. They want you to evacuate the whole canton—man, woman, and child. They also want you to get in touch with the other cantons and offer them evacuation, too, and that's not counting all the people who might want to leave when the word gets out in Prideland."

Dina's eyes popped out of her head. "Really? I wasn't expecting that."

"I was going out hunting this morning, but I've changed my mind. I'll walk over to the cantons nearest us. I'll put out the word that you're going to evacuate us and for everyone who wants to leave to get ready. That will take most of the day. Tomorrow, I'll go into the village to talk to Darcy. She'll let her people know our plan. Then you and I will walk out to your pod so you can contact your ship."

"The *Savannah* doesn't have enough shuttles to evacuate that many people."

"That's why we should contact the ship right away. This evacuation will take several trips, so we need to get started. These people want to leave as soon as possible. Some have newborn babies and sick children that they want to receive medical care. I hope your ship can handle them all."

"One way or the other, you should come up to explain the situation to your father," she told him. "He won't believe Alexander stayed of his own free will unless he hears it from you."

"He won't believe it even if he *does* hear it from me," Frank shot back. "As a matter of fact, if he hears it from me, he'll probably think I poisoned my brother or something like that. My father always thinks the worst of me. He always thinks I corrupted Alex and led him astray when it was actually the other way around. He'll believe you more than me, but if you think it will help, I'll talk to him."

"Have you talked to Elana about leaving?"

He nodded. "We talked about it last night. She wants to leave. She's worried about Finlie and her fascination with Prideland. She's worried Finlie will run away. She wants to get her as far away from Prideland as possible."

"I don't blame her. She's a good mother for protecting her daughter."

"I agree with you and I agree with her. I've been happier here than anywhere else in my life, but I'm willing to go back to the Coalition to protect Finlie—and Jule, too."

"Well, we have a lot to do," she remarked. "We're supposed to be incorporating this planet into the Coalition, not evacuating the population. I wonder what Captain Doyle will say."

"Have you thought about getting your friends out? Me getting into the village to talk to Darcy is one thing. You going back to the city and convincing your friends to escape without getting caught is another thing altogether."

"That's true," she murmured.

"You'd be taking your life in your hands going back."

She looked away.

He laid his hand on her shoulder. "Just think about it."

"All right. I will."

He moved toward the gate. "I'll see you later."

She hung around the gate for a long time after he left and thought things over. Her past was gone and she had no future. She couldn't stop her mind from spinning over all the possibilities.

By the end of the day, she didn't even bother to walk around the canton anymore. She waited by the gate for Frank to come back. Finlie and her friends ran by. Dina smiled when she saw the girl clutching her doll. At least Finlie would get out of here soon.

Hunters trickled into the canton in ones and twos and threes. Dina's heart raced every time one of them emerged from the trees. Then she wilted when she saw that it wasn't Frank. She paced back and forth by the gate trying to calm down until the next hunter came along.

The sun set and shadows lengthened through the jungle until she couldn't see beyond the first row of trees. She would have to go indoors soon. Then she saw him. She jumped up and ran toward him. He laughed when he saw her. "Don't get excited. I'm going straight back out."

"Aren't you coming back to the house?"

"I have to go back out. I have to head to the village if I want to get in touch with Darcy."

"It'll be pitch dark in a few minutes."

"I can only get into the village at night. They stay in their houses at night, so I have to wait until day to talk to Darcy. Then I have to wait for the next night to get *out* of the village again. I won't see you until the day after tomorrow."

Her smile faded. "I thought we would plan our strategy tonight."

"You'll have to do that without me. I only came back here to tell you the other cantons want to leave, too."

"How many people is that?"

"About five hundred, I would say and that's not counting the cantons we haven't spoken to. Word will spread, and when it does, more people will come forward."

Dina's head spun. "I have to talk to Captain Doyle about this."

"Wait until I get back. When I do, I'll know how the subsidiaries feel. If word gets out in the villages, you could wind up needing more than one starship to get them all out."

Her shoulders drooped. "I thought we would be setting out for the pod tonight."

He smiled and patted her on the shoulders with both hands. "It will happen soon. Don't you worry. Just wait until I get back with word about the subsidiaries. Then we'll go. We need you thinking clearly because you're going to spearhead this whole operation."

Chapter 46

Dina drummed her fingers on the chair arm. She kept checking over her shoulder that the door was still closed.

Elana smiled at her from the kitchen counter. "You might as well relax. He won't be back for a long time."

"I know. He told me he wouldn't be back until the day after tomorrow at the earliest. It just seems like such a long time to wait."

"Then stop waiting. Do something else."

"What is there to do? Do you want me to help you get the food ready? I'd be happy to help you if it will make the time go faster."

"I don't need any help with the food. I was thinking more about planning the evacuation. There must be a lot of work to do before we can leave."

"That's just the problem. I can't do anything until I know how many people are leaving and none of us can go anywhere until I contact the *Savannah*. Frank wants me to wait until he gets back."

"That makes sense. There's no point contacting the ship until you know what you're going to tell them."

"It's all this waiting that gets me. I know it takes time to sneak into the village and then sneak out. You don't have to tell me. It just takes so long."

Elana laughed. "He's going faster than he should by coming back the day after tomorrow. He wants to speed things up so you can contact your people and get the evacuation under way. He should take a lot longer getting in and out."

"I guess he does this sort of thing all the time."

Elana shook her head. "He's done it three times. The last time he went, he got chased by cats. He had to hide in the cow shed for three days to disguise his scent until they went away. The old man who owned the shed saved him by telling the cats he hadn't seen Frank hiding there when he did." She laughed. "I was really worried about him that time."

Dina stared at her. "How can you laugh about it?"

Elana chuckled over her chopping block. "If I didn't laugh, I'd die of fright. I can't imagine being chased by one of those cats. I wouldn't let him go at all if I had a choice."

"I wouldn't go back for all the money in the world," Dina exclaimed.

"He only goes back for Darcy and her kids. He certainly wouldn't go back for his brother."

"Why does he care so much about Darcy?"

"It's her children he cares about. He was always their favorite uncle and he had a special relationship with Sonya and Anthony—that's the oldest boy. It took a lot for Frank to leave them behind, but Darcy wouldn't budge. She thought it was more important for them to stay with their father than to get away from the Pride."

"Do you agree with that?"

"I couldn't say. Speaking only for myself, just about anything would be better than living in the Pride, but after two and half years since my husband died, I see how hard it is on Jule to grow up without a father. Even with Frank and all the other men around, he needs his father. It might actually be worth staying in the Pride to give him that. I'm just glad I don't have to make that decision."

"What about you?" Dina asked. "You said you're happy to leave for Finlie's sake. Would you want to leave this planet if you were on your own?"

"I can't wait to leave! The whole galaxy is waiting for me to explore. When the kids get older, I could take up studying. I might even become a biologist." She laughed out loud.

Dina smiled. "You have your whole life ahead of you."

"You'll be happy getting back to your ship."

"I ought to be," Dina replied. "I ought to be ecstatic about getting away from Prideland, but I don't like leaving Tom—that's my fiancé. He's back in the city and he doesn't want to leave."

"You should be happy. You're young, you're beautiful, and you have all your training. You still have so much you can do with your life."

"I can't go back to the life I had before," Dina replied. "I've lost Tom. I don't know who or what I am anymore. I don't think I can go back to the Armada."

"What will you do instead?" Elana asked.

"I don't know. I'll have to go somewhere where no one knows anything about me. I'll have to go somewhere where I'm not Tom Sharples's fiancé. I might even go back to Earth."

"Would that be so bad? You sound like you'd be going to prison."

Dina smiled a sad smile. "It's silly, isn't it? I should have my head examined."

Dina didn't leave the house the next day. She had nothing to do until Frank got back. She kept Elana company and helped her with the chores. By the end of the day, her agitation eased. When Jule and Finlie went to bed after dinner, Elana sat in the chair opposite Dina.

"You should go to bed, too," Elana told her. "Frank will be back tomorrow and you'll have a big day hiking out to your craft to contact your ship. That's when the preparation will really start."

"I'm not tired."

"Are you excited?" Elana asked.

Dina shrugged. "Not really. I feel at home here. I understand now why Frank wasn't sure about leaving. I feel more at home here than I have for a long time. I could get used to staying here."

"You would get bored here. You've been out in space on a starship. You've explored other planets. You wouldn't want to stay here. You only feel safe here because of the danger you've been in. This canton could never be anything but a stopping place for someone like you. You would get over your fear after a while and then you would want to get out and explore again."

"*You* seem pretty happy here," Dina remarked. "I thought you would want to stay, too, to give your children a home."

"This is the only home my children could ever have. I wouldn't let them grow up in Prideland. Prideland is no place for children. This was the only other option."

"Did you grow up in Prideland?" Dina asked. "You seem to fit in so well here and I didn't think you had the House of Man. That's why I thought you were born out here in the jungle."

"I have the House of Man," Elana told her.

"But you don't walk hunched over like the others do."

"The cat who gave me the House of Man was an old lion. His claws weren't that sharp and I was the last child he ever gave it to. I don't think he did much more than break the skin."

Dina cocked her head. "Who was it?"

"It was Lord Helion. He was old even that long ago."

Dina cradled her head in her hand and groaned. "Not him!"

Elana nodded. "He doesn't do it anymore. He doesn't do enough damage and the factors won't stand for it, but I had to get it to become a helper."

Dina's eyes widened and she gasped. "You were a helper?"

Elana nodded. "My sister and I went to the city together. We wanted to stay together, but it didn't happen. My sister went to a very nice benefactor and I went to Lord Helion. I guess he took a liking to me when he gave me the House of Man. My parents never thought about sending me to be a helper until he said he wanted me, but that's where I wound up."

"So what happened? How did you wind up here?"

"I made the mistake of confiding in my sister. After I'd been at Helion House for a week, I went to see my sister at her benefactor's house. She worked in the kitchen as a cook. I told her what was going on at Helion House and I said I didn't want to stay anymore. I said I wanted to go home."

Something in her story struck Dina as familiar. "What's your sister's name?"

"Belinda," Elana replied. "She went to some big senator and he took good care of her."

Dina's teeth chattered. She hated to hear the rest of the story. "What did she say when you told her you wanted to leave?"

"She went wild. She screamed that I was nothing but a slag and I didn't deserve to be helper to a great cat like Lord Helion. She said I deserved to starve in the mud out in the jungle. I told her I would rather do that than serve in Helion House any longer."

Dina nodded. She could just hear Belinda's voice ringing in her ears and saying those words. "So you left."

"Not then. She was my older sister, after all. She convinced me to go back to Helion House. She said it couldn't possibly be as bad as I said it was. She said I should give it another chance and that Lord Helion wouldn't let anything bad happen to me."

Dina snorted. "Yeah, right."

Elana smiled. "She didn't know something bad already happened to me. I told her, but she didn't believe me. She said nothing like that ever happens in Prideland, but I saw it happening all the time at Helion House. They all did it."

"They still do," Dina murmured.

"I thought she must be right. I thought maybe it must have been a fluke. I went back."

"Big mistake."

Elana shrugged. "That was nothing. Belinda was the one who drove me out in the end. I probably wouldn't have had the courage to leave if it wasn't for her."

"What did she do?"

"She had me visited. She told on me—that I wanted to leave."

"What happened when you got visited?" Dina asked. "What does that mean?"

Elana waved to one side. "You know. It was the usual visit—nothing special—but it did the job. I left as soon as it was over. I started toward my village, but I knew what my parents would say if I came home in disgrace. I didn't stop. I just kept going and I wound up here."

"Have you been here ever since?"

Elana nodded. "I stayed in this house when I first came here. I met my husband that same night and I married him within a month. I've been here ever since."

"I can see why you want to get off this planet. You must be hungry for something other than this canton."

"We all are. We can't even explore this planet with the cats around. We have to stay inside the fence. Only the hunters go out for food. We want our children to get an education and to see the rest of the galaxy. We want to give them the same opportunities every other child has."

"Frank must have told you about the Coalition," Dina remarked.

Elana nodded. "We all know about it, but none of us has a chance to get there. If we stay here, we'll never see or experience any of the things your people take for granted."

"My benefactor wants the Pride to join the Coalition. He sits in the Senate and he tried to convince the Pride to incorporate."

"That will never happen. Why would the cats give up their power?"

Dina sighed. "That's what everybody says, even Renfroe. He says he's the only cat in the Pride who wants it."

"Even he doesn't want it," Elana argued. "Why would he give up hunting in the jungle and sitting on the stage of the Senate? If I had to guess, he only brought it up to the Senate because he knew it would fail."

"Why would he bother? Why would he alienate his fellow Senators over something he didn't care about?"

Elana turned away and started toward the ladder to her upstairs bedroom. "Maybe he had some other reason."

Chapter 47

D ina's eyes snapped open. She threw off her bedcovers and slid down the ladder. She tumbled out of the house and ran to the main gate. Dawn broke treetops and the tree lizards barely moved in the branches overhead. Of course Frank wasn't there.

Dina slumped against a fence post. How much longer did she have to wait? Hour passed after hour. The sun rose hot and sticky over the jungle, but he still didn't come.

Hunters went out for the day. Then they started coming back with their kills. The village came to life, but Dina didn't take part. She had to be ready to strike out for the pod the minute Frank got back.

She swallowed her hunger, but she couldn't get rid of her thirst. She gulped a mouthful of water from the well. Then she went back to her seat. The sun swept over the sky and the shadows swung around the other way.

No more hunters came out of the jungle. An old man waited to close the gate for the night and he waved to her to come inside. Her heart sank, but just as she turned to come inside the fence, she caught sight of Frank coming up the trail.

He caught her eye and smiled in recognition. She almost ran to meet him, but just as she passed through the gate, something behind him made her stomach turn. A huge crowd of cats loped into view with their heads lowered and their fangs glistening.

They didn't bother to follow the path. They came straight through the jungle and Renfroe charged at the head of the pack. Fallon, Khalid, Hector, and some of the younger Helions ran behind Renfroe.

She would have screamed if the cats hadn't looked so familiar. The childish notion flitted through her mind that she could explain everything to Renfroe and stop the bloodbath. She called out to him, but he didn't hear her. Frank saw the cats and ran for the gate.

The cats streaked past Dina and poured into the canton through the open gate. Screams pierced the jungle and frightened the tree lizards. Those screams should have come from Dina, but she only blinked at those long, sleek bodies sailing past her.

The cats bounded into the canton with nothing in the world to stop them. Frank charged after them and threw himself into the midst of the cats with nothing but his knife in his hand.

The unarmed people did their best to fight and run, but most had nothing to fight with besides their bare hands. The cats slashed their claws and teeth willy-nilly at unprotected flesh. They tore out a throat here and broke a neck there before leaping to their next victim.

Blood sprayed the stilts of the houses. Torn bodies flopped to the ground, quivered, and lay still. Smaller cats jumped on the children's heads and shoulders, scratched their eyes out, and ripped their flesh from their bones. Dina didn't see where Elana and her children fell. They could only have ended up in the great piles of corpses carpeting the ground inside the fence.

Frank planted his legs wide and bellowed his challenge to the cats. He brandished his knife and bared his teeth daring any of them to attack him.

One young Helion just sprouting his mane launched himself at Frank's head with his paws outstretched and his jaws open to bite. Frank brought his knife up in a cruel slice across the lion's neck. Frank jerked his arm and slashed the lion's throat. Steaming blood spurted across Frank's face.

The lion choked once and wilted in Frank's arms. Frank hurled the body aside and spun the other way to face his next attacker.

Fallon jumped for Frank's head, but Fallon offered a smaller target than the lion. Frank couldn't repeat the same maneuver so he clubbed Fallon away.

Fallon crashed into one of the stilts, bounced off, and landed on all four feet. He didn't attack again. He trotted away to find a more vulnerable target.

Dina stood transfixed at the gate. She would die along with the others as soon as the cats got rid of the slags. Then she saw another cat heading toward Frank and she ran with all her might to stop him.

Renfroe stood on top of a lifeless body on the other side of the canton. He raised his head from crushing the person's neck when he heard Fallon hit the post. Blood stained Renfroe's jowls and whiskers and he bared his fangs to answer Frank's bellowing.

Renfroe trotted across the canton picking up speed as he got nearer. Dina ran to get between him and Frank. Renfroe would never harm her. She could only stop him from attacking Frank by blocking him with her own body.

Without warning, a hard thump pounded her body. She took a fraction of a second to realize she was watching the scene from ground level. How did she get here? A great weight pinned her down, but it didn't stop her from witnessing the whole gruesome nightmare.

Dear, kind Renfroe raced between the stilts of the houses. Her benefactor didn't spring for Frank's head. Renfroe slammed all his powerful bulk into Frank's chest.

The impact knocked Frank's knife out of his hand and the rest was history. He hit the ground full length on his back. Renfroe's jaws crunched through his neck. He tore Frank's throat out with one power twist of his head.

Black blood flooded the ground around the body. An inarticulate grunt burst out of Dina's mouth. She couldn't draw air into her lungs to scream with that weight on her back, but Frank's murder couldn't go unanswered.

Renfroe heard the noise and turned toward her. She never would have recognized his blood-stained face. A killer's cold eyes stared at her and a fiend's blood-stained fangs snarled at her. She shut her mouth and silenced herself instantly.

The massacre didn't take long. In a few minutes, only the tree lizards' calls echoed through the treetops. Nothing but the cats moved in the canton. They sniffed out anyone who tried to hide and finished off the odd baby.

Whatever held Dina down on the ground stayed there until every other human being in the canton lay dead in the dirt. Then the weight lifted off her and air flooded her lungs.

She got to her feet, turned, and found Khalid blinking at her. Then he sauntered away to help the others finish off the formalities.

She blinked after him and then surveyed what was left of the canton. This couldn't be happening, but it was. It was all too terribly real.

A creaking, rattling sound approached out of the jungle and Dina stared at the string of ox carts pulling up to the canton gate. The villagers got to work loading the dead bodies onto their carts. The cats loped away and vanished into the jungle. And who should Dina see coming toward her at that moment? Harmon Farley.

He grabbed her by the arm and marched her to the nearest wagon. He tied her hands behind her back and then he tied her wrists to her ankles. Without a word, he circled her waist with his hands, lifted her up, and pitched her on top of the bodies. She cried out in surprise, but he ignored her.

The wet, limp bodies still gave off the last of their warmth underneath her. That warmth seeped into her along with their blood. Their dwindling heat drove back the cold of approaching night.

Farley climbed into the driver's seat and whipped his oxen forward.

"Where are you taking me?" Dina asked.

"Back to the city."

"Where are you taking these people?" she asked.

"Back to the city."

The cart lurched forward and Dina fell down on her bed of corpses. Night fell and stopped her from seeing where she was going.

The bodies went cold soon enough. She couldn't think about them anymore. At all costs, she had to get the memory of the massacre out of her head. She closed her eyes and fell asleep.

She woke up when the cart stopped moving. The corpses lay hard and stiff underneath her. Her arms and legs ached. Dawn lightened the sky. She didn't recognize where she was. Only the buildings and cobbled streets told her she was back in the city.

Farley yanked her off the wagon and cut the ropes binding her. He dragged her by one arm and pushed her through a doorway in one of the buildings. Only when she got inside did she realize it was Helion House.

She stood in the doorway of the big gymnasium and rubbed the sore spot on her arm. The next minute, Farley and the other wagon people shoved her out of their way. They wrangled the bodies off the wagon, carried them through the door, and dumped them on the gymnasium floor.

Then came the most disgusting nightmare of all. The cats who massacred those people trotted in and started tearing the bodies apart. Without further ado, they pulled the bodies to pieces, chewed them up, and ate them.

Pretty soon, other cats from the city arrived and joined in the feast. Dina recognized many of them from the market and from her walks through the streets. The scene turned into a gluttonous orgy in no time....and there was Renfroe enjoying himself along with the others, the founder of the feast.

Dina stared as long as she could stand it. Then she ran. She didn't care if they caught her and killed her. She didn't care if Renfroe got mad and sold her to the Elite Battalion. She had to get out of there.

She ran through the streets of the city that had now become familiar to her. She ran all the way back to Renfroe's house, her old sanctuary. She had nowhere else to run.

She ran around the back of the house to the garden gate. She let herself in and found the portico standing open the way it always was. She ran down the corridor to her old room. She shut the door and hid under the blanket on her bed. She waited for Renfroe to come back and do whatever he wanted with her.

Chapter 48

Dina must have fallen asleep, because when she woke up, it was morning again. A full day had passed without anyone disturbing her.

She got up and left the room. Not a sound echoed through the house. She waited for Renfroe or Belinda or someone to come, but no one came. She started to worry. What was going on? What horrors could she expect next?

Then she heard the familiar rattle of utensils coming from the kitchen and she went to the door to listen. Yes, someone was in there. She went in and found Belinda at her work, but it wasn't the Belinda she remembered.

When Dina appeared in the doorway, Belinda jumped and cried out in surprise. Her hand flew to her heart and tears sprang into her eyes.

Dina gasped at the sight of her. Black bruises and weeping gashes disfigured Belinda's face. Her lower lip pouted from swelling and oozed blood from a crusty split in the swollen skin.

One eyelid drooped closed and one whole side of her face sagged in a grotesque, elephantine mask. Her nose had been smashed flat into her face.

"What happened to you, Belinda?" Dina choked.

Belinda tried to put up her old gruff exterior, but her one good eye betrayed her. "What are you doing back here?"

"Belinda, what happened to you?"

Belinda turned away to hide her face. "Isn't it obvious?"

"No, it isn't. I wouldn't ask if it was. Tell me who did this to you."

"Leave me alone!" She tried to yell, but she ended up sobbing instead. "Get out of my kitchen! You aren't welcome here. You might be Renfroe's helper so he can decide if you belong in this house, but you won't come into this kitchen again. I won't have it!"

"Belinda, let me help you." Dina's voice trembled with despair. "Tell me what I can do to help you."

"Get out of here!" Belinda shrieked. "Can't you see you've done enough?"

Dina's eyes popped. "What did I do? At least tell me what I did to hurt you."

"Don't you ever talk to me ever again!" Belinda screamed. "I don't want to see your face as long as I live!"

"Belinda...."

"Shut up!" she screeched. She covered her ears with her hands, but the next instant, she took them down and bared her horrible face to Dina's sight. "Do you see this? Do you see what you did to me? You did this! You did this to me! Now get out of here! Get away from me and don't ever come near me again!"

"But how?" Tears swam in Dina's eyes. "Tell me what happened to you."

"Can't you see?" she yelled. "I got visited. This is it. This is what it looks like when a person gets visited and it's all your fault! You did this to me! Now you know. Now get out and leave me alone!"

Dina gasped out loud. "What did I do to get you visited?"

Belinda burst into tears. She tried to wipe her tears away, but she couldn't touch her face. She winced in pain whenever she even moved her mouth to speak. "After you left, Renfroe questioned me about you. When he found out I saw you walking out the door and didn't stop you, he went off to question your friends. He wanted to find you and bring you back. I guess he succeeded."

Belinda threw herself down on the stool by the fire and burst into tears. She tried to dab her eyes and nose with a handkerchief, but that only made her wounds bleed again.

Dina knelt down in front of her. She placed her hands on Belinda's knees. Bruises and gashes scored Belinda's arms and hands. "Who did this to you, Belinda? Was it Renfroe?"

"No, not him," Belinda sobbed. "He would never do this to anyone."

Dina pursed her lips. "Who did this? Tell me who visited you."

Belinda twisted the blood-stained handkerchief in her lap. "It was Buck."

"Buck!" Dina gasped. "But I thought he was.... you know, kind of harmless."

"I thought the same thing. I thought he was a little eccentric, maybe, but shy and defenseless. I pitied him for his experience when he was younger. I thought he might be worried about someone doing it to him again."

"Maybe that's why he did this," Dina suggested, "to protect himself."

Belinda shook her head. "You didn't see his face. I did."

"What happened?"

"After Renfroe left to find you, Buck came. He locked himself in this kitchen with me for two whole days. Renfroe didn't come back. We were alone in the house."

"He must have beaten you up pretty badly."

"Not too badly—not at first. The first beating wasn't bad at all. Then he sat me down in this chair and gave me a class."

"A class?" Dina repeated. "You mean like in the village?"

"The classes are always the same. He shouted at the top of his lungs with his mouth an inch away from my face. He called me terrible names. He called me a slag and told me I belonged in the canton." Belinda broke down weeping again.

Dina listened in silence. There were worse things than being a slag.

"He kept going all night long," Belinda went on, "I thought I would collapse from exhaustion and hunger and thirst, but he just kept screaming at me, on and on and on, into the next day. He has more stamina than any man I know."

"When did it end?"

"The class?" Belinda asked. "About three o'clock the next afternoon, but after he finished, just when I started to think it was all over, he beat me up again, much worse than the first time. He tied me by the wrist to the table over there and kicked me all over. He kicked me in the ribs and the face and the back and the legs. I was lying in a puddle of blood."

"How awful!"

"That was nothing. After he finished, he untied me from the table. He sat me on the stool and started the class all over again. I couldn't see his face from the blood running down into my eyes. Every time I tried to blink it away or clear my eyes, he punched or slapped me. He told me to pay attention. He told me I obviously didn't have an understanding with the Pride. He said if I wanted to stay in Renfroe's house, I had to show that I had an understanding with the Pride."

"But you do have an understanding with the Pride. You have a better understanding than just about anyone else I know."

"Can you believe it?" Belinda cried. "He told me I had to have an understanding with the Pride—me, of all people! Ha! Who has a better understanding than I do?"

"No one."

"I didn't break my understanding. I made a mistake when I let you go. I'm certain Renfroe understands that."

"Have you asked him?" Dina asked.

"Heavens, no! I would never mention this to him. Not for all the pearls in the ocean."

"But he's seen you all beaten up, hasn't he?" Dina asked. "Hasn't he asked what happened to you?"

"Oh, no! He'll never ask. He'll know just by looking at me. There's only one explanation for me looking this way. He'll know I got visited, but he'll never ask why. The cats leave all the visiting to the factors."

"Is Buck a factor?" Dina asked.

"Don't you remember when we went to the festival? Don't you remember how he stood on the stage with the rest of them? That proves it. He wouldn't stand on that stage if he wasn't a factor."

Dina nodded. "I should have thought of that."

"I don't know why I didn't think of it, either. Maybe because he didn't say anything, I thought.... well, I don't know what I thought, but he's one of them. It only proves they have people everywhere. They're always watching for someone to break the understanding with the Pride."

"I didn't know the city had factors. I thought only the villages had them."

"The factors enforce the understanding with the Pride," Belinda told her, "and that's what Buck does. He visited me. That makes him a factor."

"I see."

"The cats don't intervene when the factors visit someone," Belinda went on. "It's none of their business, really."

"Did you tell Buck you made a mistake? Did you explain to him that you didn't help me run away? You didn't know what I was doing."

Belinda shook her head and her fat lower lip trembled. "I didn't have to explain anything. I should have grabbed you by the hair and dragged you back into the house. I knew you weren't just curious about the weather. I should have hauled you into the kitchen and beat the stuffing out of you. I should have beaten you to a bloody pulp and locked you in your room until Buck came for you instead of me."

"I'm sorry, Belinda," Dina murmured. "I sincerely wish you had."

"You just don't get it, do you?" Belinda spat. "You're a slag to your core and you'll always be a slag. If you were anything else, you wouldn't try to run away. You don't understand how important these cats are. If you did, you would dedicate your life to serving them the way I have."

"I'm sorry, Belinda. I'll do my best not to get you or anyone else in trouble again. I've learned my lesson."

"I don't care if you have," Belinda snapped. "I won't let it happen again. I won't have anything more to do with you."

Dina stepped away from her. "I understand. I'm going now. I'll stay away from you from now on."

The door swung closed. That was the end of Dina's only friendship in Prideland.

Chapter 49

Renfroe returned that evening and called Dina into the parlor. She tried to sit as far away from him as she dared. She still saw Frank's blood on his jaws. He had Elana and Finlie and Jule in his stomach even now.

"I'm glad to see you home again, Dina," he began.

What could she say to this creature, this fiend she once cared for?

"Aren't you glad to see me?" He locked his yellow eyes on her until she lowered her gaze to the floor. He knew how to make her cower. "Did you really plan to leave me? I thought we understood each other better than that."

"You understood me. I didn't understand you before, but I do now."

He tilted his head to one side. "What do you understand now that you didn't understand before?"

"Let's just say I've come to an understanding with the Pride."

He tipped his head the other way. His whiskers twitched and his nostrils flared. He could sniff out a lie better than anyone. "I don't think I understand you."

"Ha! That's a good one!" Hysterical laughter broke out of her. "You don't understand me? Sure, you do. You of all people know what it means to have an understanding with the Pride. This is what you've wanted for me from the beginning. You always told me that, once I reached an understanding with the Pride, that everything would become clear to me. Now I have and it is clear to me."

Renfroe blinked. "Something about the way you're speaking to me right now tells me you haven't reached the understanding the Pride would like you to have."

"Oh, yes, I have! I understand after seeing you and the others at Helion House yesterday morning. I understand my place in this Pride as well as I'm ever going to understand it."

"Tell me what you understand. Then I'll know whether you understand."

"It doesn't matter if you think I understand. Don't you see? What you think and what you say and whatever silly words you use to justify it don't make any difference. I understand. Do you hear me? I understand perfectly."

"You said that, Dina. You said you understand. Now tell me. What do you understand?"

"I understand my place in this Pride and I understand the place of all humans in it. I understand with crystal clarity what's expected of me if I want to live in this Pride or even to live on this planet at all."

"And what is that? What is the place of humans in this Pride, according to your new understanding?"

"We're slaves," she replied. "We serve and we clean up after the cats and we scratch them behind their ears. When the cats want to use us for pleasure, we give it to them. When the cats need toys to play with and prey to hunt, humans provide the game for their sport."

"I wouldn't put it that way."

"Humans even provide the cats with food. If the subsidiaries didn't bring cattle and lizards and milk to the market every day for the cats to eat, the cats would just eat humans. It's that simple. The humans on this planet live at the whim of the cats. They survive at the pleasure of their cat masters. You can dress it up with all kinds of fancy words like 'benefactors' and 'understanding' and all that nonsense. It all means the same thing in the end. I understand it all now."

"I think perhaps you're putting a different construction on it than exists in reality," Renfroe purred.

"Why didn't you tell me about the House of Man?" Dina demanded.

"What about it?"

"Why didn't you tell me you did that to people? In all the time I've been living here with you, you never told me about it."

"What is there to tell? You've seen it for yourself. You saw the helpers at Helion House. They walk around with their clothes off all the time. You saw the House of Man there. I'm certain you did."

"I saw it, but I didn't know what it was. I didn't know it was an injury inflicted by cats."

"What did you think it was? What else could possibly explain it."

She waved his question away. "I guess I didn't try to explain it."

"You must have realized it couldn't have been made by accident. The lines are always made perfectly straight and they must be deep enough to tear the underlying connective tissue. The procedure isn't valid if they don't."

"Valid?" she shot back. "What does that mean?"

"The person can't take their full place in the Pride. If the lines aren't made straight enough or to the proper depth, the person can't take advantage of all the benefits of a full and complete understanding with the Pride. They can't become a helper, for example."

She snorted. "Lucky them."

"Really, Dina," he murmured. "I expected a much more mature response from you."

"Have you ever seen the House of Man being done to someone?"

"Of course, I have. I've performed the procedure myself."

Dina's jaw dropped. "You have?"

"Of course. I've done it dozens of times, maybe even hundreds of times. I'm a senator. It's part of my job. In general, the larger cats perform the House of Man. That way, the lines are the proper distance apart. It wouldn't work very well for Elyse or one of the other smaller cats to perform it, would it?" His deep rumbling laugh rolled out of his throat.

The sound made Dina's skin crawl. "You fiend! How could you do that to defenseless children?"

"Their parents wouldn't tolerate it if we didn't."

"How dare you?" she roared. "How dare you put the blame on their parents? Do you think the parents would willingly subject their children to this if they thought they had any choice at all?"

"But, Dina, you must know the parents *do* subject their children to it most willingly. You saw the Children's Festival. You must have seen the parents do it."

"I saw it," she snarled.

"The House of Man is a perfect example of what you're talking about. The cats played no part whatsoever in developing the House of Man. The subsidiaries demanded that the Pride mark them in some way to show their belonging to the Pride. They demanded that the whole society use this mark to separate those with an understanding with the Pride from those without it."

She threw up her hands. "This is disgusting!"

"It's true. The slags don't have the House of Man. The mark distinguishes the subsidiaries and the helpers from the slags. The subsidiaries and the helpers demand the

House of Man, not only for themselves, but for their children. They want to make certain everyone knows they aren't slags. They wouldn't be caught without it."

"That doesn't make any sense at all! The House of Man maims them for life. They can't even walk properly after they've had it done. Surely you've seen the way the helpers walk hunched over."

He lowered his eyelids. "That has nothing to do with the House of Man."

She stared at him in blank disbelief. "You can't be serious! Of course it's caused by the House of Man."

"I don't think so."

"You must be joking," she snapped.

"I'm not joking. The House of Man is perfectly harmless. It doesn't damage the helpers in any way. We wouldn't do it if it did."

"You can't actually believe that. You must have noticed the way the helpers move during their sex acts with the cats."

"I don't know what you mean."

"You're playing stupid and you're making me mad," she shot back. "The helpers can't move their hips properly."

"You're wrong, Dina," he purred. "The House of Man enhances a person's sexual potential. That's why the subsidiaries demand it. That's why anyone who comes to the city to work as a helper must carry the House of Man. They couldn't perform their functions as helpers if they don't modify their bodies."

"You really are a master of your own propaganda, aren't you? Maybe you've swallowed that load of flimflam and found it a juicy morsel to soothe your savage soul, but I haven't."

"You're an intelligent woman, Dina," Renfroe told her. "You've received an advanced education. You must realize that people perform better sexually after getting the House of Man. You can't expect the cats of the Pride to accept a person in their primitive state with improved helpers available."

"Either you're lying to me outright or you need your head examined. You can't deliberately destroy the tendons and ligaments of a person's pelvis without permanently affecting their ability to move and walk. These people have been maimed. How do you justify that?"

"I don't have to justify it. I don't believe they are maimed at all. The House of Man makes the helpers capable of performing their duties. They serve the Pride. That's their job and they need the House of Man to do it. You've seen the helpers all over this city.

They all carry the House of Man and they all do their jobs well. That's why they get the House of Man."

Dina leaned back and narrowed her eyes at him. "If I hadn't seen you at the canton, I might be convinced that you actually believe what you're telling me. I might be convinced you'd only ever seen people with the House of Man and you've come to believe it's the normal and proper way for a person to move."

"It *is* the normal and proper way for a person to move."

"But I *did* see you at the canton," she went on. "You've seen people moving and running who don't have the House of Man, so you must know the House of Man restricts their movements. The only explanation is that it's intended to stop people from running away from cats."

Renfroe puffed out his cheeks. "That's preposterous, Dina."

Dina laughed in his face. "I saw those people at the canton just as clearly as you did. I saw the children running around. They're much better able to run away from cats and to fight back when the cats attack."

"There's no reason the cats would do that."

"Of course there is. It's the only reason you would go to such lengths to justify such a horrendous mutilation of people. It gives them a disadvantage so the cats won't have any trouble hunting them down."

Renfroe licked his lips. His voice registered the first hint of annoyance Dina had ever heard. "We don't need any help hunting people, Dina."

"No, you don't."

He sighed. "Anyway, as I told you, the cats never imposed the House of Man on anyone. The subsidiaries invented it and they demand it. The cats would be more than happy to dispense with it. Look at Elyse. She obviously finds your friend Tom very attractive. He doesn't carry the House of Man. Maybe she wants a helper who doesn't have it."

"Maybe she wants a helper who still has the full range of motion in his hips," Dina corrected.

Renfroe pretended not to hear. "And then there's you and me. I want you to stay here as my helper and you don't carry the House of Man."

"If the subsidiaries demand it, how long will they tolerate helpers who don't carry it? If I stay here, won't they eventually demand I get it, too?"

"They might start to make noise about it, but if I took a stand and told them I didn't want you to get it, they would have no choice but to accept my wishes. Elyse probably wouldn't bother. She would send Tom to the village to get it."

"So that proves it," she concluded. "The Pride *is* responsible for the House of Man."

"How do you figure?"

"You just said you could stop it if you spoke out against it. The cats could order the subsidiaries to stop the House of Man and the subsidiaries would be forced to stop doing it. So why don't they? The cats must benefit from it."

"The cats have no reason to stop the House of Man. The subsidiaries want it and it improves relations between the helpers and the cats so we allow it to continue. We even encourage it, but the subsidiaries themselves take all the responsibility for getting it done. They make sure their children have it done at an early age."

"And they visit anyone who wouldn't have it done."

"They would do a lot more than visit them. At the very least, they would drive them out of Prideland to go live in the cantons with the slags, but in all likelihood, they would reduce them."

Dina shook her head. "They'd 'reduce' them. That's a very interesting way of putting it."

"Is anything wrong?"

"You used that word again. You said they'd reduce them."

"They *would* reduce them," Renfroe repeated.

"They would kill them, you mean."

He sniffed. "We don't think of it in that way."

"Of course, you don't. If you did, you'd have to think about it as it really is. The subsidiaries would kill a person who didn't get the House of Man or who didn't have their children get it the same way you killed those people in the canton."

"We reduced them," Renfroe replied. "That's what we do with the slags in the cantons. We reduce them to protect Prideland from their influence."

"You monster!" Dina murmured. "You brute!"

"I don't understand you, Dina. How can you object to the Pride reducing slags whenever possible?"

Dina exploded. "Reduce them! You make it sound like they dwindled away to nothing. You make it sound like they blew away like leaves in the wind and you don't need to give it another thought."

"Why should I give it another thought?"

"Because you killed them!" she screamed. "They weren't reduced or cleared or laundered or whatever other idiotic word you want to use for it. They're dead and you killed them! You murdered them. They were totally defenseless and you hunted them down in cold blood and murdered them. That makes you a murderer."

"'Murder'…" he repeated. "I've heard that word from your people before. We don't have a direct equivalent for it, but I understand what you mean."

"How can you not have an equivalent for murder?"

"You mean the reduction wasn't justified. You believe we ought to get visited…. I mean, you believe we ought to suffer some negative consequence for reducing them."

"For killing them," she corrected. "You killed them. You didn't reduce them."

Renfroe moved his tongue around inside his mouth. He blinked and looked away. "All right, have it your way. We killed them, but in our Pride, there is no reduction—no killing, I mean—equivalent to your concept of murder. For us, there are no negative consequences to killing of any kind."

"That's ridiculous!" she spat. "I know you don't value human life any more than that of any other animal, but what about your own kind? What happens when a cat kills another cat?"

Renfroe licked between the toes of one paw. "That happens sometimes. Sometimes a lion or tiger loses control and kills another cat's kittens or an old male loses patience and bites and kills a young cub."

"And do you punish the killer when that happens?"

"No. I told you. Our Pride has no negative consequences for killing of any kind."

"Why not? Don't you have any sense of justice at all?"

"You must remember, Dina. We are cats. We hunt and we kill. That is our biological prerogative. No one should understand that better than you."

"I'm a human being!" she screeched. "I'm a biologist second and a human being first. I can't stand by while you kill innocent people right down to helpless women and children and babies and just shrug my shoulders and say, 'Well, they're cats. It's their biological prerogative.' No way!"

"But we *are* cats, Dina," he insisted.

"Do you think I give a snippet's fidget if you're cats?" she screamed. "Those people are just as dead. Their children are just as dead. They're just as dead as Marcus Harte."

"Who is Marcus Harte?"

He couldn't have made her angrier if he tried. "What do you care? You're a cat just like Fallon and Khalid and Victor and Hector and all the other cats. You couldn't care if you wanted to. You're biologically incapable of caring about anyone, including me."

"You know that isn't true, Dina. You know I care about you."

She wasn't listening anymore. "And to think I actually started to care about you. To think I actually thought you were a decent person. Ha! You're not a person. You're a monster just like Fallon and Khalid and all the rest of them. What a fool I was to think you were different! That's how stupid and gullible I am."

"You're not stupid, Dina."

"All any male has to do is to be nice to me and I roll over like a kitten and say, 'Please, Sir, rub my tummy.' I'm a sucker for a nice guy. It just goes to show how easily duped I am."

"You aren't a dupe, Dina, and I didn't dupe you. I care for you and I want you to stay with me. I never deceived you about that."

She turned away and he let her withdraw. They sat in silence for another half hour. When she realized he wouldn't break her neck, she left the room.

Chapter 50

D ina took her usual stroll in the garden after breakfast. Only three days remained in the Pod's power packs. She studied the plants in the flower beds and the tree lizards while she turned her situation over in her mind.

All of a sudden, Renfroe came around the corner. He looked different in the light of day. The memory of him at the canton and at Helion House afterward slipped farther into a past she'd just as soon forget. He looked like her sleek, strong protector. He sat in the dappled sunshine under the trees and blinked at the light. Dina could have mistaken him for a statue or an idol. "Good morning," he growled.

"Good morning."

"Have you forgiven me yet?"

"I'll never forgive you, but I suppose I have to accept it. It's history now."

"I'm glad you see it that way because I really do value your company. I would hate for something like this to come between us."

"It already has come between us. It will always be between us."

"You made quite a lot of trouble for me when you left, you know," Renfroe went on. "If the other helpers find out you ran off and made it all the way to the cantons and that I brought you back, they'll want to know how you got away with it without being visited."

"How did you stop me from being visited?"

"I didn't, but I suppose the other helpers understand you're my special helper. Maybe that's why they left you alone."

"Do you mean helper.... or do you mean *helper*?"

"Is there a difference?"

Dina blushed. "You know. Am I a helper like Belinda or am a helper like Tom is to Elyse?"

"There really is no difference. Any helper can do what Tom does for Elyse. It's part of their function."

"But you...I mean, a cat.... would never do that with a helper like Belinda. She's not exactly.... oh, you know what I mean.... she's not exactly young."

"Does that matter?"

"Maybe it doesn't matter to you, but all the helpers being used as sex toys are young and in prime condition. I haven't seen an old helper like Belinda being used as a sex object."

"I think, perhaps, your mistake lies in the idea of helpers having sexual relations with cats. I think, perhaps, the helpers and the cats have two different ideas about the purpose of the sex act."

"What purpose could it have other than to give pleasure? Isn't that what it's for?"

"Maybe for people it is. Humans seem to be attracted to the sensuality of the cats, but the cats don't feel the same way."

"Then why do they have sexual relations with people?"

"Because the people want them to."

"That's impossible! The cats of this Pride dominate their human subjects in every way. They control their lives down to the minutest detail. They wouldn't do this simply to satisfy human desires."

"I didn't say they do it to satisfy their desires," Renfroe corrected. "I said they do it because people want them to."

"What's the difference?"

"The people want it and they'll do a lot to get it. Once they've done it, they rarely go back on their commitment to it."

Dina frowned. "I don't understand you."

"Consider a young subsidiary who leaves his home to become a helper. He's just recovered from the House of Man. He doesn't know what he'll find in the city. He thinks that, if he doesn't like it, he'll go back home to his parents."

"That makes sense."

"He comes to the city full of all the hopes and expectations village life pumped into his head," Renfroe went on. "Maybe his father farmed a large block of land in the village. Maybe the young man's father was a village factor. Our young friend finds himself a servant in a strange city with no friends and no principles to guide him."

"I follow you so far. So what's this got to do with having sex with a cat?"

Renfroe paused. "I believe this scenario explains the behavior of your friend Tom. I never thought about it before, but now that I'm explaining it to you, it makes sense when applied to him, too."

Dina stiffened. "I'm listening."

"Back to our young subsidiary, now a young helper. He gets a placement with a cat...it doesn't matter what kind or whether the benefactor is male or female. He struggles to find his place in the city environment. Somehow, the benefactor manages to maneuver this helper into a sexual situation. Maybe the female benefactor seduced the helper by offering him favors or privileges. Maybe the male benefactor coerced the female helper into it with threats against her life or the safety of her family. It doesn't matter how our helper arrived at that situation. He or she commits the act in the end."

"Then what?"

"Then," Renfroe replied, "he's stuck, that's what. He can never go back to his family. That's for certain because the subsidiaries insist on believing no such thing can ever happen when it happens all the time. He can also never really move on to another benefactor since he'll never know for certain whether the next benefactor will expect sexual gratification as well. Better to stay with what he knows than to risk something unknown."

"And you think this actually happens?"

"I've seen it thousands of times. The cats do it deliberately. It's the perfect tool to keep their helpers in line. The cats don't much care for it themselves, but the result works so well that no cat can resist making use of it."

"This is insane," Dina muttered.

"Is it? Haven't you seen it in Tom's relationship to Elyse? I can't think of any better example than that."

"I don't see what this has to do with him."

"Oh, come now, Dina," he chided. "You're blinding yourself toward Tom because of your past feelings for him."

"My feelings for him aren't past," she blurted out. "He's my fiancé. As soon as this mission is over, he's going to marry me."

"Tom will never leave this planet," Renfroe murmured, "not now that he's committed himself with Elyse."

"He's just waiting for a chance to complete our mission."

Renfroe shook his head. "Once a person commits these acts, they never go back. They can't. Can you imagine what your Coalition would say if they found out? Would you marry a man who had sex with a cat? You know very well you wouldn't. Every time you tried to get intimate with him, you'd see him with Elyse."

Dina's mind raced. She had to find some way to undo everything he said, but even as she argued against him, she knew it was all true. "But he's still committed to the mission. You heard him at the Senate hearing."

"He says that, but he won't actually do it. How do you think I found out you escaped?"

Dina's jaw dropped. "What?"

"He told Elyse you were going to escape."

"Tom would never betray me like that." Her voice cracked. "He might be a little confused. Prideland has that effect on people, but he would never go as far as that. He's an Armada officer. He has a code of honor to uphold."

Renfroe sniffed. "That just goes to show you what his code of honor is worth."

"So what did he say to Elyse?"

"I don't know what he said or how he said it. Maybe he told her in a fit of passion. I don't know and I don't care. Elyse told me you were planning to escape, but by the time I found out, you were already gone."

Dina clapped her hands over her ears. "I'm not hearing this. This isn't happening."

"And it isn't just Tom, you know. Your other friends are committed now, too."

"What do you mean?"

"Isn't it obvious? They all told on you. Matthew and Tania told their benefactors about your escape, too."

Dina stared at him. "They did?"

"Of course, they did. I just told you. The Pride has a different way of dealing with everyone, but in the end, once a person commits himself to the Pride, he doesn't go back."

"What did they say about me?"

"As I just said, I don't know what they said. I heard about it secondhand from their benefactors. If I had to guess, Matthew probably told Fallon as a way to gain some protection for himself. When a helper finds himself hanging by a thread the way Matthew is, he'll tell his benefactor just about anything to eke out a few minutes' reprieve."

Dina snorted. "'Benefactor'!"

Renfroe ignored her. "And Tania? Well, again, I'm not sure, but from what Khalid told me, I would guess her motive was some combination of the two."

Dina frowned. "A combination of what?"

"Fear and sex. She's afraid of Khalid. She would do whatever she had to do to save herself from him."

"But she didn't give herself to him sexually—not yet, anyway."

Renfroe shrugged. "Maybe the last time you spoke to her she hadn't, but maybe between then and now, she did. You told me once she planned to offer herself to him. He gave me to understand that she had."

She cradled her head in her hand. "Oh, poor Tania!"

"Why do you say it that way? Why do you say, 'poor Tania'? I can think of worse things to happen to someone than being taken as a helper by a cat."

"But to be forced into it out of fear—that would be terrible!"

"Maybe at first. I personally believe the fear of anticipation is the worst part. Once the helpers get used to it, they no longer fear it and it becomes much more pleasant. The helpers I've seen certainly derive a great deal of pleasure from it."

"I'll bet they do," she muttered. "They have no choice, do they?"

Renfroe flicked his ears. "Really, Dina, I don't understand your attitude at all. If the helpers can get some advantage by it, either by gaining favor with their benefactors or through physical gratification, I don't see how you can object to it."

"Don't you see?" she cried. "No human being would ever stoop to it if they weren't afraid. It violates the natural imperative of separation between species."

"Afraid?" he repeated. "Afraid of what? The cats?"

"The threat of violence and death is the most powerful fear in the world. You said the cats do it to trap the helpers in their slavery."

"So what if they do?"

"So the cats exploit the helpers sexually. And what about the House of Man? The subsidiaries might enforce it, but the cats perform it. The cats are the ones who maim the population. You can't say the cats are innocent in this."

Renfroe stood up and stretched. "I can see we won't agree on this."

"Or on anything else."

"Never mind. Why don't you come for a walk with me? We can talk more on the way."

Chapter 51

"Where are we going?" Dina asked.

"Nowhere in particular," Renfroe replied. "I just thought you might like to get out of the house for a while. We can go up to the top of the hill and look at the view or we could go down to the river. The weather is nice at this time of year."

She fell in at his side. The silence soothed her nerves.

"I enjoy spending time with you," he told her. "If I didn't have business to attend to, I would spend all my time with you."

Dina rested her hand on his shoulder. "I enjoy your company, too."

"You didn't really want to leave me, did you?" he asked.

"I didn't want to leave you, but I can't stay here. I can't live like this. I had to get away somehow."

"And do you still feel that way now after your escape?"

"I didn't escape. I'm here because you tracked me down and brought me back."

"Can you blame me after all we've been through together? I couldn't just let you go without at least trying to get you back."

"Well, I'm back now. You did what you did and you brought me back, even if you did it at the cost of dozens of human lives."

"Let's not argue about that anymore," Renfroe told her.

"Anyway, I don't feel the same way. I keep thinking about what you said—about Tom and Matthew and Tania telling their benefactors about my plan to escape. If it's true, they're just as responsible for the deaths of those people in the jungle as you and the Pride."

"It *is* true."

"I believe you. I'm just amazed such honorable people could fall so far."

"Were they so honorable before you came here?"

"They were the most honorable people I ever knew. That's what makes this so shocking. Your system of getting people to commit to Prideland so they can never go back overrides everything we believed in."

"They must be honorable to stand up to the pressure the way they have," Renfroe replied. "Take Matthew, for example. He's close to death. I'm surprised he took so long to offer Fallon a concession like this. Most people would be spouting any nonsense they could think up, no matter how farfetched, just to get some breathing space. Matthew held out as long as he could. When he finally cracked, he gave accurate information that would implicate only one of his teammates and none of the others. I consider that very honorable."

Dina shook her head. "It doesn't change the fact that quite a few innocent people are dead as a result."

"For all Matthew knew, *you* could be dead as a result. How would that go down when he returned to the *Savannah*?"

Dina shrugged. "He might not return to the *Savannah*, so it won't matter."

"We could walk around and visit them if you want."

She turned away. "I don't want to see them."

"That's not like you," he remarked.

"I don't want to see them again. If I have to be here, I'd rather spend my time with you."

He walked closer to her and rubbed his shoulder against her leg. "I'm glad. I hope you'll be satisfied to stay here with me now."

"You're doing everything you can to make up my mind. My life here with you is really all I have left. There's nothing left between me and Tom, but I just can't bring myself to turn my back on him once and for all. I would have to turn my back on him and the rest of the team if I tried to leave again."

His ears swiveled toward her. "Will you try to leave again?"

She looked him straight in the eye. "No, I won't try to leave again."

"You may not want to visit your friends, but if we go up the hill, we'll go right past Khalid's house. We might bump into Tania."

"Somehow, I think we can avoid it."

Renfroe nodded. "Khalid told me she doesn't leave the house very much."

Quiet, leafy parks dotted the neighborhoods in that part of the city. Big gardens surrounded all the houses. Tinkling fountains and tree lizard calls broke the stillness. The atmosphere lulled Dina into peaceful tranquility. "It really is beautiful here."

"Prideland isn't the evil, frightening place you make it out to be. We do everything we can to make it pleasant for everyone. You must realize that."

"I admire the work you do with the Senate. The relationship between the Pride and their helpers must be a complicated one. It must be hard to manage the whole thing."

"The Senate doesn't manage anything. The cats pretty much do what they please. The factors handle the helpers and the subsidiaries, but you're right. Prideland wouldn't work without the understanding between humans and the Pride. Our society would collapse without that."

"I never said that. Being a helper to a senator is one thing. This understanding as you call it isn't anything more than the threat of mutilation and death. If these people had any way at all to fight back, you can bet your boots your precious understanding would fly out the window."

"Please, Dina," Renfroe groaned. "Let's stop arguing about this once and for all. I can't bear to have any friction between us. Let's just sit down and enjoy each other's company for once."

They crested the top of the hill. A stone bench sat at the very top. The whole city stretched out below them. Renfroe jumped up and sat down on the bench.

Dina sat down next to him. The sun glowed off the city's roofs. The river sparkled blue and silver in its gravel bed meandering through the city. The trees along the river rustled in the breeze.

"Do you come up here very much?" she asked.

"Not very much. I'm too busy. I don't even spend much time around my own house. I've spent more time at home in the last few weeks than ever."

"That wasn't because of me, was it?"

"Yes, it was. I've let my Senate responsibilities slip since you came."

"Did I mean all that much to you?" she asked.

"Do you really need to ask that? You know how much I care for you. I've told you enough times."

"You didn't tell me you were shirking your duties on my account."

"Would it have made any difference if I had told you?" he asked.

"Sure it would have. The Senate is important business."

"Not so important. Anyone can do it. It mostly involves stopping fights from breaking out between cats who want different things. Since I met you, I've thought many times of giving it up."

"Who would take over for you? Who could do as good a job as you?"

"Dozens of cats could do as good a job as me," he replied. "Since I've been shirking, almost any cat could, but since you ask, I have one of the Helion boys picked out. He's an up-and-comer, you might say."

"I'm sure none of the other Senators can tell you're shirking," she told him.

"They certainly can!" Renfroe exclaimed. "Lord Helion scolded me about it, so you know it's pretty serious shirking."

"What have you been doing to shirk so badly? It's not as if you've spent so much time with me. You've been down at the Senate building almost every day."

"When you ran away, I dropped all my Senate duties to search for you. Several important sessions took place in my absence. Some of the other Senators got annoyed when the chairman didn't show up. As a matter of fact, I'm missing a session right now."

Dina gasped. "What? You can't!"

He scanned the city below. "I can and I am. The fact is I just don't care anymore. I'd rather spend my time with you."

"But all those cats who came to help you.... reduce...the canton...How could you call on all of them for help if they got so annoyed? I thought they were your loyal friends."

"They're loyal to the Pride. They understand the importance of correcting any breach in protocol. They deal harshly and swiftly with anyone who goes against the understanding between humans and the Pride."

"So what did you do to get them to help you?"

"They didn't help me. That's what I'm telling you. I was down at the Senate building for a session. After it ended, Elyse, Fallon, and Khalid all told me their helpers said you planned to run away to your spacecraft. In the same conversation, Lord Helion told me he'd seen you in the village. I didn't even realize you were gone."

"So did you ask them to help track me down?"

"I didn't have to. I would have let you go if the decision was mine, but the Pride couldn't let that slide. All the helpers would run off if we did. I asked them to bring you back alive, but I couldn't guarantee that, either. If one of them killed you, I'd have nothing to say about it."

"Nothing to say?"

"I'd have to accept it. I couldn't get a cat punished for that, but we had no choice but to attack the canton."

"There's always a choice."

"Maybe in the Coalition of Inhabited Planets there's a choice. In Prideland, this is the way things are, but it doesn't matter. It's nothing we haven't done countless times before."

Dina shook her head. "How can you be so callous about it?"

"You think reducing the canton was something we did on your account, but it had nothing to do with you. Only keeping you alive and bringing you back to my house happened on your account. Everything else was standard operating procedure."

"Standard operating procedure! How can you be so heartless? Those were living human beings you killed!"

"I don't understand why you're making it into such a catastrophe all of a sudden. I told you two weeks ago we were going out to reduce one of the cantons and you saw us hunt down the slags that got away. You didn't bat an eyelash then."

"I didn't see it for myself. I wasn't personal friends with the people you killed."

"Reduced," he corrected.

"You killed them," she snapped. "Why can't you call it what it really is? Do you have some mental block that stops you from telling the truth?"

Renfroe sat in silence for a while. He gazed out over his city. "Whatever I did to those slags, I did it to save your life. When Lord Helion and Khalid told me you escaped and they planned to go after you, I had to go with them. They would have reduced you along with the slags if I hadn't been there to make sure you came back alive. If I hadn't helped them reduce the canton, they would have killed me, too. Remember that when you think of me reducing those slags. I did it to save you. I did it because I love you and I wanted you here, alive, with me."

She listened in silence. The same images played through her mind, but they looked different now. She could understand why he did what he did through the lens of his words.

"I don't want to fight about this anymore, Dina. Let's concentrate on our future instead of fighting about the past."

"I don't want to fight about it, either. I don't want to think about it anymore, but I can't get the images of those people dying out of my head. I can't help seeing you there with blood all over your face."

"I'm sorry you had to see that. I wish your experience of Prideland could be nothing but pleasant. I wish you'd never run away."

"But I did. I can't change that now."

"I'll do my best to shelter you from that sort of thing in the future, but you have to stay close to me. I can't protect you if you keep running off. If you try to escape again, I won't be able to save you. The Pride will demand you pay for it with your life."

Chapter 52

The sun swung around to the opposite side of the sky and began its descent.

"What would you like to do with the rest of the day?" Renfroe asked. "Would you like to walk along the river?"

"We could," Dina replied. "We've been up here for hours. Aren't you getting hungry?"

"We'll eat when we get home. I want the pleasure of this day to last as long as possible. Who knows when we'll have another opportunity to spend time together like this?"

"Will it be a long time before we can spend time together again? You said you planned to give up your duties with the Senate. If you do, you'll have all the time in the world to do what you want. You'll be free."

Renfroe shook his head. "Even if I retire from the Senate, I'll always have duties to the Pride."

"Like what?"

"Like resolving disputes between cats. Other cats will always depend on me. Whoever replaces me will need coaching to take over my position."

"You said anyone could do the job."

"I've been chairman for almost ten years. I've practically reinvented the job in my own image. The next senator to take my place will have to learn which parts of the job belong to a senator and which belonged only to me. Then the senate will have to vote in the new chairman. Whoever replaces me won't get the chair automatically. My retirement will throw the whole Senate into disarray."

"You must be torn between retiring and staying on," she remarked.

"I have no desire to stay on. My only desire is to make a home with you."

"Make a home with me?" she repeated.

"Does that bother you?"

"It doesn't bother me. You just never put it in those terms before. I didn't know you were so serious about me."

"I'm absolutely serious about you. I want you to help me make my house a home."

"How will I do that?" she asked.

"I want you to take charge of my other helpers. I want them to answer to you in the care of the house. I want you to oversee how the house is furnished and laid out and I want you to supervise the other helpers in their work."

"I can't do that. I couldn't take over from Belinda."

"Why not?"

"She's always been in charge of me," Dina replied. "She took charge of me when I first came to the house. I couldn't just turn the tables on her and start issuing orders and I definitely couldn't do that to Buck."

"I don't see why not. I'm telling you to and I'll tell them to answer to you. They'll do it."

"Don't do that," she exclaimed. "Whatever you do, don't do that."

"You aren't making any sense, Dina. I'm telling you to. They'll obey me and they'll obey you when I tell them to."

She covered her eyes with her hand. "For the love of all that's holy, don't do that. Don't you know Buck is a factor?"

Renfroe stared at her. "He is?"

"You didn't know, did you? No one did. He's kept his mouth shut all these years, but the whole time, he's been the eyes and ears for the factors. Did you know he visited Belinda for helping me escape?"

Renfroe's eyes glittered.

"You didn't know that, either, did you? Have you seen Belinda since I got back?"

He turned away. "No."

"When you see her, you'll know it's true. She looks like she got hit in the face with a sledgehammer. She won't even talk to me anymore because she's afraid I'll get her into more trouble."

"*Did* she help you escape?" Renfroe asked. "I didn't know she had."

"She didn't. She says she should have stopped me from going out of the house. She says she should have realized what I was planning to do when I went out in that storm."

Renfroe shook his head. "All this time, he kept quiet."

She laid her hand on his shoulder. "Now do you understand why I can't take control of your other helpers?"

He nodded. "I understand."

"I appreciate you wanting to set me apart from them."

"It doesn't matter."

"Can't we just keep going the way we have been? I've been happy up until now."

He looked her in the eye. "Have you really been happy here? Have you been happy with me?"

She nodded. "Being with you is the only thing that's made me happy these last few weeks. When I'm with you, I can almost forget about everything else."

"Prideland isn't really so bad. I wish you'd stop painting it as such a frightful, evil place."

"Maybe if I have more happy times alone with you, I'll stop thinking about the frightening parts. Maybe I'll come to think of it as a nice, happy place."

"I hope so. I'll try to give you more time and attention so you can think of it that way."

"You have to admit," she pointed out, "that my experience with the Pride hasn't exactly been a pleasant one."

"I realize you've had some trying times. I never said it didn't have its unique characteristics, but it isn't all bad. I wish you could appreciate its finer points."

"What finer points are you referring to?"

"The feelings we have for each other, for a start. Look at this city. It's a fine city because of the understanding between the people and the Pride. If we didn't have that understanding, this city would be nothing. It would be a jungle wasteland."

"The feelings we have for each other is a much more compelling point."

"Very well. Let's stick to that." He moved closer to her on the bench. "If you'd never come to this planet, you and I would never have met. We wouldn't be sitting here, enjoying this beautiful day together and having this conversation."

"I'm glad I met you. I'm glad for that reason that we came to this planet."

Renfroe rested his heavy head against her shoulder. "We've had some good times together, haven't we, Dina?"

"Yes," she murmured.

"And you've been safe and comfortable in my house, haven't you? Haven't I done everything a cat could do to make you welcome? I've made you feel at home."

"You've done all that and more. I appreciate all of that. I don't know what I would have done without you. You've given me the one place in all Prideland where I feel safe."

"Give me a chance to win you over," he told her. "I only want the chance to give you the life you deserve. Let me show you the beauty and kindness Prideland has to offer. Give me a chance."

She let out a deep sigh. "You already have."

He worked his cheeks and head up her arm to her neck and chest. "Will you stay with me, Dina? Will you stay with me from now on? You won't try to run away again, will you?"

He rubbed his fur over her clothes and then her skin. Waves of emotion rocketed through her. She closed her eyes. She had to shake off this overwhelming tide of longing. "There's no reason for me to run away again. There's no way for me to get off the planet now."

He tensed, but he didn't lift his head. "What do you mean?"

"Our landing craft...Its power packs only had three weeks of power. There isn't time for me to get back to the pod before they run out of power. I couldn't leave the planet now even if I wanted to."

Chapter 53

D ina glanced up the hill at Khalid's house.

"There's no one around," Renfroe told her. "You won't see Tania."

Dina looked down at the stones moving under her feet.

"Are you disappointed or relieved?" he asked.

She shrugged. "Both, I guess. I want to see my friends again, but at the same time, I don't want to see them."

"Maybe after you think a little longer about what they did, you'll want to see them again. Maybe you'll come to see why they did what they did and you won't be so mad at them anymore."

"Maybe," she replied.

At the bottom of the hill, the path turned around a thick hedge separating Khalid's house from the street. The creak of wheels announced the approach of the Elite Battalion.

The bedraggled archeologists trundled their wheelbarrow out of Khalid's yard, through a gap in the hedge, and onto the sidewalk. They stopped right in front of Dina. Renfroe didn't pay them any attention, but Dina stopped dead in her tracks.

The men stretched and two of their members hurried to catch up with the rest. They lugged a heavy burden between them. With a collective heave, they deposited the load across the wheelbarrow's handlebars behind their barrels of treasure. Dina saw it clearly and recognized Maddy.

Her arms dangled to one side of the wheelbarrow and her legs dangled the other way. Her head flopped back and forth and banged against the wheel. Her thin cotton dress twisted around her body and bunched up under her armpits. Her lifeless eyes stared away at nothing.

Dina stared at the sack of lifeless flesh. The Elite Battalion pushed the wheelbarrow down the street with the dead woman lolling and banging as they went. They disappeared around the next corner.

"Are you alright, Dina?" Renfroe asked.

She barely heard him. "Hmm? Me?"

"Who else would I be talking to?" he snapped.

"I'm fine. It's just that.... well, I know that woman."

"Who?"

"Maddy."

"Who's that?" Renfroe asked.

Dina waved toward the corner where the Elite Battalion disappeared. "That woman. She was Khalid's helper. I guess you could say she was Tania's friend."

"Oh, her. I know who you mean. Khalid's helper. I know the one."

"I met her in the city when I came to visit Tania. She didn't exactly help Tania, but she gave her advice on how to deal with her situation."

"I see," Renfroe replied.

"She told me she came from the village."

"Did you know her?"

"I only knew what she told me." She stopped in mid-stride. "Do you know what happened to her?"

Renfroe strolled on. Dina had no choice but to keep up with him. "Khalid probably got tired of her. That's usually what happens."

"What do you mean? Do you mean he killed her just because he got bored with her?"

Renfroe shrugged. "I don't know. Maybe she did something to annoy him. Maybe he thought she was getting too big in the head if you know what I mean."

"No, I don't know what you mean."

"Sure, you do. I saw that woman in the market and a few other places. She always tossed her head and laughed loudly and flipped her skirts like she thought she was something special because she was Khalid's helper. A lot of helpers get like that. They start helping their benefactors to get favors and protection. Then those favors and protections start going to their heads. They start thinking they're invincible."

"So what are you saying? They get killed for that?"

"That's usually how it happens. Once a helper starts sticking their neck out of their proper place, they have to be brought down as a warning to the others. If we didn't bring them down, we'd have the whole population on our backs in no time."

"There must be some other way you can accomplish the same thing without killing them," she argued.

Renfroe paid no attention. "You should mention this to your friend, Tom. He could be on the same path with Elyse. I don't think he has a very good understanding about the way the Pride works. He seems to think he's some higher human being who can stand on the same level as the Pride."

"So where does that leave me?" Dina asked. "How can I feel comfortable staying with you if I can't stand on the same level with you?"

"After the way he behaved in front of the Senate, I'm surprised they let him walk out of the building. The Senate only gave him the privilege of addressing them out of consideration for the Coalition and he squandered the Senate's goodwill. He'll find himself in a very unpleasant situation if he isn't careful."

"Won't Elyse protect him? Surely she wouldn't let the Senate punish him for speaking his mind. Isn't that what they called him to do?"

"I wouldn't bank too heavily on Elyse. She would dump Tom in an instant to further her own interests."

"She looked pretty fond of him to me," Dina murmured.

"Don't let appearances fool you. What did you see? You saw them engaged in a sexual act. That doesn't mean a thing. Tom is a toy to her and she won't hesitate to discard him once she's finished with him."

In the center square, the last stallholders were packing up their wagons to leave the market. Dina and Renfroe followed the river past Elyse's house. The sun slanted between the buildings and a breeze rustled the trees.

Dina looked back when she heard the same creaking noise and the Elite Battalion came around the corner. Dina watched them head for their headquarters.

Renfroe kept walking until he paused to wait for her. "Is anything wrong, Dina?"

She shook her head.

"Are you coming?" he asked.

She pried herself away and took her place at his side. The corner leading to their own neighborhood loomed before them. They turned the corner, but she couldn't drag her feet any further. She gasped out loud and her hands flew to her pockets. "Wait!"

Renfroe's eyes widened. "What's the matter?"

"I dropped something. I'll run back for it. You stay here. I'll be right back." She darted back the way they came. Renfroe stared after her with sharp eyes.

She tore back around the corner as fast as she could. She hardly knew what she hoped to find, but she had to find out what happened to Maddy. She spotted the Elite Battalion at the top of the slope. They pushed their wheelbarrow into the power station.

She ran up the path with all her might. Her lungs burned, but she didn't dare to slow down. The Elite Battalion vanished into their headquarters and Dina ran even faster. She rushed past the door to a stack of empty barrels under a window behind the building.

She climbed up the stack and prayed they wouldn't topple under her. She held her breath and peeked through the window. The Elite Battalion parked their wheelbarrow on the edge of the weir. They tipped their barrels into the water and then the same two men took their places on either end of Maddy.

One grabbed her wrists and the other took hold of her ankles. They lifted her off the wheelbarrow and, with three swings, they tossed the body into the water. They chuckled at the splash. Then they all turned their backs on the rippling waves.

Dina couldn't stay any longer. She jumped down and ran even harder back to Renfroe. She slowed to a walk when she met him coming after her. She panted to catch her breath.

"Did you find it?" he asked.

"No," she replied.

"What was it you dropped?"

She thought fast to make up a believable lie. "Just a trinket I keep in my pocket."

He glanced at her. "I didn't know you kept a trinket in your pocket. What was it?"

"Just a little...you know," she stammered. "A little.... a little thing. I always carried it around, but it's gone now. It doesn't matter."

"Was it anything of value?"

"Oh, no."

"You still haven't told me what it was," he insisted.

She cast her mind back into the past. "It was a little silver charm in the shape of a doll. I used to wear it on a bracelet around my wrist. It fell off the bracelet years ago and I kept it in my pocket. I don't know why, but it's gone now."

"Maybe you dropped it in the park," Renfroe suggested, "or it could be near Khalid's house. We should go back and get it."

"No." She started walking away. "It'll be dark soon. We should go home. It isn't important enough to go back for. It's gone. I don't mind. Let's go home."

She rested her hand on his shoulder. He took the cue and fell in by her side.

Her brain churned all the way back to the house. Less than forty-eight hours remained until the deadline. Her life couldn't end like Maddy's—in a river on some strange planet. Even if she missed the deadline and the cats hunted her down in the jungle, she had to find a way to escape.

She had to escape without a word to her teammates. Matthew would be dead in a few days if he wasn't already. Tom would keep doing his business with Elyse and Tania would carry on with Khalid. Dina couldn't trust them not to betray her again. She probably didn't stand a chance, anyway.

How would she get out of the city? She couldn't follow the road. She'd used it before. The cats and the subsidiaries would check there first as soon as anyone found her gone.

Besides, there wasn't time to walk all the way to the pod. The pod was the second place they would check. She had to get there fast before anyone found her missing—but how?

Chapter 54

*W*alk, Dina told herself. *Walk slowly. Don't hurry. You're perfectly at home here. You've got all the time in the world.*

She had to make Renfroe think she loved him and wanted to stay with him. She had to get away from him without tipping him off that she'd changed her mind.

She had to keep her plan hidden from him until the time came to break away. If she played her cards right, she just might get back to the pod before the deadline.

Whatever else she did, she wouldn't tell a living soul what she planned to do. She wouldn't see her teammates again anyway. This one was all hers and hers alone. She would stand or fall on her own legs, and if she got back to the *Savannah*, she'd take the consequences of leaving her teammates behind. At least she'd be out of Prideland.

Full dark blanketed the city by the time they reached Renfroe's house. Belinda left the lamps burning in the parlor and the fire blazing on the hearth. Renfroe and Dina sat down in their usual places. Belinda brought their food and they ate together as amicably as ever.

"I'm sorry you lost your trinket," Renfroe told her. "Perhaps there's some way to replace it."

"Forget about it."

"If you carried it with you all this time, it must have been valuable. It must at least have had some sentimental value for you. You shouldn't let it go so easily."

The lie started to take on a life of its own. "It wasn't valuable and I've carried it for so long that it no longer has any value for me. I can let it go."

"But it's your last connection to your home world. These things have a value of their own."

"I thought you wanted me to settle here," she pointed out. "I thought you wanted me to leave my connections to my home world behind."

"That's true," he admitted, "but I don't want you to lose something special to you."

She let her hand fall on his shoulder and she stroked his coat. "I can let it go now and I can let my home world go now, too. I'm staying here with you. The past can slip away into the past. I'm ready to let it go."

"Are you sure?" he asked.

Dina nodded. "I'm sure."

"Are you sure you have an understanding with the Pride? Are you sure you can accept everything you've seen and learned? I didn't think you were quite as settled as that."

"I am now. I can accept it."

"I had a lovely time with you today, Dina," he rumbled. "I'd like to think I had something to do with convincing you to become a part of the Pride."

She slid over next to him and stroked his neck "You're the only thing that convinced me. You're the only thing worth staying for."

"That isn't enough, Dina. You need a deeper understanding with the Pride if you're going to live here in peace. If you don't have anything more to stay for than me, you won't be happy."

"I'll be happy with you. That's enough."

She laid her head on his shoulder. His warmth seeped into her limbs and chased away the cold. She rubbed her face into the soft folds of fur around his neck.

"I'm happy with you, too, Dina," he purred. "I don't want to run the risk of losing you again. If you're dissatisfied, you should tell me so we can settle the issue before it becomes unbearable for you."

"I'm not dissatisfied. If anything dissatisfied me, I would tell you."

"Good." He nuzzled his cheek into her leg. He rubbed his bristly chin against her knee and purred low in his chest.

The rumble set her tingling all over. Her whole being raised its voice in one aching scream. The fire lulled her into an intoxicated trance. She leaned against his side and they fell together, side by side, onto the carpet. She rolled onto her back and he pressed his long body against her from chest to flank.

She didn't hold back. She would give herself to him, just this once, if that's what it took to get her out of here. If she had to do it with a cat, she could do it with him.

She cared about him enough to want him. For all she knew, this could be her last night alive. At least she would show him she cared about him before she died.

He sensed her willingness and, in one swift motion, he rolled over on top of her. His weight crushed the breath out of her, but she still submitted to him. She didn't stiffen or resist in any way.

He ran his cheek along her neck and up to her ear. She closed her eyes and inhaled his scent. His weight sent shock waves of excitement through her that translated into her chest and down to her belly and hips. She couldn't contain the mounting energy any longer and she flexed her pelvis upward to meet him.

The movement set off a chain reaction in him. He opened his great jaws and growled into her ear, all the time pressing his cheek against the side of her head. Her breath deepened and she wrapped her arms around his shoulders. This was it. She would give herself to him without holding back.

Their bodies pulsed and rippled against each other, rising higher and higher on pulses of energy moving back and forth between them. Renfroe moved his hips against her thighs and she spread her legs to invite him in.

His growl turned to a yowl. All of a sudden, he pulled back his lips and dug his fangs into her neck. He didn't bite hard enough to break the skin or hurt her, but she sucked her breath through her teeth in surprise. She didn't pull away. She arched her back to press herself against him even harder.

Her whistling breath broke him out of his excitement. In an instant, he returned to the sedate senator he always was. He drew back and the energy died.

"You don't have to do this," he murmured. "I know you don't really want to."

"I want to do it. If you really want me, I'm willing."

"I don't want you to compromise yourself. I know you don't really want to do it. Don't do it unless you really want to."

"I do really want to. If I'm going to be here with you, I have to do it. It won't work if I don't."

He didn't buy it, though. He rolled off to her side. He lay on the floor pressed against her, but he made no further move toward her.

His body radiated warmth all through her. She turned on her side and wrapped her arms around him. She never experienced anything like the peace and comfort of his embrace. She laid her head against his chest and listened to his heart.

"Are you mine, Dina?" he growled. "Does your heart belong to me?"

"You know it does," she whispered. "You know there's no one else but you."

"I don't want you to stay with me if you aren't mine. I understand why you don't want to give your body to me, but at least give me your heart."

"You already have it. You know that. I don't want to be anywhere but here with you."

"Are you sure?" he asked. "Are you really sure?"

She raised her face to him. "Why do you keep asking? Don't you believe me? I wouldn't say it if it wasn't true. No one else in the galaxy can come near you in my heart. You should know that by now. I wouldn't be lying by this fire with my arms around you if I didn't want to give my body to you. You already have my heart. You can have my body, too. I want you to."

He listened, but he didn't move. He knew when she was lying, but this once, she didn't have to. She loved him and she would willingly give him her body.

For some reason, though, he couldn't accept it. Something made him hesitate. He waited another long moment. Only the crackle of the fire filled the room. Then he turned away.

Dina saw him slipping through her fingers. "Renfroe, don't turn your back on me."

"I will never turn my back on you, Dina. I only wish I could say the same about you."

"But I just told you I want to do it."

He shook his head and moved away. He left a cavern of emptiness in her arms. "I don't know what made you decide to do it with me, but you still don't want to. You may be willing, but you don't really want to do it."

"I just told you I did," she insisted. "Why would I say I did when I didn't?"

"You're not doing it because you want to. You're still holding back."

"How did I hold back? Was I holding back when I spread my legs for you? Was I holding back when I let you bite me? When did I hold back?"

He didn't answer. He rolled to his feet and padded to the door. The firelight glanced off his stripes and he whisked his tail from side to side.

"Where are you going?" she asked.

He didn't answer. The next minute, he disappeared into the dark.

"Renfroe!" she cried. "Renfroe, come back!"

She sat on the floor listening and waiting, but he didn't come back.

"Renfroe!" she called. "Renfroe, please come back!"

Chapter 55

The fire died down to coals and cold took over the room. Dina sat in the same place and stared into the embers. How long had she been sitting here? She didn't know. It didn't matter. The longer she waited, the better. Maybe Renfroe would come back and he would take the question of what she would do out of her hands.

He didn't come back. She shivered and rubbed her arms, but the cold came from inside herself. No fire burned inside her for anyone or anything anymore. Nothing remained for her, here or anywhere else. Only one thing mattered and that was to stay alive.

She couldn't stay in this cold parlor anymore. She ought to go to her room, but her days in that room were over. She stood up to leave, but at that moment, the meow of a cat echoed through the open door. The sentinel cats roamed the city at this time of night. No storm would protect her if she left the house now.

She picked up the iron poker from its place by the hearth and hefted it in her hand. It was better than nothing and it was the only weapon she would find on this planet.

She tiptoed out of the room. No sound disturbed the house. Belinda would be asleep by now. Dina paused in the corridor to listen. If she went out the front door, she might rouse Belinda or Buck might come for her this time.

She crossed the parquet floor to the portico. The sky rang clear and still all the way up to the stars. The *Savannah* was sailing around up there somewhere.

Dina stepped through the portico onto the damp grass. Her feet made no sound. She hadn't broken the law yet. She could still turn back and throw herself on Renfroe's affections.

She passed the fountain and the bench where they always sat and talked. She passed the trees and shrubs where they walked together. She would never see them again whether she succeeded in escaping or not.

She walked to the far end of the garden to the door in the wall. She didn't feel the poker still clenched in her cold, stiff fingers. She lifted the latch and pushed the door open. It made no sound, either. Buck kept it well oiled.

Cats called to each other in the distance. The moment she stepped through that door, the sentinels would be on top of her. They wouldn't stop until they tore her to pieces. She would have hesitated if she hadn't been so cold. She had to hurry or go back to her room. She ducked through the wall and closed the door behind her.

She didn't hesitate again once she made that first decisive move. She knew exactly where to go. The trees blocked out the starlight on either side of the street. Her footsteps echoed off garden walls and houses. She didn't dare look back to see who or what might be following her.

She glanced back when she came to the city square. A black tide rose out of the ground, flowed through the streets, and swirled around trees and flower beds. It flooded toward her and she ran faster than ever.

The faster she ran, the faster the tide rushed her until it engulfed her on both sides. Her chest burned from running and her knees wobbled. She couldn't run any further. In a second, the sentinel cats would close over her head and drag her to the ground. The square stood wide open and empty. It was as good a place as any to make her stand.

She landed on one foot and spun around to face the cats. As soon as she stopped, the rushing flood stopped, too. She could make out individual cats running around her in droves. They darted up trees, down to the ground, and under and over one another. Their eyes gleamed in the starlight and flashed when they turned their heads.

Her fear vanished the moment she faced them. She narrowed her eyes and bared her teeth. She brought up her poker and held it in front of herself in readiness for the cats' attack.

The sentinel cats surrounded Dina on all sides so she couldn't run again. She whirled in a circle and swung her poker to drive them back. There were enough cats here to flank her even though they were only small house cats. They could easily drag her to the ground if they all attacked at once.

For some reason, though, they didn't attack. They didn't know what to do with a person who didn't run from them. They caught so few curfew breakers that they wouldn't know what to do when they found one. The helpers wouldn't fight back if they got caught.

They retreated every time she slashed with her poker. The last of Dina's fear vaporized. She was still alive so she must have won. She glanced across the square. A sea of cats barred her way.

She swung her poker faster and harder. One step at a time, she inched across the square to the opposite side. She carved a path through the cats and they parted before her.

They watched her step off the curb into the street. They put their heads together, but no sound came from them. Dina held her breath. Would they follow her? She had to make her escape unseen. She couldn't lose the element of surprise.

She backed up a few more steps, but they didn't follow. She came to the corner where she would turn toward the river. She and the cats studied each other across the street. Someone had to make the first move and she couldn't wait all night. She had less than two days left to reach the Pod and every confrontation slowed her down.

They still didn't move. Dina drew a breath and ducked behind the corner. With the cats out of view, she turned and ran again as fast as her legs would carry her. She couldn't count on them leaving her alone to escape. Either they would come after her or they would go get their bigger friends to run her down.

She retraced her steps past Elyse's house to the river. It whispered its secrets, but no one listened. It hid Prideland's dead beneath its surface where no one would know their fate. Dina would join the dead beneath the surface of the river. Alive or dead, she would go where they went and learn their secrets.

She crossed the last street. The power station sat on the hill above her. No light came from its windows. Did the Elite Battalion sleep in there on the bare stone floor? She would never know that, either.

She slowed her pace and caught her breath to approach the building in silence. Her plan hinged on this moment, but she turned away too soon.

She had just set her foot on the path up the hill when the first cat slipped around the corner and trotted toward her. The inky bodies rippled over the grass one after another. Dina didn't see any of the big cats she feared most. The same small sentinel cats must have followed her after all.

She jabbed her poker at them, but they knew what to expect this time. They outnumbered her by the hundreds and they weren't scared of her. She couldn't fight them with a flimsy poker.

They never once stopped running. The first cat jumped, but one cat on his own couldn't do much. She didn't bother hitting him with her poker. She caught him around the middle with her bare hand and pitched him away. He sailed through the air in a smooth arc, and when he fell, he landed on his feet. He hesitated, but by that time, hundreds of other cats swept into view.

Dina's heart quailed, but she couldn't back down now. Let them come. She would die fighting. That was the best anyone could hope for in Prideland. She would follow the example of the man in the jungle and take as many of them with her as she could.

The first wave crossed the street in a line. They didn't make the same mistake their comrade did and they jumped at her as one body. The starlight flashed on their teeth and Dina swung her poker and cleared the air of all of them with one stroke. She didn't have time to enjoy her victory before the next group sailed toward her.

She swung her poker back the other way and knocked the cats to the ground. Some lay unconscious at her feet. Others twitched in their death throes. The poker caught one cat in the flesh and it dangled from the poker hook every time she swung it. When the next wave attacked, the body flapped in their faces.

So many cats came to join the fight that no amount of slashing and smashing would drive them off. They no longer leapt in waves that she could knock out of the air. They jumped in one continuous rain of bodies. They would land on top of her sooner or later and that would be the end of her.

In her last act of desperation, she brandished her poker at the oncoming waves of cats. The dead cat flopped in their faces and they paused. They started at the dead cat as a talisman of her victory over them.

Dina growled through her teeth. "Who's next?"

The cats ranged themselves across the street and stared her down, but she didn't flinch. The dead cat frightened them and she used it to her advantage. When a cat stepped out of line, she thrust the dead body toward it to drive it back.

They stare at her while she backed out of sight. Cats disappeared in the back of the mob as bunches of twos and threes retreated. The tide ebbed before her eyes until only a few ranks of cats faced her across the street.

Dina's heart soared at the sight of her enemies moving off. She roared and waved her dead cat at them. In the end, she charged across the street and brandished the cat in their faces. That was all it took. The last cats turned tail and ran until she remained panting and victorious at the foot of the hill.

Chapter 56

The power station stood dark and silent on the hill. Something heavy caught Dina's attention and she looked down. The cat hung from the poker in her hand and she examined it as if for the first time.

With a few shakes, she dislodged it from the hook. It flopped to the ground, but she kept hold of the poker.

She started up the hill. She snuck past the door and behind the building to the barrels stacked against the wall. One barrel stood in a corner by itself.

She couldn't tell in the dark how sturdy it was, but she couldn't waste any more time. She had to trust her fate. Those cats would fetch their comrades, now that she'd beaten them in a fight. They would bring Hector, Victor, and Khalid—the real hunters. She wouldn't drive *them* off with a poker.

She tipped the barrel on its edge, rolled it to the water, and slid it down the bank. The water chuckled and lapped the bottom of the barrel to swallow her. She swung one leg into the barrel followed by the other. The water slapped the barrel's sides and cold sank into her bones.

Her weight held the barrel on the river bottom. She grasped the rim with both hands and rocked it into deeper water until it floated free. The current caught it and it floated down the river.

She sat down in the barrel and wrapped her arms around her knees. The river sang all around her all through the night. Its voice seeped into her dreams when she dozed off.

She only woke from her trance when light shone through the top of the barrel. She stretched her knees enough to stand up and stick her head out of the top.

Grey dawn spread over the fields and farms. People and animals still slept in houses and sheds, but the first twists of smoke were starting to curl from the rooftops.

She kept her head down. She didn't want anyone to see her head. If they saw a barrel floating down the river, they would think it was empty—at least, she hoped so. She only looked out to check her progress. How far would the river take her?

Then she spied a village she recognized. It was Alexander Mathus's village—Maddy's village. Maddy's dead body rolled somewhere in this river. The village got its drinking water from this river. Did the villagers know the river brought their own children back to them from the city?

The river carried her beyond the last house and into the jungle. She was getting closer to the pod and the jungle grew denser. How would she get out of this barrel? There was no one around anymore to see her. She stood up and looked around. Solid jungle surrounded her on all sides.

Just then, the barrel struck a rock. Before she knew what was happening, big boulders blocked the river and brought the barrel to a stop. She couldn't go any further.

She tried to climb out onto one of the stones, but the barrel tipped over and dumped her into a gravel bed no deeper than her ankles. She struggled up the bank, but she made sure to take her poker with her.

The sun passed its zenith and moved down the other side of the sky. She had to hurry. She had to leave this planet tomorrow if she wanted to leave at all.

She wouldn't find the pod today. That was certain. She had to spend the night in the jungle and find the pod tomorrow in daylight and that was assuming none of the cats hunted her during the night.

She started toward the west, though she didn't know exactly where she was. The sun went down long before she spotted any landmark. She started looking around for a tree to climb when a shadow caught her eye through the trees. She went toward it and almost burst into tears when she spotted the roof of a house.

It was the canton—Frank's canton. The fence and gate stood open. The canton stood silent and peaceful as if all the people were in their houses for the night. Only the absence of smoke coming from the chimneys told her that no one was home.

She took one step inside the fence. No cats leapt out to get her. She could rest here for the night, but she wouldn't go back to Elana's house. She couldn't bear the grief of sleeping in the same bed in the same room. She went to a different house.

The ladder up to the door still stood in place. No one set foot in that canton since the cats attacked it. Dina put her foot on the lowest rung of the ladder and listened. The silence unnerved her.

Children's shouts and laughter should have filled that canton. Women should have lingered near their ladders to snatch their last conversations for the day. Men should have finished their work at the tannery before going indoors for the night, but not even the tree lizards came here anymore. The place was cursed. Only the dead came here—and Dina.

She gave one last look around and climbed up the ladder. The house was exactly like Elana's with some uneaten food molding on the table. A black stain in the corner gave the only clue to what happened to the people who lived there.

Dina swallowed hard. Up the interior ladder in the bedrooms, she found a bed made up exactly like the one at Frank and Elana's house. Dina didn't give herself a chance to think twice. She lay down and closed her eyes. Exhaustion engulfed her and she gave herself over to it completely.

Chapter 57

T he tree lizards' chatter woke her. For a fraction of an instant, Dina breathed the fresh air of freedom, but danger drove her out of bed and out of the house. She had to get to the pod. She might already be too late. She cringed at every step and listened for any sound. She had to push herself forward. She couldn't stop.

Her heart pounded in her chest and her palms sweated. She walked faster and almost broke into a run. Her ears picked up a sound that shouldn't be there and she paused to listen. Something was following her.

She spotted the pod ahead, but its engines would take several minutes to warm up. She glanced around for a place to hide when her eye fell on an old tree just next to the path. Its center loomed black and rotten and gnarled.

She stuck her hand into the tree's rotten interior. It was hollow. She could just squeeze into it. She shoved herself into the opening when human voices rang through the jungle. Alexander Mathus and Harmon Farley led a group of village men down the path.

Farley waved his arm. "There's the landing craft. Search the area, you men. If she's anywhere, she'll be here."

The men fanned out to comb the jungle around the pod. Dina held her breath and kept still, but at that moment, the ground crumbled beneath her feet. Her weight broke through powdery rotten wood and moldy leaves and she tumbled down into a cavern underneath the tree.

The fall surprised her enough to stifle her cry and the men made too much noise themselves to hear her. She landed on her feet in a pit around the tree's roots, twisted her ankle, and collapsed on the damp soil.

Pain stabbed up her leg and she clamped her lips together to stop herself from screaming in agony. She huddled in the pit clutching her ankle and rocking while she fought herself under control.

The men walked around the Pod and even looked into the tree's opening, but they didn't see her sitting there, totally defenseless in the pit below.

Their voices faded into the jungle and Dina struggled to stand on her one good leg. She would have waited beneath the tree until dusk, but she had to get to the Pod. She clenched her teeth against the pain and straightened up.

She dragged herself out of the pit by the tree's roots and her heart sank. Most of the day was already gone. She was too late. All these unforeseen setbacks cost her time and now she'd lost her chance to escape.

She limped to the tangle of vegetation covering the pod, but she froze in her tracks when a tree limb bounced overhead. Two cats landed without a sound on the ground in front of her. She found herself face to face with Fallon and Khalid.

Dina stared at them and her courage faltered. They had her trapped. She would never get away.

Fallon blinked at the pod and then at her. "We thought we might find you here. The rest of them are all out searching the roads, but Khalid and I knew you would come straight here. You humans are so predictable. You don't offer any challenge at all."

Khalid sat down to block her path to the pod. "Your friend Renfroe wants you brought back alive. He's such a sentimental old fool, but accidents can happen to anyone. I can't wait to sink my teeth into you. I held back at that canton. Renfroe would have been upset if I reduced you along with the rest of the slags, but he isn't here now. He'll never see you again and he'll never know what happened to you."

The memory of the hunt and the man's last battle against these cats flickered before Dina's eyes and her fear turned to rage. She planted her feet wide and waved her poker in their faces.

Every move shot brutal pain up her leg from her ankle, but the pain only fired her anger against these cats. She would give them something to remember after they killed her. She wouldn't go down easily.

Fallon stared at her when she took a fighting stance. She expected him to laugh in her face. So she managed to knock around a few house cats. She couldn't expect the same result facing these two killers, but her very hopelessness gave her all the strength she needed. She would die here. No one would ever say she didn't fight to her last breath to get away from the Pride.

Khalid glanced at Fallon. "You can take her on your own, can't you? I'll watch."

"Why, thank you," Fallon replied. "I do appreciate a good fight, but this one should be no trouble at all."

Khalid sniffed. "These humans are pathetic creatures. They have no real defenses at all and she won't do any damage with a weapon like that."

The poker sagged in Dina's hands, and in a flash, Fallon sprang. Dina hardly had time to bring her poker up before he reached her. She managed to turn it horizontally across her face. Fallon struck the shaft and bounced off. He landed on his feet a few yards away.

He barely touched the ground before he launched himself at her again. She didn't have time to get her poker in position at all before he pounced onto her head. His claws caught hold of her scalp and face and his hind feet dug into her chest. He raked his claws across her face and gashed her to ribbons.

The pain ignited her fury again. She still had the poker, but no way to hit him or defend herself with it. She had to get him off. His back feet shredded her clothes and scored her chest with long, angry scratches. If he got his claws into her eyes, she was finished.

She brought the poker up hard against his body. She tried to pry him off, but when she got the poker between herself and him, she saw what she had to do. She bent her head to make a pocket between his front legs. Then she jabbed the poker upwards as hard as she could. She buried the tip in the flesh under his ribs, perforated his diaphragm, and drove the iron point into his heart.

Fallon let out an ear-splitting shriek that set Dina's teeth on edge. His claws instantly retracted and he lost his grip on her head. She fought back the urge to fling him away and dug the poker's point deeper into his chest.

He extended his claws again, but this time, he clung to her for his very life. Hot blood gushed over her hands and her fingers slipped on the poker handle. She relaxed just enough to push him off. His claws raked her skin, but he offered no resistance and hit the ground twitching.

Khalid stared at him. Then he glared at Dina. "Do you know the penalty for killing a cat?"

Dina snarled at him. "You came here to kill me, so come on and do it. What are you waiting for?"

He didn't get up. He only glared at her. She shifted her poker from one hand to the other and wiped her bloody hands on her pants. Why didn't he attack? He wanted her dead. Now was his chance. No one would see and Renfroe wouldn't ask any questions when Khalid came back without her. They both knew the law of the Pride.

His hesitation annoyed her. The longer he waited, the less chance she had of using the pod if she ever got to it. Maybe he knew that. Maybe Tania told him about their three-week deadline. Maybe all he wanted to do was delay Dina so she couldn't escape at all.

She had to provoke him somehow. She swung her poker from one hand and whirled it in a circle at her side. "Come on. You want to kill me? Here I am."

He regarded her with cool consideration. She couldn't wait any longer. She ran at him brandishing her poker. That must have been the last thing in the world he expected because he jumped up and darted away.

She followed up her surprise attack by chopping the poker at him. He leapt to one side and her momentum carried her past him. Her poker whistled through the air and he slashed his claws at her.

He caught her and yanked her off balance with one swipe of his claws. She staggered to one side and landed on her injured ankle. Her leg buckled beneath her and she hit the dirt.

Khalid jumped on top of her, but she rolled out of the way just in time. He'd recovered from his surprise and found his rhythm. He twisted and pranced and hooked her with his claws. Dina scrambled backward to get away, but she couldn't move fast enough to stay ahead of him.

He put on a fresh burst of speed and pounced on her. She pitched over backward with just enough time to get her poker into position before he landed on her with all his weight. His chest jammed the poker against her body where she couldn't use it.

She tried to shove him off, but he was a lot heavier than Fallon. He crouched on all fours on top of her and his jaws gaped in her face. She cringed, and in the face of certain death, she managed to twist on her side underneath him and roll out of the way.

He came after her in a flash. He sprang out of his crouch and swung his claws to hook her again. She twisted one last time on her side grasping her poker in both hands.

She swept the hook outwards and slashed his skin along his hind flank. The pure black fur parted to reveal the muscle underneath before blood filled the wound.

Khalid bellowed in pain, but his fangs snapped shut on empty air. Dina scurried away and scrambled to her feet a few yards away. She got into another trembling stance ready to defend herself again.

Khalid studied her, but he didn't attack. Blood dripped into the dirt and his injured leg quivered. He held his paw off the ground. He couldn't fight like this. Dina began to see a future beyond this confrontation. She might actually come out of this alive.

He took a few steps from her right to her left, but he couldn't use his leg at all. He swiveled his ears and flicked his tail. He narrowed his eyes and glanced once into the jungle.

He and Fallon came alone to catch her at the pod. They wanted to keep all the glory of hunting her down for themselves. His friends wouldn't be coming to help him any time soon.

He wrinkled his nose at her. "You can't win, you know. You'll never win against us." He sniffed in the direction of the pod. "And you won't get away in *that*."

Then he lifted his back leg and hobbled away into the thicket.

Chapter 58

D ina used her poker to slash away the overgrowth around the pod's door. She pushed the button to open the hatch, but nothing happened. Her heart sank. The power packs were as good as dead.

She pulled the manual lever and the door swung up. The air inside smelled of the *Savannah* and her spirits revived. All she had to do was get the pod into orbit.

She sat at the pilot's station and touched the power-up key. Nothing came on. The console lay dead and cold under her hands. She forced herself to breathe and then to think. It couldn't end like this, not after everything she went through to get here.

She keyed in the launch sequence, and to her amazement, the console buzzed to life. The engines didn't power up, though. A warning message appeared on the console. *Low power. Charge the power packs before launch.*

Her mind churned. She went aft and unclipped the hatch cover over the engine. Another control panel lay underneath. She shot the *Emergency Power* toggle switch and went back to the pilot's station.

This time, when she hit the power-up key, the engines whined to life. Dina broke into hysterical laughter, but the next moment, she almost lost all hope when the engines died again. She was too late. The power packs didn't contain even enough power to get the pod off the ground, let alone break the planet's gravitational field.

She only had one more chance. She went back to the aft compartment and opened the panel labeled *AutoStart*. She grasped the lever and cranked it until sweat drenched her forehead, but she already knew it was hopeless. The power packs didn't have a single drop of residual power to charge up.

She let her head fall into her hands. She clamped her lips together to stop them from trembling. Her mind scanned the pod for any source of power, no matter how small.

She found her handpad in her locker where she left it. Her hands shook. Was it possible this might actually work? She turned the handpad over and popped out the battery. It wouldn't be enough on its own.

She went to the next locker and opened it. It was Tom's locker and the first thing she saw when she pulled back the door was a photoprint of herself smiling. She shut the image out of her mind and took his handpad. She took out the battery and slammed the locker shut.

She collected five batteries from her teammates' handpads and took them back to the engine panel. The only problem was how to hook them up to the panel. She was no engineer. If Tom was here, he would know how to deal with this. She might need to find even more power sources to get off this planet.

Staring at the panel wasn't getting her anywhere. She had to take action—drastic action. She clawed the panel up with her fingernails and yanked the wires out of the switch. She found the laser welder in a compartment by the engine and welded the switch wires to the metal panel. Then she welded the battery connections to the panel, too.

She tried the power-up sequence again. The engines burst to life and immediately died. She couldn't keep trying or she would waste the little power she had left. At least she knew now that patching batteries from handheld devices to the emergency power panel worked. She only had to find a few more—maybe a lot more—to make the engines stay on.

She scavenged two more batteries from microscanners in Marcus Harte's locker, but she didn't try the engines with them. She needed more. She stood in the middle of the pod and looked around. Where could she find another concentrated source of power?

Cats could be coming through the jungle to capture her right now. She'd played her last trick with that poker. If she couldn't get the pod going, there was no point in even fighting back.

Thinking about fighting gave her an idea. She sprang across the compartment to the security lock-up and tore off the cover. Her hands trembled when she took the weapons off their hooks. Each power cell contained enough power to get the engines started. Linking them together would certainly get her off the planet.

She attached them to the panel next to the other batteries and hurried back to the pilot's station. She powered up and the engines came alive. This time, they stayed on. She keyed in the launch sequence. She didn't have a moment to lose before she lost power again.

The engines picked up power and her heart rose off the ground along with the pod. The pod broke its blanket of vegetation and cleared the treetops. Dina slipped on her safety harness. Why did she bother? If the pod crashed, she would be killed on impact.

The pod soared higher through the atmosphere. Clouds whizzed past and Dina laughed and sobbed in pure joy. It worked! She was flying away from this rotten planet forever. The sun dipped behind the planet and the first stars dotted the veil of the upper stratosphere.

Would the pod have enough power to break the planet's gravitational field? The veil thinned between her and the unlimited freedom of space. The pod shuddered and an emergency warning appeared on the console. *Low power. Charge the power packs.* An alarm sounded and the pod wobbled and faltered in midair.

She gasped and panted in desperation. She punched every button on the console. *No, no, no,* repeated in her mind. *Don't do this to me. Don't let me die like this. Oh, please, no. I'll do anything. Don't do this. Just a little further.*

The pod jolted. Every panel in the hull groaned and then the engines died. The console under Dina's hands went black. Not even the emergency alarm worked anymore. The pod floated in an endless expanse of black space with only the stars to keep it company.

The blue-green bubble of the planet's atmosphere drifted beyond the porthole. Could all the fear and confusion and pain of Prideland really be going on down there on that tiny, insignificant planet? Her memories receded with it until they didn't seem real anymore.

She turned back to the console. The engines were gone and nothing could bring them back. She didn't even have enough power to send out a distress call.

She didn't see the *Savannah* anywhere nearby. It must be on the other side of the planet. Captain Doyle and the crew would never know she was here. She would float adrift until she starved or suffocated.

She gazed at the stars. She never thought she'd see them again. If no one found her, she could die satisfied knowing she did everything she had to do to get away. She wouldn't die in Prideland.

She let out a deep breath. She went aft to the medical berth and sat down. Only now did she feel the pain in her ankle and the scratches on her face and chest. She was the patient now. She lay down in the berth and closed her eyes.

When she opened them, she didn't recognize the face peering down at her. Then he narrowed his eyes and his eyebrows stuck straight out from his face. She was looking up at Captain Doyle.

Chapter 59

Dina hugged her knees to her chest on a narrow bench that served as a bed in her brig cell. Stark white walls surrounded her except where steel bars blocked her view.

The bars hummed with enough electricity to electrocute her if she touched them. Dr. Galvin sat cross-legged on a different bench beyond the bars. She set her handpad aside and recrossed her legs the other way.

Dina refused to look at her. "I knew you wouldn't believe me."

"I wish I could believe you, Dina, but our protocols prohibit me from doing so. You know that."

"What are you going to tell the captain?"

Dr. Galvin cast a sidelong glance at her handpad and shrugged. "That you disobeyed a direct order from your commanding officer and abandoned your teammates on the planet. I have no choice but to recommend the stiffest possible penalty. You'll be demoted at the least. You might even be drummed out of the Armada."

"I don't care. I don't belong here anymore, anyway."

Dr. Galvin pursed her lips. Had Dina been looking at her, she would have seen the first hint of annoyance from the Doctor in all the years they'd known each other. "I always liked you, Dina. I told you once I thought you were a younger version of myself, but the truth is I've always thought of you more as my own daughter—without the same history, of course. I want to help you if I can."

"How do you plan to do that? The situation looks pretty hopeless to me."

Dr. Galvin picked up her handpad and touched the screen. "You keep insisting that you never actually went through with having sex with Renfroe. I find that very difficult to believe, especially when Tom and Tania both did it under similar circumstances."

"Believe what you want. It's true."

"Come on, Dina," Dr. Galvin chided. "You can't really expect me to believe that, knowing what I do about your background."

"What's that supposed to mean?"

Dr. Galvin took a deep breath. "You have a history of abuse by your stepfather, but you form bonds more easily with men than women. You bonded with your brother and you told me once you loved Tom like a brother. You transferred your bond with your brother onto Tom."

"So what if I did? That has nothing to do with Renfroe."

"Your experience with Tom and with your brother obviously contributed to your relationship with Renfroe. It made you vulnerable to him manipulating you."

"My experience with my brother and Tom had nothing to do with Renfroe. I know a good man when I see one."

"That's exactly why Renfroe was able to pull the wool over your eyes. It's obvious from the story you told me that you've fallen in love with him."

Dina didn't answer.

"You followed a similar pattern with Renfroe as you did with Tom. You were attracted to a kind but authoritative male."

"That doesn't mean I had sex with him."

"You admit you were ready to. You admit you planned to give yourself to him so you could escape."

"If I had done it with him, I wouldn't say I hadn't. I wouldn't be ashamed of doing it with Renfroe. I told you at the end I wanted to. In a way, I wish I had."

"You would be a lot more ashamed of doing it than of almost doing it," Dr. Galvin replied. "I can't believe Renfroe would back out on it when he had you right where he wanted you. You said yourself the cats use sex as a tool to manipulate their people to do what they want. Renfroe went to a lot of trouble to maneuver you into doing it. He wouldn't back out at the last second out of some tenderhearted misgivings about your feelings. He's a tyrant—a kind and gentle one, but still a tyrant. No tyrant would be so accommodating to his inferiors when he had you in the palm of his hand."

Dina turned away. "You don't know Renfroe."

"Don't you remember what I told you about the years I spent counseling the returned prisoners from the Angove War?" Dr. Galvin asked. "I recognize the effect of a controlling system on you. I've seen this a thousand times."

"I guess you haven't seen Prideland before."

Dr. Galvin leaned forward in her seat. "I'm not your enemy, Dina. I'm your friend and I'm probably the only person on board who can help you. I want to help you, but I can't do that if you don't tell the truth about what happened."

"I already told you the truth. If you don't believe me, there's nothing I can do about that."

Dr. Galvin leaned back in her seat again. "Then you'll have to stay here. I can't release you from the brig until you tell the truth."

Dina snorted. "You're using the same strong-arm tactics on me that they use in Prideland. You're no better than they are."

Dr. Galvin smiled. "You're right, but that's the military way."

"I'm not military anymore."

"No, you aren't. You're right about that. You broke the chain of command by coming back alone and you've flouted my authority ever since you came back. You're no longer loyal to the Armada. That's for certain."

"Next, you'll want me to admit I'm loyal to Prideland," Dina shot back. "Well, I'm not. I wouldn't be here if I was."

"I don't say you're loyal to Prideland. I can see you hate it. I'm not sure who you're loyal to."

"You probably think I'm loyal to Renfroe, but I betrayed him twice. Why would I do that if I was loyal to him?"

Dr. Galvin shook her head. "No, you aren't loyal to him, either. You aren't loyal to anyone but yourself now."

Dina looked up at her for the first time. "If you were in my place, you would have done the same thing."

"I'm sure I would have, but I'm not in your place. I'm in my place and I have no choice but to recommend stiff discipline to bring you back into line. If you don't fall in line, you'll be dismissed from the service. I'm sorry to have to do this. I know you worried about this very thing. It stopped your teammates from escaping and it almost stopped you."

"That won't stop you from recommending it, though."

"I'll tell you the truth," Dr. Galvin replied. "I'm seriously questioning my own position in the Armada after being forced to make this recommendation. I joined the Armada to help people, not to make their lives harder. I think I might resign."

"What about the rest of the team?" Dina asked.

Dr. Galvin scanned her handpad. "You don't paint a very optimistic picture of their future. Matthew Geromi could be dead by now judging from your description of his injuries and Renfroe doesn't hold out much hope for Tom ever breaking free."

"There must be some way to get them out."

"We have protocols for rescuing trapped personnel. The captain has to consider the safety of anyone he sends down to bring them back."

"The captain sent us down to the planet to bring back Alexander Mathus," Dina pointed out.

"He didn't know the situation on the planet when he did that. He never would have sent people down there if he'd known about this...." She wrinkled his nose at the screen, "...this Pride."

"We can't just leave them there. You might not believe me about Renfroe, but if you believe me about the danger, we have to do something."

"I already talked to the captain about this. He didn't know your team would face the dangers you did. We would not have made any attempt to incorporate this planet while it was under the control of these cats. If we mounted any rescue operation at all, he estimates we'd have to send an armed force of no less than three thousand."

Dina's head whipped around. "That many?"

Dr. Galvin nodded. "The humans on the planet are completely under the cats' influence to the point where they'll attack their own kind to defend the Pride and the humans have no weapons. That gives the cats every advantage in a fight. An unarmed human being doesn't stand a chance against a full-sized tiger or lion or jaguar. We'd be lucky to defeat the Pride even with all our weapons. The humans would defend the Pride with their lives."

"So we're just going to leave the team down there to rot?" Dina asked.

"At this point, I don't see what choice we have."

Dina cradled her head in her hand. "We can't do this. There may be time to save Matthew and Tom could snap out of it once he's back on board the ship."

"The key word here is 'could'. He *could* snap out of it. Alexander Mathus *could* snap out of it if he comes on board the ship, too. Then again, he might not."

"Don't we at least owe him the chance?" Dina asked.

"Who are we talking about—Tom or Mathus?"

Dina hesitated. "Tom, I guess."

"For the sake of argument, let's talk about Alexander Mathus. His case is much more straightforward. He told you point blank he never wanted to return to the Coalition. Tom never said that, although from what he did say, and from what Renfroe told you about people who've engaged in this kind of...shall we call it bestiality?"

Dina didn't raise her eyes from her hands in her lap.

"Right," Dr. Galvin went on. "Renfroe told you these people never leave the city, let alone Prideland, and I understand why. They wouldn't want anyone to find out what they'd done. Now getting back to Mathus. He said he didn't want to leave, and he wouldn't leave, and he wouldn't allow his wife and children to leave. Now imagine we went in with an expeditionary force and dragged him away. Are you still with me?"

Dina nodded.

"He could, as you say, snap out of it once on board ship. Then again, he could spend the rest of his life searching for a way to go back to the planet and continue to serve the Pride. Are you willing to risk your life, which you just nearly lost getting off that planet, to free him when he doesn't want to be free and will throw your sacrifice back in your face the first chance he gets?"

"I wouldn't make that sacrifice for Mathus, but I would make it for Tom. He's only been on the planet for three weeks. Mathus has been there for seven months. Tom stands a better chance of coming out of it."

The doctor shook her head. "I'm sorry. We can't allow any more Coalition personnel to endanger themselves. What happened to you is bad enough. We didn't know the state of the planet before. Now we do."

"So what are we going to do?"

"Tomorrow we'll leave this part of the Inner Corridor and continue on our previous trajectory to the Outer Ring. We'll continue with our assignment to track the Comet Integra's path into the Ring."

"Tom and Matthew and Tania's families will want answers," Dina pointed out. "What will you tell them?"

"We'll tell them exactly what you told us and what I just told you. We'll tell them we landed on that planet with incomplete and inaccurate information about the conditions and the risks. We were forced by circumstance to leave them behind. They may still be alive, but we can't run the risk of finding out one way or the other."

"I don't think I can accept that," Dina replied.

Dr. Galvin stood up and tucked her handpad under her arm. "You have no choice. Captain Doyle will explain to Chancellor Mathus that we're abandoning this mission.

He won't like it, but that's the way it is. We can't risk any more lives on this planet. The jungle can have it back."

At that moment, the door slid open and Ensign Ingram hurried in. "I'm ordered to release Lieutenant Dyer from the brig and bring her to Captain Doyle's office on the double."

A black cloud crossed Dr. Galvin's face. "You can't release her without my authorization. Not even the captain can release her against my recommendation."

Ensign Ingram shook his head and crossed the room to the bars in front of Dina's cell. "I'm sorry, Doctor. I have my orders."

He punched a button and the electric hum died. The bars slid aside and Dina stepped out of the cell. Ensign Ingram nodded. "If you'll follow me, Lieutenant...."

She followed him out of the brig and left Dr. Galvin standing there with smoke coming out of her ears. He led her to Captain Doyle's office. Neither noticed Dr. Galvin bringing up the rear.

The office door opened and Dr. Galvin barreled in. "What's the meaning of this, Captain? You know I recommended Lieutenant Dyer remain in the brig until she cooperates with this investigation."

Captain Doyle rose from his chair and straightened up to his full height. "I've read your report, Doctor, and I accept your recommendation. Unfortunately, I received orders from higher up." He waved his hand toward a chair across the room. "I think you know Chancellor Peter Mathus."

Dr. Galvin whirled around and Dina stared in shock at an older, miniature version of Frank Mathus.

Chapter 60

C hancellor Mathus glared at Dr. Galvin. "I gave the order to release Lieutenant Dyer from the brig."

Dr. Galvin faced him. "I don't have to tell you how highly irregular this is, Chancellor, especially since your order to send an unprepared team to the planet's surface caused this whole debacle."

Chancellor Mathus paid her no attention. He turned his fiery eyes on Dina. "I demand some explanation for your actions on that planet, Lieutenant. How could you abandon not only your teammates but my son whom you explicitly landed on the planet to rescue. What have you got to say for yourself?"

"I explained all that to Dr. Galvin," she replied. "I'm sure you've read her report, too, Sir."

The little man did his best to draw himself up, but he stood barely higher than her chest. "I still see no reason you shouldn't be drummed out of the service for failing to follow a direct order to bring Alex back."

"If I tried any harder to bring Alex back, Sir. I'd be dead now. Alex doesn't want to leave."

"Your orders, Lieutenant, were to bring Alexander Mathus back, not to find out if he wanted to leave. You should have bound him hand and foot if necessary."

"That would be difficult, Sir, since *I* was bound hand and foot."

"You left my son and his family in a state of abject servitude to those infernal cats," the Chancellor fumed. "You also left his children in danger of some hideous initiation rite that maims their bodies and leaves them damaged for life."

"It's Alexander who puts them at risk, Sir," she replied. "I would have got them all out if I could. Your other son, Frank, gave his life trying to get them out. I haven't heard you say anything about him. We didn't even know he was on the planet."

Captain Doyle interrupted. "I want to state for the record, in the presence of you, Dr. Galvin, and you, Lieutenant, that I never knew the Chancellor had two sons, let alone that both of them were on the planet. He only told me about the older one."

"Thank you, Sir," Dina murmured.

The Chancellor waved his hand. "If Frank got himself killed down there, he had no one to blame but himself. He always ran foolish risks and got himself into silly situations."

Dina bristled. "Frank was a brave and selfless man who gave a lot of people their only chance of escape, including Darcy and her children. He would have been a hero if he hadn't been killed. He *is* a hero to me."

"I'm not talking about Frank," the Chancellor barked. "I'm talking about Alexander. Captain, I order you to assemble another landing team. You know where Alexander is. You should have a much easier time getting him."

"I won't assemble another landing team," the captain told him. "I won't put one more person at risk on that planet. That's my final word on the matter."

"Are you refusing to follow my direct order?" The Chancellor swept his arm around the room. "You'll wind up in the brig along with anyone else who opposes me."

The captain towered over the chancellor and clenched his fists, but Dina lifted her hand to interrupt them. "Captain, Sir, and Chancellor Mathus, I think I've come up with a way to get the team and the Mathus family back and it won't require the armed expeditionary force of three thousand you mentioned, Captain."

Everyone stared at her. "What do you have in mind?"

"Alexander Mathus will never leave the planet voluntarily. He's factor of a village. That gives him extraordinary powers—for a human. Anyone would risk life and limb trying to take him or his family by force. There's only one way to get them off the planet."

"We're listening, Lieutenant," the captain replied.

"From what Darcy Mathus told me, a lot of the subsidiaries—I mean, the village people—they want to leave Prideland. They simply keep their mouths shut to protect themselves. The slags—I mean, the jungle people in the cantons—they would love to leave if they had a chance."

"What are you proposing, Lieutenant? "Captain Doyle asked.

"The only way to get them out is to instigate a domestic insurgency. We'd have to overthrow the Pride and evacuate the whole population, man, woman, and child. As long as the Pride exists on this planet, they can't live side by side with human beings without the two species falling back into this dominant and subservient arrangement."

Dr. Galvin gasped. "You're talking about inciting a rebellion!"

The captain shook his head. "It would never work. The people on the planet would be more inclined to sell *us* into slavery along with them."

"That's why whoever incites this insurgency would have to be slaves themselves," she replied. "That's the only way the Pride could fail to detect the plan. The instigators would have to be fully assimilated into the Pride. They would have to make a convincing performance of having an understanding with the Pride. Better yet, they would actually have to *have* an understanding with the Pride."

The captain's mouth fell open. "You're talking about going back! After everything you've been through, you want to go back down there. You're crazy!"

"Maybe I am," she admitted, "but I can't walk away without trying something, no matter how crazy it seems. I can't leave Tom and the others. If you won't send a force, then this is the only way to get the rest of the team out. I can do this job better than anybody. I can walk back into my relationship with Renfroe and he'll protect me from the punishment for running away. If I make him think I came back to be with him, he'll be glad to have me."

Captain Doyle narrowed his eyes. "Are you sure you *aren't* going back to be with him?"

Dina ignored the question and turned to the Chancellor. "Alexander is a factor. He benefits too much from the Pride to turn his back on it. The only way to get him back is to overthrow the system and take away those benefits. I don't see any other way of getting him or Darcy or their children out."

"You of all people understand the risks, Lieutenant," the Chancellor pointed out.

"That's why I have to go. No one understands the Pride the way I do. I already have a place in the Pride. I have a place to live and a powerful cat to protect me. As Renfroe's helper, I'll be perfectly positioned to communicate with the helpers in the city as well as the village people."

"What about the jungle people?" the captain asked. "For your plan to work, you won't be able to leave even one person behind."

"I'll have to find a way to communicate with the cantons, too. The slags are the least of my worries. They're the most mentally free to oppose the cats. They'll be the most interested in getting off the planet and the most willing to do something to make it happen. The only problem I can see is the lack of weapons. If this insurgency comes to violence, the people don't stand a chance."

"You won't be able to take any weapons with you," the Chancellor pointed out.

"I don't plan to take any weapons with me, but I'll have to come up with some way for the people to make a stand against the cats without getting wiped out."

The Chancellor slapped his thigh. "It's a perfect plan!"

Captain Doyle smacked his lips. "It's far from a perfect plan. I don't like it."

"It satisfies all our requirements," Chancellor Mathus replied. "It should appease even you, Doyle. It places only one person at risk and that person knows and understands the risks. When can you leave, Lieutenant?"

"As soon as this meeting ends."

"I can't allow this," Captain Doyle countered. "It's too risky. Tom and the others aren't worth your life, Lieutenant. I've already made the decision to abandon this planet."

"You'll do as you are ordered, Captain," Chancellor Mathus snapped. "You have your orders to send Lieutenant Dyer back to the surface."

Captain Doyle stiffened and his eyebrows bristled. "I'll do no such thing."

Dr. Galvin spoke up. "You'll support Captain Doyle's decision, Chancellor. You wouldn't want word to get out that you used your position to commandeer a ship, sent a highly trained incorporation team to an unknown planet without taking the proper precautions, and cost four officers their lives."

Chancellor Mathus pulled his head down between his shoulders. "Only one person died on the surface."

"All four were lost," Dr. Galvin replied. "Matthew Geromi will be dead within a week and the other two might as well be. We could have lost Lieutenant Dyer, too, if she hadn't been resourceful enough to escape and that's not mentioning your own son and the others massacred at the canton. Imagine the scandal when the public hears about this."

Chancellor Mathus tried to bluster, but his eyes told a different story. "Are you threatening me?"

"Lieutenant Dyer isn't going anywhere," Captain Doyle added. "We've wasted enough time and personnel running your errands. No one has to know what you did here, but if you say anything to anyone about us refusing your orders, we'll have no choice but to tell the whole story."

Dina couldn't keep quiet anymore. "You don't have to do that, Captain. I've decided to resign from the Armada. You can't stop me from going back to the planet."

The captain glared at her and Dr. Galvin stepped forward. "Don't do this, Dina. You can rehabilitate your position in the Armada. You can resume your career as if nothing happened."

Dina shook her head. "I can never resume anything as if nothing happened. It happened and it changed me. I can't go back to the person I was before. Tom and the others might not be worth the risk to you, but they are to me. I'm the only person who can save them and I'm also the only person who can stop any more children from getting the House of Man. That alone makes this plan worth the risk. I'll go back and bring the Pride to its knees."

Chancellor Mathus rubbed his hands with glee. "That's perfect, Lieutenant. You won't regret this."

Dina snorted. "I'm not doing it for you."

Captain Doyle threw up his hands and turned away. "I can't stop you if you're determined to go. I can see your mind is made up. Well, go to your quarters and make whatever preparations you need to make. I'll order a pod to take you down to the surface."

Chapter 61

Dina took Matilda from her place on the shelf and straightened the doll's little dress. What should she do with the doll?

Dina couldn't take Matilda back to the planet with her. Dina might never see the doll again. Dina surveyed her quarters. Tom proposed to her the last time she looked around this room. She could abandon everything in it, but she couldn't turn her back on Matilda. The crew would incinerate everything she left behind. Was she ready to say goodbye to Matilda forever?

She set the doll back on the shelf with Matilda's button eyes gazing out into the room. Finlie, Sonya, Matthew, Maddy, and all the others stared out through those bead eyes.

Dina put the room in order, but she didn't pack anything to take with her. She wouldn't need anything and she didn't want to carry anything from the jungle back to the city.

She looked around the room one last time and started toward the door when the bell rang. She opened it and Captain Doyle stepped inside. "Are you ready to go?"

She nodded. "I'm just on my way down to the pod now."

"Where's your luggage?"

"I'm not taking anything. I don't want to carry it and I won't need it once I get there. I'll just walk back in the same way I walked out."

Captain Doyle shook his head. "I hate to see you throw your life away like this, especially after what you've just been through getting out of there."

"It's because of what I've been through that I can't leave anyone else behind."

"It isn't your job to save the world. You got injured. You can't jump up and start staggering around on your broken legs to try to stop anyone else from getting hurt. Your job is to go medical bay and get treatment. Your job is to recover."

She smiled. "My legs aren't broken. I'm still healthy enough to stop anyone else from getting hurt."

"You're wrong. You should see your face the way I see it. You're still bruised and scratched from fighting those cats. You belong in a hospital bed. You belong back home in your mother's kitchen until you process what you've been through. This experience affected you more than you realize." He studied her face. "You've changed, Lieutenant. I hate to see how much this experience changed you and the worst part is you don't even know it."

"I know I've changed. I just said so myself."

"You used to have a fire in your eyes and a drive to accomplish something in the world," he went on. "You used to have a way of looking at things that set them on fire. That's gone now."

Dina stared down at the floor. She couldn't listen to this right now, not from him, or she would lose her nerve.

Captain Doyle turned away. "I only hope you can get back some of what you lost. I'm sorry to say I don't think it will happen, but then again, you won't get it back staying here."

"I'm sure I will."

He shook his head again. His shoulders sagged and deep lines scored his face. "You won't get it back and I won't get *you* back, either. You'll get stuck down there if you survive at all. Renfroe might be able to stop the other cats from ripping you to pieces. He might not kill you himself the minute you show your face in Prideland, but he won't let you out of his sight again. He'll be on guard to stop you from leaving and he won't let you move around enough to overthrow the Pride."

"It's not as bad as that. I think I have a pretty good chance."

"It *is* as bad as that and you don't even realize it. That's how bad it is. That's how far they've poisoned your mind and they did it all in three short weeks."

"But they didn't poison my mind. I bent over backward to stop the Pride from infecting me."

"You may have bent over backward. I'm not saying you didn't. In fact, you did a lot more than bend over backward, but you can't fight a system like this. Renfroe told you they adapt their tactics to match each person. Eventually they get everyone trapped so they can't leave or, in your case, they leave and come back."

"How do you say they adapted their tactics to trap me?"

"Isn't it obvious? Renfroe trapped you by being nice to you. He's an intelligent guy—I mean, cat. He probably realized a full-frontal assault wouldn't work on you, so he took the soft approach. He treated you nicely, even courted you, and it worked."

"That's not true," she exclaimed. "Dr. Galvin said the same thing and it isn't true."

"If I didn't care about hurting your feelings, I'd say this whole idea of inciting an insurgency is just a ruse to get back to Renfroe and the Pride. Even those people in the jungle said their young people usually don't come back. They go to the city out of curiosity and they don't come back. They get trapped just like Tom and Tania and all the rest."

"But I'm not going back for Renfroe," she told him. "I'm going back to destroy the Pride. If I'm going back for anyone, it's Tom."

Captain Doyle shrugged. "Have it your way, Lieutenant. I won't argue about it anymore. You're going and you have my best wishes for your success. I hope someday soon we can put this rotten planet behind us forever."

She started to relax. This couldn't end soon enough. All of sudden, he startled her by bursting out with unexpected passion. "You played right into the Chancellor's hands with your plan. You gave him exactly what he wanted when he ordered me to assemble another landing party. I just can't figure out why you did it."

"Don't you think my plan has any merit at all?" she asked.

"The only merit I can see is possibly getting the other landing team members back, but since the chances of that are nil, the merits are nonexistent and the cost is too high."

"I'm only one person," she pointed out.

"One person is one person too many. You've proven yourself a very valuable officer, Lieutenant. I never imagined, in my wildest dreams, you'd have the strength to escape the way you did, not just once but twice, against all odds. You're braver and stronger and smarter than Tom and Matthew and Tania put together. Your presence on this ship right now proves that."

Dina's spirit soared, but the captain's face fell. "You go on down to the landing bay now, Lieutenant. You're going and there's nothing I can do to stop you."

"How will I get in touch with you? Once I succeed in getting the people free from the Pride, how will I arrange to evacuate them from the planet?"

"I really don't know. This is your operation, not mine. You won't overthrow the Pride any time soon. By the time you accomplish your task—*if* you accomplish it—the *Savannah* will be long gone. You'd be left without any contact."

"I guess I will be trapped, then."

"And that doesn't change your mind at all, does it?" he asked.

Dina shook her head.

"Just remember one more thing. The Coalition will have to send quite a few ships to evacuate the population. If by some miracle we pick up your signal, it could take weeks before enough ships arrive. Plan on that. You'll have to keep the population ready to evacuate until all the ships get here."

"I understand."

"You won't be able to evacuate in a hurry, either," he went on. "With thirty-odd thousand people involved, it could take quite a long time to accomplish."

"I understand," she told him.

Captain Doyle fixed his eyes on her. "This is a suicide mission. You must realize that."

She did her best to smile. "Maybe not a suicide mission."

He waited for her to say something else. Then he compressed his lips and turned away. "I've said my piece. I won't keep you any longer." He walked to the door and paused to look back. Then he shook his head. "I sure do hate to lose you."

He turned away for the last time, but Dina stepped forward to stop him. "Would you do me one favor, Captain? It isn't much and I won't ask anything else."

"What is it, Lieutenant?"

Dina picked up Matilda from the shelf and handed him the doll. "Would you keep this for me just in case I ever get back?"

Captain Doyle gazed down at the doll. Matilda smiled her yarn smile up into his face. "All right, Lieutenant. I'll keep it for you."

He stepped through the door and disappeared before she could thank him, but his words gave her all the courage she needed. He might think the plan was a suicide mission, but he thought she had more strength and cunning than all the rest of the team combined. If anyone could accomplish this mission, she could. She had to.

Nothing remained for her on this ship. She didn't look right or left at the faces of her crew mates on her way to the landing bay. She couldn't stand to see the looks on their faces or imagine what they must be thinking.

It would be like this from now on. After everything she did to escape the planet, she could never really leave it behind. It would haunt her for the rest of her life. Everyone who ever looked at her would see what she did down there.

Ensign Ingram sat at the pod's pilot station, but he didn't look up or speak to her when she entered and strapped herself into her safety harness.

He went through the pre-launch checklist, but she didn't listen. She was already a thousand miles away when the engines fire up. The pod cleared the hatch without a hiccup. Ensign Ingram's fingers flew over the controls.

The pod floated down through the atmosphere and skated over the jungle. Ensign Ingram followed the coordinates for the team's first landing. He took Dina to the same spot and touched down. Branches snapped under the landing gear, but Ensign Ingram didn't shut off the engines. He kept the engines running while Dina unsnapped her harness and let herself out.

As soon as she slammed the door shut behind her, the engine wash tore the branches as the pod lifted off the ground. The tempest raged around her, and a moment later, died to silence as the pod soared away, never to return.

The steamy jungle smell stung her nostrils. It was the familiar smell of Prideland. She belonged to this planet and to the Pride now, as surely as if she'd been born there.

She hurried away as fast as she could. She followed the same paths to the road and on to the village. Corkscrews of smoke curled from the roofs. Children hung over the garden fences. No one took the slightest notice of her. She'd only been gone a few days.

She went straight to Alexander Mathus's house and knocked on the door. Darcy answered it and stared at Dina in disbelief. Slowly, her mouth opened. "Alexander! Come quick!"

He yanked the door open, but before he could speak, Dina cut him off. "Take me to Senator Renfroe."

End of Book 1.

Keep Reading

P rideland Series: Book 2: PrideMaiden

After Lieutenant Dina Dyer gets trapped in Prideland for the second time, she has no choice but to return to Renfroe's house. He's her only protection from the ruthless cats who want her dead, but things are not as peaceful in Prideland as they seem.

A freak genetic mutation is causing some of Prideland's human helpers to get pregnant from their cat overlords. The Pride starts frantically scrambling to crush the rise of a new hybrid race of Children who will throw the whole society into chaos.

With her Children's lives at stake and no other way out, Dina must battle her way through treacherous territory once again to find the one place where her Children might just have a chance to grow up. But the cats aren't prepared to let their prey escape a second time, especially not with their world on the line and Dina the powder keg that could blow it all to smithereens.

You can find it at your favorite book retailer.

Sign Up Once--Get all Theo Mann's free books including brand new releases

Sign Up Once--Get all Theo Mann's free books including brand new releases

Humanity on the brink of annihilation.

A mysterious package, a corrupt officer, and a conspiracy that goes all the way to the top? What could possibly go wrong?

When a routine mission goes horribly wrong, Warrant Officer Ewing Archer and a handful of faithful friends get trapped in a battle to save the last survivors of Earth.

The human race has abandoned the ecological disaster of Earth. Now all that remains is a network of interconnected ships, stations, and satellites surrounding the planet.

But when war breaks out, Archer becomes a firebrand that could destroy it all....or save it.

Sign up at www.theomann.com to read it for free

About Theo Mann

I write 70 books per year—and yes, before you ask, all these books are my original creative work. Nothing written under my name is AI-generated or ghostwritten because I write better than AI and any ghostwriter out there.

People don't read fiction for entertainment or to escape from reality. People read fiction to see their humanity reflected in another person's character and story.

This is my promise to you. When you read my books, you'll see your own humanity reflected in the characters and stories. I take this commitment to my readers very seriously. My books are an intimate form of communication between us. I would never disrespect my readers by turning that over to a machine or another writer. This is my bond between me and you as my reader.

I write 20,000 words per day as my daily work output. If anyone with a public platform would like to challenge me to prove this in a controlled environment, feel free to contact me on this website's contact page.

I worked as a professional ghostwriter for fifteen years. Now I'm on a mission to set a Guinness World Record by writing 700 books over the next ten years and 1400 books over the next twenty years, all originally written by me. See my website for the full book list.

I'm also the author of *Proof for the Existence of God* and the *Crimes Against Fiction* blog. You can find all my nonfiction work at www.crimes-against-fiction.com.

If you have a story idea, or if you would like me to explore a series in more depth, or if you'd like me to explore a character by writing a spinoff series about that character or world, leave me a message on my website's contact page. I answer all reader emails, so ask me anything, tell me what you liked and didn't like, and let me know where you'd like your favorite series to go. I would love to hear your ideas and find out what you'd like to read next.

Find out more at www.theomann.com.

Also by Theo Mann (so far)

www.ingramcontent.com/pod-product-compliance
Lightning Source LLC
Chambersburg PA
CBHW070403260626
47161CB00001B/252